"Jay Erickson invites the reader along as the Blood Wizard embarks on a desperate search, immersing them into the Shalis-Fey as he artfully blurs the lines between light and dark magic, good and evil. Expect the unexpected in this tale featuring adult themes and depth of characters that will keep you guessing along the way."
       - J. Wolf Scott author of *The Children of Auberon Series*

"Jay Erickson's second installment of the *Blood Wizard Chronicles* expands upon the rich foundation of fantasy fiction that he cemented in the first book of the series. Erickson's writing style vividly captures this imagined realm, highlighting the diversity and common struggles of its people through engaging character development that resonates with emotional intensity. A welcome new voice in fiction, readers of high fantasy are sure to enjoy Recreant."
       -Robert Neal Geiger, author of *The Pyramids of Norshore*

"Jay Erickson has done it again with his book, Recreant! Follow Ashyn on his plight to find his sister, and all the trials and misfortunes along the way. The descriptive power of Erickson's words blend seamlessly that is woven into one terrific story! It was hard to put down!"
       -George Kramer, author of *The Arcadis Fantasy Series.*

"Once again Jay Erickson captivates! Recreant goes deeper into the world of Kuldarr and the adventures of Ashyn Rune. New characters and old alike add dimension to the story. You get a real feeling of these people and their struggles of standing up for what's right, or their justification of their beliefs to preserve a culture. Jay Erickson continues amaze his readers on the world and characters he has created. I love his plot twists and dimension of the struggles people may face in their life."
       -J.P. Strohm, co-author of *Exactors: Tales From the Citadel*

Books by Jay Erickson

THE BLOOD WIZARD CHRONICLES

Pariah
Recreant

WAYFARER PRINCE SAGA
NOVELLAS

Stormwind
Dark Consort
Pononga
Hollow Omen (Coming Soon)

A KULDARR ADVENTURE

Barrow of Lies

ROLEPLAYING GAME ADVENTURE
MODULES

The Wild Tide
Shadow Profiteer

The Blood Wizard Chronicles

BOOK II

RECREANT

JAY ERICKSON

HALSBREN
PUBLISHING, LLC

BLOOD WIZARD CHRONICLES: RECREANT

Edited by Vickey Beaver of Obatron Productions LLC.
Cover design and layout by Jay Erickson.
Character art (Gaur) by Ashley Erickson of HardShellArt.
Photography by Jason Bigart
Model of Exemplar- Miranda Bigart
Additional art royalty free by FreeVector.Com
Headpiece template, royalty free for commercial use, by Retro Vector
Tribal elm tree tattoo art is a public domain image

Published By: Halsbren Publishing LLC. *La Porte, IN. 46350*

ISBN: 978-1-942958-08-6

Made in the United States of America.

DEDICATION

This dedication doesn't go to just one single person, but to an entire organization. To the United States Air Force. Without the military's solid character building (irony intended), I may have never developed the determination, mental fortitude, and open mind necessary to become a writer. This is a heart felt thank you for all the men and women who served and continue to serve. You taught me what it really means to stand by the person next to you, regardless of gender, skin tone, or religion. That brotherhood (or sisterhood) is far more than the pigment of one's skin, or what sex they are. To never give in when the chips are down, and to absolutely never surrender my dreams.

-Jay Erickson
Author

TABLE OF CONTENTS

RECREANT

PRELUDE

"**D**ammit boy promise me!" Xexial roared at his apprentice.

Ashyn closed his eyes and looked away from him. Tears rolled down his bloodied olive cheeks. "I promise."

Relief and pride flooded into Xexial. *This is it*, he decided, *this is how it is to end*. He couldn't think of any finer way. "You will make a great wizard one day," he told the boy, and he had never meant it more.

The branch commander had rallied her battle lines, and the Wild Elves were racing down upon them in a great mob. They weren't well organized in a large group on the empty plains, but they were a formidable mass.

"Get behind me, son," Xexial said calmly. He leaned heavily on his staff, as if it were the only thing in the world holding him upright. His charge fell in behind him.

The ground thundered beneath them as the flood of Wild Elves bore down upon them. It wouldn't be long.

With a sense of peace and acceptance that he had rarely known in his long life, Xexial said, "Be calm, Ashyn. I will show you why it is that this world fears us so."

As the first line of spears lowered towards the duo, Xexial closed his eyes. He chanted in a low, deep hum, invoking an energy that he hadn't called upon for many winters, long before he even knew the boy, back when he was a brash, youthful wizard himself.

He felt the usual pressure building in his chest. It was like going back to a favorite tome or sitting in his beloved chair. Soon the ground rumbled where he was standing, dust and loose chips of rock and earth bounced around his feet. The vibrations gathered around Xexial's fists, filling his ears with a low drone. A soft blue glow like that of his luminescent, thick-fingered gloves enclosed the elder wizard.

He couldn't see them, but could still hear and feel them. He knew the elven tide grew larger as they tore across the green earth ripping up everything in their path. The ground rumbled at their approach, adding more tremors to the spell's increasing pulsation. Xexial gathered more power around himself; he could feel the faint outline of blue energy thickening into a distinct ribbon of azure light around him. Soon it darkened to indigo, and then black. There was no turning back now. No cancelling this summons. He had called, and that magic had answered.

Xexial's iridescent gloved hands shook fiercely. Dammit, he was old! Twenty winters earlier it had been much easier to maintain. Now it felt as if he were trying to hold a rabid dog at bay. Violent tremors rattled his teeth. The hum drowned all sound.

The elves swarmed. Xexial imagined them to be only fifty or sixty feet away. Impact was imminent. Xexial raised his violently shaking staff in the air. The strain was immense! Fatigued from the battle, he wasn't sure how much more he could take. It didn't matter though, he knew. Not after this.

The rumble grew to a roar as the elves enveloped everything he heard. There was no earth, no sky, only the bitter smells of blood, shit, and angry painted flesh before him. It was so close. He could feel their lives through the spell. They were thirty feet away, twenty, ten. Through the magic he could feel the metal of the spear tips level with his chest. He fought to keep the beast at bay. He didn't have the strength he used to. He needed them closer, for Ashyn's sake. It had to be all encompassing, final, complete. *Stay calm*, he told himself, *Ashyn will be okay; it will be over soon.*

With a quick motion, Xexial slammed his staff into the ground. Chips hurled up around the elder wood. A deafening crack followed, sounding like the thunder of an immense storm and then silence. Xexial opened his eyes, to see it all one last time.

The spears slashed into Xexial futilely, dissolving upon impact with the obsidian glamour that bordered his frail body. Momentum carried the horde forward smashing into Xexial, and melting them into nothingness. Pieces of their bodies fell away like autumn leaves from a tree.

Suddenly the dark light exploded from Xexial, lifting a great pressure off of him and drinking into the earth. It then galloped along the lowland's surface like a stampede of shadowy specters. Grass, earth, and elves were annihilated on contact. It spanned outwards like a fan, as the charge of shadow and death disintegrated everything along its path.

Long cracks ripped across the barren ground shattering the once lush dirt into broken clay and rock. Thick bursts of indigo and violet light erupted from the long-trenched earth, casting Xexial's entire world into a surreal twilight.

The ground exploded outward from the severing lines in the earth, sending chunks of rock and debris skyward. The middle lines of the approaching wave of elves, trapped within the confines of the spell, were flung sky high. It was impossible to differentiate the elves from the tumbling rubble.

As the pelting terrain bounded down, it smashed hard into the remaining ranks of the Wild Elf assault. Even with everything happening, Xexial could hear the cracking of their bodies beneath the mass of stone and scree. He watched serenely as he saw the branch commander's horse rear up on its hind legs, and then she too was gone beneath the tumultuous cascade of earthen hail. A hazy cloud of murk muted the sun.

It was done. Ashyn was safe and Xexial got to witness Destruction one last time. It was a beautiful thing.

Suddenly pain seared through Xexial's chest lancing burning fires through his old withered limbs. His leg, never quite healed from his incident in the Shalis-Fey, exploded in agony as he tumbled to the ground. He had taken too much. The feedback had come calling, and now he was paying its required price.

Xexial lay on the ground looking up at his apprentice, his breaths becoming shallow and faint. Ashyn would one day be a great wizard, he knew. Though the boy could barely cast a spell, his intellect was so vast, and he was so powerful, that when he finally broke that barrier, Xexial knew there would be no stopping Ashyn Rune. The only thing hindering him from becoming the wizard he was meant to be was, in fact, Ashyn himself. It wasn't something that Xexial could have taught the boy, he needed to find it within himself.

Pain surged through his body as he felt his blood being starved the oxygen it desperately needed. The feedback was taking every ounce of life energy from him, wherever it could find it. Shadows formed around his vision slowly robbing him of his sight. He saw Ashyn looking in horror at the devastation he had wrought. Good, he thought proudly. He had chosen well. Though Destruction was a beautiful art, it came with its own costs to the soul. To see Ashyn hating what he saw, and not reveling in it, meant that he wouldn't abuse it. It was the best feeling Xexial could have hoped for.

Slowly the pain ebbed, and light faded. As he waited to be carried into the final journey beyond, he felt a new and strange sensation: energy. A raw, powerful energy was entering his body and tempering the cost of the feedback. He wanted to reach out and touch the source, but his limbs refused to respond. They had been sapped of all their strength. *We are merely its conduit,* he recalled himself saying countless times to the boy. Now it seemed even more appropriate, as the energy travelled from the source through him and fed the cost of the magic for the elder wizard.

Amazed, Xexial recognized the source of all this energy. It was Ashyn. Even though Ashyn's connection was broken to magic from the injury he had sustained, it wasn't broken through others. As his consciousness ebbed, a sudden realization struck him. Ashyn Rune couldn't be partly elven after all. Not like they had thought all those winters before. Not even an elf could do what he was subconsciously doing at that moment. The Exemplar had had the right of it. He was the *Nuchada*, Spirit Eyes; he **was** something **more**. Something more powerful than a half-elf. More powerful then Xexial could have ever imagined. It was a curious understanding in those final moments. One that he knew he would likely never find answers to as his world faded   into   oblivion.

TOME I

Recreant. It is what I have become. I have turned my back on my mentor, my master, my father figure: Xexial. I have chosen a single person over my objective. I have chosen the few over the many. I have become selfish.

When the Seven find out, and they will find out, I will become the hunted. To the ends of Kuldarr they will track me and destroy me because I am not allowed. Wizards do not suffer rogues amongst their numbers.

Even Xexial, the man who had raised me for over a decade of life said he would hunt me down and kill me if I violated the Wizard's Covenant. I did it anyway.

It wasn't to be rebellious, or because I thought they were evil or wrong. I didn't do it for riches, power, or any other kind of superficial wealth. I did it for Julietta, my sister.

Some would call me a craven for turning my back on those to whom I was supposed to have devoted everything. Others would call me a renegade and a traitor. Neither are wrong. I have become all those things and more, and given the choice, I would do it again.

Perhaps this makes me stubborn and headstrong. Perhaps this makes me an idiot. I do not care. All I care about now is rescuing my sister from the Ferhym. I have seen her scars. The Wild Elves have tortured, abused, and mutilated her. All for being what they call a 'skewer of the balance.'

Why she survived when they kill all others, I cannot say. But she is alive, and I have to rescue her, magic or not. Lame though I might be, I will not be deterred in the least from finding the fabled elven city of Feydras' Anula. And when I do, Maker have mercy on the forest-dwelling elves, because I, Blood Wizard, shall show them none.

-Journal excerpt from the Blood Wizard,
Ashyn Rune

SINISTER REASONS

Pain. Pain surged through his body like lightning. It moved from his eyes, through his skull, down his spine, and escaped through the tips of his fingers and toes. It cut a swath through him that left him drained like never before. It was excruciating, terrifying, and every moment he was without it felt like a hollow reprieve.

"Don't cut out his eyes; we need them," a voice said before him. Under normal circumstances, he would have thought the voice sultry, even beautiful. There was a certain cadence to her words, an almost song-like quality to the way she spoke. But now, in the haze of despair, her words were terror.

Hot liquid ran down his face. It mingled with the salt of his sweat, filling his nostrils with its heavy copper tinge and leaving its taste on his lips. It was blood, his blood.

The elf lingered before him. A distant memory had stirred when he first saw her. She smiled wickedly at him with dark eyes like chips of obsidian. The right side of her face was a mask of thick, pink scar tissue. From the ruined pointed tip of her ear down to the slender curve of her neck was a bubbly mass of rippled and swollen flesh. She had been beautiful once. He took that from her long ago, having destroyed their trap in a maelstrom of fire. She had been the only elf to survive, that he knew of.

Now she danced before him, waving the cruel tip of a broken spear in front of him. Its normally silver sheen glowed an orange-white. She had just finished pressing it against the coals.

"Time to seal up those wounds, dui Nuchada," she hissed.

The musical voice chimed behind him, "Don't blind him."

With her dark eyes never leaving his, her disappointment cut through her reply, "I won't." She moved against him, her body firm against his bound flesh. "I will take my time with you. I will hurt you, break you, and make you long for the death you deserve, skewer."

Her face close to his, she whispered to him, "I will make you suffer, as I have suffered. I will put you through all the pain that I have been through and more. When I am done, and my mother has all that she needs from you, I will then relish in the kill. I will burn your eyes out from your wretched skull and then I shall cut off your head for all the other vermin to see. You are a Skewer of Balance, and I will have my vengeance for what you have done to my Shedalia."

She reached back and yanked his hair so he couldn't pull away from her. Tension rising in his chest, he watched as she slowly lowered the burning blade. He felt its searing heat inches from his lacerated skin. With the twisted smile of someone in complete control, she pushed the flat of the spear against his torn face. His skin broiled and his blood bubbled. He could smell the fetid odor of his own burnt flesh as acrid steam roiled from his face. Unable to resist the unbelievable torment that quaked through his body, Ashyn Rune screamed.

He knew that was only the beginning.

FOREST OF REFLECTION

One Month Earlier...

Ashyn looked up at the dense ceiling of green above him. He had been there before. The young wizard looked at the familiar rock formations in front of him. The way they sat almost in an octagonal formation. Two larger boulders at the northern and southern points, with smaller stones of different sizes all making the other six points around it.

A pattern not easily repeated within nature, especially not within the same day. He walked up to the formation just as he had before. Perhaps these were Ferhym made. As soon as he closed the gap, he knew that idea was false.

Imprinted in the soft, verdant moss was a foot print. Large and booted. Nothing like the Ferhym's small, bare feet. It was his. It was the same formation.

With a disgruntled sigh, he sat upon the large northern boulder. His senses were normally quite keen. How was he turned about so easily?

Ashyn's grey eyes looked down at the stones. This hadn't been the first time since he set foot once more in the Shalis-Fey. It was as if even the forest did not want him to rescue his sister.

He flexed his right hand, feeling the tight muscles of his forearm extend and contract. Only days ago had he abandoned the bandages around the wounds caused by the Bristle Wolf, and now he could see the pink scars, vibrant against his olive skin. The skin had bunched around those knots of renewed flesh, and he was trying like hell to make sure that the mauling left no lasting damage against him. So far, he had been very successful.

Ashyn looked back to the canopy above him. He wished he could be just as successful in finding the Ferhym city of Feydras' Anula. But after weeks of searching, he came up with nothing. Twice he skirted by the Maze and its garish dead sentinels, and once he even spotted the ravine where he had first seen the Ferhym. Every time he thought he should be close to it, he just looped around once more to a place he had previously been. He was coming to the bitter understanding that the forest was deceptive in size. Long in length, massive in scope, and he was looking for an Elven city. Like finding a needle in a haystack.

"The Seven should have received my letters by now," he muttered quietly to himself, as if sealing an affirmation to a feeling he had growing in his stomach as of late. "They will know I am a Recreant."

Finished flexing, he reached up and took the vial of blood from around his neck. He rolled the small philter between his calloused fingers. The crimson fluid within sloshed gently, staining the glass momentarily, before seeping away to the other side.

Xexial had bled for him, as the Wizard's Covenant had demanded, and he for his master. Xexial warned him that he could always find Ashyn with the blood. It wasn't in his words, but Ashyn knew it was to stop him, if he tried to do exactly what he was doing right now.

He whispered once more to himself, "I wish you did come to stop me. Then I wouldn't feel so alone at least." Not alone, he realized. Just vulnerable.

Up in the trees they were there, watching him. The Ferhym. The Wild Elves.

It was the only explanation he could think of. Why hadn't he found a single track from the nimble elves yet? They used the trees.

Ashyn picked himself off the boulder and looked back to the tracks he had made. He wouldn't choose that route again. Ashyn began working his way north instead of east. He'd find his way there eventually dammit. He just wished he knew what the Wild Elves were waiting for.

He thought they would have made contact with him so much sooner. Though he looked the part of an elf, he was not their kind of elf. He looked like a Lefhym, a Wood Elf, and he was sure their curiosity had to be piqued. He pondered this darkly as he began to follow a bubbling brook. After all, Feydras' Anula was apparently a hidden city of elves. If he didn't find it eventually through attrition, the only way he was going to get there was as a guest or as a prisoner. And Ashyn knew the Ferhym didn't keep wizards prisoner. Not even lame ones.

WATCHER ABOVE

The young red dragon looked on as his charge walked deeper into the wooded lands. Carefully, the scaled creature slinked across the tree tops trying not to disturb its bright green surface too much. He was very heavy after all.

Just beneath him, he saw the Wild Elves also dancing through the trees following this peculiar intruder in their woods. He knew that the elves took the boy to be Lefhym, but the dragon knew better.

Xao skimmed delicately across another lush green treetop looking at the estranged wizard below. He felt the midday sun push its welcoming warmth into his gleaming crimson scales. As he moved from sturdy oaken branch to sturdy oaken branch, he kept his tail fully extended outward to help him with his balance. Xao never thought that in all his two hundred and twenty-four winters of life on Kuldarr that he would be chasing a boy across treetops. It was absurd! And yet there he was bounding from one perch to the next, eyeing the youth far down beneath him.

When Ashyn had re-entered the Shalis-Fey, Xao had surely thought the olive-hued boy mad. The Wild Elves were hunting and killing wizards. Why would he risk entering the lion's den? But then the answer was all too apparent: his sister.

Yet it created a problem for the dragon, for even though he had just recently been reunited with his ward (from his perspective anyway, since Ashyn knew nothing of his existence), the Shalis-Fey's narrow pathways and thick trees offered a serious conundrum to the rather large and wide dragon. Sure he wasn't as big as his elder hatch brothers and sisters, but he definitely was nearly the size of a human family's dwelling. One of the smaller ones perhaps, but something large enough that he couldn't maneuver comfortably in the confines of the thick, floral forest.

This left him to skirt across the massive tree tops, looking through the leafy canopy to spot the tall young man below. If Xao hadn't seen Ashyn entering the Shalis-Fey from Czynsk that one morning, the boy would have been lost to him, again. Yet, fortune had smiled favorably, and he had spotted Ashyn as he entered those dark looming woods.

Following from above had been a simple affair after that. After all, he had done it some eleven winters prior when the old wizard had sought to take Ashyn through those very same woods as a child.

Now though, things were slightly different. Ashyn was a young man bent on vengeance. Xao saw his movements through the forest less as focused and more as erratic. He was searching for something that he didn't know how to find. Following the wizard and boy eleven winters before had been an easy affair. That was before they entered the maze at least. Then it had been impossible. He had only the magical presence that Ashyn had emanated to go on, but it had been enough to save the boy before he had been consumed by a fire that the boy himself had started. Now Ashyn didn't display that presence to the dragon anymore. It was suspiciously absent, and Xao wasn't certain as to why.

Still it would soon present a new problem to the dragon. While Ashyn stayed within the thinner oaks that offered Xao slivers of vision through from the tree tops above, it was fine. But it wouldn't be long before Ashyn dove into the heart of the Shalis-Fey where the trees were as thick around as some of the eldest wyrms he knew. Those trees would be so high it would be nearly impossible to see him then.

The red dragon needed something that would let him watch the young wizard without exposing his presence, and without hindering the dragon trying to move within the confining woods. He just wasn't sure yet what it was he could do. Mireanthia would have known what to do. She had always seemed to know what to do.

He thought of his deceased hatch mother as he extended his still sensitive wing into the cold winds. The battering breeze felt refreshing against his swollen, bruised wing joint. It had finally healed enough to carry him in flight, but not for extended periods. This forced him to perch on the stouter trees of the woods, which, to his surprise, held the burden of his weight rather well.

Occasionally he would fly, but with his condition being what it was he knew he wouldn't be able to circle above the woods like a bird of prey forever. Not to mention he'd run the risk of the Wild Elves spotting him. Sure he would camouflage his appearance as best he could, but the little elves with their pointy sticks were wily ones. He knew his game would be up if they spotted him. So even though Xao had a clear vantage on the red-headed wizard now, he knew that he was working with borrowed time.

Still, his mother would have found the solution easily. She had managed to follow Ashyn's mother once across half the southern continent, never once seen by Jade or anyone else for that matter. So how could she have pulled off the feat without anyone at all noticing her? She couldn't have looked like a hillside the entire time. It would seem rather odd to be followed by a moving landmass. So what did she do?

The rustling of the Wild Elves beneath him caught his attention. He looked down and saw them hopping from branch to branch with deft speed. He peered past, eyeing Ashyn worriedly. Was this it already? Were they about to strike?

He saw the boy far below staring more at the babbling brook he was following and less at the threat above. The idiot child wasn't even aware enough to look up.

Xao thought briefly about roaring to startle the wizard into looking up, surrendering his hidden nature, when he realized that the elves were leaving Ashyn behind. They weren't going to attack the wizard after all. It seemed that they had found something else further east of the boy.

The dragon's pallid yellow eyes followed the nimble Ferhym as they performed their acrobatic acts of brachiation silently across the thick branches of the tall oaks. He was awed at how deftly they moved without making enough noise to alert the hooded man walking some ways below.

Then it dawned on him that they were moving past a great deal of the forest's tree dwelling wildlife as well. And they were doing it without giving the denizens any real thought. Some of the animals shuffled in dismay, and one bird squeaked in alarm as a Wild Elf ran too near to the nest of its young, but none of it was jarring enough to alert the young traveler beneath them all.

Soon the elves were well out of sight from the wizard walking obliviously below, and the animals of the trees were settling back into their nests. With his charge safely out of harm's way for the moment, the dragon looked once again to the natural inhabitants of the Shalis-Fey. An idea began to percolate in the dragon's mind about how to nullify his own growing predicament.

CARAVAN

J enhiro leapt frantically across the great expanse between the two oak sentinels of his woodland home. It was a distance greater than fifteen feet, which he cleared easily in near silence. He reached his callused hands outward and caught the branch he was soaring towards with the efficiency of someone who had been doing this his whole life. He swung up and over the branch to grab at the next tree branch. This process repeated for several long minutes until he was roughly a mile east of the strangely tall Wood Elf he had been following for the last few days.

Behind him, the rest of his branch followed. They, like he, were silent in their flight through the tree tops. Unlike the normal branches that answered to the Council of Elm, his was smaller. It was an elite taskforce put together by the druids, not the council. As such, they neither traveled with a councilor, nor did they ever have to answer to the Council. That was left to the druid who they were assigned to.

As a result, they spent little time at home in Feydras' Anula and most of their time traversing the outskirts of their forest home. Jenhiro couldn't even remember the last time he had set foot in the great Ferhym city. It had been months, maybe even a whole winter. He had even heard that they had a new First Councilor now, Lady Windsong.

He knew of her, of course, had even seen her once or twice, but had never spoken with the lady. He heard of her great accomplishments. She had fought a wizard singlehandedly and triumphed. Even at the loss of her own branch and life-mate, she had succeeded and brought the vile unbalancer to heel. It was truly a legendary exploit of their lifetime. That had been some winters early. Almost nineteen perhaps?

It was so hard to remember dates when he spent all of his time out in the wilderness. Even so, nineteen winters was a paltry amount of time in the long life of a Wild Elf. He knew that her accolades certainly made her worthy of being their leader. Their Spearmaiden. The one connected directly to the Spirits around them. But Jenhiro didn't answer to her. Not now, and likely not ever.

Working for the druids was different from being a traditional hunter. Their tasks were similar in that they kept unwanted skewers from their woods. But unlike the hunters who actively searched for the wicked unbalancers, Jenhiro's branch acted more as border guards for their domain. They kept trespassers out and rarely hunted for the vile blasphemers.

Druids, like the Council of Elm, like all Ferhym, believed in the balance of nature. Unlike the Council, the druids believed that balance was necessary in all they did, and often enough they sought not to kill evil but merely displace it from their lands so that balance between the light and dark, death and life, was maintained. These methods were not always aligned with the Council's, and so the druids formed their own branches to maintain this balance.

But like all things in the Shalis-Fey, the druids ultimately answered to the Council of Elm and, through them, the Spirits. If the Spirits demanded that skewers be purged, then the druids would answer, and through extension of the druids, Jenhiro's branch would answer.

Unlike hunters though, Jenhiro had to remain out of the politics of the Council, and he preferred it that way. It made things simpler.

He looked back to see that the rest of his branch had halted behind him. Slowly they were fanning out along the canopy of trees. They had to leave the bizarre Wood Elf behind, and he knew none of them had liked it. He would have at least left one of his branch to discover this strange Lefhym's intentions in their woods had it been in his power, but a more serious trespass had presented itself. And as their borders' protectors, they had to answer.

He looked down to the forest floor below. It was mid spring, and the flora was bursting through the late winter's cold and flourishing in a spectacular display of vibrant colors. Marigolds, lilies, and lavender grew interspersed between thickets of wild roses and junipers. Between it all were brambles and ivy fighting for dominance on the forest floor in the pockets of golden light peeking through the viridian canopy above him.

There was a great deal of space between the trees at this juncture of the woods. Any accustomed to the woodlands would see that between all the wild plants, there was a natural trail. A trail that led from north to south through the Shalis-Fey. It didn't endanger Feydras' Anula or any other of the condensed villages of Wild Elves within the woods. A thoroughly traveled road to those with an eye to nature. It was even wide enough for a caravan, one of which Jenhiro knew was coming.

His lead scout, Sendea, had spotted it moving through their woods two days ago. Normally, Jenhiro would have reacted immediately, but he had been far too interested in the crimson clad Lefhym that was in their lands. He had known that as a border protector he needed to quell the invaders immediately, but he had had to know more of the elf before leaving him behind.

Thus far his kin had seemed harmless enough, and even labored to take care of the woods in his passing. A welcome respite that most of Shalis-Fey's trespassers seemed to forgo. Normally he would have let the Lefhym go after that and move on, but there was something very peculiar about that one, aside from his unusual height. Something about the way he moved was not very hym-like. He couldn't deny the elf was light on his feet, or dexterous. He had watched the red-head use his white bow with accuracy only a Lefhym would possess. Still something nagged at him. Something was different. Not necessarily wrong, but different. Especially with the young elf's steel grey eyes. There was something about those eyes…

A chirping in the trees south of him brought him out of his thoughts. It was Sendea. They were coming.

Quickly, he turned to look back at the rest of his kin hidden amongst the branches throughout the line of trees on either side of the trail. None but another Ferhym would likely ever see them. He clicked and chirped as Sendea had, letting them know to be ready. He watched as one by one they drew their javelins. Each had a jagged edge at the base of its piercing head. He knew from experience that they would do just as much damage to someone's flesh coming out, as they had going in.

Like the rest of his Ferhym kin, he bore only a loincloth and the ritual body paintings of his patronage across his muscled frame. No outsider could recognize the distinction of markings from one elf to another; each set was distinctive to the very family line they either descended from or were life-mated into, unless they were Earthshorn. The Earthshorn had a woad that was completely their own.

Slowly he drew his own javelin, and like those around him, he coated his weapon in a black ichor. His was kept in a leather pouch at the base of his deer hide quiver. The druids skillfully crafted the poison using the root extract of a flower. The neurotoxin hid the javelins' gleaming metal tips. Whatever he stabbed with it would be paralyzed in seconds, offering him a greater advantage in combat. Since his branch worked directly for the druids they had spent countless months developing a resistance to the paralytic. He and his branch were virtually immune now.

He had worked with his branch for many winters. They had zero casualties for the last two winters. They knew their tactics; they knew how to work together as a team, especially in these woods, their woods.

Jenhiro went about lacquering two more javelins. Sendea was a few hundred feet ahead. It would take the slow, cumbersome caravan many minutes to get into position and he was in no hurry to waste the precious poison.

Finished, he held one javelin, while he kept the other two within a hand's distance on his right side. He knew he would need them quickly, after the first volley was loosed.

As he waited for the caravan to move into position, he took those last vital moments to prepare himself. He had a personal ritual before combat. It was a way of finding his center before the inevitable chaos of battle. He took a deep breath and closed his deep brown eyes. He tried to imagine the floral floor beneath him. The shape, its width. The distance between the nearest two oaks at the southern end and possible choke points to use against the caravan if the battle turned ill. He touched his closed eyelids with his left hand. For him, his center was all about his own senses. Not only sight, but also smell, sound, and touch.

The tactile pressure against his closed eyes helped him find serenity. He did the same to his brow, and eventually his long pointed ears, tracing their steep arch all the way above the crown of his head.

Many found it bizarre. He found it calming, and at times it opened up his own abilities to an even greater degree. Now happened to be one of those times.

As he slowly opened his eyes, his ears picked up the heavy hoof falls of his adversaries. The vibrating thrum of each settling step on the forest floor danced through his ears, drenching his senses. There was a rhythm in the movements. A harmony to the cadence as the caravan pushed forward. The owners of the weighty steps were large. Larger than elves, even larger than humans by a great margin. He could hear it in each step, feel it in each vibration coursing through the tree branch he rested upon. There were many of them.

Urgently, he whistled his query about their numbers to Sendea. Her silence lingered too long between the deep tempos of hoof falls that were moving towards them. Then he heard her response: a dozen and a half. His branch was outnumbered more than two to one. Normally that would not concern him, but these vibrations were very large.

Suddenly, the first of the mighty beasts broke the tree-littered horizon. Jenhiro sucked in a quick breath at the sight. A nine-foot creature lumbered into his view. Massive on a scale that Jenhiro rarely knew, the brute was almost as wide as he was tall. Heavy muscle flexed ominously with the thing's movements as it plodded along down the trail. Even from the distance he could see that it was only vaguely humanoid. It walked on four legs and it had a very fine layer of short brown hair from its massive ox-like head, down to its hoofed feet.

The monster's immense head pivoted on a neck as thick as Jenhiro's waist as it scouted its forward surroundings. A pair of long ivory horns protruded from the top of the beast's crown. They jutted forward like lances for almost a foot.

Jenhiro watched as its beady dark eyes looked back and forth from under a heavily arched brow. Its large deep brown snout had a bone ring jutting through its nostrils, hanging limply just above a wide flat mouth.

The wild elf moved away from its intimidating head and focused instead on the threat its physique represented. Jenhiro could tell that the mammoth beast was at least partially intelligent for it wore leather hides over its slick coated frame. In its three-fingered grip it held a stone-headed maul that was easily as tall as any wild elf he had ever known. One hit from that weapon would pulverize all of his bones.

Jenhiro realized immediately that Sendea had been correct about this… this thing. This colossal monster could be of nothing that nature would create. It was an aberration. Even the druids would not want it to live. Such a giant was clearly evil. Balance was necessary. Yet this was only one.

Jenhiro held up his hand signaling his kin to wait as the massive creature continued to pass beneath them. If they could cut it off from the main caravan, and deal a blow first to whatever the beasts were transporting, they could then handle it alone with greater numbers.

The branch commander signaled the rear guard to do just that. He saw flashes of agreement, and then they were gone, ensuring that maul wielder would not return.

Soon the caravan came into view. At the lead, two more of the bovine creatures pulled a massive, strangely designed wagon. It was conical in shape, but came to a point at the top. The entire frame was clearly shaped with wood, and the skins that draped over hides made up the bulk of its structure. Four oversized wooden wheels rolled heavily across the earth, leaving grooves in its path. As it loomed closer, Jenhiro saw three more of the strange carriages followed in tandem, each pulled by two more of the beasts. Between the second and last wagons, was a herd of goats, shepherded by another of the brutes.

On each side of the procession, maul wielders walked parallel to the hide-swathed wagons. At the rear of the entire procession, followed one last armed sentry.

Jenhiro noticed with some interest that the beasts' coarse fur ranged from beige, to brown, to black. Even the shape and color of their horns varied.

Somewhere in the back of the branch commander's mind, there was a scream of caution. That this endeavor was too much even for his well-seasoned team. They had gone two winters without a single death. Two winters! He should study them, and let them pass unhindered. They hadn't harmed anything in nature yet. He should send Sendea to find the druids and warn them of these intruders.

His dark brown orbs scanned the massive following of horned goliaths beneath him. Over half of the monsters were armed and armored, in a fashion, and each one clearly had double if not triple the strength and range of his Wild Elves.

But *they* had surprise on their side. The enemy would not be prepared to react against the elves in time. Not to mention his team controlled the higher ground. They would rain poisoned death on their enemies, while the creature's great stone hammers could do little to harm them from their positions.

He knew his team was quicker, smarter, and more agile than the cumbersome things beneath him. Even though his trained mind rationalized caution, would the druids command he drive the skewers from the Shalis-Fey, or maintain balance through elimination? Jenhiro made his decision.

He raised his finger into the air and drew it around in a circle three times. He then leveraged for a better position. With that same signal, he knew Sendea would do the same to the rear.

He lifted his poison-tipped javelin up and angled himself so that his throw would hold true. Aiming at the beast's slick-furred chest, he threw the javelin with the accuracy and strength of hundreds of winters' worth of practice.

Wild Elves rarely missed.

THE YOUNG FALL

A bellow of agony brought him from his deep inner reflections, jarring him back into the land of the living. He opened his heavy browed eyes, suddenly alert as another keen of pain assailed his ears. Blood. He could smell blood.

Quickly, the young bull jumped to his feet from his kneeling position. He had been meditating with his mentor, their pundit and shaman.

He looked at the weathered creature before him. His grey mane of slick fur, old and worn. His coal black eyes, normally droopy with age, were wide and alert. He knew of the dangers that the younger bull felt. Their herd was under attack.

The young bull watched as the elder grabbed his totem that was lying in a rack against the goat hide tarp of their wheeled pergola, and made his way to the exit flap.

The young bull looked at his pundit's totem. It was a long mahogany shaft, nearly six feet in length. At the base was a pointed spike and at the tip an egg shaped glistening white stone. Inside the stone was the natural earthen piping of green, blue, amber, and red. Though unarmed, the young bull was far from defenseless.

All around him inside was an arbor formed of horizontal trelliswork supported by a single central post. Draped throughout the workings was a multitude of vines, all trailing to the wooden floor. This was to help connect them to Brahma, the great World Spirit. Brahma would give him strength.

The great grey pundit shook his head at the young bull. "Stay where it is safe. Brahma will look after you in here."

The younger one shook his heavy head in response. His ebony horns were in full growth; he was near an adult by their standards. "I will not let our herd matrons be slaughtered, nor let our shepherds be endangered when I can assist my pundit."

The elder's eyes held firm on the young student, causing him to fidget. "This is a fragile time for you young Pan. You must wait here."

With that, the elder left the young bull alone inside their tent to listen to the screams of anguish and confusion coming from his herd outside.

Impatient, he idly toyed with a vine with his large auburn thumb, thinking of all the ways he could be out there assisting the pundit and their herd.

Something crashed hard into the side of the wheeled pergola, rocking the massive mobile construct, causing the young bull to fight to maintain his balance and sending vines swinging wildly about. He could hear the strong wood groan under the strain.

The young bull paced angrily. Though he trained all his life toward a peaceful existence, he knew well the reality of the greater world around him and of the real danger of these woods.

Again something crashed hard into the wagon, garnering another groan under the strain of the impact. This time, the left-fore wheel buckled, causing its axle to shatter. The whole vehicle tilted hard to the left, and pitched the young bull forward.

He struck the goat hide tarp with full force, his entire two-thousand-pound frame pulling hard on the trellis above him. Unable to cope with so much pressure, the bracing splintered and gave away, and then the young bull realized he was falling out of the carriage, taking half of the growing flora with him.

He hit the ground in an attempted roll, but the tarp hindered him, bringing him up short, leaving him trapped in its leathery holdings. The vines wrapped themselves around him, hampering his movement even further.

Outside, amid the bellows of pain, he could now hear screams of panic and what sounding like the chittering of some bizarre animals high above. Then he felt the impact of something piercing into the heavy coverings.

A small javelin thrust its way through the tarp and plunged into the earth inches away from his snout. Then another drove through hide and vine scoring a scratch against his belly. Immediately the wound began to burn.

"Poison," he whispered to himself. Frantically, he struggled to escape the sheeting as more javelins rained down upon him. Some penetrated the hide. Others did not. But soon they began to pierce his flesh too, adding pain and burning as he fought fiercely to free himself.

He felt the poison eating its way through his veins, and his movements gradually became more sluggish. His amber eyes grew heavy and as he fought through his lethargy, he realized that the yelling outside was becoming slurred. The poison was at work, and soon it would be his end. Pan had hoped to prove to his pundit that he was ready for his Takewatha, his spirit journey, but now he realized that his true journey was upon him. He was destined to see the World Spirit now, and begin anew in the fires of a new life, risen once again. He closed his eyes as darkness brought him into that strange new world.

...WHILE THE OLD LINGER

Jenhiro looked on with grim satisfaction as the tarp covered form stopped moving under his assailing wrath. The beasts were potent creatures, able to absorb large quantities of the neurotoxin on their javelins before it affected them. From what he could tell, at least six of the eight javelins he had thrown at that creature had pierced its flesh. Others had aided him in taking out that shrouded form as well.

Many of the monsters also had a multitude of javelins sticking from their bodies, looking a lot like extra limbs. Yet their size, and the adrenaline of battle, kept many fighting. They couldn't challenge Jenhiro's elves directly, they were too high for that, but he gave the creatures some credit to their intelligence as they went for taking down the trees instead.

Heavy hammer falls thrummed against the trees, knocking down branches and leaves. Small animals plummeted to their deaths. But not the elves. They were too dexterous for that, and they caught on after the first attack. That strategy had cost them the life of their scout.

Even with all the frantic motion of battle raging beneath him, he could see the crumpled, still form of Sendea just to his south. Looking at her lifeless eyes staring skyward sent another surge of anger through him. Seething, he hefted another of his quickly depleting javelins and threw it with all his might at the nearest ox-like beast. He watched with savage glee as the javelin pierced through its droopy ear and scored deep into the monster's brain cavity. It cried in shock and dismay, stumbled a few steps, and then collapsed. Sendea was a fine huntress and a good friend. She deserved more.

A roar of unbridled rage stole Jenhiro's thoughts. Quickly, he looked at its source. Even though he had never encountered these creatures before, he could tell that it was the elder. Grey hair riddled its body, and the beast, while still massive, slumped with age.

Unlike the others, this one bore no maul, but instead held what appeared to Jenhiro either a long thin spear, or perhaps even a staff.

Quickly, Jenhiro told all his elves to focus on this threat. If it died, it would demoralize the remaining beasts enough to make killing the rest an assured and quick ordeal.

As Jenhiro rained down his death from above, the grey-mane looked up at him with hatred in his small, beady dark orbs. Faster than Jenhiro would have thought possible the ox-headed beast drove his staff-spear object into the ground.

Not drove, Jenhiro realized. It was absorbed. There was no splitting of the earth, no rending of bramble and soil. It was as if the ground drank the item into itself. It fell smoothly into place acting as if it was always a part of the soil. There the staff stood firmly like a sapling from any of the goliath trees that surrounded them.

The grey-mane held onto the staked object and began to hum in a deep, low bass as the shower of javelins cascaded down upon him. Jenhiro stared in wonder as the grey-mane's skin became hardened as stone, shattering all javelins that came in contact with his now granite-like flesh.

Even then the beast continued to hum, and Jenhiro recognized with horror what the creature was doing. It was using magic! The magic of Creation. The ground began to tremble, shaking the trees more violently than any of the stonework mauls could have. Jenhiro struggled to maintain balance, and soon found himself gripping the trunk of the massive oak for dear life.

The ground quaked and writhed beneath him, and Jenhiro watched as it rippled like waves, striking against trees as if they were a reef. The worst happened next. His elves began to fall.

Like Sendea before them, one by one his branch began to plummet out of the trees, swallowed up in the wake of the earthen wave. Jenhiro heard the cries of shock, and then the crunch of bone and rending of flesh as dirt, stone, root, and clay ripped over and through the unarmored bodies of his elves. Soon the earth took on a red hue, and churned with the crimson morass of his fallen Elves.

Still Jenhiro held on. The ancient tree groaned in protest against the bombardment of earth, but Jenhiro knew the sentinel would weather the storm of this creature.

And weather it, it did. Soon the waves subsided, and Jenhiro let go of the rough bark that wore his fingertips bloody. He stood high above, terror stricken at the sight. His branch was gone, devoured by the earth, consumed by the nature that he had fought for so long to maintain in balance.

Yet almost all of the beasts had fallen as well. Killed in a combination of both javelin and poison. The goats, all slaughtered, and all the wheeled wagons now nothing more than splintered wood and tattered hide. Their remnants spread across the base of the ancient oaks crushed in the wake of the storm. Two survivors he could barely see disappeared into the tree-line in opposite directions.

He looked back to the elder monster, his eyes wide and disbelieving. In his decades of service to the druids, he never witnessed the magic of nature in anyone else but the elves. Even then, only the Lefhym and the Ferhym were the keepers of the secretive art of druidic magic. Yet, what Jenhiro witnessed looked to be very much the same, and from a beast no less, a skewer of the balance.

Slowly his mind adapted, the shock subsided, and he saw the grey-mane bull stumble to the pile of tarps where Jenhiro had slain the one that was riding in the strange wagon. The grey-mane was clearly drained. It was paying the price for the might of its magic. Creation was collecting. The old creature put his hands onto the tarp and began to chant. Jenhiro prepared another javelin to launch, hoping to capitalize on the monster's distraction. He aimed, pulled back, and instead found the grey one falling onto his side as he finished his chant. His flat mouth wheezed in a gasp, his whole body shuddered violently, and then he fell still. Jenhiro knew that the magic had collected fully. The old one was dead.

Jenhiro stood up and began to search the tree line. He would need to hunt the survivors one by one, and then report his findings to the druids. He moved across the branch, when suddenly the tarp moved.

Impossible! Again he drew one of his javelins and aimed down below. The fabric bundle on the ground stirred and twisted. Jenhiro prepared for whatever would arise from the shambles. Finally, an auburn hand reached out of the material and violently pulled the tarps away. The Wild Elf didn't delay as he saw the bull that was underneath.

It was massive compared to the others, perhaps almost another head taller than those that they had killed before him. It had slick auburn fur with a shock of charcoal that ran across its snout and connected to ebony colored horns like a mask. Its amber eyes searched the battlefield.

Jenhiro threw his javelin and watched as the creature grunted when it struck solidly into its abdomen. He readied another and waited for the poison to do its work. Instead, the monster ignored it, and continued to look about at the destruction of the caravan.

Jenhiro didn't know how this was possible. The creature should be dead. The neurotoxin in its system should have overloaded it. Not to mention its wounds.

As if understanding Jenhiro's disbelieving thoughts, the creature looked down at the barbed javelin protruding from its stomach. With a thick, furry hand, it reached down and grabbed the javelin. It looked like nothing more than a twig in its massive grasp. It pulled the weapon from its body. No blood was visible across its pointed tip or down the long shaft. Yet Jenhiro knew the javelin had scored deep.

The large creature didn't even seem to notice the depth that it had been inside of it. The auburn hued bull threw the javelin to the ground, and Jenhiro watched in amazement as the rent hole in its abdomen began to seal itself, leaving a small pink scar in its place. It was absurd, blasphemous! Not even their druids had such abilities! They needed ointments and salves to work with wounds to aid the magic. This truly was a work of evil.

Jenhiro prepared one of his last javelins. He didn't know how he would be able to take such a beast alone, but he had to try. Perhaps a head shot would stop it?

Again, as if reading his mind, the creature's large bull-like head looked up to his tree. Jenhiro realized that it saw him. Its eyes bored into his.

It roared at him with all the rage it could muster. It was an ear splitting, guttural sound. Then it looked down at its fallen elder, and its bellow intensified.

It slammed its hooves into the ground. Everything around it quaked and shook. Brambles and the remaining loose branches tumbled from the trees. Jenhiro thought for sure that it was going to attack his tree like the others and he held on once more to the trunk, when suddenly the bull bolted. The elf watched, nonplussed, as it grabbed the strange spear-like staff from the earth and then disappeared quickly into the woods.

Jenhiro knew at that moment that the Ferhym needed that creature. It was a skewer unlike any he had ever seen. The druids would want to study it. The elder performed unnatural magic and this creature was now a risen abomination. He witnessed its flesh heal of its own accord! And its spear-staff what kind of weapon was it? The earth had drunk it in as if it were a plant of its own, and then the waves. How had that been possible? This thing could be a bigger threat than they anticipated.

Yet, as Jenhiro looked down at the reddened earth below, a forlorn feeling welled in the pit of his stomach. It had been so long since they suffered a casualty. Two winters. Now his entire branch was gone. Good, fearless hunters and huntresses gone to just one monster and its stick. How could he capture such a creature alone and with virtually no javelins remaining? Feydras' Anula was days away. By the time he got there and back with reinforcements, the beast would be gone. He needed to catch it now. He needed someone who could take the beast at remarkable range. A marksman of uncanny quality. An elf without peer if he were to do it right.

And then he knew. He wasn't alone. There was an elf in these very woods right now, not far from here with an unusual bow. Jenhiro sheathed his remaining javelins. It was time to make contact with the Wood Elf in red.

GINGER

After another day of walking, the brook Ashyn followed turned into false hope. The small stream ended at a shallow pond with no other brooks or rivers parting from the diminutive mass of water. Disappointed, Ashyn settled down at the small bank and removed his equipment for another evening of cleaning.

Even the game was thin. After the unnerving roar of some beast he heard earlier that morning, all the animals fled or were well into hiding. As a result, he wouldn't be eating well. Only a handful of dried biscuits remained from Czynsk, and all the berries he had come across were unhealthy to consume. He wouldn't be able to help his sister if he died of dysentery before even making it to Feydras' Anula.

The small pond offered a few scant fish, but he never really learned that trade as a child, nor had he gathered much refinement on the skill in his winters within the Onyx Tower. So he would just have to deal this evening with biscuits.

Ashyn stripped out of his hardened leather, placed it carefully down, and then leaned comfortably into the mossy end of a fallen tree. His gaze drifted skyward.

Though the shallow pond was small, it offered enough of a break in the tree line to expose the world above him. He saw the vivid orange and pink hues of another dying day. He marveled at the simple beauty of the sky, and of the serene nature of the woods around him.

He found it hard to believe that something so calming and so beautiful could contain some of the foulest creatures that Ashyn knew of. The monsters of the very woods he rested in had destroyed his entire life. Be they the orcs that decimated his childhood town of Bremingham, the Bristle Wolves that ravaged his arm and nearly killed his sister, or the Ferhym that targeted him and his mentor as unbalancers, and had ultimately ruined his chances of becoming a wizard. Not to mention captured his sister and brutalized her.

Just the thought of his sister's hazel eyes scorched away, brought heat to his face and unbridled anger in the well of his stomach. He could still vividly see the small crescent shaped brands around her hollowed sockets. He could still hear the screams of her pain in his waking dreams. All because she was labeled a 'dui Nuchada'. Spirit Eyes. This was her balancing. Torture and slavery.

With no way to vent his anger, he kicked at a nearby stone, sending the rock soaring well into the darkening confines of the woods. It clamored to the ground with a loud crack, followed by the squeal of some animal that was in the turbulent missile's unfortunate path.

"Just my luck," Ashyn muttered quietly to himself. "Can't even kick a rock without pissing off someone in these woods."

As if by reply, he heard a low mewling sound coming from the direction the stone had flown. At first Ashyn tried to ignore its plaintive cries, but it persisted. Slowly the dusky orange sky disappeared above him replaced by the sanguine hues of night. Again Ashyn heard the wounded creature cry out. He sighed aloud. He knew if it kept crying it was going to bring along predators to finish it off, and if Ashyn wasn't careful, they'd finish him off too. The recent memory of those horrible cries within the woods that morning played in his head. He hoped whatever was out there was either gone now or long dead.

Again the small creature mewled in the distance. Still angry from thoughts of his sister abused by the elves, he stood up, drawing his skinning knife. The least he could do was put the damn thing out of its misery before it brought the whole forest down on him. He marched over to where he kicked the stone in search of his prey.

To his surprise, it wasn't a small ground hog or possum like he expected, but a cat. It was large, not like the domesticated kinds he had seen in his short time in Czynsk as a child. This one was easily twice, maybe even three times, the size of those cats, with ginger orange fur and black stripes running across its back and up the tips of its rather long ears. It was clearly a wild cat, and it might even be mixed with a lynx given its stripes and overly large ears.

He was alarmed to see just how much damage he caused the poor creature. He caught the poor thing completely off guard and the hefty stone crushed right into the right side of its face. Blood oozed from cuts in its fur, and its right eye was completely swollen shut. A deep tear ran across the animal's mouth and the poor thing's muzzle had caved in a little. Likely, Ashyn's careless projectile broke bones and knocked out teeth. It stared at him plaintively with its one good yellow eye.

To make matters worse the cat must have fallen. Two outcropped rocks trapped it tightly. Predators like Bristle Wolves would get at it easily, and the cat would have no way to defend itself from slowly being ripped apart. An agonizing death.

Ashyn leaned forward between the rocks with his knife, intent on ending the poor thing's life quickly for its sake. Seeing the sharp instrument coming it's way the cat hissed and spit at Ashyn, and it even swiped a free claw at him. The cat was lethargic and slow and Ashyn had no problem avoiding it. Still Ashyn was amazed, as the cat's one good eye never left his own.

"I did this to you," he said to the cat, just as much as himself. Pity overcame the young wizard. His anger caused this creature's pain and grief. His ignorance brought this on another. Sure, it was only a cat, but it was still another living creature, a life. Wasn't that what he was sworn to value as a wizard? Life itself?

Here he was about to kill this cat because he didn't want to be attacked by any predators because of its suffering, which he caused. Ashyn realized how selfish that was. Quickly he sheathed his knife and instead reached for the cat.

Again it hissed, spit, and attempted to scratch at Ashyn, but the lithe wizard was able to maneuver around its lazy swings and pry the poor animal from its confines. He set it down on the soft turf and stepped away. The ginger cat swayed briefly, and turned once more to face Ashyn, glaring at him with its piercing yellow orb. It hissed again, its orange fur standing up straight on its back.

Ashyn recanted his decision to free the feral animal. Without his armor on, his robes would do little against the feline's claws and teeth. Though it was smaller than most things in the Shalis-Fey, Ashyn knew it could still cause him a lot of pain and discomfort with those sharp claws. Slowly his hand crept back down to his skinning knife.

The cat paced in a circle, eyeing Ashyn with its one good eye the whole time, while trying to get a sense of balance. When it felt Ashyn was no longer a threat, the cat turned to run away. It didn't make it five feet. The wounded animal lost its footing and collapsed on its side. Ashyn approached it cautiously, and saw it was just lying there panting softly. The wizard reached down and touched it. The cat did not offer any resistance. With that, he picked the surprisingly heavy feline up and carried it back to the shallow pond's bank. By the time he arrived, the hefty cat was asleep in his arms.

UNEXPECTED ALLIANCE

A rustling in the hedges startled Ashyn awake. He looked up into the starlit sky. The bright moon cast its pale light down onto the small pond, reflecting broken silver shards across the small alcove. It lapped lazily, creating a soothing, rhythmic sound, as the hoary waters licked at the mossy shore. Against his ribs, he felt the weight of the hefty feline. Its chest moved up and down rhythmically, its breathing coming out in a wheeze from its slightly caved in muzzle. The cat was deep asleep. It was so calm, almost serene.

Again, the shrubs near the north end of the water shook. Small twigs broke against the pressure of whatever was atop it.

Ashyn's eyes searched his small camp. He had not set a fire this evening, and both his armor and his bow were cleansed and ready, but just out of his reach. His arrows and backpack were almost five feet away.

Figures, he thought dryly. The one night he was distracted was the night the elves decided to move on him. Then again, it's exactly what he would have done. Slowly, Ashyn inched downward, moving for his bow.

"I would not do that were I you," a voice next to his right ear clicked in the Ferhym tongue.

Ashyn froze. The elf was right next to him and he hadn't even felt it approach. Ashyn turned his head slightly. He could see the elf's silhouette vaguely out of the corner of his eyes.

"I come not in malice," the elf whispered to him. "There is a skewer ahead of you, sharing your water."

"The bushes," Ashyn answered back in the Ferhym tongue.

"Yes. Very near. There is fruit there."

Again Ashyn shifted ever so minutely to look towards what he heard earlier. There he saw a massive lumbering form sitting against the pond's shallow shoreline. Shadows obscured most of it, but he could see the long prominent horns jutting from its large bull-like head.

"Is that a minotaur?" Ashyn whispered.

The elf hovering just above him froze shortly, "You know of the beast?"

Ashyn gave an almost non-existent nod. "A little."

The elf said quietly, "They are hostile."

All Ashyn knew he had read from the Onyx Tower archives. They were a ferocious, cannibalistic species.

"Very," he agreed thinking of the black iron door back in the Onyx Tower. The one that had led below into the prison cells. It bore a relief of a minotaur cleaving a man in half with an axe. It was not a pleasant image to behold as a child.

He saw the elven hunter nod. The Wild Elf whispered again, "We take down the beast together, tree-brother. And then the druids must learn of this minotaur."

Ashyn mentally felt a sigh of relief. He had feared the Wild Elves would not have bought his disguise. He was glad he was wrong. Hushed, he asked, "What do you need me to do?"

"I will flank the unbalancer, and distract it. When it turns on me, I need you to use the bow and bring it to heel. Be warned, the beast is very resilient, and we may need it captured. With mine own eyes, I witnessed a creature of this ilk using dark magic earlier today."

"Magic?" Ashyn whispered to himself. He had never read of such a thing, but he supposed it was possible. After all, he did not know all that much about the species of bovine men.

The elf nodded. "It has killed many hym."

"Alright," Ashyn agreed.

Without a sound the elf next to him vanished. Ashyn blinked several times, adjusting his eyes fully to the moonlit night. He couldn't believe he was going to do this, help a Wild Elf with an alleged skewer.

He looked back to the bank. The creature was massive, even hunkered down the way it was. Ashyn figured it was perhaps eight feet tall if it stood upright. That would make its reach lengthy and one the wizard would not wish to be within. He couldn't see its eyes in the moonlight, but he guessed that they were dark, and full of malice. Evil.

Ashyn shook his head momentarily. Did the Ferhym not think the exact same thing about him? About his sister? What if he was wrong about the minotaur? It had not attacked him while he slept. Whose life was he supposed to value? The selfishness of his own? Or the unknown of the beast before him?

He looked down at the cat sleeping at his side. Hadn't he almost made that mistake once tonight already? Yet he had agreed to help the elf. What would he do if Ashyn did nothing? Would it die to the minotaur? Or worse would it succeed and then come back for him seeking revenge?

Ashyn felt a sudden breeze as the wind rustled across hooded head. A cool refreshing zephyr had come from the north and caught itself in the small alcove. It helped alleviate Ashyn of the heat of tensions growing within him. Seconds later, he heard a snort of surprise from the creature. The ground thundered as it jumped to its hooves. Ashyn looked up at it in shock, and the cat at his side startled awake. Its gargantuan form blocked out the moon behind it, encasing the beast in a nimbus of silver light. Ashyn could see a massive maul, the size of a small tree, that it held in one furry hand with ease. He didn't need to be able to see the bull's eyes to know it where it was looking. It was looking right at him. Something had changed. It knew he was there.

"Scent," Ashyn mouthed silently to himself. With the small breeze he had suddenly become upwind of the creature. It smelled him. The creature gave another snort as it locked in on the wizard's position.

Ashyn hunkered down against the log quietly. He wondered where the Wild Elf went. He said he was going to flank around and draw its attention, but he didn't say how long it would take, or if there was to be a signal. It was clear that the beast's focus was now clearly on the wizard. The elf needed to act quickly.

Abruptly, the creature roared. Ashyn knew then that he was out of time. He had become its prey.

The beast leapt across the ten-foot length of the pond in a single stride. It hit the ground hard with its cloven feet, rattling everything around the young man. Quickly the wizard scampered to his feet. His furry companion jumped at the trembling earth and ducked on the other side of the fallen mossy log, where Ashyn's bow and armor resided.

Ashyn didn't have a moment's break from the creature as it hovered over him. It snorted only once and then brought its massive maul crashing down towards the boy's skull.

Ashyn nimbly rolled out of the way, as the massive stone maul crushed into the soft decaying wood of the fallen tree. The weak, wet wood gave way, creating an explosion of mildew and detritus. Ashyn came to his feet half a dozen feet away from the monster, and to his misfortune, his bow as well. He stared at it and then back at the bull-like creature before him.

Its short, slick coating of fur barely contained its broad, rippling muscles. Ashyn watched in awe of the beast's power as it tried to dislodge its maul from the carcass of the deadwood. It lifted the log and maul easily with one arm, working to shake it free.

Ashyn spotted the ginger cat scattering further into the woods. It didn't seem nearly as injured as he had thought it to be earlier in the evening, and he supposed the fear of the rampaging monster was a driving factor in its desire to survive.

Ashyn watched the log swing high into the air as the beast shook at it. He saw his bow fall and tumble in a half roll, stopping just at the water's edge. His armor disappeared underneath the tumbling mass of rotting timber as the log fell apart. He looked to his pack and arrows just behind the behemoth creature. One misstep would crush everything he had. All his arrows pulverized under the monster's two-thousand-pound frame.

He needed to move around the creature and get back to his bow, but he knew the range of the monster's arm was too great. He needed to put the creature at a disadvantage.

The wizard took in his surroundings. Most of the trees were spacious enough to offer easy maneuvering, even for the bulky bull man. But after the first dozen feet, the forest thickened considerably, becoming extremely dark. If the bull had vision like his own, then he wondered how well the creature could actually see in the dark.

Ashyn backed up slowly. He knew he might be trading one monster for another, walking unarmed into the black woods beyond, but he didn't have much of a choice.

He took about three steps into the gloom when suddenly the bovine creature whistled. The keen it emitted was ear splitting, and Ashyn reflexively jumped at the horrid sound. The creature writhed in agony, swinging its stone hammer back and forth throughout the empty night air. Ashyn didn't quite understand what was happening, until the creature turned, and he saw javelins.

Two were buried deep in the meaty back of the beast, and Ashyn knew then why it had taken the Ferhym so long to assist. He could just make out the dark ink-like fluid at the base of the spear tips that jutted from the monster's flesh. He recognized it from his dealings with the Ferhym in the past. Poison.

The creature turned its back to him and stumbled into the water, trying vainly to stare into the darkness and find its attacker. Ashyn recognized his chance, abandoned his initial plan, and ran for his backpack. He quickly grabbed at a quiver of arrows and dragged the bag away.

The maul unexpectedly crashed down into the soft moss where he had been standing a second before. The young wizard saw seething hatred in the creature's coal black eyes.

Again the bull swung its huge weapon at the thin young man. Ashyn barely had time to roll away as the massive stone head of the maul whistled by above his head. Ashyn could feel the pull of the wind from the power of the bull's swing. He knew just one hit like that would reduce the bones in his body to nothing but dust.

The wizard completed his roll to his bow, grabbing it just as the monster pulled itself from the water. It lunged at him with its free hand right as Ashyn knocked an arrow. The archer fired wildly as he dove away once more.

He heard the surprising loud splash of water. When he turned to see his attacker, he found it fallen to its knees in the pond, hunched over, with its free hand covering its chest. Ashyn could see the goose feathers of his arrow sticking out between the large creature's fingers. A pool of red collected in the bull's slick coat. Pink beads swirled and disappeared in the silvery waters beneath it.

The monster wheezed violently. A strange rattling sound built in its throat. It looked up at Ashyn curious as to why so small an object like the arrow could have caused so much damage to the resilient beast, but the wizard knew why. He could see it by its placement on the bull. Slightly right of the beast's sternum just beneath its upper ribs. He must have ruptured its windpipe. The monster couldn't draw a steady stream of air. Blood was filling its lungs.

Ashyn saw a string of crimson spittle running from the bull's mouth. Blood was pooling inside the monster's body, and that was far more deadly than the wound where the blood ran down its side.

It mewled then. A hissing sound like a creature in immense pain. It sat there, dying slowly, in the small pond of water that looked like nothing more than a large puddle around the massive beast.

Ashyn approached it cautiously with another arrow knocked and ready. He could see the tired, confused look in its glassy eyes. It gurgled as the fluid completely filled its lungs. The fight was over. His attack was a fatal one.

Just behind the bull creature, he could see movement in the trees. Instinctively Ashyn went to fire the other arrow. It was the Wild Elf. It appeared as a flicker, only for a moment, saluted Ashyn, and then disappeared once more.

Was that it? Ashyn wondered. Only a momentary interaction and then the elf was gone? Was that all he could expect from Wild Elves? He knew they were insular, but hadn't the Ferhym asked him for help after all? He was hoping that he could at least ask the elf about Feydras' Anula, a location or something.

After waiting a few more moments, Ashyn shook his head in disappointment. It appeared the elf was, indeed done with him. He walked back over to the remnants of his camp. Several minutes of digging later, he pried his red Lefhym armor from beneath the twisted remains of the mossy log. He shook it free of the murky wooden chips as best he could. Three deep new scores ran vertically across the breast slicing liberally into the leather. He tested the thinness of the leather between his fingertips, frowned, and then fastened it once more to his robes.

The pond was no longer a good place to remain in refuge. The body of the bull was too large to move and it would soon draw predators.

Carefully Ashyn reequipped his backpack and quivers. Confident that he was leaving nothing of value behind, he was ready to go. It would be dangerous navigating in the dark, but anything was safer than staying behind with the dead body.

Ashyn looked at the bull once more as it finally shuddered the last vestiges of life from its mortal coil. No longer did it seem the massive and intimidating monster silhouetted in moonlight. If anything, it seemed a peaceful and gentle creature. Lost to the trials of the Shalis-Fey like so many before it.

Not the Shalis-Fey, he realized, *Me.* Another had died by his hand. Someone who was supposed to value and maintain the balance of life. He was turning out to be a terrible wizard.

The young wizard shook his head and whispered, "I'm sorry to keep disappointing you, Xexial." He turned, resuming his course northeast.

A soft meow stopped him. Ashyn turned back to his camp. The ginger cat jumped up from behind the rock where Ashyn had first encountered it. Its good yellow eye glittered in the moonlight; the other buried under swollen flesh. It looked at him once, then it looked to the southeast, and then back at him. It meowed again.

"You want me to go that way?" Ashyn asked the cat, feeling rather silly for doing so.

The ginger wildcat turned in circles, looked at him, looked to the southeast, and finally back to him once more. It meowed as if in response.

Ashyn sighed. It's not as if he knew where he was heading anyways. The wizard headed in the direction the cat was facing. Quickly the ginger feline hopped off the rock and ran to keep up with him.

Ashyn watched it curiously as it walked by his side. He chuckled to himself. "Minotaurs, Wild Elves, orcs, and Bristle Wolves in these woods, and I wind up with an orange cat as my ally." He shook his head at the audacity of it all, and continued to head southeast late into the night.

HUNTERS

For three more days Ashyn continued to follow the direction of the cat. At first, the young wizard thought himself foolish for doing so, but as they continued unerringly, he questioned just how intelligent the feline actually was.

He thought after the first few hundred feet the cat would change direction and head west or back north, but it didn't. It maintained its southeastern trek night and day. Ashyn had to stop to break or sleep at night. For the injury the ginger cat sustained, Ashyn was amazed at its remarkable endurance. He supposed it would need such inner resolve to survive the hostile woods.

And the cat could eat! They ate together endlessly, and its hunger never waned. It never seemed satiated, not once. Anything they caught, they ate, and if Ashyn didn't finish it, the cat would.

Ashyn took to calling the creature "Ginger." It seemed as if the cat didn't mind in the least. Perhaps it was just the loneliness of the woods, or maybe something more deep-seated. After all, he had not truly had a friend since he was a small child. Yet he felt a bond growing with the feline, a kinship.

It was finally midday of the third day when Ashyn encountered the Wild Elves once more. He spotted the movement in the trees and spied, only for a moment, a lone figure watching him from the lush tree line.

Ashyn wasn't positive that this was the same elf from a few nights before, but he was reasonably certain that its visibility was no coincidence. Ashyn didn't understand why now. For weeks he had wandered aimlessly in the woods, back and forth, hoping that the elves would make contact with him, yet they always remained out of sight and out of reach. Now, not only had they enlisted him for a night, they weren't even hiding from him all that hard. Was it possible that he was building their trust?

If that were the case, it was even more of a reason to be wary. One slip, one moment that they found out he wasn't the Lefhym he was pretending to be, and all that trust would be shattered. They would identify him for the skewer he was or, worse, recognize him as the dui Nuchada, and his attempted rescue of his sister would be all but gone. Ashyn pulled the cowl tighter over his head.

A small growl from Ginger brought him out of his thoughts. Ashyn scanned the densely packed horizon before him. Thick brown trunks congregated closely to one and other, their large roots entwining across the mossy floor. Any number of predators could find a shadowy recess to hide within under the thick foliage ceiling above him, even at midday.

After identifying no apparent threat, he looked to his companion. Ginger growled at the moss in front of its paws. Ashyn went over to investigate.

It took him a moment to understand what he was looking at. He knew it was a hoof print from his days trapping with his father and hunting game. But this was massive in comparison to what he was used to seeing. Larger than a horse's hoof, it took only a moment for him to remember the minotaur.

Quietly, he removed an arrow from a quiver and nocked his bow. He wouldn't allow one of the beasts to take him unaware. He had narrowly avoided the dead one's blows earlier. To not see one coming would most certainly prove fatal.

Ginger stopped growling, its yellow eyes silently sweeping back and forth across the dark folds between trees. Ashyn understood his ally completely. They were not alone.

He found another hoof print ten feet away, followed by a large scuff. It was heading in the same general direction that they were. Either Ashyn would have to go around and hope to evade the beast, which would take time, or he could skulk behind it until its path deviated from his own. That would take time, and every moment he didn't find Feydras' Anula was another his sister might be being tortured for being a dui Nuchada.

Ashyn glanced back up at the tree line high above. He could always hunt it. What if he led the elves to the bovine monster? Prove his worth. Was this what they were doing? Was this a test?

Once again, his sister's ravaged face came to mind. The crescent scars, the hollow sockets. As a child, Ashyn had been slightly jealous of his sister. She had fit in so well with the rest of the village with her joyful demeanor, where he had been an outcast. She had been his only friend in Bremingham. She had been his lifeline.

When the orcs took her, he thought she was gone forever. But it had been a lie. The wild elves waylaid the orc troop and killed them all. They took Julietta, labeled her a dui Nuchada, the spirit eyes, and then burned them out as recompense for her allegedly evil nature. She had been their slave ever since. Winters. Countless winters she remained their servant, her body beaten and broken over and over until she gave them whatever they wanted.

Anger seethed in his chest like a fire desiring to escape. But it couldn't. Something was trapping it there. He could feel it vibrating in his chest. He could feel the heat flushing his skin, but it couldn't escape.

He stared at the tracks. He would hunt the minotaur for the elves. Prove himself to them. Force them to trust him. He would do anything to get to his sister now. Even if that meant killing again.

~ ~ ~

Two hours later, he found the bull. It hunkered down in a small copse of trees so close together that the branches intertwined to form a sort of protective overhang within which the massive creature could hide. Its stone maul lay against the trunk, easily within its extended reach.

From Ashyn's vantage on a small rise of broken stone, he could he see its snout facing downward, the thickly muscled chest of the creature rising and falling gently. It was asleep.

Clever. The wizard thought. The bobble of a nearby creek ran by, churning the shallow waters violently against the stones. It masked the sound of the large creature's breathing.

The wizard drew his arrow back and aimed at the same spot he had hit the previous monster a few days prior. He knew it would be a kill shot, but it would be a slow one. An inhumane one.

Ashyn stalled as he looked down the shaft to the creature that was completely oblivious to him. A headshot would kill the creature with minimal suffering, but that was assuming his arrowhead would penetrate the bone. No, it would have to be a sternum shot again. It was their most obvious weakness.

He took a deep breath and told himself that he had to do this, had to prove to the Wild Elves that he was worthy of their trust. It was this creature's life for his sister. A fair trade, right? A carnivorous monster dies so that his innocent sister may live.

Ashyn bit the inside of his lip as he continued to stare at the monster hidden within the copse of trees. Their roles reversed, it would kill him, surely. Looking at the large hammer, he had no doubt of it.

So why did he refrain? He thought of the beast a few nights prior. Ashyn had been lying down and it had attacked him then. It had shown its true nature. Ashyn knew that it would kill him without question. So what then was stopping him from loosing the arrow into the beast's chest? What was staying his hand? It would be so easy to just let go, and let the arrow fly. Kill the monster. Earn the elves' trust. Save his sister.

He stared at the maul again. It was a weapon of battle, meant to buckle even the strongest armors, or the thickest of hides. It could crush every bone in his body in a single blow. There was something there. Something that he could see through its crude design. Was it artisanship?

He looked to the bull in the trees and saw the hides of other creatures wrapped about it. Clothing. Ashyn realized that this wasn't a dumb creature at all. In fact, if it could tailor clothing and construct weapons, it was sentient.

His arm shook and he knew he needed to make a decision. He closed his eyes. He could still make the shot without looking. He knew he could. He had to make a choice: kill the beast and earn the elf's trust, or find another way into Feydras' Anula. A longer way.

No longer seeing the bull in front of him, Ashyn heard the sizzling sound of the red hot poker over the bobble of water. He imagined it piercing his eyes the way it had his sister's. He felt his orb burst at the brand's touch. He couldn't stand the thought of her in pain any more. Of the torture's she endured at their hands. His arms shook violently, barely able to contain the pressure of the string anymore. This creature could die, and he was sure he could earn his way to Feydras' Anula. He was sure this was a test. But what would that truly gain? The death of one for what? Less suffering for his sister or for him?

He lowered the arrow and withdrew his pull, placing the string back into its neutral position and hating himself every step of the way. His fingertips were wet with blood where the string had cut into his skin.

"The few for the many," he whispered spitefully to his companion. The cat looked up at him with its pale yellow eye. "I am the few. Always the few."

Ashyn crept around the creek and continued to head southeast. Leaving his easy chance of finding Feydras' Anula behind him. He could feel his grey eyes growing hot with tears, but he refused to cry. This was his choice. The choice he had made a long time ago when he agreed to be Xexial's apprentice. When he agreed to be a wizard. The choice he had made to value all life, not just the ones of his choosing. That included what was evil as well.

He would find another way.

~ ~ ~

Jenhiro silently followed behind Ashyn after he left the hidden creature. Not taking any chances, he walked up to the sleeping bull and slit its throat. The churning brook nearby muffled its groans of shock. It grabbed its throat plaintively, knowing it did little good to stymie the flow of its rich, hot blood. Without a sound it tumbled to its side and the bull's eyes became glassy.

This wasn't the magic user. It did not have the staff. Jenhiro would find the one who did.

Ashyn continued onward completely oblivious to the death in his wake.

~ ~ ~

Neither Ashyn, nor Jenhiro were aware of a third party that watched silently from the shadows. Hidden by the power of nature itself, his amber eyes watched the two maliciously. It was time that the hunters became the hunted.

PREPARATIONS

Near black eyes stared down into the basin of water. The wreckage of the land clearly visible. All vegetation ruined. The sloping form of the gulley flattened and spread out in the shape of a V. Now only hardened clay and whitened bones remained. Scorching heat beat down upon the flat surface creating waves of shimmering heat, visible in the air.

Such power.

Such decimation.

Such **Destruction**.

A shaky voice came through the basin of water, "We know not where the wizard has gone. A scavenger may have drug his corpse away or picked his bones clean."

"No," she said, staring once more at the ruined earth. There must be something. Some sign. A lock of hair. An article of clothing. Even a piece of jewelry that was his. Keep looking, Eigron."

The druid nodded at her and severed the connection.

Brodea walked to the high-backed wooden chair on the dais. She sat, letting the hard object engulf her in its shadow. The naked wood felt warm against the bare skin of her back as she leaned against it. She looked around the room, as she always did when she didn't get the answers she sought. Usually it gave her a small measure of contentment.

Carved into a niche within the tallest elm in the Shalis-Fey sat the chamber. The council resided over one hundred and thirty feet above ground level. Behind her and intermittently at points in the high arched ceiling, there were openings carved into the wood. This was to help let in sunlight from the green canopy above. The few thin beams of sunlight were not enough to light the chamber, so torches aided, flickering their amber luminescence.

No lifts or ladders allowed anyone into the grand chamber. It was only accessible through a spiraling set of stairs that carved into very bark of the ancient elm itself.

It was a long, dangerous walk, but one worth it for the secrecy it provided. There was only one way in and the entire Council of Elm would see who joined them, when they were present. As of late, she preferred to use the chamber alone or with few in attendance.

The open expanse before her offered a view of the Ferhym city of Feydras' Anula far below them. Unlike their Wood Elf cousins, they did not naturally live in the trees, but upon the earth. She could see the many lookout stations and emergency buildings built within the sequoia trees on the horizon. They still were a people after all, and like the trees they lived around, they only felt at home with their roots planted in the ground firmly.

In the ground, she echoed in her own mind. That's what she had expected of the dead wizard. A grave to dig up, a marker, something of note. Not this foreign absence. It was as queer as her daughter was. She sighed and then massaged her eyelids with her fingers.

A voice emanated from the narrow stairs of the massive elm, "I take it his body still has not been found."

Brodea dropped her hand and looked at her lover, fellow councilor Vooken. She shook her head. "No."

The lean elf strode into the council chambers, wearing only his loin cloth and the woad of Moonspear. She could see his taut muscles playing under his copper flesh. He sat down on her right side in one of the many chairs that lined both sides of her own. "Give it time."

Brodea nodded and idly began playing with the amber bead necklace that signified her as the First Councilor. "I wanted to use his corpse to rally more to our purpose. I wanted to show that such wretched skewers of balance could be killed. That our cause is the right one, the just one."

"No one doubts you, First Councilor. We all know the Spirits speak directly to you. They demand this."

"You are right, of course." She looked upon the walls behind the dais. Long familiar were the ornate carvings of their insular societies' greatest honors. They were monuments of the smiting of the chief enemies of balance. Dragons, sentient monsters, and creatures of darkness and death all carved in dazzling displays. Each viciously slaughtered by the ever-relentless councilors. There were even a few reliefs of their greatest adversaries, wizards, victoriously defeated. Hers being the most recent, and it was already nineteen winters old.

To her, the walls were their history. They were a tribute to the Spirits that they followed. An honoring of the beauty of their cause and their way of life. But the walls were only a quarter of the way full. She hoped to add to it many more winters' worth of artistry and accomplishment.

"There is so much emptiness in these walls. We truly have so far to go." She declared passionately, "I will fill it all." The black curtain of her raven hair fell over her face. "For Ambit, I will line the walls with the annihilation of wizards."

Vooken remained silent at her reference to her deceased husband. Brodea didn't notice. "But in order to do that, we actually need to **kill** wizards. Two branches sent after the old one and the boy. Two!"

Vooken nodded.

"I was assured that at such a staggering loss, at least the old one had been put down. But now…"

"There could be any number of reasons his body cannot be found, Councilor. Eigron said the elder was dead. Rarely are druids wrong."

"But the body…" Brodea returned, crossing her arms.

"May well be contently resting in the belly of a great beast," Vooken finished. "All survivors came home, as did the remaining druid, to report what he had seen. That is the rule."

Brodea smiled thinly. "Of course." She reached over and patted the top of his hand. "These are unusual circumstances after all."

Brodea was pleased when he took her hand in his announcing, "We will crush the wizards, wipe them from Kuldarr, and achieve the greatest balancing history has ever known." Vooken's lips curved slightly. "Besides, I came with good news."

Brodea arched an immaculate eyebrow.

"I found her."

A full smile took to the Wild Elf's face. "You are positive?"

Vooken nodded, his deep brown eyes glittering with victory. "The druids took her to their cove after the battle to study."

"Then we are prepared for the Blood Wizard." She said fervently, "He will be powerless against us."

WATERFALLS

Ashyn stared at the cascading fall before him. Crystalline waters tumbled down jagged brown rocks. Each splash against the dark stone face caused an explosion of colors as rays of sunlight pierced their way through the canopy above to shine brightly upon the clinquant falls. It was an obstacle.

The waterfall was broken up into three tiers. The top ushered the thickest flows of white frothing waters that exploded against the next level in massive plumes of mist. The second tier thinned out, instead showing darker, jagged rocks between which the clear water weaved until it reached a small body of water below it. Finally, the base channeled thin drifts of cold liquid down into the brook by his feet. Stringers of the water cut through and under nooks in the stone, making it beautiful to look at and each grip questionable as to whether it would hold him or break away as nothing more than sediment.

On both sides of the falls were cliff walls. Any possible handholds covered in thick green algae. The moisture coupled with the growing heat made it feel like he was walking through air as heady as broth. They comprised the key ingredients for an impossible to scale rock-face.

Ashyn wiped the sweat from his brow as he fixated on the problem before him. He should go back and around, but that would take him over half a day. His food supplies were dwindling as was the fair game around him. He wasn't sure what part of the Shalis-Fey he was in anymore, but he knew it was nothing that Xexial had brought him through as a child. Backtracking with no food was risky.

Ginger stared stubbornly up the water face, as if it knew something that Ashyn did not. That made Ashyn even more reluctant to turn back. So far, the cat had been following a path almost single-mindedly. Not once had it taken him in a circle.

Ashyn looked to the thick foliage high above him. Somehow, even the trees had continued their upward climb through the cliffside, leaving him behind long ago. Had he been proficient in moving through them like the Wild Elves, he would have had no trouble navigating past the waterfall or even the ravine he had entrenched himself in. But of course, he knew nothing of brachiation.

He had to climb a waterfall. An ultra-slick, hard-tumbling, sharp-edged, seventy-foot-high waterfall. A single slip likely meant an extremely unpleasant fall. Death, if he were lucky.

"Are you sure there's no other way?" he asked the cat.

Ginger looked back at him once and meowed. Circled a moment, and returned to staring up the falls.

"Yeah. That's what I thought." Ashyn sighed, and shook his head. "Now I'm talking to the cat."

The wizard stepped forward and placed his hands against the wet stones. Water ran in little rivulets over his hands and down between the seams of his bracers. He could feel the mist damping his face.

Before he even made his first step he felt the weight of the cat as it bounded up the stones and landed on the top of his backpack. Ashyn grunted slightly at the weight, "Why don't you climb yourself?" he growled.

Ginger, however, hunkered down, digging its claws into the thinning leather on his back.

Ashyn scoffed at the creature and mumbled, "It's like you're trying to kill me."

He moved his soft-soled moccasin into position at the next lowest stone and hoisted himself up carefully, testing his weight against it. The rock didn't move at all. Looking above him, he saw another handhold. He reached, and got a firm hold, pulling himself a little higher.

The sparkling waters churned over his fingertips, making each grip all the more precarious, but slowly he made his way up the first tier of the waterfall until he was about fifteen feet in the air.

The two tiers above him roared onwards as he climbed another foot. "This isn't so bad," he said back to the cat, just as he reached for his next logical handhold. He felt it hold firm under his grip, and he pulled upwards.

Suddenly the handhold collapsed upon itself as the stone broke away into pebbles and lees. His right arm swung wide, and a newly created flow of water, poured roughly into his face. He gasped and hacked as the dregs of dirt and grime flooded his unprepared mouth.

Ashyn held on tightly with his left hand. Gripping with all his might, and hoping that the stone wouldn't give way. He leveraged himself against the wall and groped blindly upwards. Beyond the flowing waters his fingers brushed against what he hoped was a solid handhold. He gripped tight and pulled himself above the tear in the stone. The water pounded hard against his chest, but soon he was clear of it. He rolled on top of the first tier. Ginger hopped off him. Ashyn lay on his back wheezing as he gazed upwards at the next level.

Ginger walked up to him, the cat's fur matted down on one side with water. It's good yellow eye glaring at him.

"You wanted to ride on my back."

The large wildcat hissed at him, then backed away. Ashyn groaned and sat up, "Fine, I'm moving..." he began, but froze when he heard a loud splash from the base of the falls.

Slowly he leaned out over the ledge. He hoped to see wildlife in the brook, maybe even something he could hunt, though he was loathe to the idea of climbing back down to claim the carcass. Instead, he saw nothing.

Ashyn redirected his gaze to the canopy above. Perhaps a creature, or elf, had knocked something into the brook. Was it the elf from before, somewhere way up there? Was this his way of making contact again?

He heard another plunk in the water below. Ashyn saw nothing fall, and all his senses were alert now. Something was wrong.

He looked to Ginger who likewise looked at him quietly. It could sense it, too.

Once more, he peered down into the brook, and once more, he could see nothing in the thin, turbulent waters. What was going on?

He watched the water churn and bubble as it flowed around the jagged rocks below. The tempestuous stream moved away from the waterfall, its rough waters pushing and swirling. He couldn't see if anything fell into those waters. Though shallow, the intemperate flow pushed aggressively south. Whatever had fallen was long gone.

Ashyn turned slightly when he noticed something odd about how the water swirled at the base of the falls. The young wizard looked at it more intently. The waters themselves were separating as if they were parting for a stone. Yet there was no stone in the way, in fact there was nothing at all. The water was flowing around empty space.

That was when he saw the ripple.

"What?" he muttered.

A burst of light surged forward suddenly, and Ashyn narrowly moved out of the way as the rocky ledge he was just at exploded into scree. A new waterway tumbled from the clean rend in the stone.

Ashyn scrambled to his feet and quickly drew his bow and nocked an arrow. Carefully he looked over the edge once more, searching for whatever it was he was supposed to see.

He saw movement, a small waver in the very air above the brook, and then an eruption of energy surged forward once more.

Ashyn tumbled backwards as the ball of energy tore by, eagerly eating at the water as it passed. In its wake, it left an undulating current of steam.

Again Ashyn moved forward. This time not even trying to discern a location, he quickly fired three arrows into the brook below. One was lost to the waters, the other two disintegrated against the rocks.

He nocked another just as the water erupted behind him in a massive plum of acrid white mist. Ashyn gasped and waved away the scorching miasma. As the waters cleared, he noticed even more trouble. Vines were beginning to emerge out of the cracks in the stones. They slithered like snakes working their way towards him. He had seen magic like that before. He had almost died from it.

"Shit."

The boy knew he could not win this engagement. Not on this terrain and not even with higher ground. He needed to level the playing field, take the opportunity away from whatever was attacking him. Now that really meant he had to scale the falls.

He sheathed his arrow, threw the bow across his back, and attacked the next tier with quickness. Ginger was on him instantly, scaling up his robes and wedging itself between his back and pack.

Ashyn heard the hiss and crack as another energy ball struck the falls close to him. Cold waters poured onto his hands as he fought to find a grip against the increasingly slick surface.

Each handhold became more dangerous, each position of his feet more tenuous as he climbed. He hissed as he felt the stones bite into his fingers. He didn't have the luxury of testing the rocks to see how sharp they were.

Ashyn risked a glance back and was alarmed to see the vines were scaling the rocky wall after him. The flowing waters did little to deter the approaching creepers.

There was a sudden loud splash below him and he knew that whatever was there had just joined him on that tier. Ashyn climbed faster.

The boy made it just to the top of the second tier, forty feet above the bubbling brook, when the lead climbing plant wove around his trailing right foot. He grunted in surprise as it pulled him roughly backwards, slamming his chest into the mist laden waters. He fought and tugged against the vines as he tried to reach the skinning knife on his belt.

The vines pulled him down harder, pinning his waist painfully against the sharp rocks. Instantly he changed his mind about the knife, knowing that he couldn't support his weight with one arm alone.

Ginger bounded down his back and slashed at the green vines with its claws and teeth. Confused by the sheer intelligence of his ally, he fought to pull himself onto the next tier, straining against the strong vegetation.

Ashyn screamed angrily as he made it first an inch, then another. On his back, he felt Ginger swinging at the vines. He could hear it hissing and spitting. There was a sudden snap, and then Ashyn was loose. Quickly he pulled himself over the lip and collapsed. His arms weary from the strain, he just laid there in the thick balmy brume, exhausted.

The cold mud clung to his back, sucking him deeper into the banks. All around him the crashing water was deafening. The raging current was heaviest here as it slammed into a natural basin.

The gurgling waters churned violently, casting everything around him in a dense haze. Ashyn stared hard in the profuse mist to the ledge he had come from. Any moment he knew those vines were going to creep over.

He whispered to himself, "Get up," as he continued to stare at the ledge. "You have to get up." Tension gripped at his body. Fear coursed through his shoulders. The bitter memory of his near strangulation by the druid vines permeated his thoughts as much as the mist did his skin.

He needed to overcome this. Overcome this fear. *Move,* he told himself, *Move!*

His body responded.

Ashyn made a great squelching sound as he pulled himself out. The suction broke free violently and he immediately shot to his feet and stumbled forward in the murk. He caught his footing preventing going face forward into the basin. Once again mobile, Ashyn sought out the source of the crashing noise. He found it quickly.

Water poured down liberally before him, drenching his armor and robes. Ashyn reached for a handhold, feeling the violent waters stab at his raw skin. The pounding white water slammed against his flesh piercing his body with stinging pinpricks while at the same time trying its hardest to push him into the basin.

Ashyn looked up through the waters. It slapped hard against his chest and face, but through it all, he could see the top. Less than thirty feet away. He only need make it a little further.

He searched for a good point to climb where the tumbling falls spread thinnest. Finding a large rock, he grabbed a hold and heaved upwards. Still, even the thinnest of places was an obstacle. The wizard fought against the hard pounding waters, climbing a few inches at a time.

He groaned and strained, taking in mouthfuls of the clear waters and spitting them out. It felt like a herd of bison pushing against his chest. His thin arms were weak. They shook with every pull. Yet each moment brought him closer to the top than the last.

The waters around him roared in his ears. He knew he would never be able to hear when his hunter climbed to the next level. The watery brume blinded him to the basin behind him. He only hoped that it worked both ways, that it hid him as well from this mysterious adversary.

Finally, he made it underneath a large outcropping that split the waterfall in two briefly. Away from the assailing waters and secure in his hold on the stone he risked a look down. He was perhaps fifteen feet up. *Halfway there*, he thought.

The mist clouded thickly around the basin, but moved just enough to make out a form inside the waters. Ashyn went white. No elf hunted him.

The form lumbered forward in the murk. It was a strange sight, insubstantial. He could see the mist through it, as well as the running water beneath it. There was nothing to it, a shadow in the shape of a massive beast. Like a specter in the water.

Ashyn watched silently, as did his mud-covered ally on his back.

The shade moved slowly and with purpose, swaying back and forth. Ashyn knew it was looking for him. Once or twice he even saw what he guessed was its head tilt up to his position. It was at these moments that his chest grew tightest. Several seconds passed, and still the shadowy pursuer did not attack him.

Finally, it turned from the falls and it sloshed through the waters, cutting a large swath as it moved towards the bank. As the shadow broke the waterline, Ashyn watched it waver once more and then disappear completely.

The wizard sighed as he leaned against the stones that supported him. The thing had not seen him. Somehow, it had lost him. Ashyn reached up to grab a handhold to pull himself up the final tier. Loose stone slid down from his grip and tumbled across the ravaging waters into the pool below.

Even with the thunderous waters roaring in his ears, he heard a snort of surprise. Suddenly Ashyn saw movement once more on the bank. A swirling eddy of mist coalesced the shadow creature. Something long and narrow was between it and the water. Then Ashyn watched in surprise as that object drove into the water. The effects were immediate. Ice surged from the object, fanning out to encompass the entire basin.

"I don't believe it," Ashyn whispered harshly to himself.

As the ice touched the churning liquid, the dumbfounded wizard could only watch as it flash froze. Immediately, the humidity evaporated and a chill permeated the air.

Ice solidified the churning base of the falls, turning it into slick, glittering hillocks. Then it started to climb slowly up the falls. It was a battle fighting the turbulent white waters, but the growing ice over was winning.

"Shit! Shit!" Ashyn's pretense of stealth vanished, as he turned to climb up the freezing waterway.

He could feel the temperature shifting in the water as he struggled to climb as quickly as he could. Soon his fingers were freezing cold against the ragged rocks. Shortly after, they went completely numb. He couldn't even feel his toes in his boots.

Still, Ashyn pressed through the waters. He only had six feet left to climb, and he would be free of whatever it was that pursued him. At least he hoped that would be the case. Ashyn wasn't quite sure what was up top, but he reasoned it wasn't more falls.

He heard Ginger growl in his ear and he looked down to see the scaling ice was only inches from his feet. His wet skin stuck to the brittle stone. He climbed faster.

Above him, the crest of the waterfall was only a foot away. It was so close. His hand went over the ledge and grabbed solid stone.

Ashyn felt the ice grab his robes, pulling him roughly against the freezing falls. Ginger mewled in surprise, and Ashyn slipped, his knee slamming into the icy rocks.

He cried out in pain, and held on vainly. Ashyn tried to pull himself up, but it was too late. The freeze captured his left boot in the water. Thick ice wrapped around it and began crawling up his ankle like a spider. All remaining feeling in his leg disappeared. He couldn't climb anymore.

Ashyn stared down in horror as his leg was slowly entombed beneath the glistening ice. He tried to swing it, move it to break the ice, but there was nothing. Only a deadened limb. Anger swelled through him, and he glared down at the shadowy form. He could feel the satisfaction of the catch emanating from the creature. It had him.

Had Ashyn had his power, had he not been lame, he could have countered the ice easily. He wouldn't have even been having this fight. Now, he was powerless.

He screamed savagely at the shadowed form. He wouldn't give it the satisfaction of such an easy victory. A bloodless victory. He writhed and squirmed against his deadened limb. He was bound to the frozen falls. He felt the ice creeping higher.

Once it encompassed his torso, it would shut down his internal organs one by one, and lull him to sleep and then death. If his fatigued muscles didn't let go of the rock-face first, anyways. He wasn't sure what would give first, the ice or his bones. He cringed at the thought. Things were grim indeed.

Ashyn refused to accept defeat. He had a city to find and a sister to save! He wouldn't let these woods take him. Not yet.

The wizard reached down and drew his skinning knife. Luckily, his leg was numb, so he knew what he did next he wouldn't feel it as bad as he should have. He only hoped he wouldn't lose all his strength or bleed out before he finished the job.

Ice gripped at his other foot. He adjusted it higher up, placing him at an awkward position. It would have to be above the knee, it was the only way to be sure, without the angle compromising his grip. Ashyn closed his eyes and prepared for what was to come. He lowered the knife to his thigh. He could feel the pressure of the blade against his robes like a weight on his soul. This was the only way. The only way to save his sister.

He slid the blade quickly against the fabric of the robes splitting it swiftly and evenly. He then placed the cold iron directly against his bare flesh. "For Julietta." He breathed.

And then there was pain.

COADJUTORS

Ashyn screamed in surprise as Ginger latched on to the back of his neck, biting deeply. He dropped the skinning knife in reflex and swung to get the cat off him. He could feel his blood welling beneath the wound and running hot down his back.

"What is wrong with you!" he yelled at it. "You've just killed us!"

The ice trapping his left leg suddenly exploded. Ashyn's leg broke free. Swiftly he moved it away from the creeping ice.

Another javelin rained down from up in the canopy and destroyed the ice directly below his other foot. Ashyn looked up in alarm.

"Climb, fool!" Ashyn heard in the chittering language of Ferhym. Then a javelin soared down near the shadowy form. It bellowed in shock. Another, and then another javelin came down around it driving it back.

The wizard didn't need any encouragement. Swiftly, he reached up to the ledge and heaved himself over. It was difficult because his cold-deadened leg did little to support any of his weight. As he rolled onto the ridge, he felt Ginger leap from his back. The cat then hopped the exposed rocks to the shore.

The pressure of the water threatened to push Ashyn back over the side. He rolled away, his numb leg barely functioning, until he pushed himself solidly against one of the rocks.

He risked a glance down over the ridgeline. He could see more javelins soaring upon the shadow. Ashyn watched in amazement as the long object ripped from the water and aimed to the trees.

Balls of white energy flew forth from the umbral form, while the icy falls simultaneously thawed. After several moments no more javelins fell. He wondered if the creature below had landed a blow upon his savior.

"You need to move," the Ferhym voice came from above again. "I have no more javelins."

Ashyn knew what that meant. His pursuer was coming. Groaning, and fighting an almost nonfunctional limb, Ashyn forced himself to stand. He drug his leg heavily against the force of the water and made his way to the bank where a mud-laden cat awaited him.

"We'll talk about this later," Ashyn said angrily as he pointed to the wound on his neck.

Ginger glared at him with one ugly yellow eye, before it turned away from him, following the river.

Ashyn shook his head and followed the creature dumbly, lost in thought. The cat had known about the Wild Elf in the trees. Had it known what the elf was going to do?

And what was that exactly? What the Ferhym had just done was inconceivable. He had saved Ashyn's life. He had saved a wizard.

~ ~ ~

The shadowy figure slapped the javelins away from him angrily. He almost had it! The tall elf in red. The killer with the bow! It had been his!

He stormed back into the cold basin and reached down into the misty waters. His auburn, three-fingered hand wrapped around the glinting metal object.

Carefully he lifted it out of the water and to his snout. In one good sniff, he got everything he needed. He placed the skinning knife on his goat-hide belt and then looked up the falls. This hunt was far from over.

~ ~ ~

Night fell quickly in the Shalis-Fey, and Ashyn was overly careful in his camp this time. He didn't remove his leather tunic, though he desperately wanted to. Already, the odor emanating from the grimy, algae infused mud was drowning out all the pleasant smells of the forest.

Instead, he focused on his weapons. The scurry up the falls had cost him a number of arrows, and of course he lost his skinning knife. Amongst other needs for it, he wasn't sure how he was going to shave now. All he had now was his bow and his rapier.

Much to his surprise, and pleasure, his bone bow survived remarkably unscathed. Ashyn was continuously amazed at the durability of such a weapon. And so, fearful of sleeping, he attentively doted upon it, removing the grime built up from rolling in the mud. It was an arduous task, but he welcomed it compared to the alternative, sleeping when the shadow beast returned.

The rapier, secured in its scabbard, only needed a thorough drying so the thing wouldn't be pitted with rust. Ashyn wasn't actually sure how to dry the inside of a scabbard; he had never needed to know such weapon maintenance. He opted to lay its open end in front of the fire. He figured it probably was doing more harm than good, but his options were limited.

Ginger sat across the small campfire, vainly trying to lick away the clumped patches of fur. Ashyn felt it was a lost cause, but his feline ally persistently worked at it none-the-less.

Ashyn stared at the cat. The young wizard couldn't deny any longer that it was different from a standard cat, but what was it? It showed intelligence, problem solving skills, an intuitive sense of direction, but what did that mean exactly? His knowledge of the Shalis-Fey was very limited. He wasn't sure what variations of feline species called the woods their home.

He knew of the Bristle Wolves and their intelligence, but they were canines. He had also seen firsthand the Wild Elves and the orcs, but never any other predators, though he knew there were bears about from some of the droppings he had encountered. Only game, like hare and deer, had been prevalent up to the falls, and he spied the occasional tracks of an elk. So what other hunters truly existed in the Fey?

His mind drifted to the shadow creature. It was clearly new to him. Worse, it knew magic. That made it sentient. Ashyn saw magic like that before, with the elves. Druids. The wraithlike form didn't resemble either of them. Ashyn wasn't sure if that counted for much. Wild Elves wanted wizards dead. If they had learned what he was, it made sense to send a druid to finish the job. But if that were the case, then why the aid from the elf in the trees?

Had it gone rogue? Were the Wild Elves different than he believed they were? There were always two sides to a story; he didn't have all the answers. Not yet anyway.

He thought about the wizards themselves. Enough time passed now that the wizards could have formulated some type of response. Were they going to let him roam the woods a recreant, or would they send one the Maba-Heth?

Most of what Ashyn knew about them was either conjecture or fable. He understood they trained exclusively for the destruction of recreants and that they always worked in pairs. They were the assassins of the Seven, when not hunting rogue wizards at least.

Still he was groping blindly in the woods now. He wanted to know more. He needed to know more. More about the creatures within the forest. More about the elves. More about the wraith hunting him. More about the Maba-Heth.

He thought of the encounter, twice now, with the bull-like creatures. What he once thought were minotaurs, he now wasn't so certain. There was something to them as well.

Were they native to the Shalis-Fey? He didn't think so, and yet he just didn't know. Wouldn't the Wild Elves be at constant war with the bull-men if that were the case? With all these sentient creatures, why hadn't he seen signs of life yet? No camp fires, no settlements, no villages of any kind. Perhaps Feydras' Anula was nothing more than a myth. Was he chasing just another fairy tale?

Ashyn sighed and looked to the small fire before him. He was ignorant and he hated it. Ashyn was too far gone from his element. From books and tomes of knowledge, and even magic.

How long since he felt a connection? A lifetime it seemed. It was such a deeply empty feeling. A hollow in the core of him. Buried in his chest right next to his heart, as if a piece of his soul was missing.

Instinctively Ashyn held out his hand to the fire. In his mind he called to the flames. Beckoned them to join with his outstretched hand. Invited them to be part of him.

Nothing.

He whispered incantations to the burning pitch within the flames. He tried to feed it more air. Get it to burn stronger. He excelled as a wizard at these things. The few that he truly was a master of.

Again, nothing.

Ashyn felt the heat of eyes on him then, and quickly dropped his hand. Had he revealed too much to his elven watcher?

He looked up from the fire and saw Ginger studying him, its lemon yellow orb watching him intently, the other beginning to peek its way out of the healing mass of flesh. "How smart are you?"

Ginger studied him a moment longer, and then turned away ignoring him. Ginger resumed its futile effort to clean itself.

Ashyn ran his fingers through his red hair and blew out a large gust of air. He would get no answers tonight, only questions. The more his mind wandered, the more questions were likely. He turned his thoughts inward.

Absently he stroked at the platinum braid tied to his bracer. He wondered about the Exemplar child once more. Now she was full grown, as he was. Could she control her powers? Could he look her in the eyes? Those mysterious, quicksilver eyes.

Ashyn reached down and removed the platinum braid of hair. He rolled it between his fingers, feeling its lush softness under his growing calluses. He snickered to himself. Already he was asking more questions. Always the questions.

Xexial warned him that gathering knowledge was amongst one to the top things wizards did. It looks like asking questions was just ingrained. He chuckled slightly louder at the thought of Xexial.

He would go to the Seven once he saved Julietta. He wouldn't run from them, he decided. He would fulfill Xexial's last request to him and warn them of the war in detail, not just what was written in a letter. Perhaps he might even find something of use in Feydras' Anula. A bargaining chip for his life. After all, Xexial was dead, and yes, even though he chose his sister over his master's last request, could it not be argued that his situation was a unique one? Was he not technically without a master? That should merit something.

That was, if he was not hunted by them already. Thoughts drifted back to the specter at the falls. Maba-Heth wizards? Were the Seven really willing to risk sending a wizard into the Shalis-Fey just to quell the recreant?

It was an unpleasant, but strangely logical thought. Outside of the Ferhym, and the one encounter with the bull creature, there was no hostility by anyone else. He was not truly certain how the

Seven would respond to his letter. He had never met them. Aggression was definitely an option.

A voice broke from the darkness, "A clouded mind means a mired judgment."

Ginger jumped to its feet, hissing and spitting. Ashyn, in a blink nocked an arrow and raised his bow, enduring the pain in his hands. He leapt to his feet, and spun, looking for the source of the voice.

"At least, your reflexes are still stout."

Ashyn looked up. There he saw a Wild Elf on an overhanging branch looking down at him. For once, the stealthy creature was not hiding.

"Are you the one I owe my escape to?" Ashyn asked in Ferhym.

The Wild Elf nodded.

Ashyn lowered his bow. "Then I thank you."

The Wild Elf rolled off the branch and dropped fifteen feet into a crouch. He stood up unnervingly close to the wizard. Like the rest of his Ferhym kin, he bore only a loincloth and the ritual body paintings across his hard muscled frame. His eyes were a lighter brown then Ashyn had seen in the past, and his face was harder, more chiseled. One who spent long periods away from the comforts of a settlement.

Both sides of his head were shaven, leaving the bulk of his hair along the center. A single long, dark brown braid sat on the back of his neck.

Ashyn realized after a moment, that this curious style was to keep the hair out of his face when he moved through the trees or when he fought. Though unusual looking, it made tactical sense. He wondered why the elf didn't just keep it short, or shave it altogether.

On his back was a deer-hide quiver, now devoid of any javelins. All he had was his spear that was nestled across the quiver with some sort of break-away tether.

Across his torso, attached to his loincloth, were pouches and water skins. Unlike Ashyn, this elf traveled extremely light.

"Why have you revealed yourself now?" Ashyn asked.

The Wild Elf shrugged and said matter-of-factly, "I cannot continue to follow you, and hunt the skewer that is rampant in the Fey. I have determined that for now, you are no skewer, and you would be easier to watch if we made an alliance, tree-brother."

"Like the other night," Ashyn replied.

The Wild Elf nodded. "You are proficient enough."

Ashyn wasn't quite sure if the elf before him had just complimented him or insulted him.

"Then you know what it was that hunted me?" the wizard asked.

The elf shook his head no. "Not certain, but I have an idea."

Ashyn waited for more. Nothing. The wizard looked into the woods. "Is it still out there?"

The Elven hunter nodded. "It is, but it has become difficult to track. It leaves no traces of its passing, which is troublesome."

"Indeed."

The elf looked around at Ashyn's dismal camp. "I will adjourn to the trees, and watch from there. On the morrow we will hunt the last of the skewers."

Ashyn bit back his reply that he wouldn't kill what the Wild Elf thought were skewers and instead nodded. He would deal with that particular problem when it arose. The elf turned to walk away.

"Do you have a name?" Ashyn asked the departing Wild Elf.

He turned around and looked into Ashyn's grey eyes for many moments, as if deciding if he should divulge such information to the stranger. At last, he muttered, "Jenhiro." He disappeared into the thick underbrush.

After the Wild Elf was gone, Ashyn sat back down and smiled at Ginger. "Finally," he said aloud. The cat looked at him curiously. "A lead."

SPRIGGAN

Slowly his cerulean eyes opened to take in the morning light. His breaths came in shallow gasps. He looked around in confusion. He was in a room. Small and simple. Yellow wicker furniture dotted the confines, dirty and ragged from overuse. He looked to the floor. It was dirt. How had he come to be here? What had happened?

Then he remembered the fog. A heavy pervasive miasma that covered his body, and soaked him to the bone. There was more too…A battle. A final battle.

The old man blinked away the thoughts of the terrible fighting. He tried to ignore the smells of blood and feces that lingered in his nostrils heavily like smoke on clothing. A ghost of a memory haunted his mind.

It was over now. The battle done. How was this possible?

He tried to sit up, but his body groaned in protest. He grunted and fell back onto the cot in ragged breaths.

A squeaky, mouse-like voice seemed to answer his very thoughts, "Yes, you be alive. Sort of."

Surprised, the old man turned his head, following the peculiar sound. Bent over a brass contraption of some sort was a curious creature. Overly large almond-shaped hazel eyes stared back at the old man, just over the top of the bizarre apparatus it was working on.

It had beige colored skin and was incredibly small. Like a very young child. Its frame was petite, reminding him of the lithe form of an Elf. Large pointed ears stuck out from underneath thick brown plumes. Not plumes. Quills. As if a porcupine lain recumbent against its head.

The creature waved a three-fingered hand, "Woo-hoo."

The man sighed and leaned his head back against the cot, muttering, "A spriggan."

"Correction!" The spriggan said holding up a finger. "A spriggan who you owe your life hue-mon."

The old man sighed once more as he shook his head, "How long have I been out?"

The creature shrugged. "Few weeks. Month maybe."

"A month!"

The spriggan held his hands up helplessly. "Cannot say for certain. Time not be so important to me. It is something that you always chase and can never catch. Something you try to slow down, but can never stop. Time be always plodding forward, an unstoppable juggernaut. It will either be the instrument of our destruction, or the agent of our glory. So, I says why be dwelling on such things. Let it flow and enjoy the ride."

The human grumbled as he struggled to get up once more. Again, he fell panting upon the cot. He was so weak. He looked angrily towards the diminutive creature. "There is too much that needs to be done! There are forces at play, and I have wasted away too much time as it is."

"Time does not waste away hue-mon, only people do," the spriggan replied. "And you are here, un-wasted, you should be happy now. What presses you so, that the epiphany of your resurrection is lost upon you?"

The man did not answer right away, but turned his cold blue eyes to the thatch-work ceiling. He was alive when he should be dead. It defied everything he had ever been taught. It defied the logic of his body. Yet here he was, and though the spriggan before him was taking claim for it, he wondered if the truth of why there was still life in him lay with the boy.

"Tell me what happened after I fell."

The spriggan bounded around the strange device and moved in front of the prostate man, smiling widely with pointed teeth. The human was surprised to see the creature not only fully clothed, but with an oculus dangling precariously from a pocket on his tunic. It rubbed its hands together eagerly and then sat on the side of the cot to tell its tale.

~ ~ ~

The old man had listened to the spriggan's recounting in great detail. It surprised him to know exactly how big the New Wasteland, as the spriggan called it, was now.

"Afterwards, when all is long done, I come out from my home to investigates and claim trinkets. Not be long before I be upon your body, and as I begin to remove things, you make single breath."

"A single breath?"

The spriggan nodded fervently. "So I place ear to cold chest, may have poked you once or twices, so sorry. Anyhows, I listen and at first I hear nothing. Then when I think your breath be all in my head I hears it. A lump-dump in your chest. One heartbeat. So much time passes, but then I hear it again. Two heartbeats. I realize, amazingly, that you are alive. Not much alive, mostly dead, yes, but somewhat alive. So, I takes you before anything can gobble you up. Good thing too because these last weeks, I've even seen a dragon in these parts."

"Excuse me?"

The spriggan nodded eagerly. "Yes, yes! It's true! A dragon of red I did spot. If I knew better, which I know much methinks, I would say the dragon be looking for the boy."

The old man fell back into the bed trying to process it all. A dragon. The elves. Ashyn's survival.

"You have a name, magic man?" The spriggan asked him.

"Xexial," he responded hoarsely. "My name is Xexial Bontain."

KHYRIAXX

The spriggan held its three-fingered hand to its chest. "I be Khyriaxx."

Xexial nodded to the spriggan and looked at his strange brass contraption only a few feet away. Deep scratches crisscrossed the brass framework. "Why are you so far from your people?"

"They not be so far," Khyriaxx responded. "Closer than you think really. But in truth, I just prefer the solitude. Unusual for my kind yes, but it allows me to tinker in private."

"And yet you saved me?"

Khyriaxx scratched behind his pointed ear. His quills bounced wildly with the aggressive motion. "Yeah, well, it's not like you be talking much for the last few weeks. You be an ideal guest."

"You're evading," Xexial said flatly.

The spriggan shrugged. "So what if I am? You be easier to handle while you slept. All I had to worry about is when you be going to foul yourself, and if you be taking enough nourishment. Not so much to deal with. Now you have questions. Questions about me. Questions about time, about the new wasteland, about moving." He turned away and began busying himself with his brass device.

"Questions are good," Xexial stated. "It lets us get to know one and other. Builds trust."

"I have no use for your questions." The spriggan twisted something so hard Xexial heard it pop. "They cause too much thinking, too many variables."

Perplexed, the wizard asked, "You don't like to think?" He took in all the strange contraptions the tinkerer had about his room.

"You want to answer many problems. Hue-mons, all they see are problems. You don't narrow your focus." Khyriaxx tinkered with something then continued, "You look only at the problems, and not at solutions. People be like this. Solutions are easy with inventions though. A single algorithm to solve using steps. Machines they… they create different problems, sure, but steadier variables. It be easy to locate their root. Solve their equation. People, be not so easy." He shook his head. "They be very random."

Xexial nodded. "I think I am beginning to understand then."

And he was. For a long time Xexial had been alone, before Ashyn. He became accustomed to the solitude. Until the boy came along, he never had to answer so many questions. Yet, Xexial found such questions refreshing after decades as a hermit. Khyriaxx obviously didn't feel the same as he. People made the little tinkerer nervous. They were random and chaotic. He liked order. A path. His question about what happened was easy to answer. The spriggan eagerly shared what he had witnessed in the battle. He wondered what Khyriaxx might be hiding? Why he was so far removed from his kin?

Xexial found himself in a predicament. He needed answers. Normally he would just take them, demand that the spriggan answer his questions. Never before was he indebted to anyone for saving his life. Ashyn may be what prevented his death, but it was Khyriaxx that kept him in the realm of the living for the last month. That changed things. No one had ever cared if a wizard lived or died, except those wanting to be a wizard themselves. This creature had, knowing what he was, and thus far made no demands of him or his abilities. Xexial found that very odd.

Then he understood what the spriggan was saying about narrowing his focus. His question was very broad, more of a statement really. The real question was why the little one saved him. Given the way Khyriaxx spoke he ventured a guess, "You saved me because you think I am a solution?"

Khyriaxx looked back up from the machine, his hazel eyes sparkling. "See you solve problem on your own!"

Xexial thought long and hard to why he could possibly be a solution. He knew of no conflicts with the spriggan people. In fact, very few people even knew of the secluded race. If not for his dealings with the gnomes, Xexial would not be among them. The gnomes told him of their eccentric, tinkering neighbors at great length, yet he never expected to meet one. So few being away from their home cities.

"Are your people in some type of trouble?" he prodded, "Is that why you need me?"

"No, no," Khyriaxx answered quickly, "They be fine. Be safe. This be personal."

"Do you want to be a wizard?"

Khyriaxx's quills fluttered wildly on his head as he shook his head at Xexial. "Too many variables. No need. Keep narrowing."

Xexial thought for a while, but nothing came to mind. "I just don't know how you expect me to be the solution."

"Sometimes not all is revealed to you quickly. Sometimes it takes time." The curious creature finagled something on the device. "When you can walk, we will leave, and then you will see."

The surly wizard harrumphed. "We'll see." He studied Khyriaxx, saying again. "We'll see."

~ ~ ~

Two days later, Xexial found himself mobile enough to want to stretch his legs and get out of the cramped quarters.

Khyriaxx rarely spoke to him. If Xexial tried to engage the spriggan in anyway, the creature would just ignore him and dive deeper into tinkering with its bizarre contraptions.

It enraged Xexial to see such a simple creature ignoring his questions, but after watching the thing work, he realized spriggans were anything but simple. The creature acted otherwise in most instances, but Xexial could see a very intelligent mind. The way Khyriaxx was able to manipulate items in its home was amazing. The strange contraption he had been working on when Xexial had first awakened turned out to be a wind driven device that cooled Khyriaxx's entire domicile.

Xexial watched with much curiosity, when the spriggan finished, how it had turned the thing around and affixed it to a strange pipe that ran through his wall to the outside. Once connected, the spriggan disappeared outside and soon Xexial felt cool air emanating from the device, reducing the growing heat that was filling the room. As Xexial stared at the weird thing, he began to make out details. The front of it was covered in brass slats, like that of a keep window. The spriggan could move those slats open and close, leverage them up or down, and even left and right. The slats directed where the air was blowing.

As Xexial looked further, he could see blades turning behind the slats. When Xexial was able to move around, he checked outside to see what was the source driving the fan. When he opened the door he was amazed to see a small windmill hidden amongst the rocky fissures of the lowlands the spriggan lived in. This windmill generated the power necessary to help the small creature survive. It made cool air, made energy to run some of his other ludicrous devices, and even helped keep a fire burning in Khyriaxx's stove.

Khyriaxx had made an impressive home in the lowlands. He had a small crop farm, two goats for milk and cheese, and he had even created his own well and irrigation system, using the windmill to drive the water to and from the well to the interior of his home and his quaint farm fields.

Xexial also recognized where in the lowlands he was. He was slightly north of the crater that the Onyx Tower resided in. Dark brown and craggy, the split rocks hid the spriggan's modest dwelling from drifting eyes, and the sharp obsidian sliver that jutted skyward to his west kept most intruders at a wide berth. Xexial protected Khyriaxx all this time by his proximity to the Onyx Tower, and the wizard never knew.

"That's why you needed me alive," he said looking away from his home and down to the diminutive creature beside him.

"Hue-mons fear wizards. They be avoiding the crater at all costs. Keeps Khyriaxx safe." The spriggan nodded. "How long after you dies does the word gets out? Then many elves, many hue-mons."

Xexial chuckled deeply. For once, someone had gotten the right of it. Wizards value all life. They protected the balance of life.

"Well Khyriaxx, I will never tell you to leave this land. Fear not, you are always welcome here."

Khyriaxx smiled at him with a large toothy grin. "Good, because Khyriaxx not want to make you mostly dead again for trying."

The spriggan reached up and handed Xexial a bag. The wizard looked down with a questioning eyebrow raised. "These be all the things I find on you."

Xexial nodded and took the satchel. He would very much like to be equipped with his things again. They were an eclectic collection of items that he had gathered over the winters. Many useful, some personal. His eyes glanced at the bareness of his hand as he held the satchel. He hadn't traveled feeling so barren in a long time.

"Be you heading to where it was so important that you couldn't miss it?" Khyriaxx questioned.

Xexial shook his head. "No. Not anymore. First I must head back to the Onyx Tower to re-stock fully. Ashyn bore much of our traveling supplies and he has too long a head start. If he hasn't reached the tower of the Seven already then he will be there soon.

"If the Ferhym truly think me dead, that will give me an advantage that I would be a fool to pass up. I must know why they have started this crusade against wizards. I must know how they think they can win. Wild Elves are fervent and brave, but they are not stupid. They have something. Something they think will give them an edge. I must find out what."

Khyriaxx looked at him. "When you get ready to leave then, stop back here. I thinking I be able to help you with that."

Xexial thought briefly on asking him what he meant. If Khyriaxx had information for him, he should just give it now. Still the thought of coercing it out of him only lasted a moment. The spriggan kept him alive. That deserved a certain amount of latitude. Besides, it wouldn't hurt to stop back on the way to Buckner. Xexial hated sailing, maybe the spriggan had a device or remedy for that nauseous feeling he knew he would be living with once on open water.

Xexial nodded and turned towards the dark spike on the horizon. It was time he went home. There were pressing things that he absolutely needed to know. Like what Ashyn did and how he did it? And what were the ramifications of such an act?

Most importantly, he needed to know why he was still alive.

RETURN TO THE ONYX TOWER

Xexial climbed over the rocky crest of the crater. The ledge stretched out like four extended fingers. He wedged himself between two of the lower ones and pushed through. As he did, the green verge of the lowlands was visible on the horizon. This was it. This was the place, he told himself.

He turned towards the direction of where he last fought the Ferhym. Immediately he saw what Khyriaxx called the New Wasteland.

Cracked beige clay glared angrily upwards towards the bright blue cloudless sky above. Heat reflected off the desecrated surface in thick waves that turned the distant horizon into a mottled blur. Xexial sighed. He did this. He broke one of the sacred Wizard Tenets and took lives using **Destruction**.

At the time, it seemed like the only option. Ashyn needed to survive. He needed to warn the Seven of the Ferhym and their crusade against wizards. He had weighed the price heavily in his mind and felt there was no other way.

Now, seeing the shattered remains of the earth in front of him, knowing that in that cone of decimation there had once been many living, breathing elves, he wasn't so sure.

Xexial shook his head, *Don't be a fool*. The Council of Elm brought this upon them. No one else. It was their conflict. Their twisted, corrupt view point. Xexial was only acting to keep Ashyn alive. "You've grown too soft," he chastised himself.

He caught a movement out of the corner of his eye, and instinctually ducked behind the outcropping he was next to. Xexial looked around it.

There, scouring one of the hillocks, were half a dozen Wild Elves. Their backs were all to him. Cautiously he watched as they moved and poked at the ground with their spears. Others were rifling through the grass with their fingers.

One overturned a ripe and swollen carcass of a Bristle Wolf. A single arrow jut out from its head, its maw locked in a permanent visage of rage. The limbs were stiff and the abdomen swollen with gas. Xexial was sure that the corpse infested with maggots.

As the wizard watched, he saw that one of the elves stood apart from the rest. Where the rest had spears and javelins, this one was just standing there, holding a bowl. His head bent low to it, and he was talking to the small pewter receptacle in his native dialect. Xexial could just make out the small white shapes of bones in the elf's wild hair.

He growled, "Druid." Xexial hated druids. There was just something wrong with someone who would rather spend more time talking to animals than dealing with other people.

Xexial looked past the druid to the tower beyond. It was maybe a four-hour hike, if he moved quickly. His eyes fell back to the elves. He studied them for a long time, trying to decide if they posed a threat to Khyriaxx. He considered the odds that the hunters would find the spriggan's tucked away abode. Never once in all his long winters had he found the spriggan's place. Though, in truth, he never actually sought it out either.

These elves were actively searching for something. It could very well be Khyriaxx that they were looking for. Or Xexial himself. Once they found the spriggan's tracks, it wouldn't take much to find his home. And when they did, how long until Khyriaxx talked?

Xexial looked back the way he had come. It wasn't far. Should he warn Khyriaxx? Aid him? Kill him? Xexial shook his head, he just didn't know. His life had never before been in another's hands. He hated the feeling in his gut almost as much as he hated druids. It was like a compulsion to help the spriggan.

The only other time he felt compelled to do something like that was when he saved Ashyn from the wreckage of Bremingham well over a decade before. And that was for very different reasons.

The old wizard looked back at the elves. They would kill Khyriaxx, no question about it. They would interrogate him, label him an unbalancer of nature for the perversions he created as a tinkerer, and then they would execute him for their cause.

Xexial had no choice. If only so his edge was not exposed. He needed to use his "death" to its fullest. That meant Khyriaxx was coming with him, at least, for now.

~ ~ ~

Hours later Xexial was setting out again, this time with a confused, but grateful Khyriaxx and his two goats in tow. This was why Khyriaxx saved him. Because the wizard was a source of protection. Now Xexial had to live up to it, and pay his debt.

For the next day, they offered the lowlands a wide berth. Xexial was familiar with most of the land, and so he flanked around the crater and approached it from the northwest. Much to Xexial's surprise and relief, the spriggan was quiet for the entire journey. Either it was too distraught at having to leave behind its gadgets, or the diminutive creature knew when it was in danger.

As the sun set on the western horizon, Xexial once again found himself standing in front of the Onyx Tower. A strange well of emotions fluttered in his stomach as they stood at the large black doors. The last time he approached these doors he thought that his apprentice was going to die there. When they left, though he didn't share the news with Ashyn at the time, he thought that he would be the one that would never return to this place.

Xexial was old. The trip to Buckner, then north to the Seven, he was certain, was going to be his last. He had thought in those final moments before exiting the large black doors that his eyes would never again set themselves upon the towers vast library. He would never again sit on the Onyx Throne that resided high at the top of the tower.

Not that he really sat upon it anyways, it was far too hard and uncomfortable. But it had been one of those final thoughts nonetheless.

He intended to hand the tower over to Ashyn. He had intended many things, he realized. Things never fulfilled. There had never been time. Time was always against him.

He looked down at Khyriaxx briefly thinking about the spriggan's words only two days earlier, time would be either the instrument of his destruction or the agent of his legacy. He chuckled in retrospect. For a wizard, were those not one and the same?

Time was against him once more. Answers he needed resided deep in the library he had thought lost to him. Would he find them before it was too late? Would he get what he needed before the elves learned the truth, or before he became too infirm to make the trip to the Tower of the Seven?

Xexial's mind drifted to Ashyn, to his epiphany in his final moments on the field that the boy he raised and trained wasn't a half-elf at all, but something different. Something that could exceed even the boundaries of what Xexial thought was possible with feedback. Never in his life had he even heard of another absorbing the feedback for someone, let alone when the gift of magic was detached by injury.

Who could do such a thing? What could do such a thing? His mind shifted to the elves in the crater to the east. They called Ashyn the Nuchada, Spirit Eyes, named by their Exemplar, and marked by the same. Nothing like that had ever happened as far as Xexial knew. And now Khyriaxx says a dragon was in the area too? What exactly was Ashyn Rune?

"Take my hand," he told Khyriaxx as he extended his left hand. The creature looked at him curiously.

"Onyx Tower has wards on all the entrances, exits, and on some of the boundaries as well. These wards are powerful enough to not just shock you, but shear the flesh from your body."

"But not you?" Khyriaxx asked.

Xexial shook his head no. "I am attuned to these wards, as is anyone who is in contact with me."

Khyriaxx reached up and took his hand. Xexial opened the door and they stepped inside. Briefly, a red illumination formed around their bodies, and for a fraction of a second, Xexial felt the resistance of the ward, like trying to push through water, then the pair was on the other side. Moments later, Xexial had the goats inside as well. He would stow them in the stables.

Ashyn never left his thoughts as he escorted Khyriaxx throughout the tower, explaining what was safe and what would be lethal. He was stoic and to the point with the tinkerer. There was no reason to sweeten anything. Khyriaxx may be a guest, but he wasn't exactly a welcome one.

After he secured quarters for the creature, he quickly made his way to the top floor of the tower. Though his library was vast, only the most occult of his tomes resided up there. Xexial had a feeling that there was where he should start. He knew nothing of leeching like the boy did. If there were anything like it in the tower, it would be there first.

Upon opening the door, the dank, stale air assailed the wizard. It reeked of mildew and rot. The inside of the room was darker than the rest of the tower, having neither enchanted candles, nor enchanted chandeliers as there were in the more common areas.

His eyes adjusted to their surroundings. Instead of darkness, everything fell into a pallid grey. Obscure shapes formed where Xexial knew many of the useful items on this floor resided.

Very weak slivers of light poked through the covered windows, only further teasing Xexial to what waited within. In the back of the room he could see a goliath, towering form. He knew that to be the black throne.

Xexial never cared for the thing. It was as dark as oil, as smooth as marble, and twice as hard. The chair had no fabric of any kind. Only polished volcanic rock. He shook his head in disgust thinking about how he had thought he would never sit upon it again. He realized he would never have that desire again, even if he died tomorrow.

Xexial stepped into the large chamber. It was his master's old study. Decades passed since he had last stepped foot in there. He doubted Ashyn even knew of its existence.

By memory alone, he walked through the darkness to where the large redwood desk sat. As he closed the distance he could see candles of white, black, and red. Most burned about halfway down, creating murky dust laden puddles across the top of the heavy wood. No tomes sat upon the desk, only a quill and a long dried vial of ink. Xexial preferred a study on the lower levels. It was immensely easier to keep clean and didn't require as far a walk to the kitchens. Not to mention it let in more light than the thin-slatted archers' windows that ran the length of tower perimeter.

Xexial picked up one of the gently used white candles, and a small striker next to it. Smashing the two stones together inside the striker created a spark. Xexial position the striker over the candle and collided the stones together again, and again. It took three tries before the wick flared to life.

Immediately, the shallow orange corona gave birth to long shadows in the enclosed chamber. Xexial looked around at the walls upon walls of tomes, manuscripts, and leather-bound books that made up his previous master's eclectic tastes.

Anything that was obscure or taboo for arcane wielders such as wizards or the other **Creation**-wielding archetypes was probably located somewhere in this room. His master had thirsted for the knowledge of the written word more than any other wizard he had ever known.

Xexial had been quite different in his youthful days. He had not sought knowledge of the scroll, but knowledge from man. Everyday experience from anyone that would willing associate with a wizard was the coin with which he bartered. In his day, Xexial had mastered blacksmithing, cartography, masonry, woodworking, numerous linguistics, and alchemy. Unless the book showed him how to use his hands precisely and efficiently, he had very little need for it. Still, he found some written lore extremely useful. Cultures and languages, for instance were many of the core books he would read with frequency. Xexial was a doer, not one who read how someone else did it.

That was far from saying he didn't read. Xexial did, a lot in fact. The wizard considered himself an exceptionally educated man on all accounts, even religion. His master though, read everything. The more obscure, the more reviled the better. Dead magic, ancient races now extinct, grafting spells to flesh in the form of arcane tattoos, and even written works of myth and superstition that happened in the previous age, over five thousand winters ago. It was all here.

Xexial chuckled darkly as he remembered many adventures he had had with his master tracking down books of prophecy. He was sure many were still in this very room. Then Xexial stopped cold. Prophecy.

Watched by a dragon. Marked by an Exemplar. Could there be a prophecy about Ashyn Rune?

Xexial shook his head. He held little stock in prophecy. He always had. Xexial believed in living his own life. He did not believe anyone's life, especially his, was dictated by a handful of lunatics with lucid dreams. Still, if he couldn't find it anywhere else, he could always look for it there.

So where else to start? Xexial cast his light against the first leather-bound book he could see. On a rare whim he removed it. Dirt particles lifted into the air, scattering into millions of tiny fragments in the dim illumination. Dust smeared under the weight of his thumb causing the rough cover to change from light grey to a faded brown. It bore no outer markings.

He cracked open the seal of the book. For the first time in many winters, the dim light touched the brittle yellow pages within. *Faults and Impurities.*

Xexial shook his head, either a tome on religion, sin, and redemption, or something geological. It could even be about petrology. Maybe for mining or gem-cutting? The title was so vague. He would have to really figure out how his master had organized all his personal tomes. He placed the book back on the shelf, and as he did, he caught the sight of a movement out of the corner of his eye.

Quickly the old wizard spun the candle up to the direction of the movement. There should be nothing in the tower accept himself and the spriggan. Hesitantly, he called, "Khyriaxx are you up here?"

In his mind, he recited the formula that would beckon lightning to his fingertips. Static responded across his robes, pulling at the tattered beige fabric and raising the hair on the back of his neck.

Again, he saw a flash of movement and he spun the candle to face it. Hot wax splashed against his bare hand and lanced out to strike one of the bookshelves. The flame almost guttered. Xexial bit back the burning discomfort as the wax quickly hardened on his skin.

He called more strongly to the electrical currents in the room around him. Sparks flitted across the floor from the static-electrical buildup of the dry room. Small bursts of blue light illuminated both himself and the shelves around him, creating eerie specters out of light and shadows.

"I won't ask again, spriggan. Next movement I see, I fire."

A disbelieving voice came from near the throne, "Xexial?"

The spell-ready wizard turned to the throne, raising his candle. The golden hue sputtered and waned, but still it cast a yellowish glow on the figure before him. The old wizard took a momentary step back, and then quickly raised his hand. Bluish-white electricity effervesced between his outstretched fingertips, adding its iridescence onto the stranger.

Irises of a deep emerald green with speckles of gold flashed in the weak light. Xexial saw no visible sclera around those irises, and there were only vertical slits for pupils.

As the light took form around the person, Xexial could begin to make out scaly skin, with a small ridge of horns and frills upon its head in place of hair. There were no ears visible, instead the wizard could make out disc-shaped membranes beyond its jaw line.

It bore a blunt snout with two nostrils located above its oversized mouth. The creature before him had a pronounced overbite, its sharp dagger-like yellow-tinged teeth extended low over its lips. It reminded Xexial of a type of caiman, but the veteran wizard knew what was before him. It was a scales.

The race of the creature is not what startled him, however. It was the robes. Long black robes laced with bright jade stood out in the light. Along the sleeves and down the breast of the fabric were dark violet runes. These runes crafted an armor across the scales' torso equivalent in protection to a steel breastplate. It was the standard runes of a wizard in employ of the Seven. The colors however represented something much more sinister to Xexial Bontain. Wizard robe colors distinguished to all wizards what type of wizardry in which they specialized. Xexial's robes were tan, for a specialist in shields and wards, in which he excelled. Ashyn had worn crimson, an allusion to being a Blood Wizard, whose title was grimly self-explanatory.

Black and jade were a very special kind of wizard. Instead of talent or specialty, they represented purpose and title. They were the colors of the Maba-Heth. The wizard hunters.

GRIND

Its voice drawing long over the "S" words, the scales said sharply, "You are supposed to be dead."

"I don't die so easily," Xexial replied tartly. "What are you doing in my tower?"

The Maba-Heth turned, looking beyond Xexial briefly and then back to the wizard's cerulean gaze. "This changes things significantly."

Xexial didn't let the words deter him. Sternly he stated, "You didn't answer my question." He wanted to know why the Seven had sent a hunter here. Something was not right. A knot of tension formed in his stomach.

Then the scales did something surprising. He nodded. "Yes. I will answer your questions. It will make things more palatable I hope."

The Maba-Heth turned and raised his clawed hand as well. Xexial kept his own at the ready, power crackling and sizzling at his fingertips. All around Xexial the candles of the room flared to life. The Maba-Heth then turned his back to the wizard and walked to the throne, where he unceremoniously flopped down onto the hard stone seat. A long thick tail lounged off the side of one of the armrests.

Now in the light, Xexial could see the creature's scaly skin was a reddish-brown. The frills were a set of semi-translucent membranes running from behind the scales eyes and fanning out behind his head and slightly to the sides. The membrane itself seemed almost to decipher the scales mood. Its color would shift from cold colors like blue or green when they were at ease to hot colors like red when they were beginning to get temperamental. Currently, the Maba-Heth's frills were a greenish shade, slowly growing golden.

"I apologize for the melodramatics. I thought you might have been a looter or treasure hunter, that had managed to somehow overcome the wards of this place. I saw you enter with the small creature, but in your current state I am afraid I didn't recognize you. Until I heard your voice. I remember your voice. It is very distinctive." He put his clawed hand to his chest and bowed his head very slightly. "You may not remember me. I am Gavius Grind, Master Wizard of the Second Circle and Maba-Heth to the Seven. I was merely an apprentice when you last convened with the Seven."

Xexial nodded, but did not lower his outstretched hand. He didn't remember this wizard. "I appreciate the introduction, but you will pardon my lack of good manners in return as I find having a Maba-Heth in my tower a discourteous gesture of the Seven. I have done nothing to warrant an assassin."

Grind shook his head, "I am not here for you, Master Bontain. I was told you were dead. I have only just arrived myself. I was seeking to confirm what the Seven had been informed about your demise."

Xexial lowered his arm, "Ashyn."

Grind nodded, "I am one of the quickest travelers. I can make exceptional time. I have a certain resilience to some of the harsher environments and can move at great speeds."

Xexial knew the Maba-Heth was not boasting. Scales were known for their remarkable survivability in hostile environments like the deserts of Oganis, the Defiler's Gates badlands, or even the Wasteland. Such a thing would afford them the benefit of not going around as he was going to, but heading directly through.

"As you can see, I am not dead. My apprentice was mistaken, though indeed I was very near to that door." He kept his eyes on Grind. "Were you also here to investigate the Ferhym?"

Grind shook his head. "The Seven are looking into its validity. They held no stock in such an unbelievable story of an actual war on the wizards, until the truth of your death was revealed, and the recreant was brought to heel."

Xexial's ears perked up at the last part, "Recreant? You have a runner?"

Grind looked at him curiously. "I thought as much. You don't know do you?"

The knot in his stomach tightened further. Something about the way he said it. Something about the whole situation struck him as odd. Wizards did not often have reason to lie, especially about something as big as the destruction of the Enclave at Czynsk or the attacks on wizards by the Wild Elves.

The Seven may take a long time to debate how far the elves could actually take the war or what its true impact would be on Kuldarr. Or if the wizards should get involved at all with it being a possibly contained matter. Same with the death of a master. If Ashyn reported Xexial dead, they would have no need to dispute such a thing. They were such a dying breed that no apprentice had tried to take a master's life in thousands of winters. All of that could be discerned without sending a Maba-Heth. Regardless of how fast he was. Unless they were driven to believe it was something else. Misdirection, maybe?

"Where is my apprentice?" Xexial asked at last.

"That's what I'm here to find out," Grind replied. "I was hoping, seeing as you are alive, that he was with you, so we wouldn't have to proceed with the… unpleasantness."

The old wizard could tell right away from the scales' demeanor that he loved hunting his own kind. Xexial squeezed the candle tightly and grit his teeth. "Well, he might have been delayed. He might still be on the way to the Tower of Seven."

Xexial watched Grind shake his head again, his frill changing to an almost blue hue. "I doubt that very much." The Maba-Heth reached into his robes and removed a worn, folded letter. "Four of these arrived to the tower, within days of each other, all by raven."

He reached out, holding it in front of the aged wizard, but making no effort to leave his perch on the black throne. Xexial looked at him angrily before limping forward and snatching it out of the arrogant scales' claws. As he did, he saw how easily those claws cut through the thick parchment by the fibers it left behind on the tips of Grind's claws.

Xexial opened the letter immediately and was taken back by the flowing scrawl on the paper. It was definitely Ashyn's handwriting.

To the Master Wizards Seven,

It is with great sorrow that I must humbly report the loss of my master and friend, Xexial Bontain. He perished on the forty-third day of the season of greening. His death was not a natural passing, but an egregious affront driven by hate and violence.

We were on our way to the Tower of Seven to report an urgent situation that needs immediate rectification. The Ferhym of the Shalis-Fey have begun a crusade against wizards.

I know how extreme this sounds, but it was clearly stated by two of their branch commanders on two separate occasions. In both instances there were deaths of innocents. Casualties caught in a conflict that should not have involved them.

On the first encounter with the Ferhym, they attacked the town of Czynsk, on the western borders of Fermania. There they took hostages and held them in the Jasian Enclave until we arrived. Upon arrival, it was deemed impossible to save them, and we withdrew to report our findings. The Ferhym burned the Jasian Cathedral and all hostages and clergy within. They ambushed us that evening, and as a result of our defense, we had to kill a good number of them.

The second encounter took place on the day Master Bontain fell. East of the Onyx Tower, within the lowlands, we were ambushed once again. We drove them away, but at great cost. Xexial sacrificed himself so that I may live.

The Council of Elm is mantling this crusade. I am not sure how wide spread it is amongst the other elves, or if it is relegated to just the Ferhym of the Shalis-Fey. I do know for fact that they have the support of the druids.

I was ordered to report this to you, in person, immediately. I assume the reason for a personal accounting is so you can then determine what is to be done with me. I, unfortunately, am caught up in a rather unique circumstance. I assume this has happened in the past, or perhaps it is common that the apprentice dies with the master in combat. Yet, I have survived.

I am aware of the one master, one apprentice system. No more, no others, no exceptions.

I respect and understand the need for this system as wizards. I, however, cannot be there in person as he wished. Instead, I have sent six parcels bearing six messages to the tower in hopes that one makes it. You must heed the warning of the war with the Ferhym. It is looming on the horizon, and from what I have seen, it will be ugly.

I must now choose my own path, and I know what that means. Not only do I betray the vow to a man that had become like a father to me, I must break the Wizards' Covenant.

I do this for only one purpose, to rescue my sister. She is in the hands of the Ferhym, and she has already suffered tremendous horrors at their whims. When I have liberated her from her tormentors and ensured she is safe, I will turn myself over to the Seven and accept punishment for my actions.

I hope you can understand that I must do this. I hope there is enough humanity amongst you to recognize I did not come to such a decision lightly. However, I cannot, in good conscience, leave my sister in the hands of barbarous monsters. I have already lost too much to the Ferhym. I will lose no more. It has been an honor to count myself as one of your number.

-The Blood Wizard
Ashyn Rune

Xexial read the letter over again and again. After Ashyn's signature he went on with a full accounting of the Ferhym's battle tactics, strategies, magical uses, and exploitable weaknesses. It was thorough. Clearly the boy did everything he could to help the wizards, even while abandoning them. Abandoning him.

Xexial's hands squeezed at the edges, threatening to puncture through the thick papyrus. His eyes welled up with tears of rage. *Idiot boy! Stupid, idiot boy!* He screamed in his mind. Did he know what he had done? Did he know what he had committed himself to? He told them! He flat out told them he was taking the path of the recreant! He shook his head in disgust. He had known, of course. Knew that this path weighed heavily on the boy's mind. He knew how much Ashyn loved his sister. Still he did not think it would happen, not like this. He hoped Ashyn would have waited. Been patient and let the Seven respond to the threat. Let them aid his sister.

But no. He was impetuous and reckless. He had too much intelligence, but not enough wisdom to see what he had truly done. Ashyn betrayed Xexial. The thought of it made him rancorous because he understood the boy. He knew Ashyn's motivations.

What made him so angry, aside from the betrayal, which stung bitterly, was that he was forgoing the scale of the situation for something much smaller. His sister was one woman. The Ferhym were legion, and if united could mean the untold deaths of so many.

Had Ashyn done as instructed, had he gone in person, they wouldn't have sent the Maba-Heth, and they would have taken him at word. No one was going to take the complication of the Wild Elves seriously until it was too late. Their peace lasted for almost two decades. Those who remembered what the conflict had been like even knew that it was directed skirmish battles. The elves were burning towns to get at wizards now, and still Ashyn chose the life of a single, stupid girl.

Xexial shook his head in disgust. He trained the boy better than that. Now the scales was here, and Ashyn condemned himself. Xexial could see no returning from this unscathed.

He finally looked up at Grind, knowing why the Maba-Heth had truly come. "You will kill him."

"Wizards do not suffer recreants among our numbers, regardless of how just the circumstance may seem. You know this. He should know this."

Xexial nodded. "He does. This was his choice."

The Maba-Heth stood and flexed his scaly muscles. "Then there is nothing much left to discuss is there? This so called Blood Wizard must die." A sinister smile played about the creature's caiman-like face, revealing even more of his wickedly pointed teeth. "Are you ready to do your duty? Are you ready to hunt Ashyn Rune?"

"No," Xexial said honestly. Yet when he looked into the scales' eyes, his expression became hard and cold. "But I will be."

STALKER

The trees were changing, Ashyn noted as he climbed up a steep passage of clay and stone. The wizard looked below at the thick green heads of white oaks, elms, and a few staggered conifers, trees he had known all his life, from his time looking at the outskirts of the Shalis-Fey, from both Bremingham and from Czynsk. This is what he thought the Shalis-Fey was. He was wrong; it was so much more.

Even the maze, dreadful memory that it was, had comprised mostly elms and oaks. Now, as his gaze traveled up the steep trail that he was climbing, he could see something very different.

As Ashyn crested the top of the rise of stone and earth, he could see stands of dogwood, sugar pine, and white fir. But it was beyond them that caused him to gawk.

Sequoias.

Ashyn had read about the monstrous trees in the tomes of the Onyx Tower, but seeing them now so close, he suddenly felt very, very small.

Each trunk was, to his closest guess, about thirty feet in diameter, and the trees soared high overhead, perhaps close to two hundred feet. Some of the limbs above looked to be wider around then he was tall. He never thought he would see trees on such a scale.

Ashyn realized then that he was in a part of the Shalis-Fey that few humans ever saw. He had no idea the forest was so massive, so dense. He felt almost a fool for setting off into the woods in the hopes of finding a city that most travelers took for a myth. There was no way such a wild people could be civilized enough to form anything more than clans, they had told him.

"Keep up Lefhym!" the elf yelled from above, snapping the wizard out of his entranced state.

Ashyn chased after Jenhiro as the nimble Wild Elf tore across the treetops. Now that the ground was somewhat level again it made it easier to keep up with the skilled Ferhym. Still, the young wizard panted, his breaths labored. Jenhiro moved at this asinine pace for three days.

The apparition that pursued him was relentless as well, and seemed to have the same unending stamina as the Wild Elf. It didn't matter if Ashyn climbed, hiked, or sprinted through the flatter portions of the forest, the Ferhym remained just ahead of him, and the beast was always close behind.

Sometimes it would catch Ashyn off guard, striking violently with light and stone. Other times, they would wait for it, then drive it back with spear and arrow.

Any reservations Ashyn had about hunting this sentient skewer were wiped away the second time it had tried to kill him. There was no negotiating with the specter. It wanted him dead, no questions. Ashyn tried to appeal to it, and it wouldn't even try to hear his words. That was when Ashyn decided that Jenhiro was right. They needed to stop it.

The more Ashyn fought the thing, the more he wondered if the Seven sent it. Was this the wizard-hunter designed to kill recreants? Ashyn didn't know, and was glad for Jenhiro's intervention. The boy doubted he would've survived the last three days without him. He just wished the Wild Elf wasn't always running, swinging through trees, whatever! Why couldn't he just walk every once in a while?

Even their camps at night were swift and labored. Four hours of rest and then move for an hour or so, sometimes doubling back to make confusing tracks, and then rest again.

Ashyn understood the ploy. He left tracks; the Wild Elf didn't as long as there were trees he could use. So Jenhiro improvised to keep their hunter off-guard as much as possible.

He wished he knew what he was fighting. Jenhiro seemed to have some idea, but he would never divulge it. In fact, after the first night Jenhiro would speak of nothing else but the hunt. He never even asked Ashyn for a name, only referring to him as tree-brother, or Lefhym occasionally. It was as if the Wild Elf was keeping himself intentionally distant from his partner. Or his bait, Ashyn thought sourly. Could he really put it past the Wild Elf after all he knew them capable of?

Suddenly Jenhiro cartwheeled between two trees, breaking left. Ashyn skidded, kicking up wet leaves and clumps of clay as he altered direction. On his back, Ginger held on for dear life.

Not all was negative about the Ferhym though. Spending time with Jenhiro was giving Ashyn a new appreciation for the Wild Elves. Regardless of their zealous fanaticism regarding balance and skewers, they truly were accomplished trackers and hunters. And their agility? Some of the things he witnessed Jenhiro doing in the last few days were mind-boggling. Ashyn had no doubt that if he tried anything like what the Wild Elf did, he would be dead with a broken neck on the first attempt.

The staggered pattern of Jenhiro's movements also caused Ashyn to give up on what direction he was going. Were it not for the matter of the fact that an unstoppable shade hunted him relentlessly, he would have questioned Jenhiro's tactics long ago. But whatever Jenhiro had in mind, thus far it kept the wizard alive.

That is, alive until enough of his body hair grew back. Already he could just make out the light stubble on his arms. If Ferhym really studied him, he would see it, and then the ruse would be up. He was lucky his hair was light and his skin dark.

Still his face would give him away first. Ashyn had wiped the sweat from his face earlier that morning, and felt the rough texture of sprouting hair on his chin. It felt like a sharpening stone. Ashyn pulled the hood tighter over his head.

Just then, Jenhiro let out a shrill whistle like the cry of one of the tree-dwelling rodents that Ashyn saw. It was his code. It meant warning.

Immediately Ashyn let go of his hood and drew his bow. He nocked an arrow, and kept moving. Gradually he slowed his run to a light jog. He was going to need his energy.

The woods grew deathly quiet as the predator approached. The sequoias stood tall overhead, casting a deep shadow over him, like a disapproving parent over a rambunctious child. Ashyn raised his bow up to eye level, searching for his camouflaged assailer.

Splinters of light cut through the canopy way above, creating pools of illumination around him. In the eerie silence, Ashyn watched as tree pollen drifted lazily in the slicing beams across the forest floor. The pollen was thick like snowflakes in the lambent stringers. Ashyn was grateful he didn't have allergies. The air was dense and musty.

He waited, ears perked, grey eyes scanning the forest, looking between the natural paths for any signs of movement. Watching. Waiting.

This was vastly different from when he and his father used to hunt game. Back then, he would try to stalk his prey, draw it out, and strike. Now he was the prey. The proverbial doe awaiting the slaughter. He thought of Jenhiro in the trees again and the queasy feeling grew in his stomach. He definitely was the bait.

It wasn't as if Ashyn had much choice in the matter. This thing was hunting him, whether he wanted it or not. It had the advantage. Jenhiro needed it to move on Ashyn first. It was the only way to fight it. Knowing that didn't stop Ashyn from feeling that all of this was bullshit. This hunter disrupted everything. It put him on the run for three days when he needed to be finding Feydras' Anula. He could only imagine the unspeakable atrocities inflicted upon his sister, and here he was running from a ghost in the woods.

A ghost that left no tracks or traces of blood. No clues other than the occasional broken branch or two. How was he supposed to stop something that he couldn't see, couldn't track, and wouldn't bleed? All without his magic.

Something cracked behind him. The cat on his back grew completely still. Slowly, Ashyn pivoted around, his bow at the ready.

Dense foliage encircled him. Thick flora hanging about obscured much of what he saw. And the vines, always the vines. The vines hung and dangled like snakes, twisting and writhing before him, waiting to snatch him in their grasp.

The environment seemed to always favor the shadow-creature. Always giving it something to impede Ashyn.

The wizard studied the leaf-strewn ground before him, hoping, waiting to see something. A movement, a smear on the surface, a rock shift, a line cut through the moss. Anything at all. But there was nothing to give Ashyn a moment's advantage. There never was.

Then it happened. Ashyn saw out of the corner of his eye as a series of stones lifted from the ground. He dove into a roll just in time to escape three stones crashing against a tree just behind where his head had been. The tree groaned as bark splintered from the impact of the fist- sized rocks. Wooden shrapnel peppered his back, his leather armor and travel pack absorbing much of the blow.

As Ashyn finished his roll, he drew a shot and fired. His arrow hissed through the air and buried itself deep into a tree. In the blink of an eye, another arrow was placed against the bow, his fingers taut against the drawstring. His eyes devoured the scene before him, memorizing every nuance of plant, tree, and rock. If anything were askew, he would see it.

He swept his bow cautiously from left to right as he took it all in awaiting the next movement from his assailer. Above him, he felt the presence of Jenhiro growing closer, returning, after hearing the sound of stone on wood.

Next, Ashyn watched as the vines came to life. He was growing used to this tactic. They slithered from the trees, weaving across the ground like constrictors ready to trap their prey.

The first lashed forward, and Ashyn rolled. As he did, Ginger leapt from his back, hissing and spitting, attacking the snake-like vines in a fury.

Ashyn loosed the string on his bow, holding the arrow still, and drew his rapier with his right hand. He came up to his feet and stepped forward. The wizard may not know how to engage in a melee with the weapon, but he could chop up stupid vines with it. He swung wildly in front of him severing the vines from their overhead perches, while Ginger stayed on his side, keeping them from flanking the duo. He was growing to appreciate the cat.

A whistle cut through the air above him again, and Ashyn looked up from the snake-vines. Spotted again. But where?

Suddenly the gossamer-like being filled the air before him. Nothing more than a translucent shell of a monster.

Ashyn dropped his rapier, drew his bow, and fired. The arrow flew through the air and struck the insubstantial creature. He stared at it, as he had with every encounter so far, confounded as to how it would not bleed. The arrowhead disappeared into thin air. While the shaft and goose feathers floated ominously in empty space, as if controlled by an unknown force.

Ashyn saw something like this before, once, when he was a child. When Bremingham burned, and his family died. A creature, invisible, had saved him from an orc, and later pinned him to the ground. This thing though was not looking to protect him, but kill him.

The shadow roared, shredding Ashyn's memory, and the ground came alive at his feet. Leaves lifted from the surface, spinning and twirling in a whirlwind of vibrant color and chaos. Blinded by the wet, flapping leaves and bramble, Ashyn fell back. They slapped roughly at his arms, and face, sticking to his body like cold, wet leeches. He drew one more arrow and fired haphazardly into the curtain of flora. It missed by a wide margin and was quickly taken up into the twister.

Ashyn watched as the arrowhead that embedded in the camouflaged creature suddenly slid out from its invisible perch and fell into the spinning maelstrom. Again there was nothing. No mark, no mar on the surface of the beast, and no blood. "Ginger!" he yelled.

The yellow-eyed cat made a final swipe at a vine, and then turned and leapt at Ashyn just as the wizard spun low to grab his rapier. That cat connected lightly against Ashyn's flank and clung to his leather armor with its sharp claws. In a fraction of a second, the feline scampered across his back, to its perch. Wasting not another moment in front of the ghostly monster, Ashyn turned and ran. The chase was on.

~ ~ ~

Jenhiro watched it all from above, tracing his prey as it stalked the Lefhym. He didn't relish using the Lefhym as he did, but it was that or return to Feydras'Anula, report his failure and deaths of his branch, and possibly lose this skewer before a new branch was after it, a branch of his kin that might also die in the same horrific manner as his had. That was answer enough for him. *Besides*, he thought, *this Wood Elf in red had a surprising knack for survival.*

Being elevated from the fighting gave him a far better vantage when it came to seeing the hunter. He could see the unusual movements of patterns from on top that one could not see facing it directly. Like a piece of a puzzle sliding over the piece next to it.

Starting out similar for only a second before becoming something drastically different. Jenhiro knew that it wasn't invisibility that the creature used. It was a type of camouflage. Like a chameleon. Only infinitely more powerful. It was able to shift into multiple colors simultaneously, not just one.

But overhead the colors didn't seem to adapt as quickly, and that gave Jenhiro the advantage. That and the unbalancer's rampant desire to take out the Lefhym first.

Perhaps it was because Jenhiro was elevated, that he felt he was harder to get to, or perhaps it was because the thing saw something different in the Lefhym. Was this tall, clumsy elf somehow more powerful than Jenhiro? He couldn't see it, and yet the skewer was adamant in taking the Wood Elf first.

Jenhiro kept pace easily with the running duo down below, watching, waiting for the best moment to strike at the wraith. He knew that every minute he delayed put the Lefhym at risk, and yet he wanted to make sure he really hurt it. Though he could see the target, he wanted his aim to be true. Effective. Deadly.

Thus far the skewer seemed impenetrable to his javelins and poisons. Now all he had was his spear and dozen makeshift javelins made from sturdy branches. They were a pathetic attempt, but he had little options.

That brought the gnawing sensation to the back of his mind that he needed to return to Feydras' Anula. Or at least to a remote settlement of his kin to rearm and get help. He was afraid if he did though, he would be putting his people back at risk. Or lose the creature who was defying everything he had ever been taught.

Thoughts of Sendea's crumpled form materialized before his eyes. He already underestimated skewers once. After two winters he had grown brazen and overconfident. He had lost his humility, and it had cost him dearly. He didn't want any other to suffer for his poor judgment.

Jenhiro shook his head. No, he would do this with the Lefhym, or they would die trying. He would not endanger anymore of his people. He would either come home a victor with powerful knowledge of a skewer and a weapon, or he would die for the cause.

He continued to chase after them noting that the Wood Elf was heading directly for the thickest sequoias. Jenhiro led them here, hoping to use the size of the trees of the Upper Grove to his advantage. He was happy to see the Wood Elf obliging him. Mirthlessly, he remarked to himself, "Let's see you hammer me off this trunk."

He scaled up the thick bark, grabbing large solid handholds. Every hoist pulled him higher up the tree, but further away from the battle. Through gritted teeth he whispered, "Hold out a bit longer."

When he finally reached a branch almost two feet in diameter, he pulled himself level and continued to run after the two below. They were almost six hundred meters away from him, but easy to follow. He needed only to chase the whirlwind of leaves and needles that was pursuing the Lefhym.

Jenhiro jumped wide and far, sailing out into the open air almost twenty feet before landing gracefully on another thick branch and continuing his movements.

He looked at the ground far below. He was fifty feet up. Already he could see the trail below covering up the tracks of both the Lefhym and the skewer. How it was capable of such a feat he didn't know. Another perverse trick from its stolen magic he decided.

A roar pierced through the air once more. Must've been a good hit, Jenhiro thought of the Lefhym and his bow. "Just wish it would bleed," he grumbled as the two finally came back in sight.

Indeed, it had been a good shot. Jenhiro could see an arrow shaft buried almost to its goose feathers in the center of the camouflaged skewer. Still no arrowhead protruded from the other side, nor was there any sign of blood. It was an abomination against nature itself.

But the Wood Elf had done it! A wound that deep, the arrow would stay awhile. Now he had something solid to aim for. A true target amidst the blurred form. *Good work, tree-brother,* he thought as he caught up to them and lined himself up easily above it. He removed his sharpened makeshift javelins and set about throwing them. Jenhiro smiled as the first of the sticks bore home with a satisfying thunk.

~ ~ ~

A surprised mewling sound erupted from the shadow beast behind him. Ashyn risked a glance backward and was heartened to see over half a dozen sticks protruding from the shade. It looked like a porcupine.

Immediately he pivoted on his right foot, using his momentum to spin around. He lined up the form and fired. With a thwack another arrow disappeared within. He nocked and loosed repeatedly as it closed the gap to him. One successful hit followed another. It was a floating pincushion. Its movements slowed.

We're actually doing something! he thought gleefully. For the first time since the hunt began, they had done more than the occasional hit and run.

More sharpened sticks pelted the form. It staggered, but still came forward. Ashyn backpedaled a few steps just out of its reach and loosed two more arrows. The last hit scored a cry from it that he had not heard before.

The shadow tumbled to the left, crashing hard into a sequoia. Many of the sticks that protruded from it shattered at its impact with the tree's trunk. Others bore deeper within. It mewled once more, and for the first time Ashyn thought he recognized the sound. The swirling assault of leaf and pine straw fell apart as the spell failed. The debris dropped to the ground gently around him.

Ashyn took a step towards it, no longer fearing the creature in front of him. He could see its silhouette clearly against the tree. An outline of arrows and javelins marked the top of its exceptionally wide muscular frame. The wizard nocked an arrow and aimed where he now believed the head to be. Then he saw them.

Eyes. Keen, intelligent, amber eyes. They looked at him, worn and tired. This was his chance. He could finish it.

His hand shook as he fought to hold the string back. For some reason he couldn't let it go. In his mind he saw himself release, he could hear the successful thwack of the arrow. He could see the arrow point bore between its eyes. Watch as they went glassy and still. His pursuer becoming no more.

But its cry resonated in his head. He knew that sound. If it was a hunter from the wizards, then the similarities were very coincidental. Ashyn didn't believe much in coincidence. It was something else. Something seeking revenge for what he had done.

He heard the sliding of flesh on bark as the Wild Elf behind him skittered down the tree. Soon Jenhiro would arrive and do the deed for him. What choice did he really have? Would the Wild Elf make it as painless?

The string bit hard at his fingertips. *Just release,* he said to himself. *This thing wants you dead. It wouldn't hesitate on you.* Still, he stayed his hand; he just couldn't release. Finally, defeated by his own conscience, Ashyn lowered the bow. *A wizard values all life,* he told himself.

His eyes connected with the creature's and they both had a moment of understanding. It knew Ashyn spared it.

He felt Jenhiro approaching behind him, just as a strange white mist rolled in from between the trees. The thick miasma coalesced quickly around him and the approaching Wild Elf, once again blinding the duo. But Ashyn knew that he wasn't in danger, not this time at least.

Jenhiro appeared next to him spear in hand. "The Skewer has fallen," he said matter-of-factly.

Ashyn nodded, and looked to where the beast had been before the mist covered them. Suddenly Jenhiro lashed out with his spear towards the body before Ashyn could react.

A loud crack reverberated in their ears. Ashyn saw a perplexed look come over the Wild Elf who saw the target seconds before the haze covered them.

Slowly the fog thinned, and the form solidified in front of them once more. When it did, Ashyn couldn't help but shake his head and chortle.

There, against the sequoia was a knot of wood. All the javelins and his arrows protruded from the large bulge of hard timber. His hunter used its surroundings to escape once more.

He saw the confusion turn to rage on the face of the Wild Elf. "This abomination's treachery knows no bounds!"

Ashyn though, wasn't so sure. He recognized its cries. He heard it before. Instead, he looked down to the elf before him. "At least it learned something valuable."

Anger boiling in his eyes, Jenhiro looked up, "And what's that?"

"It knows now that we can defeat it. And if we can defeat it, it knows we can kill it. Blood or not."

The words seemed to lighten Jenhiro's rage ever so slightly. "It will think twice before attacking elves."

Ashyn nodded as the Wild Elf walked away. He hoped that was true, but somehow he doubted it.

BURDENS OF CONSCIENCE

Ashyn camped that night near a bed of wildflowers in a small clearing of the woods. Jenhiro offered a rare bit of conversation. "Many winters ago, drought struck this land," he gestured about the woods within they were making ready. "It went on for weeks. Finally, a storm came, but it offered no rain, only terrible lightning." He paused to adjust a strap. "It struck the dried underbrush, which started a forest fire that burned down nearly a dozen massive sequoias before the druids got it under control." He pointed to the flowers. "Now, these have taken over." He squatted down, signaling out a cluster. "These are Fireweed."

Ashyn marveled at their long red stems and four magenta petals. "For the color of the stem itself?"

"Appropriate as that is, no. They always bloom in the wake of burn sites. They are pioneers, leading the way for other flowers to safely grow in the future."

While Jenhiro returned to the task at hand, Ashyn's attention was drawn by what most think of as pests. There were so many insects crawling through the area or buzzing around the flowers. He wished he could capture each one and chronicle them in a tome of some kind. It had been so long since he could study them. Too long.

It amazed the wizard at how beautiful the forest seemed at times. At how tranquil and accepting the forest was. Even with the threats and dangers that he knew lurked within, he felt at home.

He looked over to his partner. The elf was a quiet sentinel amongst the legion of flowers, his spear ready at his side. Jenhiro always took the first watch. He wanted to be ready for its return. Ashyn reluctantly agreed, uncomfortable with the closeness of the Ferhym, but knowing that this clearing was their best defense against the shade. The overwhelming amount of colors would give itself away. The elf's explanation of its camouflage was logical. It couldn't keep up with so many changes in such quick succession.

It was a perfect reason to camp here. It wasn't the impending attack from their pursuer that bothered him, it was Jenhiro himself. This close, and not moving, gave the elf a long time to study Ashyn in detail. He knew it wouldn't be long before his chin hair was truly noticeable. He had maybe a single day if he were lucky. Aside of that, he feared that being this close. If he rolled over and his hood came off even a little bit, it would be disastrous. The elf would see the truth: Ashyn was no Lefhym, at least not a full-blooded one. That made him an abomination in the Ferhym's eyes, just like the creature they had defeated today.

That word, along with the elf's rage over it doing something similar to what Ashyn saw elven druids do, rankled him deeply. It seemed so hypocritical, what was allowed in their eyes, and what skewed the balance. He knew he was teetering on thin ice, staying with the Wild Elf. He was risking exposure every minute he lingered, and yet what else could he do?

Since the moment he decided to step foot into the Shalis-Fey, it had been with the intention of locating Feydras' Anula. It seemed a simple matter at the time. How large could the forest really be? Now the reality of it encompassed him. The only way he was going to find Feydras' Anula was by stumbling into it or having a guide.

Now he had a guide, but would the Wild Elf lead him? He humored the idea of simply interrogating Jenhiro, but he knew it was a foolhardy thought. The Wild Elf would never talk. There was too much strength in his character, too much resolve. Ashyn would never crack the elf's shell, and honestly he didn't think he had it in him to try.

More than once now his ability to do what it took to get to his sister had been hampered by his own moral compass. His own code and personal integrity stopped him. If it came to torture, to causing real lasting pain, could he twist that knife? He didn't think he could.

Did that made him weak? He knew if Jenhiro found out the truth, the Wild Elf wouldn't have the slightest compunction about running him through with his spear. And yet, in spite of these very real dangers, in spite of the reality of his situation, he found himself laying there in inaction.

He could hear it now, Xexial chastising him. Telling him he was a damn fool boy. But was he a coward? He didn't think so. Ashyn had stood his ground since Gregiry Bibs had struck his sister when he had been but a little child. He stood up to all adversaries, fought until the end sometimes, and even found himself reveling in the maelstrom of violence on more than one occasion.

Yet now he lay here, a wraith-like beast seeking his death on the horizon, and he was afraid. He wasn't afraid of the shade though or of the elf in front of him. He was afraid that he lacked what it took to measure up to the task before him. He was afraid he was going to fail. Afraid he would never see Julietta to safety.

"You are troubled," Jenhiro said, surprising Ashyn.

The wizard looked up at the elf who was still looking out on the horizon, searching for their adversary.

"How can you tell?" Ashyn asked, his curiosity piqued by a person he knew would probably kill him when he found out Ashyn's ears were round.

"Breathing," the Wild Elf answered.

Ashyn reached out and pulled at a fireweed quietly. The red stem broke yet the petals remained firm and strong in his hands. He studied it for a long time, weighing if he should even ask a question of the Ferhym. If it would only bring him one step closer to his own oblivion by blowing his cover.

Finally, he just let himself speak, "What guides you Jenhiro?"

The Wild Elf stopped staring at the horizon and looked to the wizard, curiosity etched across his chiseled features. "The Spirits, of course."

Ashyn nodded, "Yes, I understand that. But what drives you? You have said yourself that this skewer has killed many hym. Why do we face it alone?"

He watched as Jenhiro looked back out to the horizon and stared. "Have you ever lost somebody, Lefhym? Have you ever made a bad call that you wish you could change?"

Ashyn found himself nodding. "I've lost many people, and have made many decisions that I wished were different."

Jenhiro prodded the butt of his spear into the ground without really looking at it. "Then you know what it means to fail and have others pay the price for it."

Images of Ashyn's house surrounded by orcs flashed before his eyes. "I do."

"Then you have your answer for what drives me."

Ashyn pinched the magenta petals between his fingertips feeling their silky texture across his flesh. "I think I understand. You do not want any more of your people to suffer in this hunt."

Jenhiro's silence was enough of an answer. Ashyn thought that was the end of it, when Jenhiro asked, "Will you now tell me what it is that troubles you?"

Ashyn tried to find the right words, find something to explain himself to Jenhiro, and his fears to this person, but he didn't trust the Wild Elf. He knew what the hunter would do to him as soon as he found out that he wasn't an elf. Yet that was almost secondary to the pit growing in his stomach, a well of worry that was expanding by the day threatened to consume him. "I am afraid I will fail."

Once more Ashyn watched the back of the Wild Elf's head as it looked down briefly, and he moved the soil with the end of his spear. "You are on a quest then?"

"I suppose," Ashyn answered not really giving it much thought as to what it was. "I am looking for someone very dear to me. But the choice that I made to look for her has cost me everything: my master, my apprenticeship," he laughed bitterly before finishing, "probably my life."

"She must be dear indeed," Jenhiro replied.

Ashyn nodded, realizing the foolishness of the notion since Jenhiro was facing away from him. "She is, and that's what makes it so hard. I feel as if I didn't have a choice to begin with!" he said to the Elf, before looking back at the ground. "Not really anyways."

"Then in that, tree-brother, we are the same. I cannot rest, will not rest, until the skewer is balanced, or I am killed."

Ashyn sighed. 'Balanced,' Jenhiro said. As if changing the word made it anything less than what it was: murder.

Jenhiro acknowledged his sigh. "You do not agree?" the elf asked, curious now. "You have seen firsthand how it hunts you. How merciless it is."

"I have." He looked around. "I am just confounded as to why the Ferhym believe all balancing of nature must be in the annihilation of another species?"

Ashyn was surprised to find Jenhiro nodding. "Not all believe it. I have questioned at times. Questioned the decisions of the Council. Questioned the balancing of races. Of magic. There are creatures that I have felt did not deserve such aggressiveness. It is why I have given my allegiance to the druids over that of the Council." He turned to look into Ashyn's eyes. "But there are just some things that are wrong. Creatures that are twisted, or broken, deep within, you know. You know they must be purged for the betterment of the world.

"This creature now is such a thing. It may not have started that way. I might even be responsible for making it so, but what it is now is a skewer."

"It is alarming to hear you admit to such a thing," Ashyn replied. "Though I feel my interactions with Ferhym previous to you have been tatterdemalion at best, every one of them has always flawlessly stuck to their ideals. Even with potential facts placed before them."

Jenhiro shrugged. "I may be young, but I am not naïve enough not to see that truth is in the eye of the beholder. Faith is nothing more than adhering to your beliefs even while the facts slap you blindly in the face.

"I believe whole-heartedly in the ideals of my people. I believe in what the Council of Elm stands for. What it is symbolic of. But at the same time, it is too easy to call what we can't comprehend a skewer of balance or unnatural. I am definitely guilty of such a thing. More recently than most in fact." He looked to the ground briefly, in what Ashyn thought for a moment might be shame. Quickly the elf looked back to the horizon, constantly scouting the horizon for threats Ashyn couldn't see.

The Wild Elf continued, "It is harder to admit that sometimes we are simply ignorant. The Spirits have given my people a mission, a responsibility to defend the natural world from the perversions and abstractions that seek to unravel it. Sometimes what we *see* is not really what should be *seen*. No one likes being wrong. We Ferhym are no different. I am no different."

"So you admit to mistakes?"

Once more, he rammed the butt of his spear into the ground. "I think we both know what hunts you now, and if we are correct then it is of my own making. I recognize that now. I am responsible for its behavior just as much as it is," Jenhiro answered. "That does not mean I shall not balance it any less. It is a threat now."

Ashyn nodded once more. Though he didn't completely agree with Jenhiro's reasoning, he had a better idea of what was going on in the Wild Elf's mind. The why of it, the rage in combat, the reluctance of the use of his kind in hunting it. Jenhiro felt responsible for everything. Whatever happened to his branch and the shadow beast that stalked them now, Jenhiro felt he was to blame for it all. "We are all victims of our own creations," Ashyn said quietly.

To this, Jenhiro nodded.

"If you believe your council has made a bad call in the past, then do you think that your people could be wrong about other things as well?" Ashyn asked.

"Such as?"

Immediately Ashyn wanted to say wizards, but he couldn't. Too many people despised wizards, so he opted for why he had really come to begin with. "The dui Nuchada?" After he said it, Ashyn wondered if maybe he was beginning to press the extremes of his luck.

"You know of the term?" the Wild Elf questioned with a raised eyebrow.

"It means something akin to 'spirit eyes,' right? What makes them skewers?"

Jenhiro blurted a momentary laugh, before looking back to the horizon. "I'm afraid whoever taught you our language translated incorrectly."

"Then perhaps you could clarify," Ashyn prompted, though what he really wanted to question why Wild Elves want to kill him. Why they blinded his sister.

"It means the spirits within thine eyes. It is an older word in our dialect, and so I could understand the miscommunication from any teacher other than a Ferhym. But the key is that it is plural. Spirits."

"And most of the time the only recourse is death, yes?"

"Why?" Ashyn queried.

"Because no one should have more than one soul."

The wizard was taken aback, "Ex... Excuse me?"

Jenhiro looked back towards him. "It is a true abomination of everything natural in this world. One vessel, one spirit within. The dui Nuchada carry more. Two spirits at their core, perhaps even more. Aside from the spirit that we all have, they also contain a beast within them. A creature of immeasurable power."

Ashyn could only stare at Jenhiro in shock as the elf continued. "Their numbers are small. A very select few in this world are left. So few in fact, that the last was sighted over a decade ago. Their numbers have become so insignificant that even my own branch began to use the words 'dui Nuchada' more as myth than anything that exists in our time. Amusingly fickle when you think about how long we live. A decade is not so long a time to fade into obscurity. But before that one, it had to have been almost a century between."

"Why is it so hard to stop one?"

"The creatures look like humans, walk as humans, and talk as humans, but they carry something else within them. Something terrible, that if unleashed..." Jenhiro said, his voice fading.

Ashyn's mind reeled. A monster. A freak. After all these winters, it all came reeling back on him. His childhood, the ostracization. The name-calling, the threatening scowls, and malicious looks he used to receive. Could Bremingham have had the right of it all along? That something malign really lurked within him?

Ashyn always knew he was different. His vast knowledge, his love of reading and learning, his ability to adapt to new languages. Xexial said he was a prodigy. That his keen intelligence was a gift. Ashyn was readily accepted within the Jasian Enclave for a time for his literacy, but he knew that wouldn't have lasted once his anger was unleashed.

This was different though. This was like Bremingham again only stronger. People like the Bibs, or Old Tom Gregy, they only wanted to drive him away. They wanted him gone. The Ferhym wanted him dead. The very thought of that brought a tremor of anger to his guts.

He focused on that anger. On the times that it fulminated into something tangible. His anger was a weapon that he had used frequently. How it consumed him so fully that his world was basked in an ocherous light.

He always thought that the unexplainable phenomenon was magic. It had made sense growing up with a wizard of Xexial's caliber. And maybe it still was. But magic never answered the questions of some of his other needs and abilities. His innate sense of danger. His ability to feel the presence of something near. His lust for conflict, his need for the same aggression he accused the Ferhym of minutes before. How his desire to fight at times was so extreme that he longed to shed blood. Ashyn never liked to flee from combat. He had to be driven back.

That Xexial never could explain. Nor did he ever find any tome in the Onyx Tower that answered his questions. The closest feeling he ever had to an answer was when he had sat before the statue of Rheynnaus Craëgolshien questioning what to do about his sister. That led to another thought.

Almost in a whisper he asked, "How do you know this though? How can you tell and not risk making a costly mistake? You could say anyone is a dui Nuchada."

"The Voïre dui Ceremeia can see," he replied tapping the corner of his eye with his finger. "With their pureness of nature and their special gifts they can see into us. See to our spirit within.

"The best time is when they are children. They are at their most pure, devoid of the societal burdens and jaded teachings that bring all cultures down. When their power lashes out and attaches to you like a tick, it can dig deeply very quickly and reveal the truth of your nature. When the Voïre get older and wiser, their gifts become tempered, and controllable, the moment to peer deep within the spirit becomes veiled, more obscure, but far from impossible. It is why we respect them and do not look into their eyes. For sometimes what they see within us can be troubling to them. Or worse, us. For we see the truth of ourselves reflected in their eyes, like mirrors to our spirit. Sometimes what we see in ourselves isn't pretty."

Jenhiro chuckled to himself, "I don't know why I'm telling you all this. I'm sure since your kin have them as well, you already know about that part," he nodded down to Ashyn's bracer where the platinum braid hung, "seeing as you've been marked by one."

Ashyn reached down and touched the braid, looking at the earth. "It happened a long time ago."

"You carry a great honor."

Ashyn wasn't thinking about the Exemplar, but further into his past, before his encounters with the Ferhym, before his time with Xexial, of when he was a small child. His whole world revolved singularly around one woman: his mother.

Xexial once told him that she was the true focal point to the secret of his heritage. So little he knew of her. Who was the woman that gave birth to him? Who was the woman that showered him in her love and educated him in ways that many did not understand? Adept at so many languages, with an intellect that was probably vastly superior to his own. But now he did know. She was dui Nuchada.

This was *why* she had run. This was why she left The Shemma or wherever she had been from, why she had hidden from the elves in a small human community. She had been a dui Nuchada. It all made sense now.

Words from thirteen winters earlier rang in his ears as if they were presently spoken. *"I am well educated," Stormwind had told Ashyn's mother, "by a people who have been around for generations upon generations. I have heard the stories told. I have seen some of the signs that are in those stories."*

Stormwind had connected the dots. He had formed a true picture. The intelligent High Elf figured it out long before Ashyn even knew that he was truly different from those around him. The elf had known what his mother was, what he was, and what his sister was. He had known, and he had said nothing!

Anger flushed through Ashyn's body reddening his olive skin. He had looked up to the elf, idolized the vagabond as a hero, and the whole time Stormwind had let him live his life in a lie, knowing what lurked beneath the surface!

They both knew! His mother had lied and fled to keep others from knowing what she was. They discovered her anyhow. How many more knew the truth of the Runes?

Did his sister know as well? That something lurked within them both, like a thief in the shadows?

Ashyn didn't even try to deny it now. Didn't try to push away the idea as another deranged belief of the Wild Elves. This was something he knew it to be true. Or at least close to true. There were too many facts, too many consistencies. His mother and her mysterious past, the elves and their hunt, the powers he had, the anger he always felt bubbling beneath the surface, and the desires for conflict.

He might not be a half-elf or a part-elf at all. Or at least not to the degree like Xexial had thought. There was more to his lineage then the possibility of mixed blood. Something absolute.

It was for this reason that he was hunted. It was the reason he was hated. Old Tom Gregy and his drunken rants hadn't been far off. In fact, they might have been truer to the mark than Ashyn could have known. There *was* something inside of him. Whether it was something natural, an affliction or disease, or a spirit didn't matter. If it was a spirit, the fact that it may or may not be malignant was irrelevant. What was relevant was that it made him different. It made him dangerous. And to everyone around him, it made him a monster.

RE-TREAD

The realization that a dui Nuchada was more than just a half-elf did little to diminish Ashyn's desires to rescue his sister. He still had a job to do. Nothing changed that. Even if he was no longer quite what he believed he was after all these winters. The Ferhym had his sister, and he needed to save her. If anything, the knowledge that they were so much more than mixed breeds in the eyes of the Wild Elves only increased his drive to separate Julietta from them.

After spending the night in a bed of fireweed, Jenhiro was back on point, guiding them through the timber goliaths once more.

Ashyn followed at a slight jog, his mind trying valiantly to pick apart everything thing that Jenhiro told him about the dui Nuchada. Ashyn's initial assumptions to the multiple spirits inside one person were jolting. Already feeling ostracized, it was as if Jenhiro knew and targeted that weakness by saying that he would never fit in because there was absolutely no place for him. But as he thought more on it, he almost wanted to laugh at its absurdity.

Multiple souls in a single vessel? What did that even mean? How was such a thing possible?

Ashyn had been born and raised believing in the Maker. According to the Jasian precepts, the soul was the fire within them. Their spark, their very existence. It was what was responsible for all of their emotions. Love, hate, pain, and joy.

Not the body and not the mind. It was the supernatural concept of a source that exceeded the mundane.

Yes, his heart pumped blood through his body, and his mind controlled his motor functions and cognitive reasoning. It was his soul though that drove him day to day. It was his soul that gave him needs beyond the physical. His soul was responsible for his desires to read, to learn, to be a wizard.

It was also responsible for sin. His body didn't desire to be gluttonous. A farmer's wife's loins did not desire to pursue infidelity with a handsome merchant. It was the cravings of the soul.

The soul was the individual essence of their existence, the collective meaning of their entire life, and the only thing that would go on to the afterlife when their bodies moved beyond age and infirmity. The soul was insubstantial, and couldn't be measured in terms of weight. It simply was who they were.

For the dui Nuchada to be possessed of more than one spirit, what did that mean? Did another personality lurk within him? Did he have wants that were not his own? Ashyn couldn't ever recall feeling out of control of his own body, not unless he counted his experience with the Exemplar. Even then, he resisted her influences. He did not have a single memory that wasn't his own, and he remembered all of his actions, even when he was angry.

The only thing he could think of was occasionally, when situations seemed dire, he would garner a supernal clarity that would allow him to escape. And the voices…

Ashyn almost stumbled over a large fallen branch when he thought suddenly about the voice he heard in his childhood. The other spirit perhaps? Vaguely he remembered escaping the maze and the shadow of something large covering him. Was that his own mind creating a metaphor for the spirit taking over him?

He never told Xexial about the voice in his head. He had been afraid to. Maybe if he had, Xexial wouldn't have classified him of elven descent; maybe he would have known what a dui Nuchada truly was.

Ashyn thought of all Jenhiro had said the dui Nuchada were capable of. It was eerily on point. Ashyn was surprised that none of that seemed exaggerated. He would have figured they would lean towards the extreme with the dui Nuchada as they had with the wizards. Perhaps they knew more of the dui Nuchada then, than Jenhiro led Ashyn to believe.

His eyes glimpsed above once more as the hunter turned again. Their talk the night before put the elf in a new light. Ashyn held no illusions that Jenhiro wouldn't hesitate to kill him if the hunter thought it would protect his people. Still, even with their growing bond, the Wild Elf did not ask for his name.

It was for that single reason Ashyn did not trust him. He empathized with the tormented elf, and to some degree could even believe that they could be equals, but trust? No. There was too much danger involved in trusting a Wild Elf. And if he couldn't trust the elf, he didn't know if he could ever be friends with one.

Ashyn shook his head at the thought. Friend. He hadn't had one of those since Czynsk, and it had been all too brief. Avrimae, Macky, hells even Uriel. He smiled at the thoughts of them. How they turned up so oddly in his mind. He hadn't thought of them since he had re-entered Czynsk. He hoped they were okay. He never had the chance to find them in Czynsk on either of his returns. It just wasn't a priority.

No. Friends were a luxury he couldn't afford right now, if ever. Xexial told him once that people like him were destined to be alone. Ashyn looked over his shoulder at Ginger who sat atop his backpack. "At least I have you," he said with a chuckle.

The yellow-eyed feline stared curiously for a moment before nestling in more deeply against the arch of his back.

They travelled this way for another four hours, Ashyn's thoughts and emotions a jumble. He could now firmly see the red stubble on his forearms, and he knew his face would no longer hide his true nature. Jenhiro would find out the truth today.

Just as Ashyn was debating what he should do next, he felt the weight of Ginger shift behind him. The feline was sitting up, its forepaws pressing against the back of his neck. Though he couldn't see Ginger, he knew the cat was suddenly very alert.

The young wizard slowed down and focused on the lumbering sequoias. He could see a disheveled path across the ground cutting east. He recognized the gait and pattern of the tracks. He had learned them well. A long strider between steps, with pressure belaying that of a human. They were far lighter than normal. Ashyn recognized them because he had saw them frequently. The tracks were his own.

It was the very path they set out on that morning. Ashyn looked to his north. Between the massive timber spires, he could just make out a clearing of wildflowers. They doubled back. Why?

Ashyn glanced up at Jenhiro who was now standing solidly erect thirty feet above. The elf was scanning the dense forest floor beyond.

After spending days combating back and forth with his stealthy adversary, he needn't any more information. Slowly he drew an arrow from his painfully diminished quiver and nocked it against the white bone bow.

Raising the weapon up to eye level, he could just make out the silvery glyphs, clinquant in the piercing rays of sunlight.

The sounds of insects singing vanished. The area around him grew deathly silent. A faint breeze picked its way through the thick trees, rustling the leaves overhead and sending a drifting scent of wildflowers to his nostrils.

Ashyn slowly took in everything around him. *Will it try again?* he wondered. After their staggering victory over it the day before, would it really be so ignorant as to try again so soon? And how? Dozens of javelins had protruded from it, not to mention multiple arrow wounds. The creature had to, at very least, be wounded by now, blood or not.

The shrill whistle of Jenhiro's warning came. Ashyn knew there was movement, and it was close. He scanned the horizon once more. Where was it? The wind shifted once more, bringing another wave of fresh flowers his way. Then he felt Ginger growling against his back. The cat could smell it.

Ashyn looked over his shoulder carefully to see the general direction that Ginger was facing. Southwest. The wizard glanced in that direction and could only see thick vegetation. Some of it almost ten feet in height. A good place to hide.

Quickly he spun and fired an arrow into the thicket of flora. There was a mewling of surprise, and the ground quaked. Ashyn braced himself and drew another arrow. He awaited the usual tactics the shadowy creature had employed: vines, whirlwinds, throwing stones.

Instead, he muffled a cry of alarm as a massive Elk burst through the undergrowth. Four-foot antlers raced towards him. Their ends sported a distinctive three-point crown capable of skewering the young wizard alive.

He rolled out of the way as the animal surged past, Ginger burying its claws into his back to hang on lest it be flung from him.

The black-necked beast didn't continue its run as Ashyn had hoped it would after being startled. Instead, it turned after its pass and reared up to its full height to prepare for another charge. It had to be seven feet tall!

It dug its hooves once more into the ground. Again it rushed forward, head low, intent on impaling or trampling the young man.

Ashyn knew that elk were aggressive, but he never saw one in action before. This creature could seriously maim him, and his instinct was to immediately defend himself. Yet how would the elf respond to him killing the animal? He was momentarily torn. Did he shoot it and deal with the repercussions he might have with Jenhiro, or try to avoid it until it gave up?

The latter seemed like the right thing to do. It was also the less appealing option, not that he wanted to harm it, of course. Ashyn just knew that with a creature of this size, a single slip up, the tiniest miscalculation, and it would result in serious damage to his body. And that's if he were lucky. Death was a real possibility. He had enough to contend with, with the hunters of these woods, he didn't need to die at the hands of some territorial cow.

Ashyn narrowly avoided the Elk's second pass. Choosing to side step it versus roll again. The elk, catching on veered with him, and was almost successful. It had gotten so close on that second pass that could feel the very heat of the elk wash over him as it rushed by. It raced by. He could distinctly smell the bitterness of its sweat, mixed with the sediment from the tall reeds where it hid. The scent dominated over the wildflowers behind him.

Ashyn quickly glanced up to Jenhiro above, hoping the elf would give him some advice, or point to a place he could flee the beast. Instead the Wild Elf merely watched.

For the Maker's sake! He wanted to yell up to the trees. Didn't they just find common ground the evening before? Had they not bonded slightly? Was he really still just a pawn in the Wild Elf's eyes?

Again he thought of the unshakable bitter truth. The red follicles blooming against the olive landscape of his arm, an all too visible reminder of the differences between them. *He doesn't even care to know your name,* his own voice echoed painfully in his mind.

Ashyn refocused on the woodland creature as it turned around once more. What would the Lefhym do? His brain tried to rack through all the tomes he read about them as a child. He knew that the Wood Elves attuned themselves very closely to animals. So much so, in fact, that they had secret druidic groves just to teach the trick of it to their children. But he wasn't a druid nor did he have the affinity that the Wood Elves did.

Still, he knew he needed to play along. He needed to make Jenhiro believe for as long as he could, hair on his arms or not. If he could show, if he could convince the Wild Elf that he was a half-elf, maybe Jenhiro wouldn't try to kill him. The hunter already seemed more open-minded than any other Ferhym he had ever met.

Ashyn lowered his bow and carefully drew the arrow back to the neutral position before releasing it from the string. He slid the arrow back into his quiver.

Slowly, he raised his free hand up. "Shhh," he beckoned to the wild creature, "I mean you no harm."

Ashyn had never tried to calm a wild animal before. He had no idea if he were even doing it right. He had read that sometimes if he submitted to the superiority of the animal it wouldn't attack. Yet one look at the sharp antlers on its head, and he knew he had to keep his eyes on it at all costs. Maybe not full eye contact, but he couldn't risk looking at the ground in submission. All he hoped was that if he kept himself passive enough, and kept his voice soothing enough perhaps, just perhaps, it would calm down.

The elk reared again. Instinctively Ashyn resisted the urge to use his bow. He patted the empty air and spoke softly, "It's okay. No one is going to hurt you."

Again the creature slammed it hooves down, thick clay chipped and scattered into the surrounding the reeds. It dragged its hooves across the earth, as if readying another charge.

"I am not your enemy. I am no threat." Ashyn moved forward slowly, but remained prepared to dive out of the way at a moment's notice. He hoped that Ginger was prepared to hold on a second time around.

The elk snorted, and shook its crowned head wildly at him. Ashyn understood the gesture. It was a threat. But one it didn't want to act on. It was trying to assert itself as the alpha. That was fine with Ashyn.

"I understand." Ashyn patted the air submissively and slowly walked to the side away from the creature. "This is yours, I am going to leave."

The powerful elk's eyes followed Ashyn as he backed away and to the side. It shook its head twice more in defiance still standing firm. Ashyn stepped around it.

One foot.

Four feet.

Twelve feet.

He continued to step away from the creature as it held its ground. When Ashyn made it about thirty feet away, the elk tore mightily at the earth as a final gesture of its dominance, and turned away disappearing back into the tall reeds.

The young wizard let out a heavy breath. Never before had he tried anything like that. Even Ginger was easier to deal with. He finally let out a long sigh and looked up at the elf. Jenhiro's face was unreadable. After a moment he nodded once, and turned away to continue their hunt.

Ashyn felt a swell of pride for turning away the elk without having to kill it. He thought of how proud Xexial would have been, how amazed, to see him do anything like that. He moved onward, following the Wild Elf moving high above him, with more pep in his step.

~ ~ ~

Little did Ashyn know that it was the large orange cat on his back that had brought the elk to heel. Ginger had stared fiercely at it, over the wizard's shoulder, and let its natural pheromones exert its dominance. Now, safe from the immediate threat of the wild, Ginger comfortably nestled itself back between Ashyn's shoulder blades and his knapsack.

High over the tops of the massive sequoias, Ginger heard the distant rumble of thunder. He looked up at the shimmering light cutting through the green canopy. It didn't look like a storm was anywhere near them. Perhaps if they were lucky it would pass right by, and the elk would be all the action they would see for the day.

IDLE

Xexial stood on the roof of the Onyx Tower watching the storm sweep across from the southeast. Dark, foreboding clouds rolled towards them. A sickly green pestilence that spread across the sky like a gangrenous rot. Even from this distance, he could see traces of lightning dancing across the bloated cloud. Shards of arcing light raced across the undulating mass. Thunder followed several long seconds later.

Absently, his bare hand reached for the lanyard that hung around his neck. His thin fingers grabbed only air. He sighed and let it fall away.

Khyriaxx told him that there had been no lanyard, nor had there been a vial of any kind on his body when the spriggan found him. Immediately Xexial had known it was no deception on the spriggan's part. It was simple to deduce why the vial was gone.

"Always such a clever boy," Xexial muttered to himself as he directed his gaze to the long expanse of trees on the southern horizon.

When Xexial and Ashyn gave the oaths of commitment, both parties shed blood. The purpose stated was so that one could always find the other if they were alive. The reason sounded sincere enough, but Xexial knew of course that the giving of blood was far more one-sided. Rarely was an apprentice wizard ever gone from the master. No, this was for the master alone. It was so the senior wizards could hunt down the students if they ever became recreants. Clearly, Ashyn recognized this threat and absolved himself of the problem, or the chance of any other wizard hunting him by taking the contents of the vial.

Couple that with the fact that Ashyn's connection to magic was severed, it made it nigh impossible to track the renegade boy by traditional wizard's means. It was why Grind had come to the Onyx Tower. He had wanted the blood and hoped that Xexial wouldn't be foolish enough to keep it all on him.

He hadn't. He kept some secured amid his personal effects in a chest in his quarters. Yet somehow, Ashyn knew, and he found a way past the wards and into the Onyx Tower. He was very interested in knowing how Ashyn had managed such a feat.

The Maba-Heth's breaking and entering didn't surprise him in the least. Trained to hunt rogue-wizards, he would specialize in the subversion of wards and barriers. Ashyn never trained in anything like that though.

He shook his head of the distraction. Now they would do it the hard way. Xexial eyed the bulbous mass in the sky. The impending storm certainly would not help matters.

He had to give Ashyn credit. He planned well. Executed even better. Where Xexial thought the lad lamenting the revelation that his sister was alive and enslaved, the boy instead was plotting, devising a means to not only escape from Xexial, but make him difficult to follow for other wizards as well, namely the Maba-Heth. Xexial wondered how much Ashyn knew about them. What they were capable of. Xexial couldn't discount that Ashyn knew a lot. The kid loved to read.

The elder wizard managed to stall the Maba-Heth's desire to track Ashyn for a few days. Primarily it was so Xexial could gather strength back from his month-long coma. He also knew it was to build resolve for the task ahead. Xexial did not cherish the idea of hunting the boy. Ashyn had always looked to Xexial clearly as a father figure. A father was not something Xexial could ever be for the child. It wasn't in his character, nor could he be such a thing to a fellow wizard. Such affection was a liability.

No, Xexial saw the lad as more of a confidant and colleague. Maybe even akin to a younger brother, had Xexial ever known such a thing. Still, the liability of emotions or not, Xexial knew they existed for Ashyn. It irritated him that he had to admit it to himself. He would have to hunt his little boy brother.

"Man," he said silently admonishing himself. Ashyn was grown now. Not a boy. His decisions had weight and

repercussions. Ashyn had to answer for them. The way Xexial saw it, Ashyn's saving grace protecting him from the Maba-Heth's judgment was that, technically, he could wield no magic. When he left he was lame. No magic, not a wizard. Not a wizard, not a threat.

It was a thinly woven thread but it was something. A vain hope that when they did confront Ashyn, the Maba-Heth would be too confused as to why he had no power.

Before that could even happen, before he could even risk approaching the boy, he needed to know how Ashyn did what he had. How he acted as a secondary conduit, syphoning away the feedback that should have killed Xexial. Perhaps the real question that haunted Xexial, was could that ability be reversed? Could Ashyn afflict feedback as well as he took it? If he could, and Xexial couldn't discount the possibility of it after all he saw the boy capable of, then they ran the risk of confronting a foe they couldn't handle.

His mouth moved subtly, "Know thy enemy."

So far everything he studied in the throne room had turned up no clues or revelations. It was a conundrum that he couldn't solve, and until the arrival of the swirling dark mass in the sky, he knew he had been desperately losing time. Not so much anymore.

Next to him, he saw a set of quills bounce nervously. "Thoughts?" he asked as he glanced down to the spriggan.

Khyriaxx pulled off his monocle, cleaned it hastily on the fabric of his tunic, and then fastened it again looking at the storm. "Be gathering a lot of force in the Gulf of Malleus." He pointed a clawed finger towards the front of the cloud. It looked like an anvil head.

"It will hit us like a wall and then be sweeping over us, a torrent of rain and wind. Likely be several days of it. Look at how it moves. See how the head turns?" Khyriaxx opened his hand and spun his finger over his palm slowly in a circle. "It be cyclonic. Be like the rotor of a turbine."

Xexial looked at him with a raised eyebrow. Khyriaxx snorted his displeasure at Xexial's obvious ignorance to all things technological. "Like my fan at the home," he admonished, "It be self-perpetuating. It uses the warm water from the Ire Ocean's surface."

The lithe creature then pointed up to the sky. "It then re-condenses it into clouds and rain. This be very cool compared to ocean. That be bad."

"How bad?" Xexial wanted to know.

Khyriaxx shrugged. "Just look at the algorithm for yourself. You take these two opposing temperatures and you be mixing it with some dampness, a little wind, and perhaps a nasty storm out on the ocean and then..."

Xexial's gaze burned down at him waiting for his overdramatic stall to pass. Khyriaxx didn't even notice. "The result be a slow spin. From there it continues to pull in water and gather size and force. If gathers too much size, then it be hitting us for a long time. It will only dissipate if it breaks from the gulf."

Khyriaxx looked up at him surprised at his lack of knowledge. "Really this not be uncommon for these parts. I be seeing one or two every season of greening."

Xexial eyed him dryly. "Forgive me for not being a student of weather."

"Forgiven," Khyriaxx said with the wave of his tiny hand, clearly oblivious to the flippancy of his remark. "We really still be travelling in that?"

A raspy voice called from behind them, "Yes."

Xexial glanced back at the scales who was standing at the trap door. He looked irritated that the duo continued to stare at the impending storm for so long.

Xexial knew that if Khyriaxx was correct, and he had no reason to doubt it, they were indeed looking at a very violent tempest. "No. We won't," he countered.

Grind's emerald eyes narrowed at the elder wizard. "I will not be stopped from finding the recreant any further. Especially not due to a tinkling of rain."

Xexial chuckled and shook his head. "You know nothing of this region." The human pointed behind him to the storm. "That is not like the smatterings that Jaës sees occasionally. It is a cyclonic storm as our friend here has pointed out."

"So?"

"Have you ever seen a cyclonic storm?"

"I have witnessed some mighty squalls on the seas east of Jaës," Grind shot back at him, crossing his arms. "I was a sailor before becoming a wizard. And I've never feared them."

"Good on you. But stow your pride and think about those squalls on the sea," Xexial said as he stared hard at the Maba-Heth. "Now take that storm and push it inland. Take those winds capable of creating such massive waves, and apply them to everything you see before you." Xexial swept his arm out before him. "Imagine, as deadly as they are now mustering strength to move the immovable. Winds so harsh that they can rip trees from the earth."

"Can split rocks, too," Khyriaxx added. "And cause floods."

Xexial nodded. "Waters will pour on us by the bucket full. In these lowlands, there will be turbulent run offs and perhaps even flash floods."

Grind hissed, "This is speculation."

"This is fact," Xexial fired back. "When the storm reaches us, there will be little protection from its effects outside of the tower. And because it is cyclonic it will continue to barrage us as it pulls from the gulf."

Gavius Grind bared his sharp teeth. "All the while your former apprentice gets farther away from our clutches. Very convenient."

"We cannot track in a deluge," Xexial said flatly. Xexial added a little more quietly, "Besides, I know exactly where the lad is, you need not worry about that."

Thunder rolled behind him.

The scales issued out a hissing laughter. "Ah yes, you think to tell me the fool went into the Shalis-Fey to rescue his sister? Classical misdirection at its finest. You are the foolish one. Foolish and old."

"How long have you been a Maba-Heth? Clearly you are not very good at it," Xexial told the creature brazenly. He watched with some satisfaction as the scales' frill went from green to a deep gold.

"You would do well to watch your tongue, old man. The Seven still think you are dead."

Xexial ignored the threat and turned to face the dark forest on the horizon. "If you knew your quarry at all, like I've been trying to educate you on these last few days, then you would know the Shalis-Fey is exactly where he has gone."

"He would go to the heart of his enemy? One that he claims is now dedicated on the issuance of our obliteration to all their kin. Because of a woman?"

Xexial nodded. "Indeed he would. Ashyn is bold and headstrong. He also has a streak of nobility in him, and he feels that this is something he needs to do. Additionally, there are two things that Ashyn Rune excels at more than anyone I have ever met."

Khyriaxx looked up at the wizard curiously, just as the scales growled, "And what be those?"

"Being stupidly impulsive and surviving impossible odds."

"He would not survive the Maba-Heth!" Grind balked.

"Without my help, I guarantee he would survive you. We leave after the storm."

Grind's frill became so flushed at the insult, it was almost bronze. With nothing else in his quiver to argue with, the young wizard hunter stormed back down the hatchway. Xexial won the battle, and it granted him the reprieve he needed to continue his research, but the war was far from over. The Maba-Heth was a trained hound. He wanted to track and he wanted blood.

"You knew it be a cyclone storm!" Khyriaxx said after the Maba-Heth stomped off.

Xexial allowed himself a rare small smile, "It's not that uncommon for these parts."

Khyriaxx nodded and smiled. "It's going to be a powerful storm, but I be seeing worse. It is just speculation though, you be knowing that, right? The storm can break away from the sea very quickly and lose all its power in a matter of days."

Xexial looked down at the spriggan. "When the pouring rain and the howling wind starts I guarantee the scales will not know the difference." Xexial could hear a door slam from the Maba-Heth far beneath them.

"Besides," Xexial added, "at least this will chase the Ferhym away from your home."

The spriggan let out a toothy smile as the realization of it hit him. Then, after a moment of silence, he asked, "Is the tall hue-mon really in the Shalis-Fey?" Xexial had no reason to lie to the tinkerer. He nodded.

"That boy be brave or stupid," Khyriaxx remarked.

"Little of both," Xexial answered. He knew without a doubt that Ashyn was in those woods. And he knew the boy was still alive. It was his nature. It was who he was.

The boy was just lucky like that.

TURBULENT PATH

They were not lucky.

Within the next few hours, Ashyn watched as the once radiant forest turned dark and foreboding. Lively greens and yellows deepened to the browns and the purples of shadows. Heavy winds tore through the tree line, bending thin saplings on the ground and causing Ashyn to protect his face from a maelstrom of bramble. Around him, the wooden titans creaked and groaned. It was going to be one hell of a storm.

Holding down the billowing red hood on his head with his free hand, he looked up into the deepening shadows above. There he could see Jenhiro fighting against the wind as he jumped from one thick branch to another. *He's going to get himself killed!*

Ashyn yelled up to the elf trying to convince him to come down from the timber sentinels and seek shelter from the growing wind, but his voice was lost in the tumultuous roar of thunder above. The wizard shook his head, wondering why the elf would still push to move in conditions like this. Their hunter remained hidden all day, and was very likely hunkered down still recovering from their previous battle. There was no destination that they needed to get to that was worth losing his life in the storm. As much as Ashyn needed to get to Feydras' Anula, he could do his sister no good if he died. Furthermore, he knew he needed Jenhiro. The Wild Elf was his only shot at this point to Feydras' Anula and he wouldn't waste it over some nonsense like this.

Once more Ashyn yelled up into the treetops but even then he knew it was no use. Jenhiro couldn't hear him. The young wizard chased after Jenhiro as the Wild Elf made another reckless leap into the openness of the wind torn trees. Ashyn held his breath as he watched Jenhiro soar through the air, buffeted by the heavy winds.

The elf landed on another branch and kept running at full stride. Ashyn breathed a sigh a relief and followed as best he could. On his back, Ginger growled its displeasure as it buried its claws deep into the folds of Ashyn's Lefhym armor. For once Ashyn was in full agreement with the feline.

They made it about another quarter of a mile when the first rain drops fell. A thick, heavy globule struck Ashyn across the face. The water was warm and had a strong scent of salt. Ashyn knew that this single drop was a portent of things to come.

Growing up in Bremingham, south of the Shalis-Fey, Ashyn was no stranger to the greening season storms that would come from the gulf. They would be torrential, and many times the Bibs would lose at least one crop to the high winds and flooding. It always started out the same: a warm rain, followed by days, sometimes weeks, of downpours.

Ashyn saw it in the Onyx Tower as well, but being unable to leave any further than the gardens, he never saw how it affected the lowlands that the tower resided in. The high winds never seemed to cause any damage to the goliath structure, though he had on occasion felt it sway on the upper floors. The feeling was disturbing to say the least.

As he looked up to Jenhiro in the trees now, Ashyn wondered what a southern storm like he had grown up with, would be like in the Shalis-Fey? Would the trees hold most of it at bay?

Another drop plunged through the green canopy striking Ashyn's bare shoulder as if in answer. More brambles slapped at his legs and arms, and he knew that they needed cover urgently.

He watched as Jenhiro positioned himself against a trunk, and he hoped that the crazy elf was finally going to climb down. Lightning cut across the sky illuminating Jenhiro's muscled frame as he looked up. Quickly, darkness covered him once more.

Thunder rolled over them. Ashyn stared up, waiting to see what his ally was doing. Lightning flickered again, and Ashyn saw him.

Jenhiro moved violently to the left. *What in the world?* Ashyn thought. Fear gripped his chest. *Did a gust get him?* Quickly the young wizard scurried around the sequoia, squinting up into the growing darkness. *Where did he go?*

Ashyn moved between the trees, his hand angled over his brow to deflect the massive droplets of rain that were coming down harder now. He scanned above where he had last seen Jenhiro, and where he thought the wiry elf should be, but there was nothing.

Panic built in his guts as complete darkness ascended on them from above, drowning out all color in a deep sanguine hue.

The wind howled through the channels between the trees, and already Ashyn could feel a shift in the air. A pressure building. It was going to pour.

"Jenhiro!" he yelled with everything he could muster. There was just too much wind.

Frantic, Ashyn looked to the ground, expecting to see the Ferhym's crumpled form. It was at least a forty foot drop from the branches he was at. Easily fatal.

Still he could see nothing on ground except the swirling masses of sticks and leaves caught in the growing gale.

Ashyn continued to move along from tree to tree, as the light faded. He fought to see anything above. It was hopeless. Even if Jenhiro were still up in the trees, he couldn't see.

Then a flare of lightning blazed to life and Ashyn saw a movement a hundred feet away. He ran towards it.

He closed the gap quickly. A heavy canopy of grass and weeds enshrouded the area creating a break from the brutal winds and growing downpour. Ashyn quickly pushed inside, and had to jump out of the way quickly as a startled group of deer fled from him. He saw that they were tiny. Only three fawns broke away, and he felt bad for chasing them out of their cover. He turned to resume his search for the elf when he noticed the ground.

Flat pressed dirt with almost no visible shoots of grass. The vegetation was heavily consumed. Not that it was a surprise to him, for he knew that all deer did was graze, but this was different. The grassy alcove totaled to almost thirty feet in diameter between two sequoias. All around the ground had been eaten away to leave nothing but a handful of small stray strands of grass, and massive overturned clumps of dirt.

Ashyn recognized a grazing area when he saw one. Trained by his father as a child, he knew that a creature that could consume this much food had to weigh over a thousand pounds maybe even closer to two. Not like the tiny forest deer he had just scared off. Either this was the grazing grounds of one of the monstrous elk, or... Jenhiro's words from the night before echoed in his mind, *"I think we both know what hunts you now."*

At the time, Ashyn had vaguely thought about it. Yes, he was sure that it wasn't a wizard hunting him. It was something else. Something seeking vengeance for an act he committed.

Ashyn thought about the bull-like creature he slew at the pond. How, in the gloom, it appeared like a minotaur, a cannibal creature that ate the flesh of men. Now though, as his mind drifted back, he remembered hearing Jenhiro distinctly say, "There is fruit there." Ashyn had heard the rustle of the bushes. It had been grazing. Minotaurs did not graze.

Ashyn knew then that the bovines were not meat-eaters at all. They were herbivores. The realization hit him like a swift punch in the gut. "If we are correct, then it is of my own making."

Jenhiro killed many of them. All but the one he claimed had been using black magic.

The reason they couldn't track it by its eating cycle is because they were targeting the wrong eating cycle. It left no corpses, and that meant no scavengers, and no blood. It foraged with the Shalis-Fey's residents, side by side, and likely excreted the same way. They thought it more like them, and it wasn't. It was like the deer.

They were going about it all wrong, and the bull knew it! That's why it was so hard to trace. He had made a mistake. Ashyn had made a very tactical mistake. Worse, if his assumption was correct, then he just stumbled into their hunter's camp.

As the realization dawned on the young wizard, he heard something else amidst the roaring winds and thunder. It sounded like combat.

"Jenhiro," Ashyn whispered.

~ ~ ~

Jenhiro knew he was in trouble. Darkness pervaded all around him, and every movement he made was treacherous. He should have climbed down from the tree long before the storm swept in, but he knew they were close, and he wanted a better vantage to see it, lest they miss their chance completely.

Now though, it looked like it was destined to happen anyways. Shadows filled every direction he turned, and the winds buffeted him so heavily that even walking along the wide branches was risking death.

He looked down below, hoping to see the Lefhym still following, but was disturbed to find the signature red armor nowhere in sight.

Worse than that, he couldn't see the ground at all. Hot, salty water splashed against his face as massive globules impacted the trunk he was pinned against.

With no way to see the Lefhym, and with the impending downpour, he had no way to warn the bow-wielding elf of where he was trying to go.

Things looked grim for them indeed. They would have to weather the storm as best they could.

Then he saw something that made all the color drain from his tanned face. In the flash of lightning, he saw a form on the edge of a branch. *It can't be*, he thought desperately. *I am alone up here. Unless there was another hunter patrol?*

No, he had made sure of avoiding all other patrols. Outside of the Maze, he had taken the Lefhym and the creature as far away from the pocket villages of Ferhym as he could. He couldn't risk any other Ferhym dying for his ignorance. The only place he kept them close to was… He shook his head of the thought. No. He needed to keep away.

Thunder rolled across the sky, and another burst of light appeared and he saw it again, stalking closer. In that flash he knew he wasn't alone. The shadowy hunter had come back, this time for him.

~ ~ ~

Ashyn strained to hear any sound Jenhiro might make. The screaming wind all around made it hard to separate, but he could hear it on the cusp of his range. It was a roar, and the cry of a man. No, not man, an elf.

He drew his bow, knowing the futility of the action. The wind was too strong; he would never hold a clean shot of anything beyond point blank.

He looked down at the rapier on his hip. It was a pathetic substitute for the bone weapon between his fingers. Ashyn was no swordsman.

The wizard stepped out into the growing deluge. Water drenched him. Again he heard the roar in the distance. It was such a small sound compared to the cacophonous wind.

There was no way he would be able to find Jenhiro in time. The rhythm of the bellows was too erratic for his hearing. Then he thought about Ginger. It was worth a try.

He looked over his shoulder to the orange feline. "Ginger," he yelled to the cat on his back, "find Jenhiro!"

It looked at him as if incredulous at being commanded, and then jumped off his back, taking off into the storm.

"I don't believe it," Ashyn said to himself.

Seconds later Ginger came back into Ashyn's sight, and paced in a circle. Ashyn ran up to it, and as he did, the cat took back off in the direction it had come from.

Ashyn tore through the rain after the soaked, oversized tabby with reckless abandon. He realized how asinine it was to put Jenhiro's very life in Ginger's… paws, but it was his only option. He wasn't as mobile as the cat, nor could he see as well in the storm.

As the young red-head came around a thick cluster of intertwined sequoias, Ashyn spotted the waterlogged puss.

Again the cat eagerly spun in circles as if it were chasing its own tail. The young man ran to Ginger who upon seeing him quickly bounded up his robes and to the perch on his back. Ashyn tried to look over his shoulder at the feline, but it pressed down hard between his armor and backpack trying to stay out of the wind.

Anger pulsed through Ashyn then. He hoped that Ginger was smart enough to guide him to the Wild Elf. He knew that Jenhiro was in trouble, and now it appeared as if he had made a mistake again, and likely this one was going to cost the Ferhym hunter his life. Ashyn moved to turn away when suddenly he heard a roar directly above him.

He looked up, squinting. In the murk of the storm he could just make out a thick branch, perhaps thirty feet up. Suddenly a narrow silhouette darted across the timber arm like an apparition. As it ran by, it turned and Ashyn made out a thrusting motion.

Winds buffeted him even harder from behind, forcing him to cover his hood before it ripped violently from his head. Without warning, a makeshift wooden javelin stabbed into the ground less than a foot away.

Lightning flickered. He could see Jenhiro clearly. Fear etched across his brown eyes. In the same flash he also saw their hunter.

Water splashed across its form and ran in rivulets across its massive bulk creating a liquid silhouette. It was like water running down a pane of glass: he could see the form of what was there and see through it at the same time. The towering figure he saw before Jenhiro was without a doubt one of the bulls. And this one used magic just like a druid.

The creature stalked the elf with sure strides and were the scene not so utterly dire, Ashyn would've found it strangely comical. A bull in a tree.

This bovine seemed right at home on the precarious annex that led between the two timber goliaths. Its footing was confident and solid. It appeared equally as graceful on high as the Wild Elf did. Its ease would unnerve Jenhiro. The Wild Elf's speed and grace now meant nothing.

Ashyn attempted to line up a shot, but the wind battered against his bow and jolted his draw. The arrow was quickly lost in rain and shadows.

Jenhiro tried to make another break for it. The ox drove its strange staff directly into the long limb of the sequoia. Ashyn's eyes widened as the staff failed to splinter or crack, but melded into the tree as if a part of it.

He witnessed myriad long, pointed branches suddenly sprouted in front of the fleeing Wild Elf, barring his path with a field of flesh-piercing brambles. Jenhiro stumbled to a halt a hair's breadth from impaling his bare foot on the leading branch. Nimbly, Jenhiro repositioned his feet, breaking into a run directly for the wraith-like hunter.

The bull did not move as Jenhiro bore down on it. Ashyn blinked as more branches spread on the other side of Jenhiro, separating the two. Jenhiro stopped just short of another near-impaling. The elf was trapped.

Slowly more and more branches sprouted from the tree like mutant spears. They grew closer together, curving upwards from all directions denying the Wild Elf the option of jumping from the tree.

Ashyn knew that the Wild Elf had only seconds before impalement. He envisioned Jenhiro's death: suffering as branches slowly punctured his body, rupturing muscle, bones, and organs, leaving him to bleed out like a pig on a sickening skewer. If Jenhiro were lucky a branch would shatter his spine and render most nerves unreceptive to the agony. The wizard didn't hold out to hope.

There had to be something he could do! He thought about everything he had in his backpack. He had nothing to reach those heights. If he had his power, the gloves maybe, but he didn't. He was going to watch Jenhiro die!

Anger at the injustice of it all surged through the young wizard. He hated this! He hated these woods, and he hated that everywhere he went people seemed to die for no damn reason. People that trusted him! People that befriended him! Jenhiro, for all his faults, believed in Ashyn in some small way. He needed Ashyn to help wrong a right.

Agree or not, Ashyn respected that, and now as he stared up at the bull creature, he knew that the moment was upon him. Help or fail. Just like he failed his family. Just like he would fail Julietta.

Rage rattled something deep within him. Something that felt caged and savage. For but a single moment, it found a way out. His vision filled with golden light.

Before the realization of what was happening could set in, Ashyn reached for the javelin, taking the weapon in hand, and with all his strength he threw it. Behind the throw, he put all of his emotion: all of his built-up anger, all of his righteous rage, and all of his frustration.

The javelin flew unerringly towards its target. Nothing, not the rain, nor wind, nor even the bull, could stop the javelin from finding its mark.

The weapon struck with a crack so loud that it sounded like a thunderclap. It ripped through flesh and bone, and exploded against the long staff like object. The staff flew from the tree violently, twisting end over end, and disappeared into the darkness of the storm.

Instantly the talon-like branches stopped growing and Ashyn's view returned to normal. His vision now clear, he could see that Jenhiro was scant moments from death.

Ashyn stared down at his hand mystified at what he had just done. At what he had just felt. He had touched magic. After so long of feeling naked, he had for a moment felt its embrace once more.

He looked to the scene above him. The elf wasn't fighting the bull. He was looking back at him with a mortified expression. In that moment Ashyn could see it in the Wild Elf's eyes the realization that Ashyn was no elf. He was the dui Nuchada.

It was at that very moment that Ashyn Rune knew he had now become Jenhiro's enemy.

CRITICAL JUNCTURE

Now my friend has become my enemy. The moment had been fast approaching. He thought it would have been when the Wild Elf saw the hair upon his flesh. Instead, it was like when Ashyn had been the child in the ravine. His actions had somehow confirmed to the elf that he was indeed a dui Nuchada.

The grim moment of clarity was cut short as the bull's camouflage vanished, and it held its impaled hand, howling in pain. The power of its magic severed from the staff. It reached out with impressive willpower and pulled the long weapon through its shattered hand.

Ashyn focused on the large monstrosity, but he noticed that Jenhiro was still staring at him. He knew Jenhiro felt betrayed. Ashyn did not feel guilty. He was tired of feeling guilty for what he was. Tired of having to fight for his right to exist. If anything, he was elated. The secret was out, and by it he once again touched magic! That meant he was truly healing, and if so, soon he would be able to save Julietta.

Ashyn stowed his feelings, screaming at Jenhiro to look at the bovine creature. Despite that, he was transfixed by Ashyn. Some ingrained emotions were just too hard to shake. Hate for skewers clearly being one.

Only at the last minute did the Wild Elf sense the danger. He broke his gaze away from the wizard just in time to see his own javelin stabbing forth through the spikey bramble. He moved to avoid it, but wasn't fast enough.

Ashyn could only watch as the javelin buried itself deep in the Ferhym's chest, inches beneath his right collarbone. Blood plumed a vibrant red mist, but quickly diluted into a murky pink within the heavy rainfall.

The javelin exited his back, just beneath his shoulder-blade. Jenhiro's screams of agony cut through the wind and shook Ashyn down to his core. He looked upon the ground for more javelins, but there were none. He tried to call upon the anger again, to call upon the feeling but it was gone, the moment had passed.

Ashyn ran to the base of the tree and tried to grab onto the trunk to climb it. Water coursed through finger wide gaps between the thick and gnarled bark. Ashyn pried his own fingers into the slick gaps and forced himself to scale the tree. He made it only a foot before his fingers gave out, and his own weight ripped him from the tree taking the skin of his fingertips and pieces of his fingernails with it. He growled at his inability to climb the tree like the Ferhym of forest. He looked back to the Wild Elf.

Jenhiro, though clearly in crushing pain, continued to fight against the bull. The wiry Wild Elf used his own weight as leverage, and in a last ditch effort pulled his whole body onto the bull's extended arm.

The creature effortlessly held Jenhiro's weight, and in what it must have thought was its moment of victory, pulled the elf over the spiked bramble to revel in the closeness of its kill. Ashyn saw the tactical error. A second later so did the bull. Jenhiro, summoned his remaining strength and lashed out with his coiled feet. He kicked the bull in its wounded hand. Both feet landed so powerfully against the open wound that Ashyn clearly saw blood, for the first time, fly from the rent whole. A hot crimson spray dowsed the forearm of the massive hunter. The bull cried out and dropped the impaled elf against the thick limb, inches from the spike like branches.

Jenhiro staggered to his feet. He used the moment to his advantage. Jenhiro high kicked the goliath ox in the face. The creature, now wounded and weaponless, backpedaled, stunned. A hoof slipped on the edge of the timber arm that held them aloft so high above. The bull swung his arms wide for balance. Jenhiro gave no quarter, and rammed his knee into the creature. The bull pitched backwards, tumbling over the side.

The bovine flailed, grabbing the nearest thing it could reach. Jenhiro scooted away, but not before the hunter latched onto the end of the javelin. Jenhiro jerked forward violently as the javelin ripped back out of his body. His feet skidded across the thick branch but his pain-addled mind could find no solid perch. He made eye contact with Ashyn Rune one last time, and the wizard could see the betrayal he felt and the knowledge that he couldn't recover from this. Silently he slipped from the ledge. Ashyn watched as the Ferhym hunter hurtled to the ground thirty feet below.

~ ~ ~

Ashyn ran towards the plummeting duo. They hit the hard packed earth, one after another, with two sickening thuds. Both lay unmoving. Blood poured liberally from Jenhiro's mouth and his chest wound quickly colored the ground beneath him.

No! he thought, noticing the bull's hand beginning to heal. The creature shuddered, and the wizard heard a half dozen loud cracks as bones re-aligned themselves. The bull roared in pain as its eyes flared back to life.

Jenhiro lay still, but Ashyn could see his chest rising and falling very slightly. The elf too was still alive, but in much worse shape.

He stared down at them both. They wanted him dead, each for their own reasons. One he could relate to, the other he couldn't quite grasp. The best thing to do would be to end them both here and now. Eliminate his harriers and get back on track of finding his sister. Yet he knew he didn't have it in him to kill either of them. Not even with the obvious risk of either of them hunting him again. No, he needed to end this a different way. This battle had gone on for far too long.

Besides, Jenhiro was still his best bet for finding Feydras' Anula. The Shalis-Fey had proven to be far more daunting than the young wizard initially assumed. He had hoped his zeal and determination alone would help him find the hidden city of elves. It still may, he reasoned, but a much more obvious route lay at his feet.

Ashyn looked back to the large feline that followed him for so long, "Find us cover."

Ginger didn't need the question repeated. With eyes that fixed upon him with far too much intelligence, the cat bolted into the woods.

As much as the wizard wanted to help Jenhiro, regardless of the elf's feelings for him, he knew he needed to incapacitate the bull.

Ashyn shrugged off his pack and rummaged through the contents he took from the Onyx Tower's storage room. His eyes stopped on a pair of gloves for only a moment, and then he pushed them aside for what lay underneath.

Ashyn Rune hadn't known what to expect of the city of Feydras' Anula so he didn't want to be unprepared. He still didn't rule out the possibility that the Wild Elves did actually live in the trees. He'd packed fifty feet of strong hemp rope and a grappling hook. He almost laughed at the thought, looking at the base of the sequoia now. It was worthless trying to climb the trees here. But the strands of rope bound together were thick and could support the weight of hundreds, if not a thousand pounds. Could it hold the strength of a massive ox creature? Perhaps. It was used in tethering wagons pulled by domesticated beasts of burden.

Knowing that Jenhiro had little time, he set to work on binding the bull's hands and hooves. He was careful not to disrupt the large creature's bizarre healing process as another bone snapped back into place. When he was confident that the bull could not escape its binds he, drug the rest of the rope and tied it around a boulder.

When he was finished, Ashyn searched for anything that could help the bull escape his bonds. Minus the horns on his head, which Ashyn was not about to cut off, the only thing he found was his own skinning knife.

He grabbed the cherry wood handle and tucked the blade back against his belt. Confident his ghostly hunter was secure for the next several minutes he broke off to examine the Elf.

Jenhiro was in bad shape. The javelin had completely penetrated his body, and he had no way of knowing if it ruptured anything vital. Blood wept heavily from both holes and ran in small drips from his lips and nose. Ashyn studied the chest wound to make sure it wasn't sucking, wheezing, or bubbling, fearing that his lungs may be ruptured. Lucky for Jenhiro, that did not appear to be the case, and so Ashyn rummaged once more in his pack and found gauss and bandages.

He whispered, knowing his voice was lost to the heavy gale, "This is going to hurt; I hope the shock doesn't kill you. I still need you alive." Ashyn then wrapped the gauze around his pointer finger and buried it as deeply as he could into the raw gash. Blood jetted up from the ravaged flesh around his finger like a small geyser. Jenhiro's eyes shot open, and he gasped with barely another sound. Jenhiro's brown eyes searched wildly, and then mercifully he passed out. Ashyn removed his finger from the gauze, bundled up more, and then he pressed even further into the perforated hole in Jenhiro's body. He did the same for the hole in the Wild Elf's back. It was the only way he knew to mitigate the bleeding until he could get the elf under cover.

Doused up to his elbows in the Ferhym's blood, Ashyn was just grateful the sight hadn't made him queasy. He supposed the first few winters of his life spent hunting and skinning with his father helped. Right now keeping Jenhiro alive was an obligation. Once he was stable, or dead, then Ashyn would allow the emotions to seep through.

Ashyn searched Jenhiro's body for broken bones. He could tell by the angle of the Ferhym's right leg that it was broken at the shin, and it judging by the growing swelling of his left forearm, it looked to be broken as well. He had no idea what damage may have happened to Jenhiro's neck and spine, and didn't want to risk carrying the elf. That meant he needed to fashion a litter, in the middle of a storm.

Ashyn wiped the water from his eyes, and was disturbed to see he had created a long smear against the rich red that soaked his hands. He suddenly could feel the pressure of the blood on his face. He ignored it. There was little to be done about that now.

What he needed was two sticks long enough and stable enough to hold the elf. Wind billowed between the trees pushing much of the lighter bramble around in frenzy. Even some of the heavy sticks from above had snapped off and were now skirting across the ground in nature's chaos. After three minutes, Ashyn had what he needed: two sticks, his own leather tunic, and the cording from his armor.

Ashyn carefully laid the improvised litter down next to Jenhiro. The hot stormy waters doused his sweaty back. Trying to save the elf was tense, rigorous work.

Cradling Jenhiro's head and inching his battered body from top to bottom onto the litter, Ashyn secured the elf's upper half with more of his armor straps. His torn fingers fumbled during the attempt. The elf's pale skin added to his concern.

Shifting to Jenhiro's lower half, Ashyn engineered makeshift splints with the use of some more gauss and cording from his quiver. The cannibalization of gear left the man very much exposed.

Ginger returned, and rubbed its soaked body against the wizard's leg. Ashyn looked down, tired, but grateful. "Did you find something?"

The cat walked in two circles and then moved back in the direction it came. Ashyn hefted the litter behind him, making sure Jenhiro still looked as secure as he could possibly be. "Let's go."

Ginger took off, and the wizard followed.

~ ~ ~

The cat came through once again. Ashyn moved to the entrance and paused. What may possibly be waiting out the storm inside? Would be friendly to new visitors? He hesitation grew longer, knowing how dangerous everything in the Shalis-Fey was. When he looked to the one who had guided him there, Ginger looked back at him with an expression he took to mean "get inside the damn cave."

Ashyn sighed, ducked low, and stepped inside. From the cavern mouth the sound of the wind echoed behind him like a roar. At least he hoped it was the wind. He could hear the sound of running water all around him faintly through the overbearing winds.

As his eyes adjusted he saw the cavern opened up considerably into three sections. If he had to hazard a guess at the size of them, he would say that each hollowed out section was around the size of the dining room back in the onyx tower. Perhaps only fifteen feet wide, with a length slightly longer, the gloomy aura from the outside barely could illuminate the first of the sections. The other two sections appeared as little more than open portals that housed eerie silhouettes, only giving a dark hint at what may lay beyond, and letting his imagination get the better of him.

One thing was certain, though. He found the source of the trickling water. There were small pools, dozens of them, within the first section of the cavern. They ran against both walls and through the center, separated by stalagmites and other low outcroppings of rock.

These pools seemed to be natural to the cavern, and not a collection of the rain water from outside, though Ashyn was sure the torrential downpour was helping to brim the small bodies.

Ashyn pulled in his charge. Now out of the rain, he had to try to get the elf dry, before any kind of shock might set in.

The wizard looked around for anything that he might be able to use to start a fire. The entire cavern was humid and damp. Outside, everything was even wetter. Ashyn would have sacrificed his robes to aid the Ferhym, but they were now drenched as well. He would just have to make due.

Ashyn ached as he sat himself down with less grace than normal. Next to the wounded elf, he absent-mindedly closed his eyes. The events of the last hour replayed in his head. His heartbeat sped at the memory of the elf and the bull tumbling down from over thirty feet in the air.

Ashyn thought about the feeling he had, about the momentary surge of anger and how it had unlocked that well of magic within him for just a flicker of a moment. He was elated that he had touched it again. It at least assuaged his fear that he would never be able to use it again. After only a few weeks, already hints of it were coming back, just like when he first touched it as a child.

His emotions could reach that place where his power resided quicker it seemed than his rational mind. Now older, Ashyn began to realize why the Ferhym might find such a thing dangerous. He didn't agree at all with their methods, but an emotional dui Nuchada accessing whatever that font within them may be could be outright devastating.

Hells, Ashyn blew up a field, and took a good amount of elves with him. If all dui Nuchada were capable of such a thing... Ashyn shook his head and looked down at the wounded elf. "Great, now I'm starting to think like you. Punishment before the crime."

He replayed the moment again in his mind, the exact second his mind instinctually leapt for the magic and it broke through the prison of his injury and responded. It was at the injustice of the bull's actions. His fuel had been his own anger. His feedback had only come at the cost of his emotion. It fed on the anger and then left him strangely indifferent. He should have been terrified at losing Jenhiro. At watching the creature impale and nearly kill the elf. Now he was just apathetic.

What surprised him though was that in his rage he didn't attack the bull, but the true source of the power that was going to kill Jenhiro.

Ashyn blinked back the thoughts as the realization hit him. Instinct drove him not to attack the wielder, but its staff. A staff that controlled nature around him. Ashyn wondered if such a thing could dry out wood, or even start a fire?

He looked down to the elf who was growing paler by the moment. His saturated bandages were beginning to turn a distinctly pinkish hue. Unless Ashyn found a true way to mitigate the bleeding and control his shock, it was likely Jenhiro wouldn't even make it a day. That meant Ashyn needed fire in a water-deluged place.

Ashyn held out his hand in front of him and tried to use the anger of his predicament to reignite that feeling inside of him. If he could, he could create the fire he needed. Ashyn thought once more of the moment that had set him off, of how far he had come, and now the possibility of losing it, losing Jenhiro because of the bull. He tried to summon every bit of his anger into a single thought. Fire.

Ashyn closed his eyes and imagined what the burning ball of flame used to feel like inches from his skin. The warmth it would imbue, without burning him. He opened his eyes hoping to see it there, hovering above his outstretched fingers, illuminating the dark cavern. There was nothing.

Ashyn sighed, ran his fingers through his wet, limp hair and looked down to Ginger who was trying vainly to lick the water off soaked fur. Situated as it was, Ashyn noticed for the first time that the cat might be male. "Looks like I'm going back out there." The feline looked up, cocked his head slightly, then resumed his efforts.

"You stay here," he ordered, and before the foul weather could change his mind, he turned and walked back out of the cavern.

~ ~ ~

The rain was coming down more severely than ever. Ashyn pulled the drenched hood tighter over his head in a pointless attempt to deflect the water that already soaked him to the bone. He looked both ways, trying to get his bearings. Ginger led him to this point, and he had been focusing on dragging the makeshift litter, but he still paid enough attention that he thought he could get back to where the staff was lost.

Finding it in the storm, however, was another matter entirely. Though, since he could no longer conjure fire from thin air, the bull's staff was a long shot worth trying.

The wizard took a few steps forward and looked back. In the heavy deluge and turbulent winds, it was impossible to see the cavern behind him unless you knew where to look. How Ginger had found it, Ashyn had no clue. More to the point, he didn't know if he could get back again. Ashyn tried to memorize everything he saw, and then with shaky steps disappeared into the violent storm.

THE TOTEM

The rain ripped hard at his body, leaving welts as it pounded down on him. Flora flew everywhere striking like hammers against him. He could barely see anything in front of him, and yet he searched the ground where he thought he saw the staff land.

His torn fingers groped through ferns and thistles, trying to grasp his hands around that curious stick that had caused them so many problems.

He pushed at a ten-foot tall thicket as he blindly moved his hands back and forth across the soggy ground. He felt his fingertips probe more than once into the soft recesses of the ground and come back smeared and dark. At least he hoped it was only dirt. The grime stung the fresh wounds on his tips, but the sting from the hard pelting rain was worse.

As he forced himself through more bramble, scoring another dozen scratches against his flesh, he heard a sound that was unlike the great howl of wind. It was a mewling cry of terror.

Ashyn looked up, his grey eyes fighting to see beyond the few feet in front of him. Where did it come from? A moment later, he heard the cry again.

Ashyn moved towards the sound. Pushing against both wind and oversized plants. A few times, he ran into the massive sequoias that only appeared seconds before he would collide with them, his hands raised protecting his nose. He'd learned that lesson the hard way from the cornfields of his childhood.

Suddenly something caught his leg, and he fell forward. Ashyn braced for the impact, as his world tilted on its side. He hit the muddy ground with a splat, and then found himself in a rolling frenzy as the ground descended. Mud flung all around him, and he tore down some of the weaker verdure and wound up burying his side and half his face in the liquid laden dirt.

As Ashyn spit out the foul sludge, he sat up to see what had tripped him up so badly. There only a few feet away buried halfway in flowerage and mire he could just make out a small oblong shape. It looked like an egg.

The now filthy wizard crawled towards the object. As he did, he saw it more clearly. A white stone glistened vibrantly in the rain. Inside the egg-shaped stone he could see natural earthen piping of green, blue, amber, and red.

The wizard reached for it. As soon as he touched it, a surge of energy ran through his body. *We are merely its conduit*, the words ran excitedly through his head. He grabbed the stone and pulled at it.

Just as he had hoped, a long mahogany shaft slid from the binding vegetation. When it cleared its shrouding, he was staring at a strange staff nearly six feet in length. Aside from the rounded stone that sat on top, he could see a pointed spike at its base. This was it. This was the bull's staff, and he could feel the magic within it!

Ashyn couldn't believe his luck! The odds of really finding the staff in the storm were unfathomable. It had to be like finding a needle in a haystack, within a barn full of haystacks, on the other side of the country, buried in a landslide. So not at all in his favor.

Yet there he was, holding the staff and it indeed was the one that harried him for so long. He still had no idea how to work it, but if anything could help him connect with magic again, it would be the staff.

He stood up, and turned to head back up the rise and to the cave when he heard the mewling cry once more. It was much closer now. He recognized the sound. He had heard it twice before now.

Ashyn turned to follow the cries. He moved forward more slowly, not wanting to take another spill. The ground continued to decant downwards. Soon the foliage opened up, and he found himself in a familiar trail-like opening, with a large boulder. Where Ashyn left it, was the bull.

It was standing now, tethered tightly against the boulder with its arms caught up on its horns. The sight reminded Ashyn of how he had used to see Farmer Bib's dogs all bound up when they were tied off to a pole or their dog houses.

Ashyn noted the peculiar position of its arms pinned against its face. It must have tried to cut the hemp ropes with its horns and, in the process, somehow bound itself up.

Ashyn figured the bull, once it regained consciousness, would have muscled through the ropes somehow. He hoped to be so far gone by that point that it would have lost its ability to pursue, especially after losing its staff.

There was a crack as a long thick branch broke from the tree above Ashyn and was immediately picked up in the gust. It swung about wildly, and he ducked out of the way in time, but not before watching it bounce and bound to its new location. The boulder.

The branch, about as thick around as Ashyn's thigh, slammed into the flank of the bull creature. It writhed again, burrowing itself deeper into the coiled mess of rope. The beast issued another mewling protest from its assailer, before tumbling on out of sight.

Ashyn realized that the opening where he tied the bull down was just that, an opening. Everything caught in the heavy winds travelled through the empty space easily, and the poor creature was right in its trajectory.

Ashyn cringed as he looked around the bovine and saw detritus everywhere. The bull had been bludgeoned repeatedly ever since the winds picked up. It had tried to free itself, but now it was bound even worse than before, and to make things even direr, its weak flank was completely exposed. Not just to the elements, but to everything flying through the air.

Ashyn wanted to turn away. He wanted to leave the creature who acted as his shadow hunter for so long to its fate. It tried to kill him, repeatedly. It impaled Jenhiro, who in all likelihood was going to die. He should just take the staff and leave the beast to its fate.

There was another snap of a branch and then the loud crack of it impacting the bull. The cry it issued then, Ashyn knew that he couldn't leave it. Not such as it was. Seeing it tied against the stone, pelted mercilessly stopped him from walking away.

"A wizard values all life," he said to himself, "not just those of his choosing."

Ashyn knew what he was about to do could only make matters more complicated, but his conscience couldn't have it any other way. He thought he might be beginning to understand what it was it that Xexial told him in the fields after they left Czynsk to the Elves. "Politics are not for a true wizard. It is the people's choice to fight, not yours to fight for them. A wizard is not meant to be a champion. We are meant to keep people alive to the best of our abilities."

Through it all, Ashyn had been choosing a side, the Ferhym side. Though on many counts he couldn't bring himself to kill again, he knew he was trying to be Jenhiro's champion. At every turn he was trying to impress the Wild Elf, trying to get him to value his importance. He had done it in an effort to reach his sister. Now what seemed a simple choice of fighting what he thought was a minotaur had cascaded all the way to the very moment before him.

It was not a minotaur. Ashyn realized that for a while now. It was an intelligent, sentient creature. It controls an awesome power within the staff he held. Ashyn's decision in championing the Ferhym facilitated this feud. He helped in persecuting, tormenting, and now torturing the bull against the large stone.

No more. He was going to end it his way, a wizard's way.

VALUE

The young pan struggled against the bindings, his head pinned awkwardly against the rock by the ropes where his horns caught. He did this to himself. His anger, his fury, had driven him to this end. Worse, the elf responsible for the deaths of his herd was gone. He stabbed the foul creature with its own weapon, all but guaranteeing its death but the one in red changed things. Proverbially pulled the pergola out from under him.

He hated the red one. Almost as much as hated the Wild Elf. It smelled wrong. Acted strangely. Nothing like the elves of these woods.

It was a curious emotion, this hate. He had never known such feelings before, nor had he known the hunt before his herd was slain as if they were nothing more than diseased livestock. He always heard about the elves of the Shalis-Fey. His Pundit mentioned it during preparation for his spirit journey, his *Takewatha*. But he was denied his acceptance to the World Spirit in his death, forced back, and unable to die until his task was complete. A revenant, risen for vengeance.

The wind ripped by him furiously, slapping his body with leaves and sticks caught up in the maelstrom of the open channel he resided in. Suddenly a large limb slammed into his flank. He felt his ribs shatter under the assault. He mewled in pain. Though he may be risen, he was not immune to pain. Moments later the bones mended, and he waited again for another impact.

Lightning flashed, and thunder bellowed through the sky. He blinked the pelting waters out of his amber eyes, and then he saw a movement. It was blurry, but he knew it was there.

The pan tried to turn its head to face the movement, but he only managed to slide the ropes lower down his horn, burying his fury arms into his snout. He snorted his displeasure vehemently.

He struggled once more to try to see where the movement came from. He took deep breaths to gain its scent. No use. There were so many scents blowing by second after second, he couldn't tell what it was.

There was a flash, something glinting, like metal. The pan yanked and mewled. Though it was an unliving thing now, it wasn't sure how it might regenerate if it were say, eaten, or his head cut from his body.

Immediately its head slammed back against the stone and he felt the bindings grow tighter. The pan roared in frustration, slamming itself against the stone in hopes of giving whatever predator might be out there, a second thought before committing itself to killing him.

The lightning flashed once more, and then he saw it. The red one. Well not so much anymore at least.

The red one's armor was gone. Instead, its chest was naked. Bare olive flesh streaked in mud greeted the pan's amber eyes. The mud was thick, and he could see shoots of sward sticking out at odd angles across the narrow frame of the creature. It was strange to see something so hairless before him. It was an ugly thing, too.

In its right hand, he could see it held its knife, in the left something long and dark, probably its bow covered in mud as well.

The pan knew then that this was how it was going to finish him off. Close. Personal. Perhaps it is what he deserved. His body should not heal as it did. He should be dead three times over. Perhaps the Great Spirit, Brahma, would reward him in his *Takewatha* if he endured the torments of the knife.

Brahma never was about violence. He was a peaceful god, and the Gaur a peaceful people. At least that was what his Pundit had trained. Pan studied this for his long winters. But something was different now. Changed. Was it the Great Spirit? Or his undeath?

In his raising, he became an arbiter of vengeance. He brokered a violence that he had never known. Used his abilities to create harm to others. Those that killed his people. He sought to honor the fallen herd that died for him.

He was the reason for the migration. They were on his spirit journey. The blood of the fallen was on his hands. Perhaps that is why Brahma would not accept him. Because the deaths were his, until he could atone. He would not succumb to this hairless ape.

Still the grey-eyed creature moved forward. Pan shook, raged, and fought with all his might to break his bindings. Once he thought they might slip, and he even watched the red one take pause. Still after a moment's hesitation it continued forward.

The thing's mouth began moving, and the pan realized that it was trying to speak to him. Bizarre chittering came from its mouth. It sounded like some small dainty forest animal. What was it doing? Praying to its deities? Was he an offering?

Then its mouth moved again, and the sounds were different. It was definitely speaking to him, but he had no clue what it was trying to convey. It swung the knife in short controlled movements in front of him. Jerky little movements. Again it spoke in even more different words.

Pan didn't know what it was doing, taunting him perhaps? Showing him what it was going to do to him? Were the words a spell or an attempt to heckle him? Pan never tried communicating before with it before.

An image of one of the feathered arrows sticking out of the chest of one of his herd flashed in his mind. The slumped form, in its final resting pose, waist deep in a pond. Blood like pink ribbons moved about it in the shallow pool. The maul only a few feet away. The red one did that. The red one caused it. And there was a body of water right there. A large one. Why hadn't it tried communicating then?

The gaur roared with all its might at the approaching red one. He didn't want to talk. He looked at the puddles around him. It was possible to, but Pan was in no mood for taunts and jeers before the end. The red one wanted to kill him, and it wanted him to know it was going to kill him. Pan bucked and writhed angrily and he watched it flinch at his might. He thought, for a moment, he may have truly scared it, but was surprised when a grim determination took over its strange hairless face. Pan knew then that it was committed.

He tensed, preparing for the pain as the knife flashed forward. Instantly he felt its tip. Cold and sharp against the sensitive hair follicles on its torso. It was going to cut out his innards! It slashed down quickly.

Pan jumped away in terror at the idea of having its entrails removed. He no longer felt either the resistance of the binding or slam of his back against the boulder. Instead he moved away from the stone and the red one.

He stumbled backward, unprepared for his sudden freedom, and ended up tripping over his own hooves. He tumbled to the wet ground. He tried to brace himself, but still found his arms solidly bound. His elbow struck a gnarled root with a loud crack and he collapsed on his side.

Confused, the pan looked up at the approaching red one. He knew his entrails had not spilled out, and it was clear that the hairless thing before him had not missed. It intended on cutting him loose.

The gaur could see its knife was back at its waist, yet it still held something in its other hand. With one more ominous flash of lightning, the gaur finally made out what it was looking at. Horror set in. The red one held in its hands the pan's last chance at redemption. It was the Pundit's totem.

~ ~ ~

Ashyn tensed as those amber eyes stared up at him in malice. He instantly knew why. It recognized the staff. Ashyn shook his head. So far he tried speaking to it in Trade tongue, Ferhym, Lefhym, and even Gnomish, but it was clear the creature didn't understand him. Since principal communication was out, he knew he was going to have to rely on physical gestures. But he didn't know anything about the race before him, other than it was not a minotaur.

It slammed its bound hands down in the mud in obvious rage. Water splashed about both the wizard and the bull. Its small eyes continued to stare at Ashyn with menace.

Ashyn tapped his chest. "I freed you." He then pointed to the tree line. "Go!"

The creature snorted and stood up to its full height. This was closest he was to it while not camouflaged. It was enormous. What little light cast in the storm was muted by the shadow of the monstrosity before him. It beat on its chest and bellowed at Ashyn so closely its roar cast spittle upon Ashyn's face.

Though disgusted and petrified at the act, Ashyn noticed one thing when it roared at him. Its teeth were long and flat. Ashyn's suspicion was confirmed: the one before him was a plant-eater. He only hoped that meant it wasn't inherently violent. That everything that happened was due to provocation.

Ashyn pointed to the staff, and then touched his chest again. "I need it." He tried Draconic this time, it being the oldest language that he knew fluently. Still the effect was the same. The thing before him just didn't understand.

Ashyn watched as it slammed its hoof down and pitched its head wildly. Like the elk, he realized. It may be sentient, but its mannerisms were still like its four-legged relatives.

It was threatening him, but not attacking. It was attempting to establish dominance without violence. He supposed that was a start. Every other time it just tried to kill him. Now it was only acting as if it was going to kill him. Had Ashyn earned its respect?

No, it was trying to take control. His respect wouldn't drive it to take control. Because he saved its life, perhaps? Some code it may have. A debt?

Ashyn need only look in its eyes to know it still very much wanted to kill him. No this was definitely something else. Was it because he had the staff?

That was the only way to explain the creature's behavior. It wanted him dead. Ashyn could read that clear as day from it. And it wanted him dead for more than just the Wild Elf. If it were just his alliance to Jenhiro that facilitated the hunt, it would have never attacked him at the waterfall. No, Ashyn knew with more clarity. It was the staff. He controlled the staff. He contained the beast.

So, Ashyn said the one word that was universal in every language he knew, "No."

Whether it understood the language or not, it definitely understood the context. Immediately it slammed its fist into the boulder and roared at him with everything it could muster. Even with the pounding storm all around him, the noise was deafening. Ashyn refused to back down from its blustering. He stood tall and defiant against it, as his hawk-like gaze pierced the beast's.

Ashyn did as his conscious dictated. He spared the bull from a very agonizing death. Now he had to try to save Jenhiro, and through that elf, reach his sister.

The wizard slowly backed away. The bull, remained, staring and slamming its hooves into the ground. Ashyn made it five feet, then ten, then fifteen.

The pelting rainwaters obscured the creature's form into a hazy shadowlike wraith once more. He was almost free of it. Almost ready to take the staff back to Jenhiro and try to start a fire. Almost.

Out of the corner of his eye he saw a sudden movement. Ashyn dove out of the way as the beast charged head first past where Ashyn was seconds before. Its horns slammed violently into a sequoia with a loud crack. Dazed, it shook its head and began searching for him. But Ashyn was already running once more.

~ ~ ~

Stupid! Stupid! he chastised himself. The creature had been pinned and had he not intervened would have died. Why couldn't it see that he meant it no harm? Twice now he spared it. Couldn't it see that?

He desperately wished he could communicate with it in some way, let it know that he was only defending himself against the other one that he killed. That if there were any other way he would've taken it. But would he have though?

Ashyn slowed slightly as the thought came to him. He made the decision so quickly to kill. Agreed with Jenhiro before even knowing his adversary. He judged it on look alone and deemed it worth death.

A crash behind him shook him from his thoughts, and he pushed through the tall ferns and around another one of the massive trees.

Ashyn felt remorse for his actions of course, and it dawned on him that for some reason he didn't feel as guilty as when he took the branch commander's life, an elf who was hell bent on his death and the deaths of all wizards, and he had cried. Cried!

Yet, here he took the life of another sentient being, and all he felt was a little guilt? Was that because of his conscience, or the fact that he was hunted by its ilk? Did the fact that it looked so different from him make him think that it was somehow less of a person? That it was more animal?

The reality revolted him. That he, one who was to value all life, looked at the bull as if it was nothing more than a beast, even after knowing its sentience

He knew now how racism was born. How easy it was to judge what he feared and didn't understand and brand it. "Like me," he hissed to himself, thinking of all the winters of ostracization at the hands of the people of Bremingham for the color of his skin, for his strong intellectual mind that they couldn't comprehend. He was called a freak, a pariah, a demon.

A dui Nuchada.

"I am no different than they are," he huffed to himself while he scrambled back up the rise he had originally fallen down. He needed to get more distance between himself and the raging bull he wronged.

It was a difficult thing to swallow. That with all his intelligence, and higher learning at the hands of a wizard, he was still capable of such ignorance.

A roar and a shattering of branches behind him brought him back to the moment. He had hoped that in freeing it, that it would have left. It appeared that it was going to come down to who killed the other. The bull wasn't going to stop.

Ashyn continued to climb the mud-slicked terrain. Heat rolled from his body even though pelted in water. Ashyn's hair fell like long wet noodles against his head. The stubble on his arms and face collected grit from his trekking and had created long, grimy streaks on his body.

He thought that maybe if he could lose the bull quickly enough, he could hide in the cave and wait the storm out. As if answer to those thoughts a sudden torrent of downpour assailed him even harder. Ashyn reached out to grab at a gnarled root with his free hand to hold on lest he be hurled back down the precipice.

In his other hand, he struggled to hold onto the staff-like object. Suddenly the root gave way from the soft soggy earth and Ashyn felt himself wheel backward. Instinct drove the staff downward to try and steady himself, and he was alarmed when the staff sank into the ground of its own accord. He was holding onto an immovable anchor. He grasped it with his other hand and pulled himself close, trying hard not to question the physics of how an object only two or three inches into the muck was holding him as sturdily as one of the massive trees around him.

Water ran over the top of the grade he was standing on, and soon came tumbling down around him bringing with it all the loose detritus in its wake. It was a small landslide, and Ashyn was caught in it.

Ashyn screamed as he leaned against the staff. Water and refuse ripped at his legs threatening to pull him under. It grew in volume reaching up to his knees, tugging at his clothes and grasping at his body. The wizard's hands throbbed as he tightened his grip against the staff even more. His knuckles were white, his breaths labored and ragged. Ashyn's arms shook as the mud pulled viciously at him and his scream ripped at his throat until it died completely and all he could do was grit his teeth and hold on or be pulled below.

Then just as quickly as it started, it was gone. With trembling arms, Ashyn leaned against the staff and looked down at the churning morass behind him. Likely the bull was down there, buried now. If the creature was within that mass, it was lost.

The boy wizard looked back to the staff that just saved his life. What was it? He knew of nothing like it from any texts or tomes. The strength of it defied order. It was little more than a quarterstaff, with an unusual stone atop it, and a sharpened spear-tip at the base, and yet it was so much more.

Curiously, he reached down around the shaft and pulled, wondering if there was any way he could release it from the earth after it had anchored him so securely. He gasped as it slid free effortlessly.

He held it up and looked at it, almost in reverence in the dim light. This stick was a curiosity to be sure, but it could help him save Jenhiro, and probably help him save Julietta.

Ashyn looked back down the hill. If only he had the chance to learn more about that race of bull men. If only he hadn't been so quick to judge. He shook his head angrily.

"Learn from this," Xexial would have told him. His master believed in losing, so to speak. "There is either succeeding, or there is learning. Every failure is a lesson. And as long as you learned something from that failure then it was a valuable lesson," his mentor told him often.

He would not judge one who looked so differently again. That was the lesson learned.

Ashyn finished his climb; the rain lessened slightly making the trek back to the cavern easier to navigate. Within minutes he could just make out the craggy rock-like formations that led to the small opening. Hopefully he could figure out how to manipulate the odd staff to ignite something. Perhaps there were dried bones in the cavern.

If he could get a fire, he could treat the wounds on Jenhiro, and cauterize them to keep him from bleeding out.

Ashyn bent down and ducked his head inside the opening. The same musky, dank odor from before assailed him. In the darkness a pair of gleaming yellow eyes stared at him. For the first time in a while, Ashyn smiled.

He felt a heavy impact against his right shoulder. He looked down in confusion to see two thick mud-covered fingers the size of bananas wrap around his collarbone. Before the realization of what it was set in, he was ripped out from the entrance and sent flying.

SIPHON

A shyn hit the ground in a roll, his training overruling his natural instincts to just ball up. The staff, however, went soaring once more into the darkness. As the wizard's chaotic tumble came to a stop, he looked up.

The world tilted and swayed, but he could see clearly in front of him. The bull.

Ashyn staggered to his feet. He crashed in a deep pocket of mud, kicking up water and sludge in every direction. On either side of him were the massive bases of the sequoia trees. Any impact from those would've been fatal at the speed at which he flew.

His eyes darted back to the massive frame of the creature and then to the sodden earth before him. The staff was nowhere in sight. His eyes fell back to the gargantuan before him. At least it didn't have it.

Its eyes bore hard into Ashyn. He could see its body quiver as it struggled to breath. Long dregs of mud clung across the creature's normally slick coated body. They appeared like islands across the sea of fur.

Still the dirty mounds did little to hide the bulging muscles of the thing before him. Over two-thousand pounds of sheer mass lay between Ashyn and the cavern, and all the wizard had was his skinning knife. An odd sense of déjà vu filled him.

The bull snorted and charged.

Ashyn waited for just the right moment. Its body surged forward. A wall of sinew and muscle. Its body glistened in the rain, casting a sparkle on the slick coat of fur not covered in mud. It lowered its head down, and Ashyn saw the long, curved dark horns coming in line with his chest. Like the elk before it, it planned to gore him.

The ground trembled as it closed the distance, and Ashyn could actually see the puddles of water around him rippling with each heavy hoof fall.

When it was ten feet away and coming fast, Ashyn moved. He dove into a roll around one of the sequoias coming up just on the other side.

The bull reacted as well and turned the opposite way, narrowly skimming the thick rugged bark with its wide shoulder. It killed its momentum, tilted its massive head back and roared in frustration.

Ashyn made a run for the cave. The entrance looked too small for the thing fit through. Behind him, it bellowed again, and the ground quaked beneath his feet. Ashyn didn't look back. He just kept running.

When he was feet away from the entrance, he felt intense heat rolling off the bull as it loomed up behind him. He knew he wasn't going to make it. His eyes darted left and right. He was in the rocky channel of the opening. There was nowhere to go but forward. He braced for its impact.

Suddenly, he heard a snort of shock, followed quickly by a whistle of panic. And Ashyn was there! He made it into the opening. The boy looked back to see what saved him, and he saw, with disbelief, Ginger on the creature's snout, clawing viciously at its eyes.

Deep red lines crisscrossed the bull's snout and it swatted and grabbed at its face as if it was trying to dissuade a mosquito or a gnat. However, this was no insect. A nimble cat was ripping long creases into the bovine's flesh.

"Ginger!" Ashyn yelled, and without thinking why, he darted back out of the cave to save his feline companion.

The bull bucked wildly and slammed its fists repeatedly against its head in an effort to dislodge the feline. Ashyn saw Ginger score a wicked hit as its claws lashed across one of the bull's eyes.

The wail it produced cut through the billowing storm like a strange high-pitched whistle. It was an odd sound, and Ashyn recognized it not one of pain, but of fear. It was afraid of the cat.

Ashyn moved forward to help Ginger, when something glinted from the corner of his eyes. He turned and saw it. A long shaft sparkled under the dim light, as hundreds of diamond-like raindrops ran down polished mahogany. It was the staff. It was wedged into the gnarled roots of one of the massive timber sentinels. He put his skinning knife away. He had only one chance.

Ashyn ran for it, narrowly ducking as the creature's wild arms swung like a windmill. A corner of the creature's finger or thumb caught the back of his hood and ripped it from his head. Instinct had him trying to grab it, but he was already past. He knew losing the hood was a small price to pay for not getting crushed by one of its anvil-sized fists.

Ashyn came forward and reached out. His fingers brushed the staff, and the same spark of power coursed through his fingertips and ran down his body. His hand closed around it and pulled it from its earthen prison. It slid as free as if it was sitting in the snow. He turned right as the bull-man flung the cat away from it.

Ginger sailed away into the darkness of the storm. Ashyn didn't hear a sound. Not a crunch or a thud or a cry of pain. He wasn't sure if the cat was okay or if it was dead. The sight of the cat dislodged so callously, its life disregarded so easily, made him angry.

This cat, this animal, came to his aid. Probably had saved his life. It showed more humanity in that moment then either he, or the creature before him had in the last few days.

He looked to the bull in front of him. As much as he desperately wanted otherwise, Ashyn knew that only one of them would walk away from this.

The bull's good eye locked with his. He saw the anger, its need for vengeance. Ashyn once felt the same. He knew that need all too well. It still burned inside of him, but he had learned to temper it.

It slammed its hooves into the ground, pronouncing once more its alpha dominance. Ashyn brought the staff to bear. He didn't know how to use it, how to make its power work, but he had an idea.

Lightning ripped across the sky above them. It jumped from cloud to cloud, never touching the ground. Thunder boomed and rumbled above them vibrating Ashyn's teeth. He knew that soon they would enter the eye of the storm, where everything would be calm. Fitting he thought.

The bull roared.

Ashyn screamed.

Once more the bull charged at Ashyn, but this time instead of standing his ground, Ashyn ran at it. He ran with everything he had. He drove himself with all the energy he had left to muster.

The bull stampeded forward, foam frothed from its mouth, its one whole eye thirsty for Ashyn's blood. Ferns rent, rocks ruptured under its immense weight, and scattered branches exploded into shrapnel and debris.

Ashyn did not slow. He did not waiver. Either this was going to work, or he was going to die. But it ended here. This hunter would not pursue him any longer.

Twenty feet.

Ashyn noticed the water pelting hard against the bull's flank, its slick body glimmered in the faint light.

Fifteen feet.

He could see the scratches along its face, bright pink against its dark fur. They had not healed as quickly as everything else had in the past. It was as if the cat had somehow found a way to make that damage stick.

Ten feet.

He could feel it. Feel its heat, its intent. It was committed now, and so was Ashyn. The gap was too close, his motions fluid. There would be no way he could roll away in time, and he didn't want to.

Five feet.

Ashyn brought the staff around in front of him. The bull was so close to impact, that if it tried to punch him it could hit him without a problem. Its head lowered, and all Ashyn could see were the sharp tips of its horns, ready to gore him to death.

Two feet.

Ashyn reacted. As when he slipped, Ashyn drove the staff into the mud. The earth drank it down hungrily. And it became an anchor. It became a barrier.

He saw the bull's eyes expand in surprise, and in that moment he knew he had chosen wisely.

The crack of the bull's skull against the staff was deafening, louder than when it had hit the sequoia. It reverberated across the forest. The wind from the momentum of the two-thousand-pound bull washed over him in a sudden gust of heat. The staff held, as solid as any tree.

Ashyn watched as the bull's head split. Blood exploded along the surface like crimson geysers as it gave way to the muscles and sinew beneath. A bright line formed behind the wells of blood that was brilliant white against the darkness of blood-drenched fur. The creature's skull.

The bull collapsed onto its side. Panting faintly. Ashyn pulled the staff from the sodden ground, and hovered it above the bull's broad chest. It looked up at him weakly. It looked like it didn't have any fight left.

Ashyn struggled through the rain that ran down his face to see the beast. He knew what he had to do. *This is the only way.*

Thoughts of Julietta's torture at the hands of the Council of Elm galvanized him into doing what needed doing. He heaved the staff higher into the air and then brought it down as hard as he could. Suddenly the bull used the rest of its flagging strength and lunged at the boy. Ashyn felt pain like nothing he had even known.

He looked down confused at the bull to see its mouth moving strangely, as if contorted in pain, and then he looked at the staff. Embedded deeply in the creature's chest. He had landed the blow, and it was fatal, he knew it to be true. The bull's unique regenerative ability would not be recovering from this.

But why did he hurt so much, too? With glazed eyes Ashyn noticed the bull's arm extended towards him. He followed it all the way to his own abdomen where its large hand enclosed around something small. Slowly it fell away, and Ashyn could only stare down in shock.

Jutting from his stomach was a cherry wood handle. The cherry wood handle, Ashyn's foggy brain realized, of his own skinning knife.

~ ~ ~

Pan knew it was over. That the red one had felled him. He was content. His strike would kill the red one as well, perhaps not immediately, but it would kill him nonetheless.

As he lay there, panting, slowly letting the pain ebb away, he realized that the strange thing before him that looked like a human was not a human at all. It used the totem. It could use Pundit's totem!

It was a strange revelation as the final moments of his life bled out of him. He would have to discuss it with the Great Earth Spirit, he decided. He thought only gaur could use totems. He was told only those in touch with their bestial side could truly understand the power of the totem, but clearly this was not the case. Had he been wrong about the red one? Had he made some mistake? Did this one know of the beast within him?

Slowly, weakly, the pan reached up and wrapped his fingers around the totem. To feel the familiarity of his mentor's totem once more in his hands. In that moment he felt it. He felt the presence of the red one within the totem, and he knew without a doubt that his nose was correct. This was no human. *And* this was no elf.

There was a magic inside of it. A well of pure spirit energy that seemed almost endless, and it shifted and rolled within the red one like a caged beast.

What was he? With rising alarm at the red one's power, he realized with equal doses dread and jubilation, that the red one was siphoning the unlife essence from him. The scourge that kept renewing his body, and denying him rebirth, was drained away.

Once again he felt his spirit. He had come all this way as a creature of unlife, expecting his destruction. Instead his spirit was given back to him right before his release from this world. The red one gave it to him. A Totem-Brother.

~ ~ ~

Ashyn stared at the wall of red that was growing around the knife in his stomach. *No, no, no!* Of all the times in the past few months he thought he was going to die, he didn't think it was going to be like this! Stabbed with his own skinning knife!

He had to do something. He had to stop it. Somehow he had to stop it!

Ashyn watched in disbelief as the circle of blood turned into a sheet as it ran down his abdomen. There was so much! Too much!

His eyes burned with anger as he looked down at the bull who stared back at him. Then he saw one of the pink lacerations on its face begin to close. Without thought, without understanding how, he knew he needed that power.

He watched as the bull reached up to touch the totem. In that moment, at that tactile sensation, Ashyn felt it. An *alien* presence in the staff. It reached out to read him, and he let it. He felt its source. He felt the magic within, and through the magic, he felt the creature's power to knit its own flesh. Ashyn needed that power. Not just to save his life, but so he could save Jenhiro's, to save Julietta's. He reached out for it as he reached out for fire.

It coursed through him, cold, yet refreshing, like he just submerged himself in a mountain lake. He didn't know how to control it; he didn't know how long he would have it. But he had it, and it was already ebbing.

His hand slid down the mahogany until it brushed up against the bull's thick fingertips. Their eyes met once more, its malice replaced with awe. Ashyn pulled hard on the weapon and it slid from the bull's chest as easily as it had slid from the ground.

To both of their surprise a large gout of blood followed. The bull mewled as it stared at its own life's essence pouring from its body.

Ashyn reached down and touched the rent hole. He didn't want to waste the power, yet he couldn't leave it this way. Even after all it had done. Their eyes met, and at last both of them finally understood one and other. In that moment, a moment that was to be their deaths, they had peace.

The hole in its chest began to mend. The bull didn't fight him; it only stared as Ashyn expended all he safely could into the beast. And then, Ashyn watched as the puckering hole closed, and the bull's now healed eyes rolled into the back of its head. It fell into convulsions.

He whispered, "Feedback." It had been so long since he touched magic this way, he completely forgot. He didn't have much time.

Ashyn moved swiftly, the knife in his belly momentarily forgotten as the determination of his need set in. He made it to the cave, stumbled inside as the first wave of feedback hit him.

He stumbled, suddenly dizzy, yet held on to the staff. He felt the power ebbing away swiftly, like sand pouring through his fingertips. As quickly as he had it, he was going to lose it again. He swayed, trying to get his footing and took another step forward. His legs gave out. *No!* He crawled as waves of nausea pounded over him.

He saw the elf's still form. *Don't be dead. Don't be dead.* He drug the staff limply at his side, he could feel the pour of the magic bleeding out of the staff now. He knew he should use the last of this power to save himself, but that wouldn't get him to Feydras' Anula, only Jenhiro could do that.

The elf was only ten feet away when his arms gave out. Blackness surrounded the corners of his vision. The wizard knew he couldn't reach him. The power he had stolen was so fleeting he doubted it would be enough.

Ashyn slid the staff in front of him and pushed with all his might. He felt the knife in his side grate against the stone, pulling his own wound wider. He growled. The staff was only inches away from Jenhiro's body.

He could faintly see the rise and fall of the elf's chest. He was going to fail.

Then suddenly he was pushed. He didn't know by what, and he didn't know how, but he moved forward those valuable inches and the egg-shaped stone touched the elf.

Ashyn poured the power of the staff into Jenhiro. The effect was immediate. The Wild Elf arced his back and groaned in agony as the bones re-set themselves in his leg and arm. Ashyn watched through a fading light as the healing magic pushed out all the gauze he had squeezed into the pierced hole in the elf's chest creating an eruption of blood and wool. The hole closed. With his remaining strength, he rolled to his side. The tips of his fingers brushed the cherry wood handle of his knife. He willed the healing power into it.

He felt the beginning tingle of his mending flesh. Deep inside he felt his organs mend, and then there was nothing. The moment had passed, and the magic was once again gone.

Damn.

Ashyn's eyes grew heavy, and he knew that fate was no longer in his hands. Perhaps it was better this way. He let oblivion take him. He didn't even try to fight it.

~ ~ ~

Jenhiro struggled to open his eyes. Pain wracked his body and he felt unbelievably cold. His lip quivered and he shivered uncontrollably. Why was it so cold? It was spring wasn't it?

His mouth felt dry, and he could taste the heavy bitterness of copper on his tongue. His body was soaked in water, and yet he felt so thirsty.

Finally, with much struggle, the elf wearily opened his eyes. All he saw was blackness. *Am I blind? Am I dead?*

As if in answer, a surge of lightning blazed forth, briefly illuminating his surroundings. He was in a cave. Water trickled around him, and he could hear breathing.

His eyes adapted to the dim light. His chest covered in a mountain of used bandages, all of it sticky with crimson cruor.

His mind reeled at the memory of the bull impaling him. He desperately reached out to his chest where he expected to feel a garish wound. Instead, he felt sensitive, soft flesh. He prodded more, searching for the rend that he knew should be in his body, but there was nothing. It was gone.

Jenhiro sat up and his hand grasped something round and hard. Confused he latched onto it and drug it forward. He heard the clatter of wood on stone echo through the cave, and he realized he was holding the skewer's weapon. The very same one that the black magic wielding bull had used to kill his people. Revolted, he threw it to the ground, and that was when he saw the hand. The hand of the Wood Elf. Or Wood Elf no longer.

Jenhiro pulled himself to his feet, and limped towards the fallen body. His legs trembled; one ached like he had broken it. Still he had to know. Know if it was true.

Jenhiro hovered above the fallen boy, and his spirit broke just a little at knowing he was correct. It was not a Wood Elf. He was deceived, "A dui Nuchada."

His eyes moved from the deceiver to the staff and back again. His own fingers brushed against his reknit flesh.

It wasn't possible. He couldn't conceive it. *No!*

Jenhiro stumbled out of the cave. *No. The dui Nuchada were evil. They were skewers of the worst kind. Abominations filled with the spirits of monsters or worse.* It is what he was told. What he believed.

He reached the mouth of the cave and climbed out. He groaned as his sore body fought against him, but he needed to be away from the skewer in the cave.

Jenhiro climbed over the last rise of rock, and his eyes fell to the still form before him. He blinked away the falling rain, wiped his face, and looked again.

Twenty feet away was the bull that had hunted them. Defeated and broken, its chest rose and fell ever so minutely in the dim light.

Jenhiro bit his lower lip and spun to look back into the cave. The boy was the dui Nuchada. He was the enemy. A skewer of balance. By all rights, he deserved to die. He was an abomination. An affront against nature.

Jenhiro found himself turning and looking back to the mound of flesh and muscle defeated a scant distance away. This bull had harassed his thoughts and dreams for the better part of a month. The guilt he felt in his chest at surviving the loss of his party burned in him like white hot fire.

The dui Nuchada held up his end of the bargain. Jenhiro sighed. He helped Jenhiro protect the people from the beast. Once more he rubbed at the newly formed flesh and bone. *He saved my life.*

Jenhiro left the sight of the bull. He made his way back to the dui Nuchada. There he saw the makeshift splint out of the dui Nuchada's armor. He saw the time and attention that this skewer gave him in an attempt to keep him alive.

Jenhiro looked down and noticed for the first time, the garish wound in the boy's abdomen. Blood ran from the slit in his body. It leaked out slowly from between the steel embedded within him and his own flesh. Like the wound had begun to heal, but couldn't finish. Without proper treatment, he would be dead in a matter of days.

Jenhiro could seal the wound, but he had no way to fix the damage within the body, or to get rid of the poisonous blood that would well up inside along with other potential lethal fluids. The elf had no real way to save him, only prolong the inevitable. The dui Nuchada would die if he didn't receive proper aid.

Jenhiro was torn. All his life he hated and despised the dui Nuchada. Now, he had allied with one for days upon days, and it just saved Jenhiro's life at the expense of its own.

The dui Nuchada also delivered the weapon of the skewer and the skewer itself that plagued him. The dui Nuchada helped him. He helped Jenhiro's people.

This wasn't the mark of someone evil. Yet the Council of Elm taught... He willed the thought away. Did they not have such a discussion? Did the dui Nuchada try to tell him what he was the night before?

That decided it for him. Jenhiro reached down and pulled the knife from the boy's stomach. He groaned. Blood pumped out from the open tear in the boy's guts. In minutes it would be over, and the dui Nuchada would be dead.

The Wild Elf gathered all the materials around him, squatted down and treated the wound. He could stop the bleeding on the outside, but that alone would not be enough.

"I cannot save your life," he told the dui Nuchada honestly, "but I know those who can."

Jenhiro stood, "Spirits have mercy on me for what I am about to do." He told his fallen comrade, "For I doubt my people will understand."

The elf stared at the cave mouth once more. Yellow eyes flashed at him in the darkness. The dui Nuchada traveled with the wildcat. It looked between him and the fallen dui Nuchada. Jenhiro watched it watching him, and then it turned back out into the wilderness and was gone.

For the best, perhaps. Jenhiro figured the large feline probably thought his companion dead. He wouldn't try to find the cat; he already had enough of a burden trying to keep the dui Nuchada alive.

Jenhiro knew very keenly where he was. He came here before many times. He also knew the closest place to find help, and likely what they would do with the dui Nuchada once they helped him. Jenhiro saw little choice in the matter though. He had to try. Jenhiro was going to the druids.

PART II

FEYDRAS' ANULA

TOME II

I was once told that I should keep a journal of my exploits. To chronicle my life as it happened, so that one day my predecessors may find it and learn from me. I have often found that to be ironic since we know virtually nothing of our progenitors. Just fables, myths, and here-says.

Yet those words became increasingly wise to me as I spent time amongst the Wild Elves as a prisoner. I didn't know how long I was going to live, how long I could last. I knew then, that someone should at least know how I lived, no matter how short, and that they should know who the real Ashyn Rune was, not merely whatever legacy that would follow.

I didn't realize how important knowledge of the real me would truly become, or how deadly.

I am Recreant. At the time I committed the act it was a mar on my ego, like a hideous scar against the flesh of my mind. As time progressed, I wore it more like a badge of acceptance. It was who I was. Family came first. They gave me strength.

In hindsight I realized that Stormwind was a very smart elf. I wish I had had the chance to tell him so.

-The first journal of the Blood Wizard,
Ashyn Rune

UNSHROUDED

Ashyn was floating. He drifted aimlessly, lying against a pocket of air. Weightless like a feather caught in a zephyr. Time seemed meaningless. The burdens of his world were completely irrelevant. He tried to open is eyes to observe this lush comfort he felt himself in, but he could not. His eyes were bound shut.

An eerie sense of déjà vu overcame him. He had done this before. A long time ago. He was only a little boy back then. She challenged him not to give up and die, but to live.

"I'm not going to die this time, am I?" he asked, knowing he wasn't alone.

A melodic voice answered him, "That is yet to be seen." It was deeper now than when he heard it over a decade past. It was feminine and very beautiful, and there was a weight to it now.

Ashyn tried again to open his eyes, but no luck. "You are not going to let me see you?"

"Not this time," The ethereal voice answered him. "It would be too dangerous."

"For who?"

"Everyone," she answered simply. "We are adults grown now, dui Nuchada. Our actions carry heavy repercussions."

Ashyn did not answer. There was no need. A single thought of the lowlands east of the Onyx Tower, now a wasteland, was all he needed to know the true depth of the repercussions he carried.

"Why have you taken so long to contact me again? It has been many winters. You could have told me of the war your kind launched against the wizards. You could have warned me about Czynsk. None of our people would have died."

There was a long silence.

"Things are not so simple sometimes," the Exemplar answered. "I told you, you need to be patient."

Ashyn laughed bitterly. "Patience is a few days, maybe weeks, a month at most. I've been waiting winters."

Again, there was silence.

"You're not going to answer me, are you?"

"There is nothing to say. I am Ferhym; time doesn't caring the same meaning to me as it does to you. I did not have answers to give in the last few winters that you did not already learn on your own."

"Yet you claim to follow me?"

"I do," the voice came back honestly. "You are the dui Nuchada, and I am bound to you."

"What does that really mean? Do I have two souls? I don't understand," Ashyn queried, confused. "For winters I thought I was different because I was a part-elf…"

The voice cut in, "There is no elf within you and there never was."

"Then who am I?"

"You know who you are. The real question that burns in you is *what* are you?"

"Freak," he answered. "I am a freak."

"Perhaps to some that may be true. But I do not believe it to be the same for all. You are so much more Ashyn Rune."

"Why won't you give me a clear answer?" he pressed.

She sighed. It sounded like the soft moan of wind. He felt her breath against his cheek.

"The answers will come soon," she said, "I know what the dui Nuchada is to my people, but I don't know what it truly is to the rest of Kuldarr."

It was a slight revelation to him at that moment. She didn't really know. It was as if they were blind in this together. Bound on a journey neither understood. But she knew that they were in it together.

"But…" he began, but never finished.

~ ~ ~

Suddenly Ashyn's world tilted and jostled and he no longer felt weightless. "Exemplar!" he screamed, but she was gone.

His buoyancy ended abruptly, and he felt himself crashing downwards. He hit hard, sudden pain surging up his back. Gasping he opened his eyes.

A voice chittered near him in Ferhym, "Pick him up."

It was so dim that his eyes adjusted quickly and he wasn't overwhelmed by blinding light. A rumble of thunder sounded above him, past the green canopy overhead. His face was wet from raindrops, though nowhere near the torrent he remembered.

He felt himself lifted roughly and placed on something hard and flat.

"He's awake."

Ashyn's eyes darted around confused. A number of painted figures surrounded him. They were all Ferhym. He looked down. Only his small clothes remained. There was something strange by his stomach. A protrusion of garish flesh rose from the rest of his body. There were many of them, he realized with some nausea building in his guts. They all undulated together in a steady rhythm. Weakly he tried to touch it, when a firm calloused hand came down onto his shoulder. "Leave it."

He followed the arm up to the voice. Jenhiro. Ashyn opened his mouth to speak, but Jenhiro did not give him the chance.

"The leeches will cleanse you of the bad blood. It has filled up your body; it must be purged."

Leeches? The wizard was so confused, so tired. As if reading this, Jenhiro continued, "Sleep. It will be easier to heal."

Ashyn lay his head back, and as he did, he caught glimpse of another strange wagon to his right. Tied down was the bull he defeated.

His fate became clear. He was captured. That was the Exemplar's warning on why it would be dangerous. He understood. Ashyn let a small smile take his face. They were taking him for judgement. They were taking him to Feydras' Anula. They were taking him to his sister.

He let his mind fade away.

~ ~ ~

Consciousness came and went for what felt like several more days. He remembered catching glimpses of Jenhiro through it all, and occasionally a Ferhym with crazy brown hair with bones woven in. A druid.

He felt a curious sensation as his body was involuntarily assailed with magic. Though he knew that it was to heal him, he still felt violated. Nothing could be hidden from the healer.

Luckily, he couldn't maintain consciousness for more than a few minutes at a time. He was always too exhausted, a combination of feedback and his injuries.

Finally, he felt strength growing within him. He had long stopped moving, and he hadn't had any communication from the Exemplar again. Yet she knew he was coming.

Once more voices assailed him, pulling him from his dreamless sleeping. They were deep, male, and they spoke the Trade tongue, which confused him after speaking only Ferhym for almost a month now. Ashyn realized that they sounded human.

"Hey Yur, ye ain't gonna believe this…" the deep voice said from somewhere to his left.

"Eh?"

"It's him! Da Blood Wizard!"

That got Ashyn's attention. He hadn't expected recognition from people. He listened more intently, without trying to give away that he was awake.

"They ain't fer findin' no Blood Wizard ye fool," the one Ashyn assumed was Yur, remarked. "No wizard would do a damn thing like gettin' 'imself captured by no Wild Elves."

"I's a telling ye, Yur. Is a wizard, and I's thinks he's awake."

Well damn. So much for hiding it already. Ashyn opened his eyes.

"He is awake! Run!" the man who had been leading the conversation screamed. Ashyn heard fumbling and saw commotion out of his peripheral vision. When he turned his head he was alarmed to see the bars of a cage. They were solid wood, naked of any paint or varnish, and they enclosed him from all sides, including the top. Like he was a beast.

Across from him was another cage, and there he saw about twenty humans, men and women. They were all screaming and packing themselves into a corner. As far away from Ashyn as possible. All but one anyway, who sat still on the ground staring at him.

Ashyn sat up. A groan emanated from his lips as a pain rippled from his abdomen to every point of his body. Reflexively, he put his hand to his side and felt the puckered rigid surface of crusted flesh. He looked down and saw a fresh pink scar. It was almost two inches in length, gnarled and thick. Whoever had healed him was solely concerned with keeping him alive. He could feel the muscles bunching and spasming at his sudden motion.

He breathed for a moment and waited for the fitful muscles to calm down. The man who sat there stared at him the whole time, while the others cowered in the corner refusing to make eye contact.

Ashyn used the bars of his cell to pull himself to his feet. The exertion made him woozy for a moment. He let it settle, and then took in the rest of his surroundings past his cell.

Solid granite surrounded them on all sides beyond the wooden cages. He tried to get his bearings. *Am I still in the woods? Am I underground where the elves are rumored to live?* He gazed upwards. *What the hell? Clear skies? Not a thick canopy of trees, but sky!* A deep indigo horizon fell over him with the bright white fires of stars blazing above.

It felt like a lifetime since he saw anything but leaves and branches. He must be out of the Shalis-Fey.

The heat of the one man's eyes intensified. Ashyn stared back at the man, studying him. Filthy and in tattered garments, there was an odd familiarity about him.

Long, coal black hair tied back behind his head in a greasy ponytail. His face was round, almost comically so compared to his button nose. Yet his cheeks appeared hollow. The clothing hung limply, showing that at one time they filled a much larger frame.

Those features weren't what stood out to him, though. It was the eyes. His eyes were shade of brown, but like his nose they appeared small and beady to his oversized face. Those eyes scrutinizing him felt oddly familiar.

"Can I help you?" Ashyn asked the staring man.

The human didn't answer him, just continued to stare in an almost hateful way. Almost, because no one had stared at him with such vehemence as that of the female Wild Elves he encountered months back. With them only true hate resonated. In these eyes he saw disbelief, coupled with anger.

A cowering voice called from the crowd against the wall, "Dunna look at 'im like dat, Yur. I's thinks he's gunna hex ye!"

Yur. That sounded familiar as well. Ashyn pulled himself to his full height to address the terrified group. "Please relax," he started, "I mean you no harm."

The one called Yur scoffed, "All wizards do is harm." He spat on the floor.

"How do you know I'm a wizard?" Ashyn asked. He was curious how these people identified him by the sobriquet of Blood Wizard, when the only one to know the title was Xexial, who was dead.

Yur pointed up above, "Elves." He said and spat on the floor again. "Been showin' an image of ye, hour after hour fer as long as we canna remember now."

Ashyn raised an eyebrow. An image? How could they have captured an image of him? Did one of the fleeing elves in the battle in the lowlands draw one of him? Was their art so fine?

"Don'cha rack ye brain hard," Yur said to him. "These elves have foul magics jus' as ye do Rune."

Ashyn blinked in surprise.

"Yur!" his apparent friend exclaimed from the huddle.

The man stood then. Ashyn could see how others could fear him. In human standards, he was large. Ashyn assumed that when he was at full weight, he was a bulky man. But Ashyn wasn't of normal human standards in height, and the normally tall Yur still had to look up to him.

In terms of muscular girth, Ashyn was sorely undersized. The trials of the woods had hardened him somewhat though, mainly in stamina.

Yur walked up to and leaned against the wooden bars, and snarled at Ashyn with yellow teeth, "I remember ye boy."

"Ye'll get us all killed!" one of them shrieked. Ashyn was barely listening. He was staring back into that round face and those deep, beady eyes. Now he knew where he knew those eyes.

Quietly he said, "Yur." He looked at him, pondering, "As in Uriel?"

The man put a grimy hand to his matted hairy chest. "Ye remember me? Flattered," he said condescendingly.

Ashyn's mind flashed back to his short time in Czynsk as a child. Uriel had been one of the first boys he had met. Uriel and Macky had been in the hospice when he awakened.

Macky became a quick friend to Ashyn, but Uriel had always remained suspicious of him. Even though he and Macky were best friends, Uriel disliked Ashyn's intelligence and his literacy. He had often accused Ashyn of witchcraft. Not too far from the mark now, Ashyn surmised. He guessed Uriel sensed this.

"I always knew," the man gloated. "Always knew ye were destined for this path. Even whens we was boys."

Ashyn had no quarrel with Uriel. Not then, and certainly not a decade later. He leaned forward against the wooden bars too. "You always were smart," Ashyn agreed, trying to coax the man's ego a little. "How is it you wound up here?"

Uriel's expression turned dark. "I'm here because of you!"

Ashyn's eyes went wide. "What?"

The human stared at Ashyn with disgust. "Yer ole' chum Mactonal, ye remember him?"

Ashyn nodded, and Uriel scoffed and continued, "Idiot stood up ta the elves when they came ta town. Said we had ta fight' 'em off."

Ashyn leaned against the bars, "Macky said that?" He shook his head. "He always wanted to see the Wild Elves."

"Ta," Uriel agreed. "Until ye showed 'im strength. Never was the same after ye left with the old coot wizard."

Ashyn's ears perked up. "What do you mean?"

The wizard saw Uriel's beady eyes stare at him in a patronizing way. "After ye left, he started preachin' about hows we should stands up fer ourselves. Dat sometimes *penance* could be wrongful, and we should stand against the bishop if falsely accused, or some such." Uriel dismissed it with a wave of his hand. "He never got much backing from the other kids." Hissing, he went on, "Avrimae, though…she ne'r left 'is side in the Enclave after that."

Ashyn could already see where this was going. Avrimae had been the subject of both the older boys' hearts. They adored her, and Ashyn knew that unless she rejected both of them, one day she would cause a schism between the two.

Uriel continued, "Long story short, he became a leader of sorts. Did odd jobs fer a mason when 'is charity was paid and he and Avrimae moved in together.

"Didn't las' long though. Tis one thing in the hospice, nother on ye own. She couldn't take it; he couldn't live up ta bein' the man she thought he was. Had a brutal break up." He added with a dark smile, "So Mactonal joined the Enclave and became a priest."

Ashyn flinched. Macky had been a member of the Enclave. He knew the Enclave had burned to the ground because the Wild Elves didn't get the fight they had wanted from Xexial and him. Not that Ashyn hadn't wanted to give it to them at the time.

"I don't know how to tell you this," Ashyn said somberly, "but the Enclave is gone."

Uriel nodded. "We was there." Then he looked sharply up at Ashyn. "No thanks ta ye, wizard."

It wasn't like that, Ashyn wanted to tell him, but he knew Uriel wouldn't understand. In a monotone voice he surmised, "So Macky is dead."

Uriel gawked at him. "Hells no. Not yet, at least."

Ashyn looked up at him in alarm.

"Dat's what I've been trying to tell ye, before ye interruptin' me. Mactonal thought he was some type of leader after ye left. Even all dem winters later, when the Wild Elf scouts first came in ta Czynsk, Mactonal wanted ta fight 'em."

Ashyn blinked dumbfounded, but didn't say anything. He needed to hear it all.

"First elves came in week's a'fore and 'twas helluva surprise. They was civil enough, speaking strange fractured Trade tongue, tryin' ta find a way ta contact ye wizards. I knew the bishop knew how ta get in touch with em, seens it done many times when I was a kid. I told em so."

Ashyn wanted to yell at Uriel and tell him he was a fool, that he had helped invite the destruction of the Enclave, but he knew he couldn't. As much as he may not have been friends with Uriel when they were children, if the elves had been civil, he could not have known what was going to happen. He hadn't had to flee from them for days on end through the Shalis-Fey.

"They go to the Enclave, and Father Mactonal," he sneered as he said it and Ashyn realized that Avrimae's choice in Macky over Uriel must have thoroughly destroyed their friendship, "he turns them away." Uriel looked Ashyn in the eyes. "Cuz he says he knows da truth about dem. Dat they hunted ye fer days in the forest. Overheard it from ye mouth and the wizard's. Even winters later, he stood up fer ye!

"They leave, angry," Uriel continued, "and returned two days later. This time they came in force. Marched right through town they did, straight to the Enclave, and demanded ta have a message sent. Otherwise dey would start a balancing.

"Fool ass still told em no, but in da interest of saving lives, the Bishop relented and sent ye wizards a message. Bishop told em, that the wizards' be comin' in a few days' time. Elves left."

Uriel blew out a sigh and sat down with his back to Ashyn, his hatred of the wizard momentarily lost as he recalled those events. "We heard thunder for the next three days in the Shalis-Fey. Then on day four, a day afore ye arrive, they march out from the woods.

"Scariest of things we ever did see, wizard. So many came. Too many. They came right up to Czynsk and surrounded the town. Their leader said that they were there to balance it! That us just having a way to contact the evil wizards, marked us as corrupted. Imagine that! Theys ask us ta do sometin', we dos it, and we are evil? Hypocrites!" Uriel threw his hands in the air.

"They executed the bishop on the spot for being a collaborator. Then pitched 'is head into our water well so that we'd all taste the bitterness of his corrupted spirit or some such."

Ashyn heard a few of the others begin to sob as Uriel recounted the events.

"Then they says, any others who resist would be balanced, lethally.

"There were outcries, and Mactonal even orchestrated a rebellion of sorts against 'em, preachin' that if it be their time then the Maker would smile upon 'em for standing up for 'emselves against the tyrants." Uriel preached, and then spat, "Me wife was among the volunteers."

"Your wife?"

Uriel nodded, "The rebellion was a pathetic joke. A ridiculous blunder. We not be warriors trained to kill like the elves. The first few were slaughtered. Cut down like wheat by a farmer's scythe. They gathered the rest and sought to use 'em as bait against ye. Rile ye up inta violence. But ye fled like cowards afore they could." His eyes were as bitter as his voice.

"As they were wheeling our people away, claimin' ta take em fer reclamation, I took my chance. I tried ta free me wife." Uriel looked down at the disheveled clothes on his body, "I failed, and dey took me, too."

With a deep sigh he looked up at Ashyn. The hatred that burned fervently a moment before now was lost to sorrow. "And the rest is history."

Ashyn leaned his back against the bars. "Where is Macky then?"

Uriel nodded up above the rock face. "The worst of us skewers are up there, near the pond. On the real bad nights, we canna hear them screamin'."

Ashyn didn't want to ask, but he needed to know, "And your wife?"

Uriel nodded and looked down to the ground. "Ta. She's up there too, somewheres."

Ashyn had no clue what up there looked like. He was confused as to why they had placed him in his own cell to begin with, let alone left him with the general populace. Unless they didn't know he was there.

No. Ashyn answered to himself before even trailing that thought too far. He remembered the look on Jenhiro's face. He remembered the betrayal of seeing a dui Nuchada. Why then was Ashyn even alive? Perhaps the same reason he had kept Jenhiro alive. They had needed each other.

Pain stabbed through his thoughts, and Ashyn looked down to his abdomen. He was alarmed to see a green fluid seeping through the puckering scar where he was stabbed.

Ashyn touched it. It was tacky. When he brought it up to his nose, his senses were quickly assailed with the sharp piercing odor of mint.

Must be a healing remedy of the druids, Ashyn thought, or at least hoped, anyways. It didn't seem infected or gangrenous. The scar, though severe, wasn't swollen, painful, or red. The only pain came from the spasms and contractions of his injured muscles. Everything seemed okay, minus the fact that he was generating the green liquid, of course. He had no idea what druidic healing consisted of. It might be normal.

Once more he felt the heat of Uriel's eyes on him. Ashyn looked down to see Uriel's beady gaze analyzing him. "They hurt ya good?"

Ashyn looked from Uriel to the crowd of scared people cowering in the corner. "Nothing I won't overcome."

Uriel stood back up and walked towards the crowd of people. "I knew the boy, afore he was a wizard," Uriel said loudly. He turned and looked Ashyn in the eyes, the flare of anger had returned. "Watch your back, Ashyn Rune, for you have no allies here."

~ ~ ~

"Dui Nuchada," a voice said in the darkness. Ashyn opened his eyes wearily. Though well rested from his ordeal, he knew he still had a long way to go until healed, and he knew it was likely, once the Council of Elm found out he was here, he would find very little peace and rest afterwards.

The voice whispered harder, "Dui Nuchada." Ashyn became suddenly more alert. The voice hadn't come from the cage next to him, but from above. Ashyn looked up. It was some hours later after he spoke with Uriel.

There standing against the moonlight he could see the outline of a male figure. Pointed ears cut like sharp daggers across the night sky. A Wild Elf.

The voice whispered, "There is little time, and after this moment we must be enemies." Ashyn recognized it then.

He stood, whispering, "Jenhiro."

"Shhh! Just listen to me. I do not know what the council will have in store for you, dui Nuchada, but you saved my life. I, in turn, have spared yours. I do not know if you will live or die at this point, I don't know if I have placed you in hell, but we are even. That is what I want you to know. We were allies in the Fey, now in Feydras' Anula we must be enemies."

"I understand."

Ashyn sat back down and looked at his hands. There really couldn't have been any other way. The Wild Elves swore to the balance of life. Everything about Ashyn was counter to that in their mind. At least Jenhiro confirmed that he was in Feydras' Anula.

Ashyn looked back up to where the elf was. To his surprise he still saw him there, watching, likely lost in his own personal conflict.

The two survived the hunt from a powerful adversary together. They bonded in blood and sweat on a field of battle. Though they might call each other enemies, Ashyn thought that there was more to them now. At least, perhaps it was a dream. Seeing Jenhiro still above him, perhaps it was more than just hope.

He whispered, "Elf," not daring to use Jenhiro's name again so that he may protect him. The Wild Elf's eyes gleamed down to him in the moonlight. "My life is irrelevant. If you really want to be even with me for saving your life and bringing your unbalancer to justice, find the skewer they call Julietta. She has hair like mine, and we share the same complexion as well. You will know her when you find her for she is..." Ashyn took a breath to control the anger he felt rising in his guts. "...she is blind, with crescent-like scars around her eye sockets."

Jenhiro continued to stare down the hole at him, as if weighing the young wizard's words. Then Ashyn felt a flood of relief as he saw the elf nod. "I will do this for you." And the elf was gone.

For the first time since he had learned of Julietta still being alive, Ashyn had hope.

SWALLET

Morning came quickly, and with it, the dawning reality of his position. Ashyn Rune was captured. He looked down at the clothes he was wearing. His armor was gone. His knapsack with all that he had taken from the Onyx Tower was gone. His bow was gone. His skinning knife, too. Ashyn was defenseless.

Even his cat Ginger was gone. Did the feisty feline survive? Last he saw, the bull flung it into the night, and then nothing. No crack, no thud, no cry of pain.

The one thing they had not taken from him though was the single braid of platinum hair. It remained, attached to the bracer on his wrist. For how long, he couldn't know. Still, he would not be deterred. This was what he wanted. Not necessarily in this fashion, but he had accomplished what he set out to do. He was here, and if he was here, Julietta had to be here too! All he needed was a way to find her, a way to escape his confines, and then a way to get out of a mythical hidden city.

He would figure out what direction to go once he had her and how they'd escape a legion of Ferhym who were hell-bent on the destruction of them both. He had to outwit some of the best known trackers on the continent and survive the magical prowess of the Druids. All while having almost no connection to magic and towing along someone who was blind.

No problem.

Suddenly the cage jarred. Ashyn grabbed the nearby bars to hold himself upright. A hand lanced out of the opposite cage and locked around his wrist tightly. Ashyn looked over in surprise.

Uriel had his arm in a vice-like grip, his crusty cracked nails digging into Ashyn's tanned flesh. "Time to go to your fate, Blood Wizard!"

Uriel let go and Ashyn pulled his arm back quickly. Uriel smiled wickedly at him with filthy yellow teeth. "I'll be listening for your screams."

Ashyn ignored him as he noticed that they were rising. The wizard looked up to see vines wrapped around the four corners of the cage and they were slowly slithering back up the craggy rocks to the world above.

Druids.

In reflex of the thought, Ashyn flexed his once wounded forearm. It had taken weeks to heal, and now, like his stomach, it too bore a bright pink scar against his dark-toned flesh. No, he wasn't fond of druids.

Ashyn watched as another set of vines slithered like snakes to the other cage, latched on, and pulled it upward as well. People in that cage whimpered and cried. Ashyn could only guess at the horrors these humans were going through in order to achieve their reclamation.

They blamed him for it too, just as Xexial said they would. Blamed him for abandoning them. He understood. He felt like he abandoned them. Soon the first signs of more than rock crested over the edge.

He was in a glade. Rolling green plains stretched out before him, for maybe a mile, perhaps two. Beyond them, he could make out a cliff-face, how high it was he wasn't sure at his distance and vantage, but he recognized the massive trees that grew above it. They were the sequoias. He looked back and forth along his horizon. It was all the same. The glade boundary always ending in a rocky wall with the massive timber sentinels standing watch high above.

Ashyn laughed darkly to himself. How close did he get and didn't even know it? How long had Jenhiro skirted him around his destination? A day, a week?

Ashyn turned around to see if the cliff face continued all the way around. He gasped. Dozens upon dozens of buildings lay before him. They averaged one or two stories in height built from the woods around him. The small squat structures were naked.

Devoid of any kind of paint or varnish, the wood on most of the homes was beige to dark grey.

All of the buildings had thatched roofs, much as he had seen growing up in Bremingham. These thatches were made from branches instead of the traditional hay. The roofs were flat, not arched, and Ashyn knew growing up that a flat roof with no way to dispose of running rain water often leaked heavily or even collapsed under enough weight.

He could see here that it was no different. After the storm passed through, a number of elves, and what he assumed were skewers, were busy rebuilding at least twenty roofs.

Ashyn assumed that the hidden Elven city of Feydras' Anula would have buildings, but what he didn't expect to see was what they surrounded. Looming high above all the buildings was a single elm tree.

Its size defied everything Ashyn knew about the deciduous tree. Growing up on the outskirts of the woods, and even having a small copse of elms by his house in Bremingham, the tallest elm he had ever seen was no more than one hundred feet. This one put all of those to shame. In fact, Ashyn was positive that it was even larger than a sequoia. The elm before him had to be almost four hundred feet tall, with a trunk at least forty feet in diameter.

Like other elms he had grown up with, the elm supported a canopy like an umbrella over the entirety of the city. Since it was spring, the leaves were bright green, and even from where he was at he could make out small purple flowers dotting the lush crown. The wizard had no doubt that this was his destination, and now he understood why they were called the Council of Elm.

Over one hundred feet up the tree he could make out a gnarled knot that was twice the width of the trunk. It looked that at some point in the tree's life it must have been diseased or struck by lightning, and then continued to grow resulting in such a natural deformation.

Within that warped ball of wood, Ashyn could see an alcove cut into the tree. Winking lights flickered inside telling him that was where the council oversaw their people.

He could just make out a series of steps carved into the tree from the alcove circling downward.

Just then his cage shuddered to a stop. Three Wild Elves stood before him.

Like Jenhiro, and the branch commanders he had seen before, these elves wore nothing but loin clothes to cover their genitalia. The females wore bands of leather to hold down their breasts.

All across their skin was their woad, paintings on their flesh that seemed different from one elf to another. Today their woad was white, and Ashyn hoped, like Jenhiro, it meant that these elves were not part of the wizard hunters. For those that had attacked Czynsk had worn red and brown like the blood of an animal.

They all held their spears, and he could see the deer hide quiver of javelins on their backs.

Ashyn watched as the wooden bars warped and bulged, creating an O from what had once been tight, straight bars. The lead elf beckoned him forward.

Ashyn did as he was bade, but he looked around for where the druid may be. He didn't see it. Neither had he seen the druids right away when they created the fog that descended upon Xexial and himself in the lowlands, nor had he ever seen the one that controlled the Bristle Wolves that attacked him and his sister in the fields.

His forearm tightened once more at the thought, but he also grew curious at that. At what range could they manipulate the tendrils of magic? How far could they beckon to it and it answer? Ashyn's training, the use of magic had always been directly at the source, him. All magic flowed through him and he focused it elsewhere, well in theory anyhow. The only thing he had been extremely skilled at was using fire, and for some reason he had very good control over wards.

Even then, the farthest he had ever propelled fire had been no more than fifty feet. As Ashyn looked around, he could see no druids, which meant their range went much farther.

The trio raised their spears to Ashyn's chest. If not for his predicament, Ashyn might have smiled at the sight. Normally when pointing a weapon at an adversary it was level, or lowered. These elves were almost twenty inches shorter than he was. Most of their spears rose above their heads to make it level with Ashyn. Still he knew how talented the Ferhym were with those spears and the humor was quickly lost.

The leader motioned with his spear to head towards the tree. Ashyn knew what he wanted, and he obliged. The only way he was going to be able to find Julietta was to look for her, and he couldn't do that standing in front of the cage. Ashyn headed towards the great elm.

Behind him he could hear Uriel heckling him every step of the way.

~ ~ ~

It didn't take long for Ashyn to see the pond that Uriel had mentioned the night before. It was where his escort was leading him.

As Ashyn passed down the narrow fairway he looked at the Ferhym in their natural environment. He was surprised to see that they weren't all training to be killers, and that there weren't daises with elder Wild Elves preaching about skewers and the need for balance. In fact, everything that they were doing appeared rather normal.

The males worked in fields, tending crops, or herding elk, while the females busied themselves in their domiciles, cleaning, cooking, or making wicker objects of use. What surprised Ashyn immediately, perhaps due to his lack of experience with the opposite sex, was that all the women were topless.

Ashyn felt his ears flush red as his eyes fell to one female's breasts. Flustered he quickly looked away at anything else he could find, something else he could learn.

He wondered why these females were topless while the ones he saw on the battlefield and even behind him had their breasts covered. Was it something to do with station? Was there the rank structure amongst the Wild Elves? Upper class, lower class, poverty, and such?

Curious at that thought, and thankful for the mental diversion amongst seeing so many half nude females, Ashyn tried to categorize the town while searching for his sister.

Aside from those few skewers who were rebuilding the damaged roofs, there were no others in sight. None visible tended the livestock or tilled fields. Ashyn had no idea where they could all be, unless there weren't as many as he thought.

A cold feeling entered the pit of his stomach. *What if Julietta isn't here?* He hadn't encountered her in the woods after all, but out in the fields. *What if they were scattered amongst the Shalis-Fey?* Then he might have gotten himself captured for nothing.

He pushed the dismal thought to the back of his mind. It was too soon to think like that. He hadn't even been awake a day yet, and by the looks of the glade he was in, there was a lot of land he was going to need to cover. He couldn't afford to give up so soon before even trying.

He felt a sharp jab in his back, and Ashyn realized that he had stopped walking. He glared at the Wild Elf who had poked him with the spear and was surprised to see the Ferhym wither a little under his glare. They were afraid of him.

Ashyn stood up straighter and continued walking towards the elm. He wondered to what extent they feared him. He resisted the urge to rub the pricked part of his back though it stung like the dickens. He needed to appear strong.

Soon they broke away from the domiciles and a large series of ponds came into view. To the east he saw more tilled farm land growing crops, as well as irrigation channels running away from several of the ponds and into the fields. Beyond them he spotted more buildings on the horizon. To the north, and closest to him, was a brackish looking circle of water, and the land around it turned surprisingly craggy. Broken rocks stuck out in jagged lines against the filthy green water, skeletal fingers trying to grope their way out of mud.

As Ashyn got closer, he saw long slender bars of wood that ran about twelve feet into the air, ending at sharpened tips. Soon he realized that this fence ran the entire perimeter of the craggy shore. Ashyn found it curious, until he saw movement on the rocks.

They made a prison cell out of the shoreline? Ashyn thought incredulously. That made no sense. All one needed to do was jump into the water, swim to the other side, and they were free.

He watched as the bodies mopped across the ragged granite in shuffling gaits. As Ashyn passed by the bars of the cell he knew why the Ferhym didn't fear these skewers would flee.

Hollow empty eyes looked at him through gaunt sallow faces. Atrophied limbs shook as the people tried to remain erect enough to walk by the cell to see this new skewer. They were a defeated people.

One person, a woman with shaven scalp whose hairline was so thin, there were actual balding spots, wrapped thin, wiry fingers around the bars and looked at him.

Her eyes lacked the life in them like all the others, but when they fell to Ashyn's own, he saw a spark. She smiled. Hideous cracked teeth, black and rotten, filled her mouth through pallid, thin lips. Her mouth croaked hoarsely, "Meat." She waited and whispered again, "Meat."

"I have nothing to give," Ashyn told the woman apologetically.

Arms so emaciated that Ashyn could actually see her bones tried to shake the bars. He noted how they didn't budge. "Meat!"

Ashyn shrugged. "I cannot help you."

Narrow, threadlike fingers reached out for him. She growled as she grabbed the tattered fabric of his small clothes. "Meat!"

That spark in her eyes that Ashyn thought might have been hope turned wild as she ripped at him. Her shattered teeth chattered, and she leaned her face between the pikes and distended her jaw trying to get at him.

A spear flashed by Ashyn and the woman howled. Ashyn stumbled away from the woman suddenly. He looked down to where she had been holding him, and he wanted to vomit. Her hand was still gripping the fabric of his clothing. Yet past her wrist there was nothing. Just a well of red seeping out of from the gripping hand.

The woman grabbed her forearm staring at the stump where her hand had once been. "Meat," someone said from behind her.

She turned and looked away from the Ashyn who followed her gaze. Another person looked upon her through deadened eyes now flickering with something feral.

"Meat," another voice said from behind him.

The woman backed against the bars hissing and spitting at the men, as blood poured down her arm. Ashyn looked back to the guards expecting them to do something.

The one who had severed the woman's arm prodded his spear forward once more at Ashyn. The boy quickly moved away just as he heard the weak men fall on the even weaker woman. Her screams turned into a gurgle. Ashyn distinctly heard the wet squelching sounds of tearing flesh. His stomach roiled and he quickened his pace.

Right behind him, her own people were devouring her. All because they saw her blood and the elves did nothing to stop it. He had learned about the Wild Elves from Xexial, but not this.

"Maker help me," Ashyn whispered as the reality of his predicament settled on him. How had Julietta survived this for so long?

They pushed him along the perimeter of the piked fence until he reached the other side, and he found himself standing at the base of the massive elm tree. So close to it now, he found its sheer size unfathomable. It was an Elm. An Elm! The sequoias were large, but an elm tree? The one that dwarfed him now looked just like any other elm he saw as a child except for the fact that instead of a four-foot base he was looking at a forty-foot wide trunk. And in that trunk were carved steps no wider than ten inches circling upwards. The Ferhym behind him pointed with his spear.

Ashyn looked from the elf to the stairs raising his eyebrows. "You want me to climb that?"

The Ferhym eyed him with dark orbs and brought the spear forward sharply. Ashyn raised his hands. "Okay, okay."

The wizard looked back at the narrow stairs and then upwards. He could see the thick knot way above him. Ashyn was not afraid of heights, but looking at the narrow path before him, with no rail on his right and nothing but rough bark on his left, he knew it would be a straight drop to the earthen floor if he stumbled.

Ashyn eyed all the roots rising from the ground nearest the ancient tree. They were thick and sturdy, and hitting any single one of them on the way down would shatter his bones like glass.

The elf chittered in Ferhym for him to move, and Ashyn knew he was testing their patience. After watching how callously they disregarded the woman's life just moments ago, he knew it was likely that they would kill him just as simply. Ashyn ascended the narrow stairway to whatever lay above.

~ ~ ~

The climb didn't take as long as Ashyn feared. Though when he reached the top, at the thickened growth, things looked harrowing. The stairs flared outward from the bark, and pitched him into open space. It was completely disconcerting, and he felt at any moment he was going to fall over the side. He now found himself in a most curious chamber.

Immediately Ashyn could see that the route he had taken was the only access into this carved room. There were no lifts, nor ladders, nor obvious ways to escape.

To his left, the chamber opened up before him and offered a view of the Ferhym city of Feydras' Anula and the glade upon which it rested. To his right was the inner sanctum. Deeper within, intermittently at points in the high arched ceiling, there were openings carved into the wood.

Ashyn knew the design was to let in sunlight. The few thin beams that entered were limited. Torches aided, flickering their amber luminescence in recesses of the room.

The floor itself was the tree, sanded smooth and polished until it shone. Ashyn could see the rings of the tree within and he was amazed. They were so tightly compacted next to one and other that he knew without a doubt that this tree was millennia old.

In the center of the room there was a singular pillar, with a basin of water. Ashyn approached it cautiously and looked within. Still, tranquil blue waters reflected worn grey eyes back at him. Ashyn saw beginnings of a red beard in those waters, and even though he knew it was his reflection, he did not recognize the man within.

The cold, hardened expression his eyes now wore was not one of playful, childlike jubilance, but one of a man who had seen too many things. The ghosts of his memories rippled across those eyes in the water.

Ashyn looked away, feeling sick. He did not need to see that boy again. Did not need to see his own haunted visage. Nor did he want to see those lean features of his face, so set, so hard as if he was solidifying himself into something.

The wizard focused his gaze past the basin to a short dais. Twenty high back wooden chairs sat in a semi-circular fashion towards the back of the chamber. They, like all that he saw thus far, were naked of any adornments or colors other than the natural wood. Unlike other council chambers he read of in tomes, there were very little to the chairs that showed any kind of comfort. The wood was hard and natural, only polished smooth through centuries of use.

They sat so close together that he imagined the elves' knees must touch, if not have their legs interlocking with one and other. He could only imagine the heat generated by having twenty bodies so close together.

Behind the chairs, against the long expanse of carved wall, Ashyn saw a relief. It took up, perhaps a quarter of the length of the wall, its true measurement hard to decipher due to the curved nature of the chamber. Entranced, it occurred to him what he was looking at. This was their library. This was how their stories were conveyed. It was their history.

There were great monuments to the smiting of the chief enemies of what the elves considered balance. Ashyn saw dragons. He saw strange monsters that were clearly sentient by their garb and weaponry. Ashyn noted creatures of darkness and death. Carved in remarkably dazzling displays of action and violence, the details were so acute, so real, that it reminded him of the Rheynnaus' chamber in the Onyx Tower. This was a place of reverence for the Ferhym. A place where they honored the accomplishments of their ancestors.

Ashyn turned to regard his entourage. They watched him quietly, though they looked slightly more at ease now that he was up here. Was it because he had nowhere to go? Or was there something else? Perhaps protection from magic, wards, or glyphs that he couldn't see? With his attunement to magic in such a state of flux, he couldn't feel anything like he used to. He couldn't even feel the threat from the Ferhym as he had in the past.

Ashyn looked back at the relief certain he had missed something. There must be wards of some sort. The elves had feared him up until this point. What would cast them at ease so readily?

The young wizard moved around the high-backed chairs and examined the exquisitely crafted artwork closely. Each scene depicted was of an elf viciously slaughtering a skewer. Ashyn was amazed to see so many creatures he hadn't even known existed.

As he searched, he found himself looking for the bovine hunter that had harassed him for weeks. He didn't see any such a beast present. *Perhaps Jenhiro will now earn a place on this wall,* Ashyn thought. The wizard was certain that they wouldn't let him take credit for it, even though the act gave him no comfort. He hadn't a choice he reminded himself. Ashyn had extended his hand in peace too often only to have it batted away.

Ashyn reached the end of the relief and was about to give up on the idea of wards when something stopped him. It was a very familiar image. There was a bearded man in robes. He looked larger than a human, and Ashyn could see that his canines poked up from his lower lip giving him a bestial appearance. The amazing detail of the work gave the man a strange cracked look, as if he were made of rock. In one hand he was holding a tome, in his other a long tendril lashed out from his palm. Ashyn saw this only once before. It was from Xexial on the day he died.

The elder wizard had lashed out with an obsidian-like whip of magic that severed the legs of a druid right at her knees. There had been no cutting or breaking of bone. No tearing of muscle or ripping of flesh. Just the absence of what once was. Where there were muscles, sinew, flesh and blood, now there was simply nothing. A complete line of emptiness, and a wave of unnatural cold. Ashyn shuddered at the memory. It was **Destruction**.

Ashyn studied the concepts enough with Xexial, but never committed to the magic. He hadn't been ready. Ashyn knew the picture he was looking at. This was a wizard.

The image wasn't alone. Within, as in all others, was the hero to the elves. This one was a female. She was much smaller than the wizard was, and she had ducked nimbly underneath the whip of magic. In her hand, she held what looked like a crystal. She was driving it towards his heart.

A feminine voice suddenly spoke only inches from his side, "That was nineteen winters ago." Her words were in heavily accented Trade Tongue.

Ashyn turned and felt the color drain from his face. A Wild Elf female stood before him. Not a Wild Elf. The Wild Elf, the one he had just been looking at in the relief. The wizard killer.

She was very short. His chin almost touched his chest as he looked down upon her. This elf looked similar in complexion to many of the other Ferhym females. She bore raven-colored, shoulder-length hair and copper-hued skin. Her eyes were dark, like chips of black glass, and she looked at him with sharp intensity. Those eyes didn't resonate the usual hate he felt, nor did they show fear. They showed him confidence and through that confidence was power.

Unlike any of the other Ferhym he had ever met however, she wore leathers. It was still scant, by human standards, only a short leather tunic that bared her midriff, and a barded leather skirt that cut off at mid-thigh. She had no bracers or greaves, revealing tightly woven cords of muscles in her arms, legs, and abdomen.

Also unlike the other Ferhym, she wore jewelry. A necklace sat upon her breast, a string of thick amber beads. In those beads, in the Ferhym script, he could see words written, names. The name that was clearest was on the central bead. It was turned slightly downward, but he could just make out the word: Windsong.

She was different from the other Ferhym, that was clear. More so than everything else that identified her were the markings on her skin. Ashyn saw these markings many times now. A woad in various patterns across their bodies. Often it didn't make much sense to him, just swirls and slashes, crescents and circles, or vines twined together. The colors were either in white paint, red, or brown.

But this was different. It was a deep red, almost maroon, and it wasn't made of paint that crusted and flaked. This was part of her, etched into her flesh like a tattoo. The surface was not raised, but as smooth as the rest of the coppery landscape. Even more striking to him was it looked like it glowed in the light. Ashyn almost wanted to reach out and touch it.

She was beautiful and dangerous, and oddly familiar to him. She held her spear casually in her right hand, indicating that he was no threat to her.

As Ashyn took all this in. He responded, "Funny. I'm nineteen-winters-old." Not his most elegant moment.

Her dark eyes sparkled, "Truly? You are but a child."

Those words rankled Ashyn a little, but not as much as the way she was eyeing him now. Those eyes were hungry for something that she knew he had. Ashyn didn't delude himself into thinking this exotic elf was attracted to him. No, this hunger was not carnal; it was feral. "What is it you want?"

The elf's eyes traveled across his narrow body, to Ashyn's growing discomfort. She even walked around him, observing him from all angles. "What do *I* want?" she repeated coyly. Ashyn was surprised at how easily the words tumbled from her lips in Trade Tongue and how unique a Wild Elf's voice sounded when forced to talk so much slower than their dialect usually dictated. He doubted few, if any people, were graced with hearing such a unique accent.

"Why, I want your help," she told him.

Ashyn couldn't help but to laugh, even knowing he was surrounded by imminent death. "My help?" He looked to the three guards one by one, his laugh apparently startling them into raising their spears towards him. "You have tried to kill me," Ashyn fired back darkly, then added, "Repeatedly."

The raven-haired elf nodded, "Yes. And now we need you."

Ashyn watched as she gave a subtle head motion to one of the guards. He walked to the edge and whistled in six short bursts, forming a quick, strange melody.

"Follow me, Blood Wizard," the elf told him, as she walked away from the reliefs.

Ashyn reluctantly did. She didn't take him far, just off the dais and towards the edge of the compound. She stood, comfortably, at the very edge, her toes extended over the hundred and thirty foot drop below. Ashyn walked behind her and to her right, but kept a full step from the precipice.

The elf noted this. "Do heights bother you?"

Ashyn shook his head, "Just the fall from them."

"You know what we do, yes?"

Ashyn stared out at the vista before him. The glade was a stunning sight to behold. He could see everything from this vantage. Even the cliff-faces beyond, the sequoias high above and all the Wild Elven settlements dotted throughout the glade.

She didn't wait any longer for an answer. "We maintain balance from those that seek to skew it for power, be it personal or otherwise. We protect nature from something like this ever happening again", she said with a flourish of her left hand to the glade before her.

Ashyn looked at her confused, "This is gorgeous. It is lush and green, and well cared for by your people. It is one of the most impressive natural wonders I have ever seen."

The dark-eyed beauty nodded, "Now, yes. It has taken millennia to make it this way. Before that, it was a circle of devastation and blight caused by a skewer."

The tattooed elf spat with sudden vehemence. She cursed for a moment in Ferhym, before looking back at Ashyn. "I know not how to convey the words in your tongue."

"Then tell me in yours," Ashyn answered back in Ferhym.

The wizard heard the three behind him shift as he spoke. The elf before him showed no surprise. Instead she nodded, and spoke in her own language. Who was this Ferhym?

"This land is a swallet. Do you know what that means?"

Ashyn shook his head no.

"Over one-thousand and six hundred winters past, a being of great power sought to destroy the Ferhym. He came and chose this spot, which was thick with the strong sequoias you see on the horizon. It was beautiful, and isolated, but it was also where we would meet for our annual summer joinings."

Ashyn didn't know what summer joinings meant, but still he listened. He never read this in any tomes.

"He came using powers that no one should possess. A power of wizards," she told him. "When all of the Ferhym were in one spot," she said pointing down at the ground below, "he destroyed the very earth beneath them."

"Like the lowlands?" Ashyn asked, thinking of the destruction that Xexial had wrought.

She shook her head no. "Not quite, but infinitely more awful." She gestured, "Look around, Blood Wizard. Do you see that cliff-face in the distance?"

Ashyn nodded.

"All of this actually used to sit above that face. It was a hillock that rose high over all of the Fey."

The wizard's eyes widened as he looked around now at the cliff face in the distance. It had to be two miles away, in all directions! Not to mention its height! The level at which it sank was unimaginable, especially if it was a hill first.

The elf continued. "Yes. There were many of us back then. We flourished. We loved nature and ignored the wider world around us. Then my people were virtually annihilated on one single day. Very few of us survived."

"Wh-why?" he stammered. "Why would someone do this to your people?"

Her void-like eyes looked at him curiously for a moment before she answered, "Because it is in your nature. There is no logic for your kind. You have power, you abuse power, and nature suffers."

Ashyn shook his head. Colder than he meant to, he responded, "I have done nothing to your people that hadn't been provoked by them first." The sting of Xexial's death still burned in him. "I just want to live."

"But how can you truly live when your very existence perpetuates the suffering of others? Of the pestilence you inject into the very ground you walk upon? Of the lies you spit from your venomous tongue."

Ashyn ignored her fanatical litany. He heard it before. Instead he countered with his own question. "So this man who waylaid your existence and destroyed all this is the reason you hound wizards?"

"One of many," she answered. "His ruination enlightened us to a very real truth. An epiphany if you will. We learned our calling.

"After my people recovered from the effects of our assailer, do you know what is it we found?"

Ashyn shook his head.

She pointed to their feet. "This tree. This single Elm survived where all the sequoias around it splintered and fell. This solitary elm was left behind amongst the tragedy of death and destruction. It remained tall, unwavering, and firmly rooted, even though the soil beneath it may have changed.

"The Ferhym learned from this tree. That though the world around us may fall to chaos and discord, we cannot. With our roots in the soil, with nature as our ally, all things heretical must be set right. To merely live life, ignorant to those who seek to abuse others, is no true life. The skewer's unnatural, defiling power showed us that we, as nature's servants, are here for a reason. That we survived for a reason. The spirits of our deceased did not demand vengeance. They demand balance.

"Our world is skewed, Blood Wizard. Everyday something unnatural bends the order of our world to fill their twisted devices. Dragons, wizards, monsters, and creatures of pestilence and death. They are a blight, you see. A sickness that wastes away at the land, tilting it towards darkness and decay. We seek to eradicate that skew and put the world on its right path. That is why we are here. It is our cause."

"Pretty words," Ashyn told her, "but how does the action of one person, no matter how revolting, condone everything you have done down there?" The wizard pointed down below, to the rocky outcropping next to the pond. From his vantage he could see a red stain on the slate grey rocks. He knew it had been the woman. And further he could make out stone forges, billowing white smoke, something he missed on his initial approach. There he could see humans hauling buckets of stone.

"Harbingers of chaos have many acolytes. Any seeking to parlay with the skewers inevitably cast their lot in with such evil. They seal their own fate with their choices; we release them from it." The elf's dark eyes glittered with intensity.

Ashyn knew she believed every word she said, that the men and women below were guilty, just through association whether with him, or Xexial, or even the Jasian Enclave. *She's mad*, Ashyn thought bitterly. *They are all mad.*

"We offer those who are not truly lost a chance at reclamation. They learn how to care for and love the land. Like all children, they must first start by working it."

Ashyn grabbed the bridge of his nose and closed his eyes. "Working the land?" he repeated her words. "Reclamation comes at the price of slavery?"

"Ferhym serve nature. The reclaimed too must serve."

Ashyn knew slavery. He had once thought himself a slave to the Jasian Enclave as a child. His salvation came at a price. A Charity Fee, which his toils of labor had to pay back. It had made him harsh and bitter to the bishop at the time. It took Xexial's explanation to help Ashyn see that while he was indeed living a life of indentured servitude, the reasons for it were not for profit or malice on the part of the Enclave, but to keep a growing population of orphaned children under control.

What this elf before him was telling him was nothing like what Xexial explained. These people were suffering hard labor because the Ferhym didn't agree with their ideals. Because they thought that those below were in league with skewers. His stomach rolled in disgust, leaving the bitter taste of bile on his tongue. He fought down his growing anger. He needed to know about Julietta.

"So what does that mean for the Nuchada?" He asked. "Am I to be reclaimed as well? Are we parlaying for the Spirits' forgiveness now?"

The elf laughed at him. The sound was dark and cruel, and Ashyn knew she was mocking him. She shook her head no. "There are no terms here, wizard. You are a skewer of the foulest kind. You are the terror our people have fought beyond centuries. You desecrate all you touch. You are a poison."

"Then why are we talking?"

The elf smiled widely at him. Ashyn noted that she had perfect white teeth. "Even though your spirit was damned the moment you came into this world, Blood Wizard, you can still save those you care for."

Ashyn heard struggling, and he saw two guards pulling a figure up the narrow stairs. He could tell by the shapely form that it was a woman. But there was a bag draped over her head. She wore tattered white robes, so filthy they now looked beige, held together by a cinched cord at her waist wrapped around several times and now frayed at the ends. He could see that the robes liberally ripped at her leg line up to her hips. Her arms were thin and emaciated, and Ashyn felt his world begin to fall apart. How did they know?

They threw the woman to the hard wooden floor and she tumbled down with a cry of pain. Ashyn was on her in an instant, helping her sit upright. He reached behind her head and loosened the cord that kept the bag pinched tight around her neck.

Quickly he pulled the bag away from her. Ashyn stared for a moment dumbfounded as a tumble of straw-blonde hair cascaded down around her head falling down past her shoulders.

Elated that it wasn't Julietta, yet slightly confused, Ashyn reached up and parted her hair so he could see the face that lay underneath. Worn blue eyes, in sunken sockets, looked up towards him. Ashyn could see dark freckles dancing across her face. She was older now, a woman grown, but he knew that face.

"Ashyn?" she whispered.

"Avrimae?" he responded in disbelief.

She launched upon him in a tight hug, heaving in deep sobs. Ashyn put his arms around her as well, and he let her cry. He looked up at the female elf, hatred of his own for her now burning in his eyes. How did this elf know so much about him?

Another elf walked beside her then. A male. He was taller than her by half a head and he had long dark brown hair that was pulled into a ponytail. His face, like many of the Ferhym was covered in paint, and through that paint he could see deep brown eyes staring down at Ashyn. In those eyes he could see pride and triumph.

The elf was holding some sort of tome in his hands. It was thin, and seemed to be made of some kind of leather binding. It definitely didn't look to be made by the tribal Ferhym. It looked old. Ancient.

The female took it, and held it up for him to see more clearly. The cover was indeed nothing the Ferhym had ever worked with. The binding of it was aged and well worn. There were no discernable markings or words to be seen, but he knew a tome of its sort when he saw one. The Onyx Tower had many just like it.

"Here is what you will do, Blood Wizard," she said matter-of-factly. "You will decipher this book for us, and," she paused long enough to accept a strange shard from another elf, "you will teach us about this." It looked like a crystal that emanated a strange, cerulean glow. The male who'd handed it to her looked as if he'd dreaded even touching it.

Ashyn gently pushed Avrimae off him. She continued to sobbing gently. He ran his arms across her shoulders in an effort to comfort her. She nodded at him, grateful, and held her hand to the back of her nose to stifle her tears.

He stood and walked back over to the female elf. Even though he towered over her, she wasn't intimidated in the slightest. She held the book up to him.

Curious, Ashyn opened the crumpled leather binding, and gently touched the archaic yellow pages within. He recognized the harsh scrawling letters across the page. Draconic.

Though there were many markings across the page, it only translated into a single word, which he whispered, "Craetorian."

The elf's dark eyes were alight with fire. "What does the next page say? Just the heading, if you will."

Curious himself, Ashyn gently turned the page. There were many words on this page, but one word lingered there boldly. "Netherphage."

"Netherphage," she repeated.

Ashyn looked from the tome to the crystal. Was this the Netherphage? "What is that?"

She held it towards him. As Ashyn reached out to take it, his fingers brushed the smooth crystal. An unearthly cold penetrated him instantly. It felt like he was thrust into a frozen river. He gasped. He felt this before. When Xexial had saved him from the druid.

This shard contained **destruction** magic.

Ashyn withdrew his hand. He tried to cover up the recognition in his eyes but it was too late. She said flatly, "You will decipher the book."

Ashyn closed the tome. He knew now why she wanted him to decipher the tome. The Ferhym wanted to learn how to wield **destruction**. It was a wizard's most coveted magic, and none but master wizards knew how to call upon it.

What the elves did not know was Ashyn had no power over **destruction**. He had not finished his training. Though he may have turned his back on the Wizard's Covenant to save his sister, he would not betray his people of his vow. He knew how to read schemata. He could figure out the principles of the spell even if he couldn't cast them. He looked down at the closed tome and then handed it back to the elf, the words of the first two pages seared into his mind. Craetorian. Netherphage.

"No," he answered her.

Faster than he would have thought she could do, she swiftly backhanded him. Like a snake launching forward to bite its prey. His lip mashed against his teeth. The pain was instant and fierce as he felt his lip split. He could feel blood trickle from the wound.

Anger like a blazing inferno showed in her eyes, "You are in no position to tell me no skewer!"

Ashyn reached up with the back of his own hand and held it against his bleeding lip. Salt and copper touched his tongue. He had to wrestle within himself, fighting down his anger. He was here for his sister, he reminded himself. His eyes fell on Avrimae. And now her and Macky too.

Still, what they were asking him to do? What unseen horrors could these people unleash? What was Netherphage? The young wizard looked back out to the natural earthen barrier than separated the glade he was in from the rest of the Shalis-Fey. What if the tome possessed the same access to that? Or worse.

In the past, he would have thought such a thing ludicrous. Now, seeing what Xexial had done to the lowlands, hearing what he had done with the firestorm he created, it didn't seem so unimaginable anymore. Xexial had learned the ability from someone, from somewhere. Just as Ashyn had learned his meager abilities.

Most of that came from tomes of knowledge. Vast books of spells, and scrolls of the arcane. He looked down at the book in his hands. Ancient. Who knows what devastation the Netherphage may bring?

The very words were enigmas to him. Craetorian. Netherphage. They felt archaic, born from a time so long ago that their use was now defunct and forgotten. Yet, there was something that resonated in that first word. Something familiar to him. What answers could he find? Perhaps even answers to his own injuries?

He thought to barter for the freedoms of everyone he loved. He could free Julietta, Avrimae, Macky, and everyone else. He could give the elves what they sought, and earn those he loved a quick reclamation.

All he had to do was teach them. Teach them how to use a magic that was denied to them. He could do that couldn't he? He could teach them the art of **destruction**. In his heart, Ashyn knew he could learn the incantations, even if the magic wouldn't answer him personally. He could do it.

Besides the wizards were likely hunting him now, were they not? Bent on destroying him because they didn't count rogues amongst them. They didn't allow Recreants. They wouldn't hesitate in destroying him. Why shouldn't he give the elves equal footing?

No.

Ashyn steeled himself. With more conviction he thought to himself, *No.* If he agreed, they would kill those he loved anyway. If he agreed, it would only strengthen the Ferhym's campaign against skewers and even more would die or become enslaved at the hands of these crusaders. Even if he tried to lie to them, the druids would pry it from him. They would find a way to get the truth from him. This was the one time where his own ignorance could protect the ones he loved.

But if he defied them, would they kill him? If they killed him, how could he save Julietta, Avrimae, or Macky?

Indecision gripped at Ashyn. In his mind he could hear Xexial's voice, deep and powerful, telling him that there was no real choice. Death was his only true option. "Few for the many," the old man's voice echoed in his head.

What was his death, or Avrimae's, or, as much as it ripped him to shreds inside to even consider, what was Julietta's death in comparison to what the elves would do if they could wield the power of wizards?

Ashyn looked into the lead Ferhym's dark eyes. They needed him. They wanted him. This is their chance, and he had delivered himself so simply to them. He had given them an opening, a chance to command a power they felt no one but they should have.

Ashyn did this. "Xexial, what have I done?" he whispered. Standing before this elf with her tattoos etched across her flesh, and seeing the thirst in her eyes, he knew he'd erred in deviating from his promise to his master.

He should have gone to the Seven. He should have pleaded and rallied the wizards. Now he gave his enemy a modicum of strength. An advantage against those he respected and those he loved. He did this.

Ashyn snorted then at his own idiocy. His very presence may make it worse for Julietta. His best option, his only option, was if they didn't know she was his sister. That meant he had to defy them, even if it meant his death.

Xexial's words were so loud in his head that he thought the elves before him should surely hear it. "Would you rather they die violently, glorifying you? Or live long lives, hating your very name?"

Ashyn did exactly as Xexial had said the day they left Czynsk. He mistook the obvious choice for the correct one. His judgment was so clouded over his sister; he didn't see the bigger picture, until this very moment. He gave the Ferhym exactly what they wanted. Worse, he had done it from the very beginning. How many mistakes had he made in his hellbent quest for Julietta? How many people died, or still may die just for her? Or for him?

His anger fled him then. He felt empty and hollow. Just a vessel that no longer deserved his humanity.

Few for the many. He looked at Avrimae, at her blue, tortured eyes. "The few for the many," he said aloud.

He dropped the book at her feet. It landed with a dull thud. "I will not teach you what is in this book." Ashyn spit a glob of his blood right next to the book. It splattered against the yellowed pages. "Not now, not ever."

Her eyes exuded fury, but her voice came out calm, "We shall see wizard. We shall see."

THE VOÏRE

Brodea stood at the rim of the council chamber, her toes slightly extended past the edge of the tree. The calluses on her feet from centuries of moving amongst the trees left her hardly feeling the coarse bark scraping against them. A gentle southern wind pulled at the great elm, rustling the leaves and pulling her raven hair outward like a billowing flag. She knew very soon the council would be angry with her for keeping the Blood Wizard alive. It was a calculated risk, she would make them see reason.

Soft padding against the smooth floor alerted her that she was not alone. Brodea's keen ears picked up the gentle swishing of fabric against the floor. She knew who approached.

"Yes, my Voïre," Brodea said, turning, but not looking the platinum-haired Ferhym in the eyes. It was tradition that she respect the Voïre dui Ceremeia regardless of her position over the young elf.

"First Councilor," the Voïre dui Ceremeia replied equally as curt. She bobbed her head, and approached the wide opening to stand beside Brodea. Brodea, in return, looked back out into the swallet that was her home, her domain.

"You have him?" the Voïre asked, ignoring all pretenses.

"Yes." Brodea said flatly.

"May I see him?"

"No."

Brodea looked out the corner of her eyes at the Voïre to see her reaction. The young elf was emotionless, staring out into the city beyond. "Are you never going to let that go?"

"You marked a dui Nuchada," Brodea declared bluntly. "And worse, that dui Nuchada has become a wizard."

The Voïre seemed unfazed by the obvious facts. "Yes."

Incredulous, Brodea continued, "And you are okay with this?"

"You know my reasons."

Brodea folded her arms, and turned to face the Voïre dui Ceremeia, looking politely at her chin instead of her eyes. She spoke as forcefully as she started, "Because of your aversion to justice."

"Violence," the Voïre corrected. "I watched Whísper commit horrors on that day."

"You watched her balance skewers for the cause!" Brodea declared.

Now the Voïre did look in her direction. Brodea could feel those swirling quicksilver eyes upon her. It never got any easier feeling the magic washing over. Passionately and full of anger she replied, "I was a child."

"You are a Voïre!" Brodea snapped. "Your bloodline has been gifted with you. The Pure Hym. You need to act like it."

The Voïre snorted, "Act like a pure hym. Counsel me then, Lady Windsong, how is a pure hym supposed to act? For it seems to me that my choice in sparing Ashyn Rune that day has in turn benefitted the cause greatly. Do you not have everything you need for the tome? A wizard and a dui Nuchada. Rather convenient, is it not?"

The Voïre dui Ceremeia turned away and walk towards the stairs.

"Where do you think you're going?" Brodea demanded, not finished with the feisty young elf.

"Are you going to let me see him?" she asked without turning around to face Brodea.

"No."

Brodea saw her head nod, "Then I'm going to find the hunter that brought him here. I have a great many questions about this Blood Wizard. And if you won't help me, First Councilor, I will seek help elsewhere."

And then the Voïre was gone.

Brodea dropped her arms and sighed. She looked back out into the valley, realizing that the Voïre dui Ceremeia was right. If

Whísper captured or killed Ashyn Rune all those winters ago, then she might have never found the one she needed to translate the tome and bring balance to all of Kuldarr.

She watched below, and after several minutes the silver-haired Ferhym appeared, heading west. Perhaps it was the will of the Spirits this Voïre marked the dui Nuchada. Perhaps it was precognition. Perhaps it was simply luck. Brodea couldn't ignore the truth of the Voïre's words, though. The Voïre's choice in sparing Ashyn Rune would benefit the cause.

Perhaps it was Brodea that needed to open her eyes and accept it. Perhaps this very particular Voïre could be extremely useful in the days to come. She would have to wait and see.

NOT THE SAME

Jenhiro silently nodded to one of the Feydras' Anulas protectors as they passed him. The guard didn't nod back. He probably had things that he needed to be doing.

The hunter returned his gaze to Eigron, who was with the Elder of Vines. He did not know this druid. The Ferhym was young; he had not even seen a full century of life. Yet he was now working side by side with the most venerated druid in the Shalis-Fey. How this fidgety druid managed such fate was beyond the hunter.

Worse, this Eigron questioned every single part of Jenhiro's story on the capture of the dui Nuchada. Jenhiro did not like it; he had to keep his story vague. It was the only way to keep the dui Nuchada alive, as well as honor his fallen brothers and sisters who died by the skewers.

As branch commander, no one but his superior, Fen Treeshaper, or the Elder of Vines, should've questioned him. The fact that this junior druid felt he had any direct authority over Jenhiro bothered him.

Jenhiro risked much, just tracking down the small cove near the cavern where the dui Nuchada fell. He risked even more when he convinced those druids to mend the dui Nuchada's wounds. He used his stature as a branch commander to get them to do what shouldn't have been done. He even used the fallen Bull and its weapon as leverage. And now this petulant child was trying to catch him in a lie.

Jenhiro knew that he was supposed to be humble, that it was their nature, especially as hunters, to acquiesce to the wants of druids. But interrogated, even chastised, by an upstart youth, rankled the branch commander. Fen would have never spoke in such a fashion to Jenhiro. The druid respected the skills and prowess of Jenhiro and his hunters. But Fen wasn't here.

Fen Treeshaper was currently at the druid's sacred cove, Soum' Shalis, many miles to the East. Was the druid busy on matters of such great importance that they wouldn't notify him at the loss of his entire branch?

That was completely unlike Fen. The druid helped pick Jenhiro's team. He knew each and every one of their names. That meant that Fen's inability to speak to Jenhiro came from another source. The hunter suspected that source was standing directly in front of him. This Eigron was really beginning to piss him off.

With no direction coming from Fen, Jenhiro reported to the Elder of Vines. Master of the Druidic Order of Ferhym. Who just so happened to be at Feydras' Anula.

Now the hobbled, old druid was busy studying a long mahogany object in his thin frail hands. Jenhiro looked at it briefly. He had seen it so much that its very sight was beginning to make him ill. For about the hundredth time since he united with the druids, he heard the word, "Fascinating."

The Elder of Vines looked up to him, and the branch commander stood at attention. "The horned beasts made this you say?"

Jenhiro looked to the spear-like staff. "I have seen two separate bull-men use it with devastating effect." His insides felt cold. How many times were they going to ask him the same questions over and over again? Everyone looked at the monster, and every single one of them couldn't believe it was capable of using the same magic that they did. He hadn't thought it possible either, until it hunted him for weeks using the similar tactics of the druid.

Every time they asked how an animal was capable of using their magic, they wanted him to explain the nature of the spells he saw. So he would, which dredged up the pain of losing his unit each and every time. They died. And now for what? A stick?

When Jenhiro had brought the weapon to the druids, it was because he knew it was a threat to his people. He watched one of the skewers turn hardened soil and stone into undulating waves of death and destruction. He bared witness to the travesty of his people being ground into mulch. Slickening his beloved forest in a thick crimson mire.

The cries of the fallen echoed in his mind. The grinding of bones and the rending of flesh flitted about the inside of his skull like a fly trying to escape a jar. He wanted them to fear it. He wanted them to protect his people from it.

Instead they were in awe of it. Eigron's dark eyes were intent upon the smooth shaft. "Can we use this against the wizards?" he asked the elder, hopeful.

The Elder of Vines nodded. "The magic within is Creation. Even if we can't use it, we can learn from this. Brodea will be most pleased, most pleased indeed. Especially since her precious book tells us so little."

"Wizards?" Jenhiro asked alarmed. "I thought we were at peace with wizards."

The elder shot him a puzzled look, and then a smile crept to his lips. "My dear branch commander, I forget how long you have been at field. First Councilor Brodea Windsong has received words from the Spirits that our hunt of wizards must resume in full force."

"I thought surely you knew," Eigron interjected, adding insult to the fact that this boy knew something Jenhiro did not. "I mean you are, after all, a hero to the people."

Jenhiro stepped back startled. This was new as well. "Hero. I have done nothing."

"The prisoner you brought to us..." Eigron said, a smile growing with every new piece added to the mosaic.

"The dui Nuchada."

Eigron shook his head. "The Blood Wizard."

Jenhiro's pulse quickened. "Blood Wizard."

Eigron nodded, eagerly. "You didn't know whom it was that you captured?"

The Elder of Vines came around the table and patted his shoulder. He felt the thick calluses of the senior's fingers against his bare shoulders. "You have done the Ferhym a great service. You have brought us a weapon to use against the wizards and brought the First Councilor the dreaded Blood Wizard all in one swoop." Eigron added, "A warrior without peer."

It was too much for Jenhiro. He traveled with the Blood Wizard. Hunted with the man. It was hard enough to know that he was a dui Nuchada, but this? A wielder of Destruction. A master of unbalance?

"But he used a bow."

Eigron reached under a threadbare tarp and removed the slender bone bow with silver runes. "A most lethal weapon as well," the druid commented. "I watched many die to this device. All at the hands of the Blood Wizard. He is a savage. In fact, our own First Councilor's daughter was almost among the number of deceased. The burns upon her flesh…"

Jenhiro nodded. He had seen Whisper. Her once beautiful features were reduced to a mound of angry red flesh on the side of her face.

"There was more…" Eigron commented looking around. "A pack with artifacts. There were gloves…"

The Elder of Vines looked to the Genrus Eigron and shook his head. This seemed to irritate the young druid, but Jenhiro's mind was still reeling at the idea of the dui Nuchada being more. As if seeing this, Eigron instead added, "The Blood Wizard is a master of fire."

"I saw no such thing," Jenhiro commented before he could think better of it.

Why am I defending the dui Nuchada? He wondered. *Why am I denying what the Druids are saying?* He always listened to them in the past. They were about balance above all else. They weren't invested in politics like the Council of Elm. Why was he denying himself the words they were telling him? Was it because he didn't like Eigron? Was his separation from his people really making him so shallow?

Jenhiro bowed his head. "I'm sorry, that was very discourteous of me," he apologized before he aroused the ire of the druids. "This is all very sudden."

Elder of Vines squeezed his shoulder again. "Wander your home; it has been a long time since you've seen its paths with your eyes, felt its grass beneath the pads of your feet, and witnessed the majesty of the Great Elm. Seek Windsong, hear her words."

Jenhiro nodded, "You are wise, Elder."

Jenhiro suddenly wanted to be away from the druids. He wanted to be able to collect his thoughts. Besides it felt weird being in doors when he spent so much time only under the canopy of his trees.

As Jenhiro walked away from the two druids, he heard Eigron ask the elder, "Now how best do we use the beast?"

"It seems too stupid to understand what it was dealing with," the grandmaster Druid returned.

Jenhiro turned and looked back to them. "The beast?"

The Elder of Vines looked up and smiled. "The bull creature. The one that you say used this staff."

Jenhiro could only blink in disbelief. It was on the verge of death when the druids took it away. He thought for sure it was going to be dissected to learn how it was capable of such magic.

"You've kept it alive?" Jenhiro asked shocked.

"For study," Eigron replied.

"A creature just like it is responsible for the death of my entire branch!"

The Elder of Vines smile disappeared. "Do not raise your voice at us! We are not naive little hunters that see a set of dancing lights and calls it magic. We are servants of nature and masters of balance. This little sow you brought home is no danger to the likes of us." He added hefting the staff, "Not now that we have its weapon."

Rage gripped at his chest. How could they? Fen Treeshaper would have never acted in such a way. These druids... what has happened to them? They don't care! The elder doesn't care! He doesn't care that his people died so violently! Doesn't comprehend the threat made when Jenhiro foolishly had his branch attack the bulls. The druids only seemed to care about how those deaths benefited them and the cause. Jenhiro could still see Sendea's broken form at the base of the tree. He could still see her wide, terrified eyes.

This was not a people he remembered serving so proudly. "I want to speak with Fen," Jenhiro said defensively. "I must speak with Fen Treeshaper."

"And I have told you he is not available," Eigron sternly protested. "You should accept such an answer from your betters."

Jenhiro did not miss the warning or the look in either of the druids' eyes. He turned away and stormed out of the druids' quarters and into Feydras' Anula before he did something he knew he would regret.

~ ~ ~

Once outside he breathed a little faster. He was away from the staff. Away from the sudden burst of knowledge of how unimportant his people were. Away from the druids that seemed to care little for the fact that he lost everything.

Sendea should be praised for her brave and noble sacrifice in the protection of her people. All of his branch should be. Instead, their sacrifices in trying to keep balance within the Shalis-Fey went completely unnoticed, and it was he that was going to be praised, not even for the balancing, but for a weapon. And for defeating an alleged wizard. Jenhiro was a hero in the minds of his people, yet what he felt like was the villain. He was bringing death to those he swore to protect, and they loved him for it.

Jenhiro tried to take a deep breath as he felt his heartbeat quicken. He didn't deserve to be a hero. He didn't even deserve to be alive. Now, he learned that he brought an enemy to the very walls of Feydras' Anula. The one thing he avoided for weeks with the bull, and now it was here, and so was a wizard!

What have I done? What have I committed my people to? The druids didn't know the danger of the creature. They didn't respect it as he warned! Fen would have, but Fen was out of reach.

Breathing suddenly became very difficult. He tried breathing through his mouth, his firm chest heaving up and down. He couldn't get enough air in his lungs. He felt deprived, starved.

Anxiety gripped at his heart like a gauntlet. Crushed underneath it. His chest tightened. He was unexplainably jittery. His hands shook, he breathed faster.

It was all falling apart. Everything he had planned. What he desired to do for the druids, for the fallen, for his people. The hunter's head grew light at the thought. A movement from the corner of his vision startled him. He looked up quickly. Only too late did his mind recognize the green dress or the long platinum hair, before he was looking into her eyes. The swirling silver eyes of the Voïre dui Ceremeia. Instantly all that he feared came to life in those eyes. He saw his reflection. The reflection of his soul. The reflection of a coward.

"Excuse me, are you the branch commander that captured the dui Nuchada?" she asked in a song-like cadence.

Terrified and unable to cope with what he saw, he needed to be away from her. He needed to move. It was all too much. He had to bleed this excess energy out of his body. The anxiety was overwhelming. He wanted to scream. He wanted to cry. He wanted to run.

Jenhiro stumbled away from the Voïre dui Ceremeia without so much as uttering a word. He moved as quickly as he could away from the druid's small, squat structure against the base of a rocky outcropping. His footing was unsure. He couldn't get a sense of equilibrium, and it only caused the tension to mount in his core. The hunter thought he might rupture. Spill all his energy, all his emotions, and all his life out onto the stones in front of him.

His palms grew sweaty, his breathing quickened even more, but it didn't feel like enough. There was just not enough air to fill him. His head swooned. Everything became blurry. Jenhiro bent over and grabbed his knees. He screamed at himself to calm down.

Jenhiro fought against his emotions and grasped at his breathing. He needed to slow it down. Consciously, he breathed in through his nose and out through his mouth very slowly.

At first it didn't feel like it was doing anything. He didn't think he was getting enough air. He wanted to breathe more quickly, but he wouldn't let himself. Once more he took a long deep breath in through his nose and exhaled.

The tightening restriction on his chest loosened. He actually felt like he had gotten just a pinch of air in his lungs.

Though hungry for more air, he inhaled slowly again. He exhaled. His heart calmed down even more. He could feel his anxiety ebbing. Jenhiro's vision began to clear, and his footing felt sure.

It was time to get away. Away from the druids, away from the squat buildings, away from his people whom he had terribly endangered.

An hour later he found himself miles outside of the city. He climbed a sequoia, and sat on the thick branch overlooking Feydras' Anula, the hidden city of his people. Though it looked the same for the most part, it felt alien to him now. He was no longer its inhabitant. He was the stranger.

It has only been a winter! his mind yelled. *A single winter, nothing has changed.*

But it had. Nothing felt the same. The druids seemed eager, almost reckless now. Their pursuit for more powerful magic was all encompassing. Where was the balance in that?

In the distance he could see a great quarry being dug that was never there before. Lines of humans were moving the stone in large baskets. Others at the end of the line took the heavy baskets full of stones into newly constructed forges. Long trenches were dug so that cages could be stored for holding skewers, hoping and toiling for their reclamation. The numbers that he saw were staggering. First Councilor Tehirs rarely demanded so many skewers be reclaimed. It was a work force. Slave labor pure and simple.

Who was Brodea Windsong? He knew of her of course. Everyone did. She was a legend among hunters and councilors alike. She defied the odds at every turn. She defeated a wizard single-handedly. She balanced more skewers than any other elf alive. And she gave birth to three daughters!

Elves had a hard enough time bearing one child. Two was looked at as a blessing. Three? Until Brodea, such a thing was unfathomable. The Spirits had chosen her it seemed.

But aside from these accolades, who was she really? What gave her the right to rule as the First Councilor? He shook his head at the thought. He had never questioned politics.

"What am I missing?" he asked himself aloud. "Why do I see things with different eyes?"

Before he met the dui Nuchada, he rarely questioned the will of the Spirits. Mostly because he had the luxury of working for the druids and their coves. Now though it was not the same. The druids always answered to the Council of Elm, but never did they produce what they were producing now. Weapons of war.

And Jenhiro just delivered them a very big stick. Which if you asked him six months ago, he would have been fine with it. Now he was beginning to question the First Councilor's motives.

Did the dui Nuchada do this to him? Did the man cloud his mind somehow? Put him under a spell? Use illusions against him? Was Jenhiro questioning everything because the wizard cursed him?

He was taught that wizards spoke honeyed words that dripped with a foul poison. That their tongues could produce sweet sounds, but beneath, their breath reeked of blasphemy and pestilence. He never felt that way with the dui Nuchada. The man's words were never honeyed; they were bold and questioning. He constantly challenged everything. Jenhiro had somehow found that inquisitive mind refreshing.

Again Jenhiro closed his eyes and willed himself to breath before another panic attack came on. It unnerved him that he had made an alliance with the dui Nuchada. It bothered him more that due to that alliance he now questioned everything he had ever learned.

Part of him was desperate. He felt that he did that which he feared most. He brought the enemy to Feydras' Anula. But another part of him, the one that had really spoken to the dui Nuchada, thought of him as a man, not a monster. And he questioned did he really bring terror to his people?

The dui Nuchada did not seem like a wizard, it was true. In fact, he did not seem like anything other than an elf that was diligently trying to find someone.

Julietta. That was all he desired. All he wanted. To get to her. Not to fail. Now he was in a cell, and it was likely Brodea was going to kill him brutally.

Jenhiro told the dui Nuchada that he would find her. He vowed that he would make sure she was safe. If the man was an evil wizard, should he still help? Could he?

Jenhiro believed he was a man of strong moral character. The dui Nuchada risked himself to save Jenhiro's life at great cost. All he asked from Jenhiro was to find Julietta. How could he not repay that?

But if the man were a wizard? Jenhiro didn't think he could bear it if the dui Nuchada hurt any of his people. He brought him here. Their blood would be on Jenhiro's hands.

No, it would be worse. There would be so much blood that it would consume him, drown him in it.

But if he helped the dui Nuchada find Julietta, it may ease the man's mind. Jenhiro chuckled cynically to himself as he stared out at all the moving elves in the distance. For first time in a very long time, a hundred winters at least, he was uncertain of what to do.

In the field, as a branch commander it was different. He saw a threat to his people within the Shalis-Fey. He neutralized it. Life or death. Out in the wilderness it was simple. Clean, unforgiving, and final.

Now he was too uncertain. Uncertain how he now fit in in this city. With his elves. With the hunters. With the very world.

He watched the sun climb high into the sky, reach its apex, and then slowly begin to descend, encapsulating his beloved city in the beginnings of dusk. He spent the day lost in thought, and in the end he came to a single, very simple conclusion.

He would get no answers here. They needed to come from somewhere else. Someone else. He would go to the man. He would see the dui Nuchada. Tonight.

ENDURE

Ashyn knew that it was going to begin like this. He knew it the moment they took him away from her. He took one thing away with him though as they drug him out of that council chamber. A name. Her name.

Brodea. This was the name of his enemy.

And just as he knew the moment he defied her, it wasn't a surprise that night when his cage climbed back upwards to the glade above on its own.

Uriel jeered up at him from the other cell, and gave a mock salute as Ashyn went alone, skyward, "Try not to die too fast wizard."

He needed to be strong, Ashyn told himself. He needed to be brave.

It happened almost too fast for him to register. As soon as the lift of his cell stopped, the elves were on him. He tried to defend himself, but he didn't have anywhere near the martial skills they did. Fists and feet lashed out at him, striking him all over.

Pain exploded in so many places at once it was dizzying. He felt a pop at his side, and he knew that one of them broke his rib. Then he was down on his hands and knees, blood streaming like crimson waterfalls from his nose, mouth, and ears. He coughed and spat, struggling to hold himself up. His entire body wrenched with pain.

More kicks against his side, another pop, Ashyn groaned in misery. His arms quaked as he tried to sustain himself, tried to hold on.

What happened? He thought they feared his magic. What gave them strength?

A foot caught him under his jaw jerking his head violently backward. A bloom of fire raced across his mouth, down his throat and gripped his spine. He fell backwards gurgling and choking.

A form moved over him quickly. Almost protectively. "Do not kill him!" Ashyn heard one of the elves chitter quickly. He recognized the voice instantly. It was Jenhiro.

Grateful for the reprieve, Ashyn rolled to his side coughing and wheezing. Thick stringers of blood hurled from his throat and left flecks of red spittle across his lips and chin.

He felt another one of them hovering over him as well. He glanced upwards. There was something in his hand. It was balled up and lumpy.

Jenhiro knelt down next to Ashyn, and held out his hand. The elf placed the compacted object into Jenhiro's out-stretched hand. The wizard could see it more clearly. It was a bag.

Ashyn tried to speak, but only sputtering grunts came from his mouth. His stomach clenched tightly, his whole core in violent spasms.

They shared eye contact, and Ashyn wasn't sure what it was he read in those dark eyes. Guilt, pity, sadness. One thing he was certain of, Jenhiro was deriving no pleasure in this. That brought him comfort.

Jenhiro unraveled the bag, whispering, "You need to endure, dui Nuchada. I will find her, and then you will answer questions." He pulled the sack over Ashyn's head.

His world went dark. Ashyn felt himself jerked to his feet. Another wave of pain laced through his body. Then he felt his hands bound tightly behind his back. The rope was so tight that it bit into his flesh. The moment the final knot pinched against his skin, the elves dragged him away from the cells.

They were careless in how they moved him. Repeatedly he slammed into rocks, logs, and stumps. His head banged into low-hanging objects. Forced to hang his head, the aches in his chest grew.

His blindness added another level of terror to the whole ordeal. He was aware of his own wheezy breathing. It sounded like thunder in his ears. He also heard the elves talking amongst themselves, but it was broken and hard to understand. Like slang. He knew they were talking like that on purpose. He gave away too soon that he could understand them; it forced the elves to come up with different methods.

Where were they taking him? What did they not want him to see? He tried to detect where he was going by his sense of smell, but everything was so saturated in the smell of copper that he could barely distinguish one odor from the next.

He stumbled along for what felt like hours until he realized that he wasn't surrounded any more. There was only one person each in front of and behind him. It was then he realized he was climbing.

He knew where they were taking him. He also knew that if he lurched suddenly to the right, everything could end before it even began. How long had he been climbing? Was it only a few feet or did he hit around fifty or more? He wasn't sure.

If he risked it and was wrong he would probably just break his legs, and that would put him in a worse predicament. Was he even capable of suicide? It was a question he asked himself when he knew what Brodea wanted from him. Would he be capable of killing himself to stop her from translating the book?

He realized even with fear beating his heart that the answer now was the same as before. No. His desire to live was too strong. Was it greed that he wanted to live, or just his love of life? His mind was so jumbled, he didn't know.

The bag was soaked with sweat and blood by the time he finished the climb. He could hear the whistling of wind from the massive portal at his left side. On his right, he distinctly heard the crackle of torches.

He was forced to stop, and then brought to sit. He felt the hard granular surface of a wooden chair beneath him. His hands were bound to the back of that chair.

The bag was violently jerked from his head, and he felt the piercing torchlight assail his eyes. He heard a collective series of gasps around him. He squinted his grey eyes into the room, but it was hard to make anything out. There were many murky forms around him. Strange silhouettes.

"Blood Wizard," one of them muttered in their tongue.

Another spoke with a hint of fear, "You have brought him here?"

Another cried, "Quickly, bind his liar's tongue!"

Ashyn felt a rope pulled tightly over his mouth, pulling his cheeks back, and curbing his tongue.

Soothingly, a voice he instantly recognized as Brodea's broke in, "Councilors, relax. We have taken precautions against his dark ways. He has been depleted of energy. Were he to try and cast on us now, he would be killing himself, am I correct?"

Ashyn saw one of the forms move forward, the top of it, its head he assumed, bobbed vigorously. "The feedback would claim his life, in his current state, absolutely."

Ashyn felt his head loll to its side. He barely had the strength to lift it. But the images were solidifying, and the first thing he noticed were feet. Dozens of bare feet, all intertwined with one another.

"First Councilor, what is the meaning of this?" a different, slightly elderly voice demanded.

An elf stepped in front of him, her well-muscled thighs just in his field of vision. Her coppery skin was slick with sweat. Brodea.

"First Councilor!" another said alarmed.

Brodea pulled his head back so he could look up at them, at her. His grey eyes burned with malice as he looked towards her.

Triumphantly she announced, "The Blood Wizard is powerless right now, Councilors. Keep him taxed, and his body won't be able to handle the stresses of a spell."

"And what would be the point?" another asked, "After Tehirs joined the Spirits, you were quick to end his peace with them. Why keep this one alive?"

Brodea looked away from Ashyn. He could tell by the painful grip tightening in his hair that the Wild Elf did not appreciate the challenge. "Tehirs followed the guidance of the Spirits at his particular time, now I follow their guidance in a different time. I believe this one can help us."

"Help?" the elder spoke up again. Ashyn could wearily hear the murmurs around him. How could their enemy help them?

Brodea released his hair and walked away from Ashyn. Once more his head slumped low. He tried to look for Jenhiro, but all he saw were rows of dirty feet. He noticed among those feet quite a few who were discontented. Their legs twitched, and a few members tapped the ground with the pads of their feet, clearly nervous.

Then she was by his side once more, as was another. Ashyn tried to find the strength to lift his head and look up, but it was so hard. He wanted to learn all of them. He needed to know his enemies if he was to find a weakness in them.

His head raised only an inch, before it was grabbed by Brodea once more and violently yanked towards the other elf. She was holding the tome.

Ashyn managed a muffled grunt, "No."

Brodea had clearly chosen to ignore his weak words as she spoke over him. "As you know, the druids can do no more with this book; the Elder of Vines has even stated that only a wizard can decipher the rest. Something to do with Destruction. Well, now we have a wizard."

Out of the corner of his eyes, he could see the crowd of Councilors staring at him warily. "Why should he share such information? And even more, why should we believe anything that comes from that poisonous tongue of his?"

"Pain has a way of getting all men to speak," Brodea stated so coldly, yet so surely, that it sent a shiver down Ashyn's spine. "We will break this wizard. The Spirits demand it be done."

He could see looks of concern etched on the faces of the elves around him. Good he thought. Let them worry. He would not give Brodea what she wanted, no matter what.

"And when will you begin?" the one Ashyn recognized with Brodea before, asked.

Ashyn could feel Brodea's smile by the heat radiating from her body. "Immediately."

Ashyn closed his eyes and took a deep breath. If Jenhiro was not here, then Ashyn knew why. The hunter couldn't be. That comforted Ashyn in some small way. He needed to endure this. He only hoped he had the strength to do what was necessary.

~ ~ ~

Ashyn watched as the councilors stood and filtered out of the chamber. They were just going to leave? Leave Brodea, their First Councilor, and the wizard alone?

His head hurt, his brain was foggy, and yet he couldn't understand why they would do this? What happened to the fear of a wizard's magic? Even if they were right, that he wouldn't risk a spell now, what about later?

After many minutes there were only three people left in the open chamber with Ashyn. The First Councilor, the male who he could now tell was a druid, and a very different elf.

Instead of the naked flesh that he was growing accustomed to, the figure before him was dressed in a simple long flowing green dress. Her hair was a silvery-blonde that ran straight and pure down her shoulders to the small of her back like spun platinum. It cascaded around her body like captured sunlight. Elongated slender ears poked out of the mass of her silvery hair and rose to sharp points just above the crown of her head. She had a heart-shaped face with a soft, round nose. Her lips were perky and curved upwards in the corners. It seemed as if the young elf was constantly smiling. No markings covered her flesh, but he knew what she was: an Exemplar.

The Exemplar walked right up to him and bent down to look into his eyes. Ashyn tried to look away, but Brodea grabbed his head firmly, and held him in place with incredible strength.

Ashyn closed his eyes, Xexial's words to him as a child still echoed through his head. "The magic has a way of ensnaring anyone who looks in the eyes of the Exemplar. You become bound to them in ways you don't truly understand. Some say it feels like love, others ecstasy. Either way you become enraptured by the magic."

Ashyn realized now, how truly disadvantaged he was. Of course they would use the Exemplar in this way. How could they not? He almost wanted to laugh at the irony. The pain put a stop to that. He was still nothing more than an ignorant child. He thought that the elves should fear him. Of course they would fear him, but they had someone that could control him. Someone that could look into his soul. He couldn't allow that to happen.

"Open your eyes," Brodea commanded from above him.

"No," he croaked out.

There was a sudden pressure at his right shoulder-blade. "Open them," the order came again, simply and powerfully.

"Never."

Ashyn gasped in shock, as he felt a thin object pierce through his body and slide up underneath the bone of his shoulder.

"Open them."

He shook his head violently as sweat beaded his brow. Pain exploded through his back as he felt her rotate whatever blade-like object pierced his back. It grated against the bone. A moan of agony escaped his lips.

Fire ripped through his body as he felt another penetration into his body. His left shoulder this time. His whole frame convulsed as both objects twisted inside of him, leveraging against the bones of his shoulders, pushing them outward away from his body.

Suddenly, Brodea's mouth was against his ear, "This will end if you open your eyes." His mind foggy with pain he wasn't even aware that she let go of his head.

"No," he tried to say. In reality, though, it came out as a plaintive cry.

He could feel her hands against his back manipulating the torture devices inside of him. "If you don't open your eyes, it will get much, much worse. We will have to start cutting things off you. Things that are important and won't grow back."

She slid around to the front of him, he kept his eyes shut but felt the heat of her mouth only inches from his. Then she slid her knee up between his thighs, driving the point home. "Things you might want to keep."

Ashyn felt her grip around him, like a hug, but the fire in his back returned anew. Her mouth was back at his ear. "And when we have removed all we can from your body without you bleeding to death, we will be forced to cut off your eyelids so you cannot shut them anyhow. Making all of this pointless resistance futile." As she finished, she bit down on his earlobe so hard he felt her teeth tear through the ball of flesh. Blood dribbled against his neck from the wound.

Tears leaked from the corners of his eyes. He squeezed them shut tightly. The pressure of her body lifted. He braced himself for more pain, for another stabbing feeling somewhere in his body. He prepared himself for the worst pain he could think of, a knife down by his loins.

It didn't come. He waited, the tension building in his chest. He knew it was inevitable, to feel the pain again. She was just toying with him. Like a cat playing with its prey.

Then it happened. It wasn't at all what he expected. There was no rending of his flesh, no burning intense fire in his loins. There was only a sound. A simple crack.

There was no pain. No physical pain anyhow. No. The sensation that bombarded him was completely his alone. He knew the sound intimately. He felt the whistle of wind surge past his cheek. His mind was thrust back a decade as the biggest terror of his childhood gripped him.

A whip. His eyes flew open in fear, and he was enveloped in the swirling platinum eyes of the Exemplar. Magic danced and rippled across her eyes. Her pupils looked like twin hurricanes as the liquid mercury twisted around their black forms. He could feel the power in them, and the power between them, and he knew the First Councilor was right. It was futile. He was hers.

THE OTHER ONE

Ashyn felt himself floating. It was an all too familiar feeling as his body drifted like a feather, weightless and in nothingness. She knew! She knew he feared the whip, but how? How was it possible for her to know so much! Then he realized where he was. The same recurring dreamlike sensation he had every time he was near death. The place the Exemplar brought him.

He opened his eyes, and there she was before him. Platinum hair and swirling eyes.

"It is you," he said in shock, recognizing the Exemplar that was in the council chambers with him where he was being tortured. "You have betrayed me," he spat, surprised at the venom of his words. "You told her, didn't you?" He continued, "Told her my fears."

The Exemplar before him cocked her head to the side like a confused animal. "How would I know your fears, until before I looked into your eyes?"

Ashyn slammed the palm of his hand to his head, "because you are in here. You seem to always be in here!"

Her large silver eyes blinked at him, and then looked around. "You have been here before? You manifested this?"

Flabbergasted, at the elf Ashyn yelled, "Yes! Twice at least, I've been here. And no, you made this, not me!"

She eyed him suspiciously, "You will do as I say."

Ashyn suddenly felt himself drawn to her. A strange allure that he found impossible to resist. "What. Are. You. Doing?" he growled, as he took a step towards the Exemplar through the fog.

Ashyn's head clouded, and he felt himself growing lighter once more, his control on his own mind slipping. "Stop this!"

"You resist me?" the Exemplar said incredulously.

Ashyn fought to direct his gaze somewhere else, anywhere else. The cords in his neck bulged as he strained against his own body. Finally, his vision shifted half an inch to her shoulder. Instantly his feet slammed to the ground and he grew dizzy.

"How did you..." the Exemplar trailed off. He felt her eyes searching his body, and then involuntarily he raised his own arm. The arm with the platinum braid on it. "Where did you get this?" she demanded.

Oh shit, Ashyn realized. A thought of both Xexial's words and the Exemplar's rolled through his head. The Exemplar warned him. Their actions carried repercussions and they needed to be careful. That was why she didn't allow him to see her.

Xexial warned him that the Ferhym have Exemplars more often than any other Elves, and that it wasn't uncommon that they have two in a single generation. Ashyn assumed because she had platinum hair and eyes that it was the same person, but it wasn't. This wasn't his Exemplar. It was another one.

As this epiphany dawned on him, he could see now that her features didn't exactly match those of the child he had met.

Ashyn changed tactics fast. "How did she know?" he countered, challenging the Exemplar's question with his own. "How did Brodea know I would fear the whip?"

The Exemplar shook her head. "I do not know. The First Councilor is extremely resourceful."

"And you are helping her." His voice hissed disdainfully.

Ashyn's personal control within this bizarre dream state seemed to unnerve the platinum-haired beauty. She took a step backward. "I am Ferhym. I serve the Council of Elm. You are a skewer and the dui Nuchada! Your words are poison."

"Why are we here?"

The Exemplar blinked at him several times, clearly dumbfounded. "You are going to serve me. You are going to read the tome."

Ashyn shook his head, his strength gaining. "No. I serve no one.".

The Exemplar's voice quavered, "This is not possible. You will serve me!"

Again he felt a powerful allure to do as she bid. When he resisted her, it was like his head was being slammed repeatedly with a war-hammer. She could control him without making eye contact, he thought.

Then he remembered that the eye contact was already made. This was a fight inside his mind. He lost the first battle; he refused to lose the second.

His eyes searched for anything that could distract him from the powerful Exemplar. After a moment they fell on the dangling silver braid hanging from his wrist. Almost immediately, he felt the powers ebb.

Ashyn stood to his full height. He was suddenly towering over the Exemplar. At this moment she looked incredibly young. Like a child. She looked up at him terrified.

"Tell your First Councilor the answer is still no."

His strength regained he slammed his hands together and the dream dissolved.

~ ~ ~

The Exemplar screamed and fell away from Ashyn. The young wizard gasped as his body was once again flooded with a stinging pain.

His eyes burned and watered, but he saw the Exemplar huddled over on the hardwood floor. She was crying. Immediately, Brodea was there, hunched over the Exemplar.

The silver-eyed elf cried, "He's a monster. He resisted me. What does it mean?"

Brodea looked back at Ashyn, her eyes blazing, "It means we have to break the skewer even harder."

The Exemplar spat angrily. "He's already broken. To the magic. I saw it."

Ashyn stared at the Exemplar in disbelief. How could she have seen it? How did she know?

"Really?" Brodea asked.

The Exemplar nodded, "Something has caused his connection to weaken. It only comes sporadically now. Like water lapping a shore, occasionally it creeps up far enough that it brushes his feet."

Brodea stood up slowly and faced the druid. "Is such a thing possible?"

The druid looked from Ashyn back to the First Councilor. "It is, and it would explain much. Like how Hunter Jenhiro was able to defeat him."

"Indeed." Ashyn watched Brodea's reaction. A smile crept on the corners of her lips. "In that case, bring me Whísper. It's time we fueled this interrogation with a little raw emotion."

Brodea's cold, dark eyes fell on Ashyn, "You will wish you had complied, dui Nuchada. What I have done to you is only a pittance to what Whísper shall do. By the time this night is over, I doubt you'll even remember how to pronounce your own name."

~ ~ ~

Hours passed and only one thing filled Ashyn's mind. Pain. She was right. Everything grew foggy under the endless waves of torment. He forgot her name, he almost forgot his own.

Pain surged through his body like lightning. It moved from his eyes, through his skull, down his spine, and escaped through the tips of his fingers and toes. It cut a swath through him that left him drained like never before in his life. It was excruciating, terrifying, and every moment he was without it felt like a reprieve, but also felt hollow.

"Don't cut out his eyes. We need them," a voice said before him. Under normal circumstances he would have thought the voice sultry, even beautiful. There was a certain cadence to her words, an almost song like quality to the way she spoke. But now, in the haze of despair, her words were terror.

Hot liquid ran down his face. It mingled with the salt of his sweat and permeated his scent and his lips with a heavy copper tinge. It was blood. His blood.

The elf lingered before him. A distant memory had stirred when he first saw her. She smiled wickedly at him with dark eyes like chips of obsidian. The right side of her face was a mask of thick pink scar tissue. From the ruined pointed tip of her ear down to the slender curve of her neck was a bubbly mass of rippled and swollen flesh. She was beautiful once. He took that from her long ago, having destroyed their trap in a maelstrom of fire. She had been the only elf to survive, that he knew of.

Now she swayed before him, waving the cruel tip of a broken spear in front of him. Its normally silver sheen glowed an orangish-white. She just finished pressing it against the coals.

She hissed, "Time to seal up those wounds, dui Nuchada."

"Don't blind him," the song-like voice chimed behind him.

With her dark eyes never leaving his, her disappointment cut through her reply, "I won't." She moved against him, her body firm against his bound flesh. "I will take my time with you. I will hurt you, break you, and make you long for the death you deserve, skewer."

Her face close to his, she whispered to him, "I will make you suffer, as I have suffered. I will put you through all the pain that I have been through and more. When I am done, and my mother has all that she needs from you, I will then relish in the kill. I will burn your eyes out from your wretched skull and then I shall cut off your head for all the other vermin to see. You are a Skewer of Balance, and I will have my vengeance for what you have done to my Shedalia."

She reached back and yanked his hair so he couldn't pull away from her. Tension rising in his chest, he watched as she slowly lowered the burning blade. He felt its searing heat inches from his lacerated skin. With the twisted smile of someone in complete control, she pushed the flat of the spear against his torn face. His skin broiled and his blood bubbled. He could smell the fetid odor of his own burnt flesh as acrid steam roiled from his face. Unable to resist the unbelievable torment that quaked through his body, Ashyn Rune screamed.

He knew that was only the beginning.

PROGRESSION

Brodea stared at the limp and twitching form on the floor in front of her. A small puddle of blood was beginning to ooze underneath him from the hundreds of wounds both she and her daughter inflicted. After every session, the druids healed him just enough so that he would live, but not enough that they couldn't attack the already sensitive and damaged flesh.

For three weeks, they tortured the Blood Wizard, and still he refused to translate the tome.

At first, his strength enticed her. To see him resist so firmly, so surely, where so many others broke down. Of course, she knew immediately that the problem was that she set limitations on the torture itself. She forbade blinding him, even one eye. She needed him to be able to see. She also forbade breaking his fingers in case somatic gestures were required to teach the druids. Finally, she absolutely refused to have him castrated.

This was one of the first things they did. When at risk of losing their manhood, most generally became cooperative. But she needed him whole, and that meant taking away one of their most useful techniques. Whisper had begged each day to sever his phallus or testicles from his body. Still Brodea refused.

Truth was she wanted the wizard broken, but not ruined. She had great plans for this one. He was young and virile, and still easily moldable. Though she knew the council would never understand, she knew that if she were to destroy the wizard threat forever, it had to first come from a wizard.

Under First Councilor Tehirs, the council had become too narrow-minded. He had sorted out the wisdom of the elements, of magic. Slowly druids filtered out of the councilors. As the old retired, or returned to the soil, their positions were filled solely with hunters. People that only knew combat against the skewers.

Brodea too had been a hunter, and she had no love of magic, that was certain. Yet she knew how well her kin handled it. She respected the druids' attunements to both flora and fauna. She saw how they were needed for the cause.

Tehirs' council was blind to their importance. They saw only to themselves, and the people of Feydras' Anula. Their cause, dictated by the Spirits themselves, was a distant, abstract thought. Ferhym preached humility, and yet the council bore one thing that Brodea saw too often as of late: pride.

Not for Brodea. She may be proud of her accomplishments, and proud of her ability to serve the Spirits so fully, but her life was the cause. She made a promise to her late husband Ambit, who was now one of those spirits, and Brodea intended on keeping it, for him, for all of them. It was her sacred vow and her destiny to do so. And if that meant dirtying herself to purify and balance nature, then she would do it. The Spirits demanded no less. That dirt meant magic.

Brodea knew that wizards often preached that no one understands a wizard, but a wizard. Now she had one, and he would eventually help her understand. Because knowing your enemy was the key to victory. She would fight fire with fire, and ice, and blood if need be.

Still, at three weeks they were no closer to breaking down any barriers on the wizard as they were on the first night. Somehow this child could resist their Voïre dui Ceremeia. To say that infuriated Brodea was an understatement. The gaze of the Voïre was magic incarnate. How the dui Nuchada was capable of resisting the purest strain of magic itself made no sense.

The Voïre dui Ceremeia was the greatest connection to nature. Nothing short of another Voïre should be able to resist a trained adult, not even another hym or even a trained druid. The power of their connection was that strong. Even Brodea couldn't resist the influences of the trained adults, should one ever try.

This young wizard did, and she was determined to find out why. Brodea knew she should use both against him, but she decided to refrain from using the second Voïre for now. It was bad enough she was risking one of theirs, she would not risk both until she was positive the Blood Wizard was no threat to them.

They were taking a small respite now. As talented and driven as Whisper was, Brodea knew when her daughter needed rest. They taxed Ashyn so far the night before, Brodea was sure they nearly killed him. She knew what drove him, but how he managed to keep going under such duress confounded her.

She heard the echo of another approaching. She looked up awaiting her visitor. As the man-child lay on the floor, shattered, and alone, Vooken came up the narrow steps. They made eye contact, and he quickly came her way, sidestepping the husk of a wizard.

Brodea barked, "Anything?" She was waiting for Vooken for hours now. She could read the rejection in his eyes before he even shook his head no. Brodea slammed the Councilor's chair with the palm of her hand in frustration. "You said we had her!" She spat.

Vooken sat down next to her. "We did," he agreed before adding, "until the druids said they found something unique in her. Thank your precious Genrus Eigron for that one. Now they have her and don't want to give her back until they can figure out why she is so resistant to magically generated fire."

"We are the Council!" Brodea argued. "We answer the will of the Spirits!"

"And the druids maintain the balance of magic with nature. Unfortunately, she falls under their jurisdiction on this."

Vooken's eyes drifted to Ashyn. Brodea answered the unasked question, "He's exhausted and unconscious. He cannot hear us at all.".

"You are certain?"

Brodea nodded.

Vooken said sympathetically, "You risk so much, keeping him here like this. You risk yourself. He is still very dangerous."

"I must be here. I must be synonymous with his pain. Every time he is in agony, it must be my face he sees. Besides, as long as the boy thinks he can rescue his sister, and as long as we keep him exhausted, the wizard is no threat to us," she reassured Vooken and put her hand in his.

"It will only be on the dawning of that moment that he realizes there will be no saving her that he will become uncontrollable."

"Then we must continue to feed him hope, while simultaneously bringing him down," Vooken angled. "And then we will control him."

Brodea smiled and squeezed his hand. "You read my mind. Ashyn will break. He just doesn't realize it yet. Now, he thinks he has succeeded; he thinks he has infiltrated Feydras' Anula by his own will. I will be there to bring it all crashing down around him. In that moment, he will know true failure, and then he will be ours."

Vooken raised an eyebrow, "You are planning something else other than torturing the boy?"

Brodea's smile grew until it almost touched both ears. "My dear Councilor, there are many forms of pain. Physical is the least of them all."

~ ~ ~

"I am sorry, Mother. I told her she wasn't allowed to come." Whisper said, with her head bowed to Brodea. Only minutes after Vooken left, Brodea found herself accosted by the very two people that couldn't stand to be around each other.

The Voïre dui Ceremeia stood with her hands on her hips, her mercurial eyes dancing wildly. "Weeks the Nuchada has been here. Weeks! Not once have you consulted me. You take her! A blunt instrument, but not me. I can help you!"

Whisper scoffed, "Just like you helped our branch when you foolishly marked the boy. Good hym died that day because of you."

"They attacked a wizard," the Voïre shot back towards Whisper. "In fact, you'd think you'd be grateful. Didn't that little incident grant you a field promotion?"

"Why you little bit..."

"Stop!" Brodea growled at the two Ferhym. "Not in front of our guest."

The three elves turned to regard the still unconscious form lying on the floor.

Whisper said defiantly, "Perhaps if our precious Voïre knew how the mark worked, she would realize that such a bond would let her into his mind at all times. Then we can have what we need."

"Absolutely not," Brodea responded. "We cannot risk the Voïre being in his head like that. We would have no control over him should he dominate her."

"I can do it," the Voïre offered.

"No," Brodea said adamantly. "Absolutely not."

"You're too weak anyhow," Whisper said, driving the spear deeper. "He would conquer you faster than we conquered Czynsk. You heard what he did to the superior Voïre didn't you? You wouldn't stand a chance."

Whisper spit a wad of phlegm on Ashyn's prone body in disgust. "You should let me take his testicles. That will break him."

"Why? Are yours not big enough as it is? Or was it Shedalia who played the male? I've always been confused," the Voïre sniped.

Whisper wheeled to strike the hym, but Brodea was quicker. The First Councilor lashed out and caught Whisper's clenched fist. The Voïre didn't even flinch.

"You... never... strike... the Voïre," Brodea growled between each word. "You will end this prattle now, and conduct yourselves properly as a branch commander, and as a Voïre dui Ceremeia. This is childish and beneath the two of you!"

Whisper looked wildly at Brodea, before her dark eyes calmed. She dropped her arm from Brodea's grasp and bowed her head, "Yes, Mother. You are right, forgive me."

The Voïre looked at her, Brodea wasn't quick enough to look away and felt the shock of her controlling magic only for a second before the Voïre also bowed her head. "Yes, First Councilor."

Finally! Brodea turned away from the squabbling duo and walked back to take her seat. "You are right, Voïre. I have excluded you. Mostly to protect you. That will end today."

Again Whisper's eyes went wild. "You can't be serious? She marked him!"

Brodea stared coldly at her daughter, "And now we have him. The very wizard our Voïre dui Ceremeia marked. Ironic, is it not?"

Whisper cocked her head to the side, confused.

Brodea looked between the two of them, back towards Ashyn. "It is time we changed the rules of how this game works. The dui Nuchada is admirably resistant to pain; perhaps we need to approach this differently."

The Voïre folded her arms. "I'm listening."

Brodea nodded. "Good. It's about damn time."

~ ~ ~

Four hours later, Ashyn was awake, and Brodea went to work once more. Using the punctures under his shoulder blades, Brodea had him mounted to the ceiling using long hooks.

"You must be absolutely still," she told him, "for a single movement, a single shudder will permanently damage you. If you are lucky it, will only cripple you. If you are not so lucky, well," she paused, "continuous drooling might be the least of your concerns."

Ashyn whimpered in pain as he hung from the bone. Brodea smiled as he grit his teeth and looked at her menacingly. Such defiance!

Brodea unfurled the whip, and watched as his grey eyes went wide. Yes, he feared this object. It was a powerful weapon against the wizard, perhaps her greatest for the time being. Brodea knew that the moment she broke him it would be a great day for her people. It would be the beginning of the end for wizards.

There was a slight rustle behind her, Brodea turned agitated. Unless it was Whísper, she instructed Vooken to make sure that they remain undisturbed. It wasn't Whísper.

Before her stood the Wild Elf who was responsible for all of this. The one she desired to laud as a hero to her people, and yet he turned down the accolades. Humble, as he was trained to be. Just like her. Humble before the Council of Elm, before the druids, and before the Spirits themselves. And yet now here he was, in the council chambers, uninvited and unannounced. The idea of it brought anger flaring to the tips of her ears, yet she pushed it down. He at least earned a little leeway. Only this once.

"Hunter Jenhiro," she addressed him as if his interruption meant nothing at all to her, "how can your First Councilor be of assistance?"

She watched curious as his eyes drifted from her to the wizard hanging upon the ceiling like a rack of meat. He stood there for a while, just staring. He muttered quietly after many moments, "Dui Nuchada."

Brodea nodded. "A terrible beast disguised in the flesh of a man. You have done us a great honor in capturing this monster. You have protected Feydras' Anula and countless Ferhym."

His eyes did not break away from the wizard, and instead he bowed once to Brodea without ever making eye contact. "Forgive my intrusion, First Councilor. It was rude of me to come without first seeking an audience," he said clearly, before turning and walking back down the stairs.

Brodea watched him go. She was confused as to what it was about. Then she remembered. He lost his entire branch in the woods. All dead to a creature that could wield magic like a druid. He defeated some large animal and the dui Nuchada. The wounds of loss were still fresh.

She knew intimately what such loss felt like. He was here because he was confused now. He wanted vindication. He wanted to wash the blood of his kin from his fingers because he felt guilty. He wanted vengeance against those who took them away.

And why shouldn't he? She had been in that very same position nineteen winters before and Tehirs had tied her hands.

Jenhiro felt bound by the rules, like a weight weighing heavily on his conscience. Her anger at him deflated. She knew exactly what he was going through. When Whísper took over later, she would track down the hunter and speak with him. Privately Ferhym to Ferhym, and not as his First Councilor. He believed in the cause. Jenhiro was one of the Ferhym that she knew she needed to keep. He was a survivor.

Brodea nodded to herself. That is exactly what she would do. But first, she needed to weaken the wizard. She cracked the whip across the floor, and smiled as the tears streamed from the boy.

GROWTH

Jenhiro moved down the stairs briskly, almost bordering on recklessly, as he strived to get away from the council chambers. Sweat soaked his hair and body, but it wasn't from exertion. It was from nervousness. He snuck past a Councilor and approached the Council of Elm uninvited. That in itself was worthy of remedial punishment. But he took it even further and confronted the First Councilor.

He needed to know that the dui Nuchada was still alive. He still had questions that the wizard needed to answer. Jenhiro took a great risk in what he just did, but he had to.

In the few weeks since he brought the dui Nuchada to Feydras'Anula, it ate at him more and more. Had he done the right thing? Perhaps it would have been better if he let the boy die.

The sight he saw just moments ago certainly made him feel that way. What was happening to him was barbaric. It was not his place to decide how to balance skewers, but he knew wrong when he saw it. And that was wrong.

Jenhiro reached about twenty feet from the bottom of the stairs and moved towards the edge of Water Pens and leapt off. Councilor Vooken was at the bottom of those stairs. He didn't need to be caught now, though he was sure the First Councilor would say something.

Jenhiro moved away from where the worst of the skewers were kept. The Water Pens was a place of punishment that said that these skewers were closer to death than reclamation.

He didn't approach them, but found a rocky outcropping a few feet away and sat upon it, just staring into the pens. Staring at the pathetic things that were hanging onto their lives by a thin sliver. Be it of hope, faith, or hate.

Jenhiro sat there for hours, just looking into to a different world. Watching those forlorn and destitute spirits meek out their paltry existence as animals. He put them there. None of these poor bastards, but in the past he had put an occasional skewer in those pens. Living out the last of their wretched days as the very beasts the Ferhym claimed them to be.

Never in Jenhiro's life did he think of anything but the wellbeing of his people. Even when he was using the dui Nuchada as bait to the bull, his people came first. As a child he often heckled the skewers within the Water Pens. Threw sticks at them, and laughed when they grew starved and desperate enough to turn on one another.

That thought turned his stomach now. He was older, and he was looking at things through different eyes. His people still meant the world to him, but he was also so very jaded.

Jenhiro's branch was dead. Slaughtered because he had clung to a code and claimed the bull-men monsters. He made them monsters. Now his people paid the ultimate price for it.

What was happening to him? He felt so weak. Having his life saved by the dui Nuchada left him confused. He used to serve the druids without question. Protected his kin. A protection made possible by keeping skewers out; not torturing them, enslaving them, or killing them. His life was about preserving balance.

Looking at the skeletal figures shambling across the slick broken rocks within the pens, he couldn't call that balance. He didn't even know what crimes they had committed to warrant such a fate.

A beautiful voice sang sorrowfully next to him, "Hard to look at them, isn't it?"

Jenhiro looked up into quicksilver eyes. He quickly looked away. "My Voïre dui Ceremeia," he said standing up. He nodded politely. "You honor me with your presence."

Jenhiro saw as her chin turned back out to the pens. "Do you think they deserve this?"

Staring at the ground he immediately offered, "The Spirits demand it be so." Jenhiro was alarmed at how easily it rolled from his tongue. How second nature it seemed, even though his heart was now questioning such a thing.

The Voïre dui Ceremeia nodded. "So the Council of Elm teaches us, yes. But I am not talking to a Councilor; I am talking to a branch commander for the druids, am I not?"

Jenhiro was nervous, which was not in his nature. In fact, ever since he came back to Feydras' Anula, so much was not in his nature.

Where was this going? Was the Voïre here because he snuck into the council chambers? Did Brodea send her? The Wild Elf knew that just looking into the eyes of the Voïre was opening his spirit to them. That they could read his feelings, thoughts, and emotions like he wrote them out on a scroll. Had that glance he had given her, already told her all she needed to know? He felt suddenly transparent.

"I was the one who tried to speak with you, a few weeks past at the Druid Cove, but you were seemingly preoccupied." If she could read his conflicted emotions, she betrayed none of it.

Jenhiro suddenly remembered her outside the squat building. "Yes, I am sorry. I very was distracted."

She sat down on the craggy rock next to where he had been sitting, folding her green dress beneath her legs. "It is okay. I no longer have questions about that topic anymore. I know the First Councilor has the dui Nuchada. There is little I could ask you, that I couldn't get from her now."

"Oh."

"I come here often," she told him, suddenly changing the subject.

Jenhiro found himself curious. "Why?"

"To question if we are doing the right thing."

Still extremely wary, Jenhiro felt compelled to hear more. He lowered himself down next to her. "So you come to the Water Pens?"

The Voïre nodded. "Look at them," she paused briefly,"I mean really look at them, and tell me what you see."

Jenhiro did as he was bade, and he looked at the creatures in the pen for a long time. Moving along, suffering, a haunted hollow look in most of their eyes. An empty life. Many of their clothes were torn and filthy. Their heads all shaved to keep the rampant lice problem down to minimum. "I see broken creatures."

"Who?" she asked.

Jenhiro nodded to the pen. "Them."

"So you identify that if 'they' are broken 'they' must have feelings, by the way 'they' suffer?"

"I guess."

"So if they are capable of emotions, then what else are they capable of?"

Jenhiro shrugged, "Anything."

"Precisely," she answered back. "Emotions have a wide range, and many things have them, including animals. One thing though separates those from the pens, with the common creature."

She had his attention now. "What's that?"

The Voïre answered in a low tone, "Choice. Everyone in that cage is capable of making a choice."

Jenhiro looked at her, but didn't object. A silence built between them and he was hoping she would continue, but she didn't. Her swirling platinum eyes merely stared out into the pens where the people lingered.

People.

She looked to him, and he quickly looked away. She told him, reading him in that single moment, "Now you understand the nature of free will." The Voïre patted his knee, and stood up. With those final parting words, the Voïre walked away.

Jenhiro let out a breath. He did understand. They were people, not monsters, but people. Living, breathing, people with loved ones, families, hopes, desires and dreams. People that his kind didn't understand and they labeled skewers out of fear and ignorance. Jenhiro indeed was beginning to understand. His very world was unraveling at its seams. Everything he had come to understand as truth was now revealing a different side to it. The reality of it all left him stunted.

He valued the life of his people. Whose lives past theirs did they value? Clearly not the men and women in the pens before him. He just didn't know what the hells someone like him could do about it? The Wild Elf found his eyes climbing the length of the great Elm to the council chambers above.

~ ~ ~

Days passed, and as they did, Jenhiro found himself going to that same rock again and again, hoping to see the Voïre dui Ceremeia, hoping to ask her questions. He wanted to know more. He was beginning to question himself. He was beginning to question the cause.

He also wanted to know about her. Twice she entered his life, and both times she mentioned the dui Nuchada. It was curious.

He had the impression, talking to her for those few moments, that she was very lonely. His people put the Voïre dui Ceremeia on pedestals, never to look at, never to talk to, never to touch. He wondered what it would be like, not to have any connections?

He found it a surprising and welcome distraction from thinking about his fallen comrades. It pushed his guilt over surviving into the back of his mind. It gave him focus. He wanted to learn more about her.

Jenhiro overheard that the First Councilor went to his home on the night he stayed by the pens. She was looking for him. He feared to know why. He had the feeling it wasn't a social call. He took a risk, visiting the dui Nuchada, and he now placed himself in her line of sight. Jenhiro was well versed in making himself a target, and when knowing not to.

So he hid from her. It wasn't elaborate in anyway. He hid in plain sight, and she, being far too busy, was none the wiser. If Jenhiro learned anything at all from the dui Nuchada, it was that the easiest place to hide was right under the adversary's nose. Brodea wasn't a stupid hym; she just had other matters to deal with. He was low on her priority list.

So he spent his days, watching and learning, looking for the Voïre, and hunting for Julietta. She was an enigma, this Julietta, a conundrum. The more he thought about it, the more it rankled him. Jenhiro found nothing about her. It wasn't as if he hadn't tried either. He went to every pen that the Skewers were locked in, and not a single one fit her description. He questioned other hunters. It shamed him to know that they didn't take the time to really look at the Skewers. They were nothing more than evil beasts in the eyes of his brethren. It was the same for him until recently.

Jenhiro was coming to the unwelcome realization that she was either well hidden somewhere where no one wanted her found, she was not in Feydras' Anula at all, or worse, she was already dead.

If she wasn't dead, then who was Julietta? What made her special enough that she wasn't locked away with the other skewers? Was she dangerous? Was she another dui Nuchada? Or was she even worse?

After Jenhiro gave up questioning hunters. He moved to the guardsmen of the pens. They too didn't remember seeing any women who fit that description in the recent insurgence of skewers they had.

It wasn't until he was all but ready to lose hope that he decided to ask the Earthshorn. The farmers and gatherers of Feydras' Anula. The lowest caste within the Ferhym peoples. It felt almost below him to even talk with them, but he made a promise, and he vowed to see that promise through.

It was with those field hands that he received his first real lead. A red-headed, blind girl had worked for over a decade de-husking vegetables, and cleaning the livestock. She had a rare talent for it and did this for many winters. She was occasionally visited by the Voïre dui Ceremeia, but little interaction was ever made.

After seeing the Voïre at the Water Pens, that didn't surprise Jenhiro. If the hym watched those people, then her watching a blind skewer in the fields didn't seem far of a stretch. He learned that a few months ago, Whísper Windsong suddenly and unceremoniously pulled the blind skewer to the vanguard that led the attack on Czynsk. She hadn't been seen since.

When Jenhiro asked why they didn't know her name was Julietta, he received an odd look from the field hand. "One does not associate with skewers. Just as much as one does not name the wheat that we plow."

"But you name your animals?" Jenhiro interjected.

The look from the Earthshorn seared into his mind; it was as contorted and abhorrent as Jenhiro had ever seen. It was as if Jenhiro told the Ferhym he had been born from a sow. His words were equally cruel. "Animals are the balance of nature. They are innocent and pure. Gifts from the Spirits. They've earned the right to names. Skewers are their disease. Evil, corrupt, and foul. Skewers only earn condemnation, and at most the promise of a quick death to release their corruption upon this world."

"Not reclamation?" He pushed.

"Reclamation is reserved for only the deserving. If the blind girl was so deserving she would have received it long ago. She must have been far from that."

Such strange news sat with Jenhiro over the next few days. How could an Earthshorn, the lowest member of their society, not believe in reclamation? In advancement in station? What about the blind girl could seem so alien to them that she was beyond salvation? Odder still, why was she pulled to Whísper's vanguard against the humans of Czynsk? He knew that his only hope of learning about Julietta and her fate were now with the very people that were torturing the dui Nuchada. Very few survived Whisper's failed vanguard and those that truly knew the most were Whisper and Eigron. And, of course, Brodea.

Jenhiro watched the traffic coming and going from the council chambers after that. The first two days it was apparent to him the Councilor Vooken was Brodea's proxy. She routinely called on both him and her daughter, Whisper, to work on the dui Nuchada. So Jenhiro stalked each one, and learned everything he could about them. It was weird at first, targeting his own people. Yet he quickly adapted.

Whisper mated to Suneris. It was immediately evident that not all was well at home. Whisper rarely spent time there or time with him. Over the days Jenhiro learned that Whisper really wanted nothing to do with Suneris. She only performed what was necessary, when it was necessary, in an effort to propagate their species. There was never any intimacy between them. It was a job, a chore, and nothing more. The only time he saw her happy was when she was going back to the council to torture the dui Nuchada.

Vooken was a very different matter. He seemed indifferent to the torture. He was only going through the paces because of the end result. He was a motivated and patient hym. He was a forward-thinker. That made him someone to watch for. Vooken was looking for something, waiting for something. Something that only the dui Nuchada would be able to give him.

That meant the boy was still alive. Part of Jenhiro was relieved that he endured for so long, but part of Jenhiro wished the boy would just give in and end his misery. Deep down Jenhiro knew that Brodea wouldn't let the dui Nuchada die. And it was likely the dui Nuchada wouldn't give up either. He wouldn't give up until he knew Julietta was safe. Just like when they were hunted, the dui Nuchada would not relent until he was sure of his goal. For that, he needed Jenhiro's help.

Eighteen days Jenhiro continued to do this without fail. It was always the same. Whisper up, Whisper down. Vooken up, Vooken down. The hunter was ready to move on Whisper when he spotted someone else climbing up the steps of the great Elm. Eigron, Genrus of the Druids of the Vine.

The Wild Elf hunter hadn't seen the young druid since their first encounter. It left a sour taste in his mouth, and he wondered if he purposely ignored the Ferhym because of it.

No. Though he did study the druid with great interest. The young hym climbed the steps with a sure gait. This was not an elf who followed anymore, but an elf who led. He held a sense of dominance in his posture. In fact, as Eigron approached the top, Jenhiro could see him interacting with Councilor Vooken. He spoke to the senior Ferhym as an equal. Druids, though higher than Hunters, were still beneath Councilors in the caste system. Eigron's blatant disregard for this system angered Jenhiro. It was obvious that there were many changes under First Councilor Brodea's reign.

If Eigron was no longer a Genrus of the Vines, then what was he? The Hunter waited for the druid to come down from the council chamber, and as he had with Whísper and Vooken, he tailed Eigron.

The druid was definitely not taking an established route as he met with two other Ferhym. Though Jenhiro didn't recognize the elves, he could tell by the way they respected and addressed Eigron, that they were hunters for the druids. A separate branch, perhaps Eigron's own? The trio then walked through the field hand slave pen areas examining each person.

This made Jenhiro curious. Who was Eigron looking for? Why did it make a difference? Had the dui Nuchada finally cracked? Was Eigron trying to find Julietta? The Earthshorn said she worked the fields for many winters.

Jenhiro quickened his pace at that final thought. Though he was unable to find the woman, Eigron might know where she was.

He watched, outside of the pens, always keeping an eye on the druid. After over an hour of searching, Eigron reached out and grabbed a human woman.

The branch commander nearly froze at that. If Eigron was looking for Julietta, Jenhiro was too late. The druid spun the woman around to look at her, and Jenhiro knew immediately that she wasn't Julietta. Her hair wasn't red, but a brownish-blonde, like the color of wheat. Her complexion didn't match the wizard's description. Most telling was that she was not blind. Jenhiro almost let out a sigh of relief, until he saw what the hunters did next.

They pulled a sack over her head and she screamed in protest. The elf watched appalled as they beat her mercilessly. She cried and screamed and the druid and his two cronies continued to beat her with their feet and the butts of spears. She stopped trying to block the rain of blows falling upon her, and tumbled to the ground. The horror didn't end there. The trio began ripping at her clothing next, pulling it away from her body, exposing her crème-colored flesh.

Nudity meant nothing to Wild Elves, but Jenhiro knew that it meant much more to humans. With the little strength she had remaining, she fought to cover her exposed flesh. The assailers whittled away at her again with more blows.

Soon her curled form slackened, and her hands fell from her body. The trio grabbed and pinched, twisting her flesh, leaving tracks of vicious red welts. The other skewers cowered away from the three elves as the guards waved their weapons in front of them to keep them at bay. They laughed at what they were doing to her. Laughed!

A red swell of anger filled Jenhiro's belly. The Ferhym threw her over so that her bare bottom was facing up at them. One of the guards moved his loincloth away, and Jenhiro could see what was going to happen next. Rage at the acts of his own people nearly blinded him in a senseless fury for justice. This was not balance! This is not what they were taught! What he was taught. She may be a skewer, but redemption was about seeking forgiveness from nature for their affronts to it, learning through serving the land. This action was pure malice. There was nothing balancing with what he was going to do to her. It was deplorable.

He rose to stop it. Stop them. They were acting as skewers now. It was his duty to set things right. He felt a soft hand come down on his shoulder.

Quickly, he looked up. It was the Voïre dui Ceremeia. Her mercury eyes looked terribly sad. He stared into them, unable to look away, violating everything he ever learned about respecting the Voïre. She didn't care.

Jenhiro shook his shoulder and pulled away from her. He was going to go and help the human woman who was being violated in every terrible way.

Slowly the Voïre shook her head no, and brought a single finger to her lips. She bent down next to him and whispered in his ear, "It is not yet time. That will only get you killed."

He looked to her in puzzled shock. How could she approve of this! But accepting what he saw in her eyes, he read her as she could read him: she didn't approve. What their people were doing to the woman destroyed her on the inside just as much as it destroyed him. He understood. They were in this together now. And they both watched in horror, absorbing every terrible moment so that they would always remember. Remember what it was that they were going to fight for next.

Jenhiro knew at that moment, with no words between them, that it was her. She was what his true people represented. That the Voïre was everything he defended and everything he believed in. Not the druids, not the Council of Elm, and absolutely not the three Ferhym in the pens committing the atrocity. Those were hym no longer. They were skewers. And just as he was trained, he was going to balance them as their hunter.

CONTROL

Ashyn hung limply from the ceiling, his hands tied to stirrups. His arms extended so far that the pulling pain engulfed everything in him.

His consciousness came in flickers now. When it did, it was nothing but bursts of pain, and a litany of questions he refused to answer. Brodea kept him teetering on the edge of life, but never took away the pain. She didn't want him to die of an infection or to bleed out. She needed him after all. And that's what kept him going.

He had no idea what day it was anymore. Had it been a week? A month? An entire winter? Thoughts of Julietta circled in his head. They kept him strong. She endured this and stayed alive. He could do the same. He would do it for her.

There was a commotion at the stairs. It was laughing. One of the druids approached. One he saw before, Eigron, Brodea called him. There were more with him.

He raised his head wearily to see what they had in store for him now. It wasn't as if he cared. They already hurt him in almost every conceivable way.

The voice that he had come to despise crooned, "You're awake. Good." Ashyn looked over at Brodea with abhorrence. Her hideously scarred daughter was with her. Ashyn said nothing to either of them. He didn't want to waste what little energy he had.

Brodea continued, "I hoped not to have to resort to this. I hoped you would have proven smarter and realized that helping us was helping those you care for. You have proven to be most resistant to learning however. For that, wizard, you have brought this upon yourself." Whísper's wicked smile towards him made his stomach turn.

They drug a woman in, her clothing torn almost completely away. They dropped her battered, mostly nude form on the floor, a sack pulled over her head. Welts lined her emaciated body as well as garish bruises in their infancy.

Ashyn the felt his stomach drop completely. "No."

They ripped the bag from the woman's head. It was Avrimae. As she lay there, he could see blood oozing from dozens of cuts. Worse, she was bleeding from between her legs. A fleeting glance at Brodea showed a flicker of surprise and horror as well. Was there humanity within the elf? Then the cold expression returned on her face, and Ashyn knew the answer.

Whísper reached down and lifted Avrimae's head up for him to see. Her face, swollen and splotched with broken blood vessels.

"Noooooo!" Ashyn roared as he struggled against the binds. His arms popped and agony ripped through him.

Whísper smiled at his reaction and let go. Avrimae's head thumped against the hard floor.

He vaguely heard Brodea tell the druid in a clipped tongue, "Eigron, a word." To her daughter she added, "You are in charge of this, Whísper. Do what needs to be done."

He watched the scarred elf nod. She looked at the two that came with Eigron, "String him up so he can watch." Ashyn didn't know what Whísper was talking about. He was already tied up.

Then another figure was drug in to Ashyn's field of view by two more elves. He was tall and skinny with a pale complexion. His trousers hung limply from his narrow frame and he had no shirt. Dirt and mud clung to him. He, too, had a sack pulled over his head.

They strung the man up across from Ashyn, hanging much as he was. Between them both laying on the ground was Avrimae.

When they secured the man, Whísper walked up to the man and grabbed a handful of the sack. "Remember dui Nuchada, you could have stopped this." She smiled and added, "But I'm glad you didn't." The huntress pulled the bag away.

The man's face was pock marked. He bore the scars of bad acne in his teenage winters. He had a pointy nose, but it was crooked, likely from multiple breaks. His head was completely shaven, but it was a rough job. Multiple scabbed over lacerations dotted his head between fresh growing brown stubble. Doe brown eyes looked wildly in all directions. Those eyes locked onto the beaten form at his feet.

"Avrimae!" he wailed and started pulling violently against his bindings. "Avrimae!"

Ashyn stared in shock. He knew those eyes. He knew that voice. It was Macky.

Macky ripped and pulled at his bindings in a frenzy. "What have you done?" He roared at the elves. "What in the Maker's name have you done to my Avrimae!"

Ashyn looked on at Macky with pity. He knew it was only the beginning for them. Macky had no idea what was yet in store.

Ashyn pleaded, "Let them go."

The wizard saw Macky's eyes follow the sound of his voice. He shared eye contact with the man, and saw his mouth shape Ashyn's name in confusion.

His voice came out stronger in the Ferhym language, "I said let them go."

Whisper walked around from behind Macky, taunting Ashyn. "And why should I do that?"

"Because it is I who is the skewer, not these people."

The Wild Elf laughed. It wasn't cruel or condescending; it was an actual genuine laugh. The honesty of it threw Ashyn off momentarily.

"These collaborators were picked up long before I even figured out you were still alive. They are very much skewers, Ashyn Rune. Especially this one," she said pointing to Macky. A quick glance and Ashyn could tell Macky had no idea what they were talking about.

"He continuously preaches about a heretical false idol, even while being relegated to the Water Pens. He stood firmly beside the wizards when I asked him to contact you, and on more than one occasion has tried to stir uprisings amongst the Reclamation groups. I think he is long overdue for this."

Eigron's crony walked over to Whisper and handed her the whip that Ashyn had come to hate so much in her hands. She cracked it once behind Macky, gathering a sharp piercing sound that echoed in the hollowed out chamber. "I could be persuaded though. If you give me something I can give my mother." She offered, "Read to me the third page."

Ashyn shook his head, "No."

Whisper looked at him with a mock expression of sadness, "A shame." The Wild Elf then walked up to Macky and whispered in his ear. It was loud enough that Ashyn could hear every word. "Your friend, the wizard, can make this stop. He has the means to do so. Remember that. All he has to do is give me what I want." She said it to him in Trade Tongue and despite from her accent; he was able to decipher every word clearly.

Ashyn stared at her menacingly. He looked over to Macky, whispering, "Be strong."

"Yes, be strong Father Mactonal," she told him condescendingly. "Be very strong for your *friend*." She spit the last word from her mouth as if it was something repulsive. She pushed his head away from her roughly, still reeling from the word as if it were like acid burning her tongue.

"You did this for me," Macky said, as he looked Ashyn in his eyes, "I will do this for you."

Ashyn nodded his face stern.

Whisper laughed at the both of them. "Oh no, Father Mactonal. Not you."

Macky stared at Whisper confused. She then looked over to the two cronies. "String her up for me."

Ashyn paled, "What are you doing?"

Whisper ignored him as she paced around to the lip of the opening that looked out onto Feydras' Anula. She turned her back to them as she studied her city.

"I said, 'What are you doing?'" Ashyn demanded.

Whisper didn't even turn to face him when she spoke. "The only thing I will hear from you now, skewer, is 'Yes,' or 'I will.' That is all." Her voice was hollow and cold, so much like Brodea. "The time for games is over."

Avrimae moaned as they hung her from the ceiling. They pulled the remaining clothes from her body. Panic grabbed at his chest.

"You've made your point, huntress. But it is me that deserves this. Me that deserves the torture."

"I am torturing you."

The whip lashed out racing a long red line across Avrimae's right breast over her collarbone and against her back. The slash immediately ripped her from unconsciousness. Her eyes grew wide in horror and her face contorted. She shrieked in pain.

"Stop it!" Ashyn yelled simultaneously with Macky. Macky looked at him in horror, and Ashyn realized that those words were directed towards him, not Whisper.

The whip flew forward again biting into her. Blood trickled from her wounds.

"She cuts so easily," Whisper remarked. "She has nowhere near the endurance that you do, Blood Wizard." Again the whip reached out etching a line from the bottom of her neck to the top of her right buttock. Avrimae wailed, crystalline rivers pouring from her eyes. She had no time for words, only agony. Macky ripped at his bindings, tears also flooding from his eyes.

"You should know, Father Mactonal, that I have to keep Ashyn alive. My mother needs him after all, and he knows this. But Avrimae? Well that is up to him, or the Spirits. We shall see who claims her first."

Macky fixed Ashyn with a look of terror so pure that it broke Ashyn's heart. "Tell her." He spat. "Tell her what she wants."

Ashyn's vision became blurry as he felt water build up in them. "I can't."

"Yes, tell me." Whisper cajoled. The whip ripped a new line across Avrimae's belly. "Did you know she is a mother? Mother told me. Before you came. Avrimae was about to be reclaimed, but you put a stop to that by refusing to read the tome. That was why they brought her to you that first day. A warning. Yet you are so prideful, wizard. So strong. What's happening is your fault. Right now her child is wondering where her mother is. Wondering if she will ever see her again. Ever be held by her, loved by her. You can make that happen. You can put an end to all of this by reading one," she lashed Avrimae, "single," another lash, "page," she said, punctuating the statement with a third one that sent the woman into convulsions.

Ashyn stared through leaking eyes at the deep red gouges in her flesh. She had cleaned his wounds after his punishment. This was a woman who cared for him time and again, who held him when he cried. She helped bring him back from the brink of death and this is how he was repaying her?

"Fuckin' tell her!" Macky roared at Ashyn. A level of terror and hate filling his words so fully that it shook Ashyn to the core of his being.

"I can't!" Ashyn yelled. "I can't!"

Macky ripped at his bindings. "Where is the Ashyn that I once knew? Where is that boy who took a lashing for me because he didn't want to see his friend in pain? Did becoming a wizard change that in you?"

Ashyn shook his head, "You don't know what it is you are asking me to do, Macky. What it is that they are after."

"Is it worth Avrimae? Is this stupid thing worth her life?" He cried.

He heard the snap once more, and Avrimae arched so bad he was afraid her spine would break. Blood was running down her back in sheets now. Between the previous beatings, starvation, and rape he didn't think she had enough left in her to keep going. He was going to commit his friend to death for a few words on a piece of parchment!

Not words, Ashyn reminded himself. Power. A power that he couldn't let the Ferhym wield.

"I am sorry," he cried. "I am so sorry."

"Fuck you then, wizard," Macky hissed. "The boy I knew loved me, and he loved Avrimae. You are nothing now. Nothing but a sinner and a murderer in the Maker's eyes. You will rot in the hells for this! The Ashyn Rune I know is dead."

Macky's words wrenched at his heart. They devastated him. He *was* a murderer. A killer. A taker of lives. Her blood was on his hands.

Ashyn's eyes went wide in understanding. What was it that she said to him while he held the branch commander, bleeding her life away in his arms?

My Whisper. She will have you.

He looked at the burned elf with a sudden understanding of the female's hate. The branch commander, she had been Whisper's lover. The elf he killed with his knife was the same one Whisper called Shedalia. That was why Brodea used her. That was why Whisper was so passionate about his pain. She would do anything to hurt him. Anything to cause him grief. She wanted to kill him more than anything. More than anyone. Because he already caused that pain to her, tenfold.

He needed to use that. Use her pain. She was a coiled viper ready to strike. The only way to do that was to give her some bait. It would save Avrimae. It had to.

If not, Whisper would kill her. And even with her death they would still use Macky against him. Build a hate in the man so powerful that Macky might try to kill Ashyn himself. The wizard didn't know if his heart could take that. He could take pain though. He had been doing it for a long time now. Besides, Whísper admitted it herself. Brodea needed him alive.

It was time to dangle the mouse.

"I hate you!" Ashyn yelled at Whísper, summoning what little energy he had left to put it into words, "And I will kill you!" He growled, "Just like I killed your beloved Shedalia."

Whísper's eyes widened in disbelief.

"She begged you know."

Whísper dropped the whip.

Ashyn almost wanted to sigh in relief. It was buying Avrimae a much needed reprieve. Whísper stormed over to Ashyn and before he could ready himself, she struck him fully in the mouth.

Once.

Twice.

Three times.

Pain detonated through his skull like an exploding star. His vision blurred, and he felt his nose crunch. Blood filled his mouth from his torn lips. He spit it on the floor and looked at her. Her whole body quaked in anger and unbridled rage. "I am going to bleed your girlfriend dry, and let you watch as she fades into nothing more than a memory. Just like you did to me."

Whísper turned to hurt the nude woman once more. She was close to the precipice. Ashyn had to keep her there, for Avrimae's sake. That meant more pain. A lot more pain. "She called out for you in the end," he said to her back. "It's your fault that she died scared and alone. It should have been you!"

Whísper wheeled on him. She reached up and grabbed his face roughly, her nails digging pits into his cheeks. The Wild Elf yanked his head so that he looked down at her. His blood ran freely from his mouth and nose down her hand and onto her forearm. It slickened her copper flesh in a blanket of red. He whispered, "You know it, don't you? That it should've been you."

Her eyes were murder. This was what Ashyn needed. He had her. Whísper was so focused on him, that it kept her away from Avrimae and Macky. If she beat him into unconsciousness she would have no need to keep hurting Avrimae. It didn't gain the elves anything hurting the woman while Ashyn wasn't awake to suffer for it.

She drew the broken spear that Shedalia tried to take his head with from the frog that held it across her back. "I...will...kill...you..." she huffed, flinging spittle in his face with every word.

"You can try."

With a single slash, she cut a thin line across his chest. He grunted at the impact, but was long past feeling pain on shallow cuts.

Whísper lifted the spear tip in front of his eyes. Ashyn could see the red of his blood through his blurry vision. She licked the spear tip, and then spit the blood upon the ground.

"Your words are poison," she hissed. "It is time I cleanse this world of your putrescence."

In a quick, deft motion she cut his bindings off the wall. He tumbled to the floor striking his knees roughly against the hard wood and then rolled onto his side.

Ashyn curled up in the fetal position, but he didn't have a moment's respite. Suddenly she was at the rope pulling him across the floor by his arms. Ashyn groaned as he was strung out and drug across the polished surface like dead game. He had no strength to stop her.

As she reached her destination, she hefted him up, and Ashyn was alarmed at her immense strength. She held him by the rope and the hair, and he was staring out into- emptiness.

He was at the edge of the chamber looking out at the sequoias beyond. Ashyn's heart hammered in his chest. He wasn't fond of heights.

"It is said that the dui Nuchada possess the spirits of dragons," she said to him in a bitter laugh. "Does that mean that they can fly?"

Whísper spun him around so he could look into her dark eyes one last time. "My mother will find another wizard," she told him. She let go of the rope and held him up only by his hair. She leaned against him so that the ridged flesh of her burned cheek rubbed the side of his bloody jaw. She whispered in his ear, "Scream for me, boy."

Ashyn gasped as lightning tore through his body. A pain so electric that it coursed to every nerve ending he had. He looked down in wide-eyed disbelief. Lodged in his abdomen was the broken spear.

The wizard was only vaguely aware that Whísper let go of his hair, and he tumbled backwards. His surprised eyes locked with Macky's for a single instant, and then he was falling. There was no floor beneath his feet. In fact, there was nothing at all. Ashyn pitched off the side, and he saw the ground then. It was a long way off and rushing towards him fast.

Ashyn Rune obliged Whisper as the reality of his situation finally hit him. He screamed.

He screamed the whole way down.

~ ~ ~

Brodea returned up the stairs just in time to watch an enraged Whisper drive the spear into the wizard's guts. The First Councilor broke into a run, scrambling to make it to the wizard in time. Whisper let go of his hair and let him fall away. Brodea screamed as she reached out for the plummeting boy but she was too late. He toppled over, and tumbled down below, screaming the whole way.

Brodea straightened and looked to her fury driven daughter. "What have you done?"

Whisper didn't give her satisfaction of an answer. Instead, her dark eyes flashed with the contentment of cold-blooded murder. "Find yourself another scribe," she said icily, "I have a head to claim."

Whisper then plowed past the First Councilor and proceeded to walk down the stairs. Brodea was in a state of shock. What could she do? What would she tell the council?

She tried to listen for anything from the Spirits. Any guidance at all, but there was nothing. Her thoughts were hers and hers alone. And they were dark.

SOURCE

Xexial grunted in dissatisfaction as he closed another tome. Slowly he massaged the exhaustion from his sore eyes.

After a moment, he blinked away the throb and looked at the table before him. Stacks of tomes lined the tabletop like tall buildings in a thriving town. Little alleys wove between the towers with the occasional crumpled papers, hopeless notes scrawled on each.

Two empty ink jars sat by his left elbow, and a quill sat just to the right of more parchment, above his most recently finished tome.

He picked up the tome and added it to one of the ever growing towers. It was becoming a fruitless endeavor. Xexial reviewed countless tomes in both his old mentor's throne room and now in the great circular library. He researched no less than three hundred manuscripts all with no solid leads on what Ashyn was. Did he imagine it? He was on the brink of death, could it just have been luck that kept him alive or someone else? Was this all for nothing?

Xexial looked between the forest of leather and parchment to his stalwart aide. Khyriaxx was fastidiously documenting everything of potential relevance, even what seemed to be the minutest. Xexial knew it was because the spriggan classified himself as a tinkerer, so every equation, every computation was important to him. They had worked at it for weeks.

After the hurricane cleared, the Maba-Heth was eager to hunt for Ashyn. That left Xexial in a predicament, for he had no way of researching everything in the Onyx Tower in time without help. The elder wizard didn't trust Grind. Not one bit. Additionally, he didn't want the wizard hunter to know that his future opponent might not be entirely normal. That would only condemn the boy all the quicker.

If Ashyn could challenge the title Recreant, then he wanted to give him that chance. Xexial knew Ashyn's reasons, and his reaction wasn't that surprising. It was why the wizards were supposed to choose people who had nothing left to live for. It was the very reason, in fact.

Ashyn simply chose family first.

If he could present a strong case, then there was a minute chance to rescind the declaration of Recreant. That is what made Khyriaxx a perfect candidate to help Xexial. He already proved himself trustworthy in keeping Xexial alive for over a month. Not to mention how resourceful and analytical the little creature was. Khyriaxx was always studying variables, and when Xexial approached the spriggan with the fact that Ashyn may be something other than human, or may have discovered an ability to harness magic in a new way, the problem-solver leapt at the chance to delve into something new.

Immediately, the spriggan interrogated Xexial on everything he knew about Ashyn. Once they completed that, he began systematically tearing apart the throne room for tomes of relevance, using any mentions of history, or races before the Era of Enlightenment.

To classify Ashyn as something that they hadn't seen before wasn't out of the realm of possibility. So much history was lost to the wars of the Forgotten Era. So much lost of people, races, cultures, even magic. For all Xexial knew, what Ashyn did to him might have been commonplace five thousand winters ago.

The real trial was keeping it secret from Grind. The scales was very wary of the two of them, and did not trust Xexial. The wizard knew it was a well-earned distrust. He was slowing progress on hunting his apprentice considerably.

Still, their hunt did begin. He couldn't delay it forever. Xexial convinced Grind that they should begin tracing Ashyn's steps. First was Czynsk. Though this was contrary to the fact that Xexial knew Ashyn was in the Shalis-Fey, he still knew Ashyn went to Czynsk before stepping foot into those woods. The letters reached the Seven after all.

So when the flooding from the hurricane cleared enough for travel to be possible, the trio began. Khyriaxx carried a few tomes at a time, to study for Xexial, and the old wizard helped where he could. Most of the time he spent distracting the Maba-Heth from asking too many questions.

Czynsk turned out to be a lucky break. Two people admitted to seeing someone who fit Ashyn's description. They also confirmed that he indeed headed towards the Shalis-Fey. Xexial thought Grind would accept this. He did not.

Grind wanted to explore all their options. That meant the Dark Elf capital of Tilliatemma, the human bastion of Buckner, the deserts of Malten, and the Shalis-Fey. Grind, thought that Ashyn couldn't possibly want anything to do with the elves. That it was all misdirection. Therefore, he demanded they go to Buckner.

Xexial humored the scales, but not before re-provisioning at the Onyx Tower and gathering new tomes for the tinkerer to study.

Buckner proved to be a large waste of time in locating the recreant, but it did provide the old wizard insight into how the Maba-Heth tracked their prey. Xexial had to admit that Grind was not stupid. He was immensely skilled in fact. Were Ashyn able to wield magic, and had he not reacquired his vial of blood, Xexial had no doubt that Grind would have found his quarry long ago.

Ashyn covered his tracks well. But it at nagged Xexial like an itch. How did the boy get into the Onyx Tower?

Of course the real question he was trying to avoid was, was Ashyn still alive? He told Grind that the boy could survive ridiculous odds, and Xexial firmly believed it. But going up against the Ferhym while he was lame, to save a blind woman? That was stretching it even for Ashyn.

Again he rubbed his tired eyes. They had arrived back from Buckner two nights ago. Grind announced that the two would stay for a week or two in the tower while he reached out to his connections in Tilliatemma. He left immediately afterwards, claiming he could cover the ground far quicker alone. Xexial didn't argue with the scales, for the elder wizard knew how to make good use of his time. Khyriaxx and he immediately set themselves into tackling the large circular library. They hadn't slept since they began, and his power waned.

"You should be resting. You be worn and need recovery of your energy," Khyriaxx remarked without looking up from his books. Like he just read Xexial's mind.

"I need answers," Xexial protested.

"You will be finding none like this."

Xexial wanted to argue with the tinkerer, but knew he was right. Xexial was far from a young man, and the traveling was draining enough as it was. Let alone the aggressive reading for the last two days. Xexial nodded at the spriggan. "Just a few hours."

"Few hours," Khyriaxx agreed.

Xexial stood, stretched his sore old body, and limped to his quarters to get some much needed rest. He would only need an hour, maybe two.

The wizard looked out a passing window to see the sun high in the sky. Yes, two hours would be good.

~ ~ ~

Xexial barely felt like he had any rest when he felt himself being shaken awake, eyes slowly opening. Overly large almond-shaped eyes were staring right back at him, inches away.

"Gah!" Xexial yelled as he pulled away from what he thought was a monster.

As his eyes focused more he saw that it was the spriggan. "What are you doing?" He asked incredulously.

Khyriaxx leaned forward again, "I be waking you ups."

"You don't need to be so close."

Xexial looked out of the window of his quarters. A dense void of black greeted him. There was no light. Not a star in the sky.

"What time is it?"

Khyriaxx shrugged. "Past the midpoint of night I be guessing. I be telling you time means little to me."

"Apparently," Xexial grumbled, "I said an hour or two, you let me sleep for almost twelve."

"Who be caring," he replied with a sparkle in his eyes. "I be working the variables, and I think I be finding a part of the solution to your problem."

Xexial sat up faster. "You found something?"

Khyriaxx nodded and handed Xexial a sheaf of parchment. The old man looked down at it and stared at it in confusion.

There was only a series of lines and scratch marks across the paper.

"What is this?"

"It be the first solution to your conundrum."

Xexial turned the parchment around. "Is this a puzzle, or a map or something?"

"That be my writing!" Khyriaxx stated offended.

"This is writing?"

A small three-fingered hand ripped the parchment back from Xexial's grip, "It's Spriggish. Clearly you aren't as cultured as you thought!" he harrumphed. "I can read your messy language!" the spriggan added.

"Just tell me what it says."

The spriggan affixed his monocle to his large eye, looked down and read his notes aloud.

"The first part was found in a journal called; *Patrius Monerch, Exactor.*

4381 EoE- I have witnessed a terrible thing today, which has forced me to recant my decision to be an Exactor for the Jasian Enclave. I thought the religious nation was more civilized, but I was wrong. What they have done today is nothing short of barbarism, and it disgusts me to admit that I am part of it. Worse than part of it, I was the instrument wielded by the Enclave to commit the foul deed.

The Enclave says that it is protecting humanity from the evils that have escaped from the Forgotten Era, and if it not for my actions, I would have believed them. But nothing could prepare me for what I did today. There can be no atonement for my actions most foul, nor can I ever be rid of the taint I have placed upon my own soul. I killed a woman. A woman fully pregnant with child.

They called her a monster. They called her a witch. They said that she was a siphoner. A manipulator of feedback, a stealer of life-energy. A wielder of terrible magic without temperament or training."

Xexial looked up hearing those words. Ashyn used magic without training.

Khyriaxx nodded and continued, "*They say her kind is a plague placed by the Defiler, and only their eradication could protect the world from their treacherous ilk. And so, as commanded by my Purist Commander Amdehain, I ran her*" *through, terminating the life in her womb, and I removed her head from her shoulders.*

I have never felt so wrong in my life. I have never felt, so evil. What have I done? What did she truly do to deserve such a fate? The Purist called her Craetorian. I don't even know what that means."

Khyriaxx lowered the parchment for a moment and looked at Xexial. Xexial noted there was some pride on the spriggan's face. "There were many more entries in the journal. The man ended up abandoning his life as an Exactor after the act and even tried killing himself. He be found in Malten and taken here to the Onyx Tower to become a wizard. That be when this journal ended, and he started a new one as a wizard's apprentice. I cross-referenced all the other words that you told me of: Feedback, Conduit, Life-draining, Feeding, etc., and could find no other references. However, when I be looking for Craetorian I found something most compelling."

The spriggan held the paper up again and read a single sentence, "The Second Inquisition; The Craetorian Purges. 4365 EoE- 4390 EoE."

"The Second Inquisition," Xexial thought aloud. The old man stood up slowly muttering the word repeatedly as he walked toward his dresser. He reached atop it and drew his long-stemmed pipe. He packed it with leaf and then lit it taking a long drag. The tobacco often calmed him and helped him think.

"This other tome, not the journal, was it a novel called *The Second Inquisition*?" He asked blowing out the smoke. He was surprised that there was no substance to it, no flavor. Discouraged he emptied the contents out, and put the pipe away.

Khyriaxx shook his head no, the quills bouncing on his head like braids. "It wasn't a tome at all; it was a single sheet of parchment that was slid between two documented history tomes of Fermania. It gave the dates of the inquisition but nothing else. When I looked in the two historical tomes, there was no referencing said inquisition."

Xexial nodded. "That's not surprising." He looked at Khyriaxx. "The Jasian Enclave doesn't like to have a tarnished looking record of bad decisions. Even though it took place five hundred winters ago, this Craetorian Purge sounds like it may have been a huge travesty. That slip was probably added by the former Exactor Patrius Monerch, as a way of acknowledging to himself that the purges were real, and should be remembered."

"This be sounding like what you are looking for, yes?" Khyriaxx said with a smile.

"It does indeed," Xexial admitted. "The Jasian Enclave has a long tradition of dislike for any magic other than healing magic. I've always found it hypocritical really, considering they proclaim that the Maker bestowed us with the gift of Creation. Yet, anyone that uses said magic for anything other than healing is a bastard in their eyes. Ashyn would fit that category. He was able to manipulate fire with no training, only emotion."

"So we have a focus now. None of your silly hue-mon broad topics. We have our variable." the tinkerer said.

"You are correct, lad, we do. We finally have a name to research: Craetorian."

WEIGHT OF THE SPIRITS

Brodea sat on her high backed wooden chair staring hard at the dried blood that stained the polished wooden floor. Most of it was Ashyn's, and she was fine with that. It was the traces of brown that she knew belonged to Avrimae that bothered her.

She couldn't tell the blood apart of course. It all dried into a crusted mass, but she knew some of it belonged to the human woman.

Brodea wasn't opposed to her torture; she had ordered it after all. But what the three did before that was not within bounds.

She told Eigron to gather two of the druids' Hunters of the Vine that he trusted to balance a skewer. Avrimae was thoroughly abused to show Ashyn what his refusal was doing to others, not just himself. Either Eigron had not understood, or she herself was not clear. They went too far.

When she saw the woman's groin, what they did to her. It revolted her to think that she ordered such a thing. Brodea tried to rationalize that Avrimae was a skewer, and she made the decision to have such an act performed on her when she stood for the wizards and worshipped a false idol. But Brodea was female too, almost raped by a wizard on the very day of her mate's death. Haunted by the pressure of him against her loins to this day.

Now her people had raped a woman to psychologically wound a wizard and it left the First Councilor troubled. The cause always declared that the balancing of nature required sacrifice, and that it would be done by any and all means necessary. And she agreed with it her entire life.

She forced her daughter to marry a male, instead of allowing her to be a lover of other females. She had her own hym killed because the cause demanded the sacrifice.

Avrimae was a skewer, and an expendable one at that. She was an unbalancer. So fate decried that she must be balanced. But rape? How did such violation serve the Spirits? How did it serve the cause?

Eigron assured her that it did. He was distressed that he upset his First Councilor, but he told her that the result would be most effective on the Blood Wizard, and on the skewer they called Mactonal. He was completely right. The effect was apparent on them immediately, but a byproduct of that, was that it also affected her. Worse, it caused Ashyn to become reckless to the point of pushing Whísper into throwing him from the chamber ledge.

Brodea's eyes drifted to that ledge. It was such a long way down. Now she was left at an impasse. Whísper went too far. She was too unstable. The loss of Shedalia broke Whísper in ways that Ambit's death never unhinged her. Though Brodea and Whísper may share the same appearance, and even the same values and determination, her middle daughter lacked Brodea's strength. She lacked the foresight to see this through.

Whísper was unreliable. She was no longer an option. If Brodea wanted to see the tome translated at all, she would need to employ different methods. The rest of the council would demand it. She may be First Councilor, but she still answered to the majority.

Luckily for her, Eigron was beginning to prove himself invaluable and solved that problem for her. She was assured that it would arrive any day now.

Brodea was practical, she knew worth when she saw it. Though he was young and ambitious, Eigron was resourceful. He saved her daughter's life after the burns. He was the sole-surviving druid of Whísper's failed vanguard on the wizards. He warned her of the Blood Wizard's impending arrival. He was advance scout when looking for the corpse the elder wizard. And now he informed her of weapons found from both the Blood Wizard's arsenal, and that of the beast in the Water Pens. Items the Elder of Vines failed to mention.

He was the only ray of sunlight that she had received recently in the thick dark canopy of her despair. That was why his lewd actions against Avrimae hit her so hard.

On top of everything else, their resident hero had disappeared. Jenhiro, the sole-surviving branch commander that not only captured the Blood Wizard, but also provided the druids with the new weapons Eigron was excited about, was now missing. Though he turned down the accolades, and remained humble, it didn't mean that the hunters denied his contribution to the cause.

Already Brodea lined up artists to add the relief of his tribute to the great wall. They were going to begin within the week, and yet the hym of honor was nowhere to be found. Brodea feared that the survivor's guilt was too much for the elf. It was only a matter of time before he turned up dead on the outskirts of the city.

Brodea sighed and rubbed her hands over her face. She glanced down at the tome that she desperately wanted, no, needed translated. It sat there, taunting her.

The First Councilor opened the tome and moved her fingers across the page. She felt the raised words against her copper flesh. Craetorian. She thought she felt the power within them. She turned the page. Netherphage. This was the power to change things. The power to make a difference. To rightfully bring the world in balance. To fulfill their cause.

Whisper took that away from her, from her people, in one incredibly selfish moment. It went against everything she trained to be. It disappointed Brodea as the First Councilor. It shattered her as a mother. Brodea already had one daughter turn her back on the Ferhym. She was lucky that up until this point Whisper was so successful as a branch commander. Now with rumors spreading like wildfire of her dalliance with Shedalia, and her rage attack against the Blood Wizard, it would soon grow that the First Councilor could not control her wild children. Something had to be done. The cause demanded it.

Once again Brodea's mind drifted back to Avrimae. To her naked, violated form. She sighed in disgust. She needed to get this out of her head. Needed to get over it. She was stronger than this. Stronger than her daughter. Stronger than all the Ferhym. She survived the trial. She was the First Councilor!

Brodea stood and paced. She walked to the edge of the chamber and looked out beyond into the great city of her people. Fire lights flickered in all the abodes in the distance, and the sounds of toiling hammers at the forges rang in the distance. The city was alive with nervous energy. A war loomed before them, and they weren't ready. A war she promoted. The thought of it tightened Brodea's chest.

She needed to vent this pent up frustration. She needed to pour out her energy into something, leave her body exhausted, and lathered in sweat. She paced back and forth, looking longingly at the sequoias in the distance. Her days of hunting skewers were over. Her days of running amid the trunks and swinging across the branches were a decade behind her. As the First Councilor her obligation was to the Spirits, to the cause, and to the people. Not to her own desires of the hunt. That was what the rest of the council was for. And they were hunting until morning.

There could be no release that way. She needed to purge another way. A spar or a fight perhaps? But who would dare fight the First Councilor?

As if the Spirits heard her pleading cry, she looked down from the balcony and saw Vooken ascending the stairs. In his hands he held a bottle of amber wine, and two goblets.

This was the answer. A different kind of sparring. Though crude, and lacking the refinement that she was accustomed to, it was exactly what she needed. Brodea wasted no time. When Vooken finally reached the landing and looked up for her, he stopped cold. Her leather bracing and skirt were gone. She sat posed erotically on the throne with her legs open. With a single sensuous finger, she motioned him over.

The goblets tumbled out of his hands and shattered against the hard wood as he stumbled forward. Luckily, he had the presence of mind to put the bottle down before it suffered a similar fate. That was good. The goblets weren't necessary. The wine was. She planned to get good and drunk, even if she had to drink if off his body.

Brodea was ready to swap being in demand as First Councilor for having her demands met. With Vooken's arrival, she would not be denied.

PROPER BALANCE

The wooden bars animated themselves slowly winding shut, braiding together as easily as strands of hair. As the last skewer stepped into the cage, one of the hunters reached out and squeezed her right buttock. She screamed and jumped in surprise. The three elves laughed. The hunter jeered at the woman, assuring her that she was next. The human could understand none of it, of course, but his compatriots did, and they laughed even more. The bars locked themselves into place, and then the druid Eigron lowered the cage down below using vines.

As they fell below ground level, the other hunter moved his loincloth aside, and urinated on the people beneath them.

Most screamed and scattered, others who had given up didn't even acknowledge it. Worse, some who were desperately dehydrated actually tried to drink it. This elicited raucous laughter from the three elves.

When the humans were lowered fully, Eigron made sure they were secure. The three of them laughed some more and walked away. Jenhiro followed the trio from the shadows, noting all their movements, and most importantly, their stops. Jenhiro shadowed these three for the last two weeks. Their routines were predictably similar, with the small exception of Eigron, whom was different on any given day. He was the most difficult.

Eigron answered directly to the First Councilor, now, and no one else. Jenhiro wondered how the Elder of Vines felt about having his position so unceremoniously usurped by an elf who hadn't likely even seen a century of life come and go?

Jenhiro didn't know what to expect at first. He guessed that these particular elves would somehow act evil at all times. That those actions would carry over into everything else, labeling them clearly as something sinister. The truth was after they were away from the human skewers, they acted no differently than any of the other elves. They went on with their lives, working, praying to the Spirits, spending time with their families, playing with their children, and loving their mates.

The hunters were each gifted with the luxury of a child. They both had loving families. The children were relatively young too. They were at an age where they could even play together. A rare honor for elves.

Both hunters wed to very comely females. It appalled him to know that those lovely hym were likely clueless as to what their mates were doing to human women when they were supposed to be guarding them.

It was around the skewers that they degenerated to something far worse. Jenhiro hoped their actions were isolated only to Avrimae, but Eigron's amnesty for his actions fueled the fire. Now the three spent days handpicking which human women they would sexually conquer next. Any human men that objected to their actions were handled severely. Many beaten into unconsciousness, and Jenhiro actually witnessed one of them killed outright. Eigron covered it up quickly as an accident.

Since most of the Councilors couldn't speak Trade Tongue, and neither could Jenhiro, the plaintive cries from the skewers went unheard. Sadly, at this point, Jenhiro knew that even if the Councilors could understand the humans, it was likely there would be no action forthcoming. They were skewers of balance. Defilers of the will of the Spirits. Their lot in life was to be balanced. Only through reclamation was there any hope for them. And so far, the Voïre du Ceremeia was right. He hadn't seen a single human reclaimed yet.

This left no one to defend the unbalancers from the malice of the few that treated them so poorly. No one to stand up for them, or protect them. No one to stop the growing carnal fascinations the trio had for the human women. No one, but Jenhiro.

The branch commander knew he waited long enough. Tonight was the first night he was going to act. Jenhiro was careful to learn everything about them. He needed to know what he was doing was the right thing. That it was the will of the Spirits. So he learned everything. How they worked, what they ate, how they made love to their mates. He canvased them.

The hardest was the children. In the past when he defended the Shalis-Fey from intruders, the lives of children didn't have as much weight to him. They were skewers after all. They were less than the Ferhym. But these children were different. They were Ferhym.

Jenhiro tried to rationalize that if those children knew what despicable acts their fathers were performing before seeing them, or if their mates knew where their soiled bodies were before accepting them into their beds, they'd recognize the unbalance. Jenhiro shuddered. This was the Spirits' work.

Jenhiro followed them past the domiciles as first Eigron broke off to attend whatever matters Brodea had for him. This was good for Jenhiro. It made things much easier tonight. He only had the two hunters and he knew their routines intimately.

The pissing hunter's name was Mehris Willowfallen. He would go to his family dutifully tonight. He did so every night after he soiled the sanctity of a human woman's virtue. Jenhiro would let him go home this evening. It was the last hunter, the pincher, Hengrit Elkhunter, who was going to be first.

Jenhiro didn't even turn to acknowledge Mehris' routine as the hunter slipped into his home to hug his daughter, and kiss his mate. The branch commander's eyes were set solely on the pincher.

As always, Hengrit had other plans before going back to his family. Like a dark ritual, he sought Avrimae. Jenhiro didn't know if Hengrit was always so cruel, or if it was something more deeply rooted to the fact that Avrimae was the first. What Jenhiro did know was that it was repulsive. It was monstrous. It was wrong.

Soon Hengrit was all alone in front of a single ground level cell where Avrimae slept. As she lay there, catatonic, the pincher opened the wooden door. Slowly he hovered over her. Watching. Jenhiro could see his chest rising and falling, his breath quickening. Hengrit moved his loincloth aside. Already the elf was prepared. Just the sight of her, his first victim, stimulated the elf. Hengrit took his weapons off and placed them to her side. He looked around to make sure they were alone.

Jenhiro crouched lower to the ground, well out of the elf's sight. Though it chafed his spirit, he had to wait for Hengrit to begin. It would place him in his greatest position of weakness. If Hengrit was committed to the act, he wouldn't be ready for Jenhiro.

Jenhiro took those last vital moments not only to distract himself from what was going to happen, but to prepare himself for what he was about to do. He began his own ritual that he partook in before combat with a skewer. The way he found his center before the chaos. He took a deep breath and closed his deep brown eyes. He imagined the cage before him. The shape, its width. The distance between the walls at the southern end, and possible restrictions he would have if Hengrit were somehow aware of him. As he did so he touched his closed eyelids with his left hand. His center was all about his senses; sight, smell, sound, and touch.

The tactile pressure against his closed eyes brought serenity. He did the same to his brow, and eventually his long-pointed ears, tracing their steep arch all the way above the crown of his head.

As he slowly opened his eyes his ears picked up the heavy erratic breathing of his adversary. The thrum of each inhalation as it quickened in anticipation of what the elf was about to do. It soaked into all of Jenhiro's senses. He could taste the bitterness of Hengrit's desire for Avrimae in the very air.

Hengrit turned the unconscious woman over on to her stomach. Jenhiro knew that this was the way Hengrit liked it. From behind, where he could get the best leverage, the deepest violation of her being. It was how he could exert the most control.

Avrimae flopped over easily. She was heavily sedated. It was so she could sleep and heal. Anymore, when she was awake, she was hysterical. Jenhiro watched her every day hoping she would snap out of it, but he didn't think she ever would. The woman was broken now. Light pink scars arched up her back from where Eigron healed the whip lacerations. But there was no amount of healing magic Eigron could perform on her that would fix the damage he did to her psyche.

Her scent touched Jenhiro's nostrils, along with the sour tang of her sweat. When that scent changed into something more pungent, he knew the elf would be at his most unaware.

Hengrit aligned himself atop the inert woman, spreading her thighs with his knee unceremoniously. Jenhiro moved slowly now, drawing a thin cord of tightly woven vine from his side pouch. It was tethered together with two small knots of wood at each end. Jenhiro spent the last few nights carefully creating the weapon.

In most cases, poison would be preferable, but Hengrit was a hunter. Like Jenhiro, the pincher was trained to build up a tolerance to the toxins they used. This meant Jenhiro needed to alter his tactics. Blade work was messy, and spears would be too cumbersome. He had to get close. Part of him wanted to be close.

The elf went to work on the woman with his fingers, and her scent changed as her body was reacting naturally to the violating elf's commands. Were she awake, Jenhiro knew she would blame herself for what the elf was doing. That even though she fought him, she still somehow wanted it. Jenhiro wished he could get through to her. Tell her it wasn't her fault, no matter how much she might think it was. That it was just the body reacting to what was happening. He wondered if she could even accept such a thought. He wondered if he could, were the roles reversed.

Hengrit positioned himself over her, ready to commit her body to him once more. He pushed forward, penetrated, and gathered a momentum. Jenhiro acted.

Like a bolt of lightning Jenhiro struck forth. Covered in the sweet ground paint, his scent was the only thing that Hengrit caught wind of before he was on him. Jenhiro effortlessly wrapped the makeshift garrote around Hengrit's neck. He twisted and pulled.

There was no sound, only a thin wisp of trapped air escaping Hengrit's lips. Jenhiro twisted the wooden knobs again, cutting the vines tighter into Hengrit's neck, crushing his windpipe shut.

Hengrit bucked backward like a wild animal, but Jenhiro had leverage. He pushed Hengrit down against Avrimae. He anchored his arms into Hengrit's back, using his elbows against the elf's spine to draw him further down.

Hengrit tried to reach back for Jenhiro but his angle was too good, and the crude oil against Jenhiro's body was too slick for Hengrit to get any kind of grip. Jenhiro buried the side of Hengrit's face into the ground right next to Avrimae's. His body flopped like a fish as it was starved of its vital oxygen. Jenhiro leaned close to Hengrit's ear. He desperately wanted to whisper, "Look closely at her, skewer." He wanted those dying eyes to be on her face, as he let Hengrit know that she was the last pure thing a true unbalancer like him was ever going to see.

But he didn't. He stayed silent. The plan demanded it. Jenhiro cranked hard against Hengrit's neck. The elf's eyes bulged horrendously. Jenhiro twisted one last time. He heard a pop as the cartilage of Hengrit's throat gave way, and the elf's larynx caved in on itself, collapsing his windpipe completely. Jenhiro held firm atop him until after a few more seconds Hengrit's convulsions stopped.

Jenhiro stood up, breathing hard. He reached down and untethered the garrote. Blood pooled against the skin where the tether was tightest. It created a growing line of ruptured blood vessels around Hengrit's throat. The skewer's tongue sagged from his mouth like a fat, bloated slug. A puddle of drool formed against the dead elf's cheek.

Jenhiro's hands shook so badly he could barely hold onto the garrote. It took three tries before he secured it into the pouch. His breaths quickened. It was getting hard to get air. Jenhiro looked down at the body atop Avrimae, realizing fully what he had just done. He had taken the life a Ferhym. He killed his own kind. He committed murder.

He stared at his quivering hands in disbelief. *What have I become?* his mind screamed. It was so easy to rationalize. Easy to stalk, and to hate, and to think about what he wanted to do. But now he did it. He murdered an elf!

Jenhiro backed against the wooden bars of the cage as another panic attack assailed him. His back cracked against the bars hard, but his mind didn't register the pain. He stared mortified at the empty glazed eyes of Hengrit. He wanted to run away screaming. He wanted to turn himself in to be put to death. He deserved to die. Jenhiro was a monster. Only a monster would kill his own kind.

Then he followed Hengrit's death gaze to Avrimae. The sight of her, the innocence of this human slowed his breathing down. His heart steadied. Regardless of whatever crimes made her a skewer in the eyes of his people, she did nothing to deserve the fate that was bestowed upon her. Nor did she deserve the repeated assaults that were thrust upon her while in her fugue state. She had gone from criminal to victim.

Jenhiro took a deep breath. It was done he told himself. He did what he was trained to do. He had committed the world to balance once more.

One down. Two to go.

AN AWKWARD TURN

Suicide. A terrible and taboo subject. Very few cultures accept it as anything close to honorable. Most religions revile it as something that guaranteed the worst possible afterlife. A coward's escape.

The Ferhym are no different. Brodea knew to take one's own life was selfish, and it hurt their cause. A single death of a Ferhym crippled their sacred mission. Self-induced harm was tantamount to attacking the mission itself, handed down to them from the Spirits. She was raised believing that should one take their own life in such a cowardly fashion, that their spirit would forever dissolve, unable to join with the Spirits of the after to help their people fulfill their solemn duty.

Everything about who they were would no longer exist. That included any reliefs of history made in their honor. Their name stripped and banned. The mate would retain their original family name, as would the child. Unless there was the rare brother, or cousin who bore the same honored surname, mere mention of it abolished for no less than a century. After that time, it could be carried again by the child or a new family, if they so choose. It was rarely chosen.

Brodea knew all of this painfully well, so when Eigron and Mehris found Hengrit slowly swinging from a vine noose the next day, it sent the entire city into an uproar.

The First Councilor had spent the night in the council chambers. She had drunk greedily of the amber wine. And she had taken greedily from Vooken's body. She had not been humble. She had wanted and he had been more than willing to share.

Now though, her head throbbed from over indulgence, and a furious council sat around her, demanding to strip Hengrit of all of his accomplishments over the last two centuries of his life.

Brodea wanted to cover her ears and just will it all away. She received her much needed release, but now it seemed as if things were compounding upon her in even greater measure.

Suicide. A hunter hadn't committed suicide in ages. Why Hengrit Elkhunter?

One look into the Druid's eyes before her and she knew the answer. Hengrit was one of the three.

She wanted to groan and cover her head with her arms. She in no way was weak, but now to have one of the rapists dead. Was it guilt at what he did? Was she the cause of this?

Eigron looked at her plaintively. She could see that Hengrit's passing troubled him deeply. She pitied the elf. He did so much for her.

Around her some of the councilors continued to rage at Hengrit's suicide while others spoke of Whisper's actions and throwing the wizard off the precipice. They were talking about stripping Whisper of her rank and status as well. Brodea's own daughter! As if Brodea wasn't even in the room!

Anger at everything happening welled in her like a building storm. She said in a whisper, "Out."

No one heard her; they all continued to argue amongst themselves, their din sounded like a cacophonous howling in her throbbing skull. Louder, "Out."

Still the Councilors spat amongst themselves. Eyes darted to Brodea, but she didn't think that they were concerned about her. Quite the opposite, actually. They looked accusatory.

"Get the hells out!"

Everyone went suddenly silent, and looked at her in shock.

"I must commune with the Spirits. Now." Her voice was razor sharp, there was no denying that she intended for them to leave right this moment.

"First Councilor…" Vooken tried to plead next to her.

His brown eyes shimmered. How the hells did he escape from the effects she was feeling? She looked angrily at him. It felt like the boulders tumbling through her head were part of a landslide, and Vooken looked no worse for the wear. In fact, he seemed refreshed.

Brodea lifted hand and pointed out to the city beyond. Her voice came out in a growl, "If you don't leave right now, I will throw each and every one of you off that ledge just like my daughter did to the wizard!"

Instantly, a few of the Councilors scurried from her. No one wanted the wrath of the Spirits to come down on them. Vooken merely stared at her, disbelief at being turned away especially after the night before, clearly written on his face.

She looked away from him. She was the First Councilor. She didn't need to answer to him. She heard his seat skid across the floor as the ponytailed elf stood and headed towards the stairs as well.

Brodea turned to look at Eigron. The druid still stood there. She mouthed, "You stay." He nodded.

As the Ferhym fled from their enraged First Councilor, Brodea looked up just in time to see the Voïre dui Ceremeia watching her with concern. Her eyes swayed like mercury. The expression on her face, on the corners of her downturned mouth reminded Brodea so much of someone she cared for, so long ago.

"Would you like me to stay?" the Voïre dui Ceremeia asked. Her voice sounded, hopeful.

Even though she was First Councilor, Brodea did not make eye contact; she stared down at the smooth floor. "No, Voïre. I will have this young druid with me to convene with the Spirits."

"I understand," the Voïre dui Ceremeia said, and Brodea could hear sadness in her voice, and even a touch of, was it disappointment? But why? The thought of it made her angry all the more. How dare someone so young even think to question her!

The First Councilor heard the flutter of the green dress and then the Voïre filed out with the remainder of the Ferhym. The whole ordeal took over twenty minutes, but when they were all gone the mad pulsing in her head softened considerably. It wasn't gone completely, but it was a dramatic improvement to what she had been suffering minutes before.

Sure that no one remained, Brodea stood up and strode to where the druid was standing. "You found the body. What else do you know?"

Eigron's expression was tight as he looked to the stairs. "The Voïre..."

"Is of no concern to you," Brodea finished for him. "What is it that you know?"

"He was murdered," Eigron said flatly.

Murdered? Brodea wanted to laugh at him. Wild Elves who stayed true to the cause did not kill one and other. Not in Feydras' Anula anyhow. That happened to the other cells. The forests further north. Never in their home city. Yet the look in his eyes. "You are serious?"

Eigron nodded. "Under his fingernails was the sweet ground paint that our hunters use."

Brodea baulked.

"There is more," Eigron interrupted her before she could make a snide reply. "There is something you need to see. You will not like it."

Brodea didn't like anything that was happening in these last few weeks. What more could there possibly be?

~ ~ ~

Staring in fury at the last moments of Hengrit's miserable existence, she roared at Eigron, "Stop it!"

The basin of water showed a clear view of the back of Avrimae's head, her back, and her naked buttocks. The body beneath him was immobile, sedated, and she could hear Hengrit's hard breathing and a steady wet clap. She wasn't an idiot. Her mind churned at the thought of what that miserable, soulless, spirit forsaken, piece of shit was doing.

"You need to see it all," Eigron told her.

Seething, Brodea wheeled on him striking him across the face so hard it brought the druid to his knees. "You do not tell the First Councilor what she 'needs' to do!"

The grunts were getting louder, but Brodea did not look into the basin of water where Hengrit's final act was playing out.

"I told you that was to never happen again!"

Eigron covered his mouth with the back of his hand. Blood ran freely from the corner and from his nose. She saw fear in his eyes. A fear she hadn't seen from him in many months. He had grown too confident around her.

"It wasn't supposed to!" the druid pleaded. "I was unaware that Hengrit had continued."

Brodea stared hard at the cowering druid. It felt like a lie. She was going to hit him again for lying to her when she heard a curious sound come from the bowl. The heavy breathing stopped suddenly. Too suddenly. Replaced with a single, small wheeze. Her ears were attuned to the sound. Someone's air just was cut off.

The First Councilor redirected her eyes to the pool of water by her side. She fought back the nausea of seeing Avrimae's position. Yet she was curious now at what she was seeing. Hengrit was jerking far too violently for it to be in coitus, no matter how rough.

The corners of the pool of water were fading. A tunnel-like vision closed in on the hunter. She could see Hengrit's arms flailing in front of him. Suddenly he moved down hard into the small of Avrimae's back. Not moved, Brodea realized, driven.

There was no sound coming from Hengrit. No gasping, just silence as he continued to writhe. Then he was viciously slammed to the ground so that all Brodea could see was the catatonic face of Avrimae staring at her at an awkward angle. The vision focused on her face, and then there was a gut-wrenching popping sound. Cartilage breaking. Brodea knew it well.

Everything faded to black.

Brodea stared quietly at the black waters for several minutes. Was it her imagination or was there a ghostly silhouette of the human woman still in the dark waters? She didn't even notice when Eigron picked himself up off the floor.

"You are being hunted," she said in a whisper. It didn't seem possible, but there it was, unmistakable. Brodea was a hunter for centuries. She knew how to kill quietly like that. She had done so many times when camps of Skewers had out-numbered her and she needed to whittle them down silently. The First Councilor damn near perfected the technique. Strangulation. It explained the mock hanging. Brodea looked up to the wounded druid, "Have any of the humans escaped?"

Eigron shook his head no. "They are all accounted for. Even the deceased. Every single one. I checked myself after witnessing this vision."

Brodea stood away from the basin. "They made this look like suicide. Whoever did this knew that the council would never accept that he was murdered without proof. They are trying to destroy everything about him." Brodea's eyes widened. "They are balancing him." The revelation made her shiver.

"Then we show them Hengrit's final images. We don't let the killer get away with this!"

Brodea scoffed, "And reveal that we condoned him raping a human woman? Even if we deny any affiliation to his actions, the council will be abhorred at his actions. Not for what happened to the skewer, but for the fact that he could have created an aberration due to his continued lustings! A half-Ferhym aberration!"

She shook her head. "This will not come back to me, Eigron. Destroy that image. I'd rather he die by suicide than be responsible for creating a reviled skewer from his own loins."

Eigron nodded. "Then the killer wins," he mumbled, but Brodea barely acknowledged it. Her mind was working in high speed now. Thinking ahead. If this was going on the whole time, there was no telling how Avrimae's womb was handling it. Humans were far more susceptible to pregnancy than the hym ever were. Even blasphemous hybrids were easier to come about than pure hym. She saw her Goldhym kin time and again make the hybrids, the man-hym. Diluting the purity of their species. It was weeks since the first occurrence. If Hengrit continued all this time…

"You have to kill her," Brodea said suddenly. The thought made her stomach roil.

"I just spent weeks trying to nurse her back to health!" Eigron said astonished, "Now you want me to kill her?"

"Apparently healing wasn't the only thing you were doing to her!" Brodea snapped. "There's no way to know what is going on in her body until she is further along and it begins to show. You are responsible for this Eigron. He was under your command. I will not have a skewer half-breed born amongst our numbers. I will not! You have done this Eigron, your continuous negligence after all I have elevated you to."

He shook his head no, and stuttered, "First Councilor, I had no idea Hengrit was still performing those acts on her! I thought it was only that one time, I swear."

Again she could feel the wrongness of his words. He was lying to her. Lying to her to cover up his heinous actions.

Her hand lanced out before her mind could comprehend what she was doing. She grabbed Eigron by the throat, his eyes widened. She squeezed, cutting off any more blasphemous lies he might try to tell. "No… more… lies." She hissed. "I have elevated you, perhaps wrongly, to this position and now you have fumbled. You have one chance to make this right, or you will find yourself as less than what you were when you sulked home in defeat from the Blood Wizard months ago."

Brodea watched as his eyes bulged and his skin turned purple. She continued, "Whisper has long sought vengeance for the pain you caused her when you brought her back to health."

She tightened her grip, drool oozed from the terrified young druid's mouth as he was starved of air. It was pathetic. He didn't even try to fight her. A hunter would have. Hells, Hengrit would have. To think only an evening before she felt grateful for him? It disgusted her. What had she been thinking? Part of her wanted to end it right now. He was only a Genrus, no one would notice if he disappeared. She could simply say she sent him out on a mission directed by the Spirits, and he never returned.

No. She needed him. Someone had to take the fall if this all turned south. An overeager druid who refused to accept his station and remain humble. It would work perfectly. Eigron was still useful, even as a patsy.

"You fail me in this again druid, and I'll see Whisper gets that revenge." Brodea released her grip.

Eigron coughed and sputtered as he tried to breath.

"No more delays from the Elder of Vines. I want you to bring Julietta here. I want that staff you keep telling me about. And I want Avrimae dead from 'natural causes' all before this season is through and people begin to suspect. Am I understood?"

Eigron was bent over in a coughing fit, but he managed a nod. He gagged reflexively a few times, and Brodea thought for a moment he might vomit.

"And what about the killer?" he rasped. "Clearly they must know something?"

"Perhaps." The First Councilor thought about any of her people who had shown any leniency towards humans in the past. Only one came to mind, and that was when she had been a child. It was more than likely dissidents who still wanted things to be as they were when Tehirs had been First Councilor.

There was a semi-vocal minority of Ferhym who were displeased with Brodea reinstating the war against the wizards. They voiced their discord, mainly with the Council, but up until this point none was so bold as to take any direct action against her. This thought intrigued her.

"Call it incentive," Brodea quipped to the Druid. "You deliver to me Julietta, and I'll take care of your hunter problem personally. And you handle Avrimae."

Eigron composed himself and stood up straight. Only his strained voice belied that he was still in pain. "You will have her by the next council convening. I hope that is adequate."

Brodea smiled. One week. The Druids of the Vine had been dragging their collective feet for months, and now he claimed she would have the woman in a week!

This was the release that she sought. Not Vooken, not alcohol, or some crude half-fulfilled sexual exploit. She would hunt. She would finally have a chance to do what she was good at, and against the worthiest of prey, another hunter. The best part was she didn't even have to leave Feydras' Anula to do it.

It was for the cause, she reminded herself, stopping herself from letting her conscience dictate that fighting a Ferhym was wrong. This hunter killed one Ferhym, and at least two more were on the menu. One week. She looked at Eigron. "Let's hope for your sake, my dear druid, that you make it that long."

~ ~ ~

Jenhiro remained completely still as he held on to the bark of the great elm. Thick moss clung to his body from the sweet ground paint. Were anyone to look up at him, they would be no wiser to his presence. He was perfectly camouflaged. He had positioned himself there, over a hundred and twenty feet in the air the night before, just after he had staged the mock suicide.

He needed to see how the council viewed the suicide. He also wanted to see if Eigron would take the last moments of the hunter. Jenhiro didn't realize that the druid would then bring the truth to Brodea. The revelation of his First Councilor both disgusted and infuriated him. The taint went deeper than he would have ever thought. She was the heart of the problem.

She was the pestilence. She was the disease. Eigron was nothing more than a boil. He was a superficial surface wound compared to the cancer that ate away at his beloved culture from within.

He couldn't afford to be aggressive though. She would have to wait. Eigron was still his target. The druid knew where Julietta was. That was good, and it answered many questions for Jenhiro as well. It made sense why he couldn't find her. She was at the very place he refused to go since coming back to Feydras' Anula.

And why wouldn't she be? A dui Nuchada was searching for her. It would make sense to keep her surrounded by magic.

What disturbed Jenhiro though, was that Brodea knew about her as well. Either that meant the dui Nuchada broke down, or she had been expecting him. And if she was expecting the dui Nuchada, then that meant she was willing to bring the threat to her people. That did not bode well with Jenhiro's already burdened conscience. The more he learned, the less this dui Nuchada appeared to be his enemy.

Jenhiro knew his priorities now. Hengrit's death had riled the nest of vipers, and now they were poised to strike. He needed to put a stop to Eigron and his hunter accomplice Mehris before they killed Avrimae. She didn't deserve to die because Brodea was afraid she carried an abomination in her womb due to rape that Brodea endorsed!

When all was concluded he knew he needed to find a way to Julietta, and he needed to save Avrimae. It would be tricky, and he couldn't be two places at once. He needed help. He needed a team.

Jenhiro looked down below to the lone figure watching the Water Pens. He shook his head at the very idea running through his head. *I must be mad,* he decided. There was no other way to explain what he was going on in his head.

The branch commander would build his team. He would retrieve Julietta, and he would save Avrimae. Then he would deal with the heart of the problem, and save his beloved Ferhym from the rot that was consuming them all from within.

He only hoped his instincts were right, and that he could trust her. Jenhiro slowly and methodically climbed down the tree, unseen by all. He was going to risk everything. He was going to reveal himself and his intentions to the one person who could do the most harm. He was going to ask for help. He was going to contact the Voïre dui Ceremeia.

It was all going according to plan, more or less.

GAUR

His life was pain. It enveloped every facet of his being, encompassing his entire existence around a single quantifiable moment. Waiting for it to end.

Consciousness came in small glimpses. He saw images. A large three-fingered hand reaching for him. A beautiful elf's heart-shaped face looking down at him with intense concern. Her silver eyes not swirling. Some sounds were mute, others noisy and indistinct. Every time he awoke, the smell of rot prevailed his nose. And he hurt. It was indescribable. He hurt, everywhere.

Elves moved around him. Druids. Moving, speaking, and rubbing things on his body. Things that were cold. Things that felt like fire. They seemed confused. He was confused. Once he saw the First Councilor. He choked on her name. Hate flowed through the broken fibers of his body.

Then he saw humans after the elves were gone. He began seeing groups of them. Some had concern etched on their worn faces. Hunger and desperation on others. They seemed trapped away from him, only an arm's length away, yet it might as well have been a chasm.

Finally, after what felt like an eternity, he opened his eyes, and they stayed open. Sleep did not take him immediately. It was a curious feeling being back in the world of the living. He was still exhausted, and sore, but he was awake.

He looked around. His neck was tight and every movement caused spikes to shoot down his spine. Like bursts of lightning from the base of his skull. He dealt with it. His curiosity was overriding the pain.

He was in a pen of some sort, and his back was against the wooden bars. With an ache of unused limbs, he used a bar to pull himself into a slouch. A piercing sting stabbed through his side, an agony that cut through all others. He reached to it. His fingers came away tacky and green. His robes had long since eviscerated to mere scraps of fabric.

A fetid odor touched his nostrils, and he heard the shallow sounds of lapping water. He looked up to see garish brown waters slowly pushing their way against wet, moss covered rocks. Each rolling of the water against the shore left rubbish behind that looked very much like feces. His pained stomach turned.

He heard something like a scraping of rocks. He turned towards the sound. It was dark. The massive canopy obscured the moon above. He must have awoken sometime at night. An indistinct form moved in the darkness. He struggled to see it, with his tired, unfocused eyes.

Then it came forward, suddenly. Whatever it was, he knew that it was the one in control; he had nothing in him with which to fight. The figure was there, before him, standing like a towering behemoth. A seven-foot frame hulked over his slumped form. It leaned forward, and amber eyes glistened in the faintest of starlight. It was the bull.

He wanted to back away, but it took too much of his strength pulling himself into the disgrace of a sitting position he was in. There was no way he could defend against it. The bull that stalked him for so long finally had him where it wanted him. He was absolutely powerless. It bent low and scooped him up. It was strangely gentle. He was a doll in its arms. Carefully the beast carried him over to the putrid waters.

Ashyn Rune cringed as he was lowered down right next to the foul smelling liquid. He felt the waste that was on the shore squish and ooze underneath him. To enervated to move, he wanted to wretch.

The bull hunched over right next to him and stared into his eyes. It raised its left hand before him, and moved it over the water. Ashyn watched, petrified. It could kill him. It could crush his skull like a berry in those hands. It could bludgeon him to death with the rocks about, or even drop him in the sludge where he would drown.

It didn't.

Again the bovine creature lifted its hand up before him and then hovered it over the water, waving at him to do the same.

Shakily Ashyn raised his hand and held it over the foul pond. It was exhausting. The bovine dipped his fingers into the water.

Ashyn scrunched his face in disgust. The bull pulled its fingers out and put them back in. With its other hand it signaled for him to do the same. Ashyn shook his head no. He wasn't putting his hand in that filth. Just the thought of what he was laying in was revolting enough to make him want to vomit.

Once more the massive creature before him dipped its fingers into the water, and nodded for him to do the same. Knowing he would anger it or frustrate it, and not wanting to have his head squashed like a melon, he relented. Slowly he dipped his fingers into the disgusting shallows, stifling the bile thick in his throat.

I am ga…

Quickly he ripped his fingers out in surprise as a deep voice assailed his senses. He looked up in surprise at the creature. The bull continued to stare at him. Slowly he lowered his fingers back into the murk.

I am a gaur. What are you?

He blinked in confusion. The bull nodded his muzzle towards the water.

"I, ugh…" his voice rasped.

Quickly it shook its head no, and looked to the water.

Use nature. I am a gaur. It repeated. *What species are you?*

Tired and exhausted, and unable to even fathom why he was still alive, Ashyn simply thought, *You can understand me?*

The gaur shook its massive horned head and repeated again. *I am a gaur. What species are you?*

Ashyn was bewildered. Not only was it truly sentient, they finally could understand one and other. *I'm not sure anymore.* He answered it honestly.

The gaur cocked its head curiously at him. Did he understand what he meant? Then to Ashyn's surprise it nodded.

Water is the universal path to all life. The gaur explained. *If one knows how to traverse its pathways, then they can speak to all who use it.*

We are speaking through the water? Ashyn asked.

The gaur snorted, in what Ashyn assumed was a yes. Then another question sprouted to his mind, and he asked it before he could suppress it. *Why are you not trying to kill me?* He looked up in horror at the thought, realizing what he did.

The gaur was unfazed. *We are Totem-brothers now. You bore the power of the Pundit's Totem, and removed me of my curse of un-life. You released me back into the cycle without the loss of my vessel.*

Ashyn had no idea what it was talking about, but he didn't object. If the gaur no longer wanted to kill him, then he was more than happy with that.

So does the Totem-Brother know his species? The gaur asked again.

Ashyn shook his head, *when I was a child I thought I was human, and then when a wizard found me, we thought that I might be a half-elf. I went by this assumption for many winters, only recently have I learned that I am neither. The elves here call me the Nuchada.*

Nuchada.

Ashyn nodded.

I have never heard of the species of Nuchada.

Ashyn chuckled. It hurt. *Join the club.*

What is a club? It asked.

Ashyn shook his head at that, *Never mind.*

The wizard looked around a dawning crept over him. *I'm in the prison by the pond.*

Water Pens, the gaur replied quickly. *You flew from the Great Elm and landed in the water.*

Landed?

The gaur rounded its shoulders at him, and Ashyn realized it was shrugging. *It was not graceful.*

How did I get out? I don't remember.

The gaur patted its other hand against Ashyn's leg. *You are a Totem-Brother now.* It answered simply.

Ashyn then looked down to his torn robes and slowly opened the brown-stained fabric to see a new jagged pink scar lined with green fluid, just next to the one that the gaur had given him. *I seem to be collecting these lately..*

The gaur rubbed the circular pink scar against its own chest, reminding Ashyn that he was the cause of that one. *As have I. But now it is different.* It remarked. *We are both prisoners to these creatures, and your species is capable of using the totem.*

That has never happened before, to my people's knowledge. For the time being, that makes you a brother.

Enemy of my enemy. Ashyn returned. Again the gaur snorted.

They do not like you, Nuchada. The burned one tried to cut your head from your body, but the silver-eyed one forced her to stop until their Bos Gaurus arrived.

Ashyn shook his head, trying to understand the thing in front of him. He understood burned one, and silver-eyed, but Bos Gaurus confounded him. He told the creature so.

Your herd does not have a Bos Gaurus? The gaur questioned.

I do not have a herd. He replied.

The creature leaned back alarmed.

My herd was destroyed, in a raid, Ashyn corrected, catching on.

The beast let out a heavy sigh. *Most of my herd too has been lost. These small sharp-eared things interrupted our exodus. My Pundit is dead, as is the Herd Matron.* It looked to the ground morosely. *Even you slew one of my herd.*

I'm sorry. Ashyn replied. He didn't know any other way of conveying his feelings on the matter. He was fighting for his life, and he made a choice.

I understand, now, The gaur replied, and Ashyn realized once again that their thoughts were bridged together by the water. *You were trying to survive.*

Ashyn thought it best to change the subject, otherwise he would risk losing the gaur's fragile alliance with him. *How is it that the elves have placed you in here?*

The gaur snorted, *I am too big for their tiny cages, and their magic-creatures that keep bones in their head fur have no place for me. Yet they need to keep me for study. They do not understand how to use the totem. So I remain alive, and fed, until they can discern its function.*

That meant this totem he was talking about was something mobile. Understanding swept over him. Ashyn had used it already. That was why the gaur was calling him a totem-brother. *The staff.*

It is not a staff. The gaur replied with a slight hint of anger. *It is the embodiment of the elements forged into a symbol of great purpose for the gaur. It is our icon, our talisman.*

I see. Ashyn replied, though he still wanted to call it a staff. Looks like a duck, quacks like a duck. The gaur's amber eyes sent him a patronizing look. *Okay, totem got it.* He really needed to learn to take his fingers out of the water.

Another question came to the wizard. *Why am I still in here?*

I do not know. I cannot understand these narrow-minded creatures' tongue. When their Bos Gaurus came, she chirped as a bird does, and then they healed your wounds and left. At least they thought they healed your wounds.

I don't understand.

The gaur shuffled closer to Ashyn, his fingers traced a line in the foul mire, and Ashyn watched a piece of excrement bounce off the gaur's thick digits and spin away. His stomach roiled.

I am a pan, it continued, closer to him, *I served my Pundit, my…* Ashyn saw it studying Ashyn's eyes as if trying read his memories. *Your words call him shaman. I was his student; we were on the Takewatha, a journey to our progenitors, so that I may humble myself before the Brahma, our Great World Spirit. It was to be my spirit journey. I was to become the next Pundit of my herd. The next Shaman.*

The gaur lowered its head in shame. *I have failed that journey, but moreover it has left my herd without its Pundit. Without a Pundit's guidance, the Bos Gaurus will not have access to the Great World Spirit, when looking for direction to lead his people.*

Ashyn sat absorbing it all. If he was good at anything, it was listening. The large creature continued to project its conversation into his mind.

I am trained in use of the elements. In use of nature. My totem is my guide. Still, I am capable enough without it. I am strong. The elements nourish me, and through me I nourished your flesh.

You have been healing me? Ashyn replied surprised. It was so startling he almost spoke aloud.

The gaur snorted. *You removed my curse of unlife, and then used the totem to heal my fatal wounds. Though we believe in the cycle of all things, I felt I needed to stop your return to the cycle. It was within my power to do so.*

His thick finger pointed to the green fluid around the gnarly pink scar. *The sharp-eared creatures do have talents though, and they know nature well. It was a combined effort, but they do not know I helped, nor do they realize what I can do without the totem. I am difficult for them to understand.*

Ashyn couldn't believe what the gaur was telling him. After hunting him for so long, it was now telling him, it was responsible for saving his life. If Ashyn didn't know better, he would say that the creature seemed rather proud of the feat.

He was a student. He told himself. He had a mentor, just as Ashyn had, that meant he was...

Our lifetimes do not flow like yours. The gaur interrupted his thoughts with an answer. *We believe in a resurgence of our one spirit through a great number of vessels. The age of this vessel is what you would call nine.*

Nine-winters? You are only nine-winters-old? It was so big.

The bull snorted. *We measure cycles differently. Just like there are multiple elements, our lives measured are multiplied by all of the seasons, not just one like your species chooses to do.*

Four elements, four seasons, Ashyn thought as he nodded at the gaur's words. *That would make you thirty-six by my people's reckoning then.*

It rolled its shoulders in a shrug again.

You are right. Ashyn replied. *Age is irrelevant. What is relevant is that we are both prisoners of the Wild Elves, and they have something we both want. That makes us allies, and allies share names.* He touched his chest. *I am Ashyn Rune. Do you have a name?*

Again he watched the gaur's powerfully intelligent gaze drift to the ground. *Had I completed my Takewatha, I would have taken over from my Pundit as Strides with Spirits. It is the name carried by all Shamans. Until that time I was just Pan.*

So I can call you Pan?

The gaur shook its head no. *When the sharp-ears poisoned me and ended my life, and the life of my Pundit, I ceased to be Pan. I now carry no name, for I am nothing until I can be reunited with my totem.*

Well I have to call you something? Ashyn said. *It'd be rude of me to continue to call you gaur the whole time.*

The creature lifted its gaze. *What does it matter?*

Consider it an investment, Ashyn replied.

The bull cocked its head confused.

A name carries weight to it. It makes someone real to the other person. When you share a name, you identify with them. That identification makes them tangible. It's hard to place why, but attaching a name to them makes them a part of your life. It makes them real. As a result, you care more about them. Think of your herd, those at home, and those you've lost. You miss them right?

The gaur nodded.

Now think of the elves that were killed, do they seem real to you? Give it some thought.

Ashyn could see the gaur really thinking about it. After many moments it replied, *Knowing a part of something, someone, creates an acceptance of them in your world.*

Ashyn nodded and continued, *By not knowing a name, it creates less of an acceptance of their reality. Think of soldiers on a battlefield. Every one of them knows that the opponent they face has a family at home. Those people have others that they love and are loved by. But every soldier still fights the other to the death if need be, recognizing that they are committing untold suffering to those left behind in that man's wake. Families now made to struggle on without someone to care for them, feed them, educate them, and love them. Yet that soldier will still take a life, will he not?*

Though your words confuse me, I think I understand their meaning. My herd does not have the soldiers you speak of, but I think the comparison would be our Shepherds. They look out for and protect the herd from dangers, especially orcs.

What you are saying is that we know the names of our Shepherds, and they are endeared to us, but the orcs have no names to us, and are just an enemy, though they too must have some sort of social structure. In that social structure someone must care for them, which means they would have names too.

Ashyn nodded. *The same goes for these elves. The scarred one that wanted my head, her name is Whisper. They call the silver-haired one a Voïre dui Ceremeia.*

Knowing each other's name will strengthen our bond to each other, making it all the more likely we will work together to escape.

Ashyn watched as the bull looked up to the tree, its eyes climbing up the length of the trunk slowly. *Your words carry much wisdom.*

Ashyn chuckled aloud, and shook his head, getting another confused look from the gaur. *Sometimes I feel like I'm just making this stuff up as I go.* He told it. *I didn't realize the importance of a name either, or its significance to another person until I killed one of these elves. How real it makes them. Of course, that wisdom came with a heavy price. Not only did the elves lose a loved one, but also so did I with the death of my mentor.*

Ashyn pulled his fingers from the water for only an instant. He didn't want the gaur to know that he had also used a name as a weapon as well. Though that weapon had almost cost him his life, it hopefully saved Avrimae. Was he committing his own emotions to more turmoil by learning this gaur's name? Would it feel like a betrayal, if the creature turned on him? Would it feel more real?

Ashyn didn't have answers to those questions, but didn't want the creature to know he had his own share of doubts. The wizard strongly needed allies here. He was all alone, and he was suffering. He hadn't seen Jenhiro since the elf said he would find Julietta, he didn't know if he could trust him. That in itself felt like a betrayal.

It was a betrayal that Ashyn certainly knew was coming, but when it did happen, it didn't hurt any less. Jenhiro had never wanted to know Ashyn's name. It made the separation and disassociation that much easier.

Yet he was also afraid to involve anyone else. The inclusion of Avrimae and Macky had thrown him off. Worse, what they did to Avrimae in particular, just to hurt him, was horrific. How could he ever justify that to another? How could he justify it to his sister? Had it already happened to her as well?

He slipped his fingers back in the water hoping to distract that unpleasant thought. He wondered if the gaur noticed?

It didn't seem to.

Finally, it looked up to him. *To have a name again would be good, but I am unworthy of such. You have risen me from the curse of unlife, and liberated my spirit from an eternity of damnation by allowing it back into the cycle. What name would you suggest?*

Ashyn blinked, suddenly surprised by the question. *It is not my place to give you a name,* he said apologetically.

You are a totem-brother now. And the herd always assigns us our class name, and then when we assume the mantle of our destiny in this cycle, our station name, the gaur explained.

And you were Pan, and were supposed to become Strides-With-Spirits?

The bull snorted its agreement.

But we cannot use those names now?

It dishonors those worthy of the position, It replied instantly.

A word the gaur used lingered in the back of his head. He still felt awkward at naming the gaur for him, yet he also felt it was somehow fitting.

Rye –zen? The word came back awkwardly into his mind.

Risen. Ashyn returned. *If you are risen again to try to piece together a new life. Risen once more to continue your cycle. Risen from the wreckage of an unlife and back into the world of life. It is a fitting name.*

Ashyn watched as the Gaur contemplated the name. Finally, it snorted. *Rizen it is.*

Ashyn realized that the gaur was being very heavy on the S and intentional or not, it seemed appropriate. *Rizen,* he agreed.

With a smile, painfully stretching the battered and bruised muscles on his face, Ashyn looked at the newly named gaur. *Now that you have a name Rizen, I think it's time we start discussing how we can get out of here. It is time we collect what is ours and go home.*

The gaur snorted powerfully, and stamped a hoof on the ground. The act made Ashyn jump, pulling his hand from the water in surprise. Slowly he lowered it back in, and they both looked into each other's eyes.

I'll take that as a yes.

REACQUANTING

66"You're alive!" A voice exclaimed from behind him. Ashyn rolled onto his side to see a crooked-toothed smile beaming down at him. It was Macky.

Rizen suddenly lunged to his feet snorting and hooting. He began stomping his hooves on the ground. Macky backed away from the barrier between them, terror etched on his filthy face.

Ashyn quickly raised his hand to the gaur. "It's okay," Ashyn, told it.

The gaur continued to hoot.

Shit, Ashyn realized. It couldn't understand him without water.

The wizard reached upward and grabbed one of the posts he was lying against. He gripped it firmly, and with every remaining ounce of strength he had remaining, he pulled himself upward. Slowly he positioned himself between Macky and the gaur. Ashyn pointed towards the water.

The gaur wheeled its massive horned head in an aggressive gesture, but Ashyn could see it. Rizen was telling him no. He understood. Rizen wanted everyone to think he was just a mindless beast. They didn't speak aloud. They spoke through the water. Did Ashyn just blow it? Had Macky heard the words?

The wizard risked a glance backwards to see the terror gripping his old friend so deep that, no, he probably didn't hear Ashyn at all.

Ashyn turned his head back to Rizen and nodded very slightly. He began looking down pretending to be terrified.

Hopefully the gaur understood that Ashyn was in on the ruse. If not, things might really become terrifying, as he doubted the totem-brother bond would carry through if it meant death for the gaur.

Ashyn needn't worry. Rizen was far more perceptive than he gave him credit for. The apprentice Shaman slammed its hooves twice more in a show of superiority, and then wheeled away, as if going to stalk a worthier opponent.

When the gaur was far enough away, Macky came back to the cage, his trembling. His voice tight and abnormally high, he gushed, "We have to get you out of that side. I've been terrified for days now. I was sure that the monster was going to eat you."

Ashyn looked over to Macky and smiled weakly, "It's okay, Macky." Macky reached over and grabbed Ashyn's hand on the pole, gripping it for reassurance. It was a foreign gesture to him after so long, yet the sensation meant so much. Quickly the young wizard's mind raced as to how he could explain why he was safe on this side. "The creature does not eat meat."

Macky looked up towards it skeptically. "Are you sure? It seems, well, monstrous."

Ashyn nodded. "It is, but," thinking of the elk he encountered and how similar the two acted when they were provoked, he explained, "as long as it doesn't think I'm trying to take over its territory. As long as it thinks it is dominant, I am safe."

Macky blew out a sigh of relief, before letting go of his hand and collapsing next to him on the other side of the bars. "You always were smarter than me, Ash. Maybe that's why you left with the wizard that day."

Speculating or baiting? Ashyn wondered.

Before he could answer, Macky continued, "I always knew that the orphanage was too limited for you. I trust you got a strong education with the wizard?"

Ashyn nodded. Strong was an understatement. Xexial pounded his growing mind with languages, literature, history of the sixth era, mathematics (which he was already quite good at), and, of course, training in his craft: magic. It was grueling, almost relentless, and yet Ashyn absorbed it like a sponge. Xexial taught him more in the first winter than he ever learned from his mother's books. "I am well educated."

The wizard looked at Macky; there was a strange expression on his face. Confusion and apprehension, maybe. After a moment the priest shook it from his face and regarded Ashyn with a somber look. "How is it ye are alive, Ash? I mean, after that elf threw you from…"

Ashyn tilted his head and saw Macky looking towards the council chambers from the corner of his eyes. The simple man shook his head, "I would like to think the Maker has his eyes upon you Ashyn. That it was his grace that spared you."

That look returned. "But you don't believe that?"

Macky sighed, arching his back into the poles making them sway gently. "Wizards are evil, Ashyn. That's the way it's always been. That's the way it will always be. And you chose to go with one. Worse you were willing to let us be tortured to protect those evil beliefs."

Ashyn winced at his last statement. Mostly because it was true. Not necessarily the evil part, but he did willingly let Avrimae get tortured. What kind of friend did that?

One choosing the many over the few, he answered to himself. A wizard's beliefs. Macky was right in that at least. Ashyn decided not to argue with the young priest. Instead he changed the direction of the conversation to something he needed to know, "Avrimae?"

"She's alive," Macky told him.

Ashyn let out a sigh of relief.

"After you, um, fell from the ledge, the one that was in charge, the dark-haired elf, she had Avrimae treated by the healers rigorously. I can't explain it Ashyn. It was all very confusing. She seemed concerned about Avrimae. As if her elves took the torture too far. The leader, she helped minister the bandages herself, and wouldn't let anyone else near Avrimae's wounds. Especially the part where she was…" Macky choked on the words, and Ashyn could hear Macky sniffle away tears. He didn't finish. He didn't need to. "After that, Avrimae was taken away; I hope it was to heal. They threw me back here in the Water Pens. I haven't seen Avrimae since, but I know the Maker is looking out for her."

Again Ashyn remained silent. It wasn't that he didn't believe in the Maker, he was raised by his parents to worship the Maker. The village of Bremingham, where he spent the early winters of his life, was dedicated to the Jasian Enclave's teachings. Later, when he first met Macky, he was an orphan in the Jasian Enclave's hospice. He toiled for them for a short time before being re-discovered by Xexial.

He just didn't know how to answer such remarks about the Maker. The comments that he would hear, such as it was his god's will that things like Avrimae's rape should happen, left a bitter taste in his mouth.

Sure the most pious would blame the Maker's adversary, the Defiler, for the rape, but it was always the Maker's will that we overcome such adversity. Ashyn liked to think that he had some control of his own destiny, no matter how small, or how limited it may be.

Besides, Macky was a priest now. A man of the cloth. A servant of the Maker. Any possible counter Ashyn might even give would lead into nothing more than a stern lecture.

Aside from that, the knowledge he just learned of Brodea confounded him. Brodea hurt him terribly. Hung him from hooks by his own bones, why would she care so much for Avrimae? For her violation?

Ashyn looked back to Macky to see the man staring at him. "What?"

"You have grown so much."

It was true; Ashyn was a head taller than Macky. "I was only a little boy when we were friends."

Macky shook his head. "That's not what I meant." He looked back at Ashyn. "But I admit I never thought you would be so tall. No, what I meant was that you were ready to die for her. Ready to die to save Avrimae."

"I wouldn't say I was ready to die," Ashyn replied. "I certainly never thought Whisper would throw me off the edge like that, let alone stab me."

Macky shook his head again. "No, deep down you were ready to make the ultimate sacrifice for those you love. Perhaps you didn't even realize it yourself. I've always respected your character Ashyn, ever since you stood up to the Bishop all those winters ago. Even after you left to become something which I can't even begin to understand."

Ashyn opened his mouth this time, but was stopped by Macky raising his hand. "Don't try. You only spent a few months with the Enclave, I have spent winters. The Jasian Enclave views Destruction magic as vile, and the acts of a wizard reprehensible. Anything you say I will just counter with an argument. Even now I feel the strong urge to counsel you on turning away from your path of darkness. It's ingrained at this point."

Ashyn nodded, that was fair enough. Ashyn didn't think he had the strength to argue anyhow.

Macky did say one thing about it though, "I mean, I always knew you would leave the Enclave. It was never going to be a fit for you, but seriously of all the lives you could choose, you pick a wizard?"

Ashyn chuckled. It hurt. "Yeah, a little wild, huh?"

Macky laughed at that. "Yeah, a bit."

It was then that Ashyn realized something about Macky. He wasn't using the slang of the lesser educated that they did as boys. That Uriel still used. That many townspeople used.

"When did you learn to speak like this?" Ashyn asked.

"The Enclave," Macky responded, obviously understanding Ashyn's query. "When I began studying for priesthood, it was important to be clear and concise for sermons. I learned to read, too."

"Count?"

"Let's not get crazy now."

Again the two laughed. It felt good, really good. It hurt, but he needed it.

"It looks like you are the one who has grown up, Macky."

The priest shrugged. "I've made my share of mistakes. Suffered my own trials. I have had many wonderful winters, and some less so. I have loved, and had, for a time, been loved." He looked down between their feet, "Then I lost the woman I loved to another man."

"Avrimae."

Macky's head bobbed slightly. "She was my world, Ashyn. I am not afraid to say it. She always was, even when we were kids. After she married and had a child, I couldn't take it. There was finality to it that I could no longer ignore. It was over. Even if Avrimae still loved me, she was wed with another now. The Enclave forbids adultery, and the penance for such an act is terrible for the women."

"Why didn't you just leave then?" Ashyn queried.

"There was nowhere for me to go. I toyed with the idea of going to Buckner, but my heart wasn't in it. I am a simple man, Ashyn. I needed a simple town. Czynsk is that town."

Ashyn nodded. Macky gathered joy from the smallest of things around him, and he always kept his aspirations low. Excepting Avrimae.

"Do you think she still loves you the way you clearly love her?" Ashyn asked his friend.

Ashyn felt the bars quiver against his back as Macky shook his head. "I don't know, Ash. I want to think she does. Sometimes she looks at me and I think..."

Ashyn looked back between the beams to see tears rolling down the man's face. He shouldn't have pried so deeply.

Macky took a deep breath and continued, choosing not to finish his last sentence. "Knowing that I was bound to Czynsk, I did the only thing I could think of to protect Avrimae, and try and save what was left of my sanity. I joined the clergy.

"I thought that if I could fill that void in my heart with something greater than my own desires, I would mend and move on with my life. I have always been quick to love friends, and strangers alike. I know people might find that childish and gullible, but I thought perhaps I could use that, you know? Direct it towards something that could benefit not just me, but everyone? Perhaps I was merely being arrogant. Perhaps it was pity and selfishness, or maybe I was justing giving Avrimae the tools necessary to let go, because ultimately, I lacked the strength to do so. I became a priest."

"How long?"

"I've only been an actual Father for a little over a winter, but I've been training for about four or five winters now. I've lost track of time here. The people of Czynsk seemed happy with me though."

"And Avrimae?"

Macky's shoulders shrugged. "She never attended my sermons. And being a man of the cloth, I could not exactly attend many of the local taverns. Imbibing grain alcohols is prohibited for the clergy. I figured she moved on with her life, I needed to as well. You should've seen her in Czynsk, Ash. The way she is with her daughter. She loves that girl so much. It'd melt your heart. That's why I was surprised to say the least when I tried to rally the town to turn away the Wild Elves that she was among the first to stand with me."

"Turning people away seems very unlike a father of the Jasian Enclave," Ashyn postulated.

"Well, hounding one of my best childhood friends through the Shalis-Fey and trying to murder him may have made me slightly biased, I'll admit."

"Fair enough."

"We are only human after all," Macky added.

Ashyn sighed. Only human. He knew it was merely an expression, but how much did that even apply to him anymore? Ashyn felt normal. He looked normal, too. Yet what was it about him that made him so different inside?

Nuchada. Bearer of multiple souls. How did that even work? How could it work? It seemed impossible. And yet, he was not human, and not Elven either. So what in the hells was he?

Once again he felt Macky looking at him. "What is it now?" Ashyn asked without even looking his way.

"That's eerie Ash," Mactonal replied. "Is that some sort of magic thing?"

Ashyn shook his head. He hadn't felt magic since the totem. "No," he said. "Just my own unique trait, I guess."

"Weird."

"What's the question Macky?"

There was a long silence. Ashyn knew that Macky was thinking long and hard on his question. It was written in his body language, before his mind could even formulate it to his lips. "Have you ever been in love with someone, Ashyn?"

"No," Ashyn replied quickly.

"Never?"

"Never."

"It is a terrible privilege," he said after a moment's hesitation, "to give your heart so completely to someone. To honor someone more than you honor yourself. To have someone's needs come before your own so fully that it is a reflex. It is not servitude. You want to do it. There is nothing quite so amazing, or rewarding. Nor quite so terrifying."

"I love my sister," Ashyn said at last.

"As we love all our siblings and parents," Macky replied. "It is different to love someone other than kin. I don't want to say it is stronger, for I do not believe it is, but it is definitely a very different kind of love. That in itself seems a gift of Creation."

Ashyn thought about his words. Subconsciously his hand reached out and stroked the fibers of platinum hair that were woven into a single braid. The only one now, whom he could truly say he loved unequivocally, was his sister. He was here for her.

"My sister… she is still alive," he said quietly to the priest.

The answer came simply from Macky's lips, "I know."

Ashyn summoned the energy to turn and look at the man. He grasped the bars desperately, leaning into them just as much for support as for a need to know from the man. "How? How do you know?"

Macky nodded to the water. "The elves have an ability with their magic…" He stumbled, and Ashyn could see he was in unfamiliar territory with his scope of knowledge. Had Ashyn not just had a conversation using water, he too might have had difficulty understanding what the priest was going to say next. "They can make these images appear in the water."

"Appear?"

Macky nodded. "I watched you fight an elf through her eyes. I watched you kill her."

Ashyn leaned his head against the bars at hearing the words. Though he ran them through his head for the last few months repeatedly, to hear them from the mouth of a peer…

"You had no choice," the priest told him reassuringly. "She left you with little option, the Maker knows this, your soul is not yet damned, not for her death."

"Not yet…" Ashyn agreed, but let the words hang.

"I heard what you asked her. I heard the name," Macky motioned back behind him to the straggling people on the rocks, "We all did. Julietta."

His body spiked with a surge of energy at hearing that they all heard the name. Perhaps Macky knew where she was, perhaps anyone of them did?

He pressed hard against the bars, as if someone trying to convince them of his need to get on the other side. His eyes frantically darted to the other forms in the background, their importance suddenly taking on a new meaning. Urgently he asked, "Do you know where she is? Do any of them know where she is? She has red hair like mine, and she's blind, with crescent brands around her eyes."

Ashyn felt that energy bleed from him as Macky shook his head no. "The elves asked us. Many of them were very aggressive about learning where she was. None of them ever heard the name Julietta before, but if it will put you at ease I will ask them again. Just be aware that I can pretty much assure you that we have seen no one that fits that description. Like your complexion, she is unique for the region."

Ashyn slammed his head against the bars in frustration. "I know."

He felt a pinch against his scalp and reached up confused. Ashyn drew his fingers back to find them wet with blood.

"Careful," Macky told the wizard. "If the bars feel threatened, they bite."

"Bite?" Ashyn pulled away from the bars to see a tiny beak protruding from the wood. Within a minute it receded back within the bar and then faded completely.

"They're safe to lean against," Macky told Ashyn. "Took me weeks to figure it out. You can rock them a little. A jostle here or there and they're fine. Just don't shake or slam against them, and whatever you do don't try to pry them apart. That's bad."

Ashyn nodded and touched the small wound again. That was when he realized there was something different about him, that he didn't notice when he first awoke.

He ran his fingers gingerly over his head. Spiky stubble stabbed at his sensitive fingertips. His long hair, it was gone.

Macky could apparently read this new revelation in Ashyn's eyes. "Lice."

Ashyn looked at his friend, "What?"

"They shave our heads because lice are a huge issue amongst those in the Water Pens. We can't exactly clean ourselves in the water after all. Our filth builds up to high levels and we are covered in small insects they call lice. If they don't keep our heads shaved the lice will bite and cause rashes on our scalps. We will itch the inflamed flesh and tear open wounds. Then those wounds turn into grotesque infections."

Ashyn could see the scabs on Macky's shorn scalp. "So they keep our heads free of hair. That is about the only service they provide. They care very little for many of us in these Water Pens. We are here because there are those held elsewhere that do care. We are leverage, nothing more. I have no doubt that when our use is done, we will be exterminated like the vermin they think we are. All I can do is pray to the Maker for salvation for my people."

Ashyn was still alarmed at what his fingers were telling him. What Macky was telling him.

"I watched a woman torn apart by the men and other women in there. They just moaned 'meat' over and over as they cannibalized her."

Macky looked down, murmuring, "Glorine." Speaking up a tad, he went on, "She was one of the orphans with us as children. I don't know if you ever had the chance to know her?" Looking to the ground he added, "I whispered many prayers to the Maker that night. As you will soon learn, the Water Pens suffer the punishments for many of our people's poor work out in the quarries or whatever other tasks the elves have us do for our reclamation.

"Before your arrival, it was a particularly brutal time. The elves keep us on a very jejune diet. They need to keep us too weak to revolt. Any human found rallying in the other cells is sent here to one of the pens to isolate them and destroy morale. They do it through hunger. Many of us hadn't received more than a sip of water in a week's time. We had not eaten food in near to a month. We were dying a slow, agonizing death. The ultimate morale crusher. Starvation is a terrible way to die, Ashyn.

"What my own people did was horrifying. To know how low we can fall that we would consume our own is unconscionable. Worse, to know that the elves were willing to let us go that far is contemptible. It is hard to pray to the Maker for forgiveness when a people show such lack of humanity towards one and other."

Ashyn nodded. He could understand the dilemma the young priest was faced with. Even though the Ferhym were the enemy, the Jasian Enclave taught that all races were the Maker's children. That all should receive absolution for their sins. Ashyn knew how hard it would be for Macky to pray to the Maker to forgive the actions of the elves.

"They fed and watered us two days later."

Ashyn was at a loss for words. He had seen and heard despicable things come from the Wild Elves; he witnessed the violent murder of Glorine. To hear the pained words come from his friend's mouth, to know, without asking, that Macky was part of the starved that had partaken. Ashyn didn't want to know.

The churning water lapped behind him, reminding him of its presence. "But water…"

Macky shook his head no. "It is fetid. Any who attempt to drink that filth will die of dysentery, guaranteed. We've seen it happen."

"And the leaders of the revolts?" he prompted.

"Once broken, we are thrown together in this large pen. There is an overwhelming sense of hopelessness Ashyn. You have not seen it. You have not been here long enough. Most of the souls you see here conspired at one point. They tried to lead. Now look at them. They are emotionally dead. They've given up on all but life, and soon they will give up on that too."

The wizard slammed his palm against the wooden pillar in frustration. Instantly, a dozen beaks lashed forth out of the bar.

Macky vaulted away from the pole, surprisingly dexterously. "Ashyn!" he hissed. "I just told you!"

Ashyn stepped back. "I know. Sorry. Just they've taken everything sacred! How can I not hate them?"

The beaks kept moving forward on snake-like vines. Snapping and hissing at the duo. The two moved further away from each other. The vines kept coming.

"Sometimes anger can be righteous Ashyn, but never hate. Do not confuse the two. We'll talk again later. Tomorrow Maker willing. I think you've pissed these things off too much for tonight."

"Right," Ashyn agreed. "Tomorrow then."

Macky turned away from the vines and ambled back towards the collection of worn people. The vines stopped pursuing and quickly receded into the bars.

Ashyn moved all the way to the waterline before the protective snapping vines stopped coming forth out of the bars. They stretched out to four feet in length. Very much like the way Rizen's totem forced the tree to grow sharp spikes from a branch. It was a curiosity, and something that he knew he would have to ask the Gaur about later. Macky's parting words forced Ashyn to think for the first time, why was he truly here?

To save his sister from torment? Or because he hated the Wild Elves so much that he wanted them all to pay for what they had done to her? To him? To Xexial? The longer Ashyn thought about it, the more disturbed at the idea he became.

TURN

Eigron was moving quickly through the hunter's living quarters of Feydras' Anula. Jenhiro was right behind him. The druid was acting fast now. He didn't seem desperate, not yet, but he was definitely getting there. Brodea's ultimatum towards him put the fear of the Spirits into him. She was a councilor. She was a hunter. That made her a killer. Something the druid clearly was not. Jenhiro could see it as clear as day.

Eigron may be many terrible things to their people, but a cold-blooded murderer was not one of them. So when Brodea told him that he needed to kill Avrimae in order to keep what they did a secret, Jenhiro knew she put him in a difficult place.

Jenhiro saw it before. Desperation could drive people to do the unexpected. Even unthinkable. Eigron was not there, not yet. So that meant he would turn to someone else. Someone who was a killer: Mehris.

The question was would the hunter do it in broad daylight? It had to look natural or accidental. That didn't leave the druid much time to plan. Jenhiro tried to put himself into Eigron's head. How would it best be done? Suffocation? Or perhaps a slip and fall? Poison?

Eigron slid through an intersection full of elves. They were busy feeding the local elk, though they did notice the wild-haired Ferhym as he slipped through the throngs' intent on making his destination. Jenhiro followed through the crowd just as deftly. He needed to know the plan before he could protect Avrimae.

If he waited by her pen for Eigron and Mehris to show up, he could compromise the illusion of his disappearance or further risk Avrimae's life. His impulsive decisions already cost enough lives. No, he would study his prey. Jenhiro maintained a safe distance, while Brodea's last few words to the druid resonated in his head, "I'll take care of your hunter problem, personally."

She was in the game. Jenhiro knew that Brodea had centuries more knowledge at hunting than he did. She knew all the tricks, all the angles. She knew that if Eigron was truly hunted, that he would have a tail. And that meant Jenhiro would have a tail, unless he could remain elusive.

Mehris' home, however, was likely on the very place she would scout out her quarry, him. He needed to be invisible.

He learned how to do that in the forests. He blended with the trees, becoming a shadow. He never had to hide in plain sight among his own people before. No hunter had. For that he needed new tactics. He hoped to divert the First Councilor. He took a trick from the dui Nuchada. He changed his appearance to look like someone else. Not as drastic as going from a human to hym, but something aggressive enough among his own kind.

He became an Earthshorn, one of the farmers and gatherers of Feydras' Anula. It is the largest family of Ferhym to be precise, the lowest and most common caste of Ferhym. Unlike the prestige of hunters, druids, and councilors and their extended families, the Earthshorn all bore the same markings upon their flesh. Their particular woad was identical amongst them all, and not a single one stood out. Unless an Earthshorn born showed talent as a hunter or druid or found favor with one, none of their woads ever changed. Not all Ferhym could be hunters after all. Not all battled the skewers for the balance of nature. Only the most talented. Only the most devoted.

Jenhiro's fingertips traced the alien markings upon his breast subconsciously. He never wore another woad before. He never disguised himself as *someone* else before. It was bizarre, and uncomfortable, but he couldn't deny that it was effective. A single look at the markings on his body, and every hunter ignored him instantly. He was no longer Jenhiro Windreaver, branch commander for the Druids of the Vine. He was no longer a hunter in their eyes. He wasn't the hero who had brought them the dui Nuchada. He was a peasant. And he was invisible to everyone.

The Ferhym also wore his dark hair unbound, so that it fell down around his face. It only helped to make the illusion more real. Very few Earthshorn kept the sides of their heads shaven. There was no need. So he adapted as necessary.

Would his disguise fool Brodea? He doubted it. She knew his face. Yet for now it worked on everyone else, including Eigron and Mehris, and that was all that mattered.

Jenhiro kept alert as he pursued Eigron. Any set of eyes that fell on him could be an agent of Brodea's. He did not know the lengths of her power as First Councilor. How far the tendrils of her influence spread? Already she penetrated the sanctity of the druids with Eigron. Did she have all of the councilors too? The hunters? The Voïre?

He couldn't reach the platinum-haired beauty and it concerned him. Did Brodea know what he was thinking? And what of the Voïre dui Ceremeia herself? He looked into her eyes. Had she seen all that she needed to judge him? And if so, what was the verdict?

Jenhiro slowed down briefly. He touched his eyes, extending his senses. He needed to focus on Eigron; the rest would come later. When he opened his eyes again he was ready to find out what the druid had in store for Avrimae. He set out once more, centered. He knew the First Councilor was out there, and that was all he could do.

~ ~ ~

Eigron turned out to be fairly predictable. After trying to lose his tail in the crowds of Ferhym, he wound up at the small abode of his hunter accomplice. Jenhiro watched, three houses away, as the druid curtly greeted Mehris' mate, and then pulled the hunter from his home. Jenhiro could see Eigron talking swiftly to the hunter, agitation apparent in the aggressive motions he made with his hands.

The branch commander wished he could get closer to the duo, but he was too wary of Brodea. She would have Mehris watched. She would have his family watched. No, closer was not an option. In fact, he was beginning to have reservations about even following Eigron to Mehris in the first place.

Jenhiro pushed himself tighter to the house, and tried to appear nondescript to any who may look his way. A random Earthshorn taking a break underneath the overhang of a public house wouldn't appear out of place considering they were surrounded by passing Earthshorn. Confident in his security, Jenhiro watched the two, trying to learn what he could through body language alone.

Mehris nodded at everything Eigron said, and though Jenhiro couldn't hear a word of it, he could see the growing comprehension in Mehris face. His worried eyes roamed the other houses as Eigron talked, and flitted across every elf that passed by. He was a hunter searching for danger. Jenhiro could make out the flickers of paranoia playing in the corners of Mehris vision, the concern over flashed movements between passersby.

"You cannot trust anyone," Jenhiro muttered very quietly to himself as he watched the growing apprehension on the hunter's face.

Then Eigron hit a point in his explanation that made the hunter rock on his feet. Did he explain that Hengrit was murdered? That his fellow conspirator kept raping Avrimae long after the initial assault? Or did he tell them of the First Councilor's ultimatum?

It didn't matter, Jenhiro decided. There was little he could do from his vantage, to learn of the conversation between the two elves, and he never held an affinity for reading lips. His life as a branch commander was about birdcalls, hand signals, dead drops, and trail signs. He didn't have to actively spy on anyone to determine whether or not he felt they were a skewer in the Shalis-Fey. Other than the dui Nuchada anyways, but that had been by choice. And curiosity.

Finally, something Eigron told Mehris made the hunter run back into his house. The druid wasted no time, and left, traveling deeper into the district. Seconds later Mehris exited his home and headed in the opposite direction. Journeying towards the public cells. The direction of Avrimae.

Jenhiro leaned back against the wooden slats of the home as Mehris passed. The hunter's eyes darted across everyone, but as Jenhiro knew, Mehris was only interested in another hunter's woad. When Mehris' eyes looked at the Earthshorn markings on Jenhiro's chest, they moved on to their next target, never making eye contact with the branch commander.

This had taken a turn in a direction Jenhiro already considered. While he assumed Eigron would gather Mehris and together they would go to Avrimae, where one or both would do the deed, this was different. Eigron wanted Jenhiro to follow the hunter. It was a ruse.

Jenhiro could see the bold move playing out two paces ahead of the duo. Mehris was a hunter and yet he left with no javelins or spears. That was not a mistake any hunter made, not even in the security of Feydras' Anula.

Eigron on the other hand, traveled further into the denser population of the elves. This was alien in and of itself. When Jenhiro was a child, he rarely saw a druid. He thought them as uncommon as an albino Bristle Wolf. It wasn't until he was older, and a hunter, that he learned the truth about nature's elite.

Druids congregated in their cove. In most cases they were social pariahs, only communicating with the Council of Elm or with their hunters at most. Even then, only a rare few could handle that. Many druids never socialized outside of the comforts of their circle. It wasn't unusual for them to ignore Jenhiro, even within their cove.

Jenhiro had at first thought that the druids were elitist and prudish, thinking they were better than other elves. It wasn't until he became a branch commander and had to deal with his own assigned druid that he learned a valuable lesson. They weren't arrogant and self-righteous against the other Ferhym. They were aloof and distant.

Learning to care for nature the way they had, separated them from their own kind. The only ones to really understand them were of course other druids. To protect nature the druids disconnected themselves from society.

Eigron was a Genrus of the Vines. He was no different. Until his sudden elevation in station Jenhiro hadn't even known the Ferhym existed. Eigron was even more insular than usual. Jenhiro worked for the druids for many winters. Though he hadn't spoken with many, he knew their faces. Until his return to Feydras' Anula, he had never met Eigron before.

A true druid's nature wouldn't head where there were more people, but away. Eigron should have left towards the Cove of Vines, or back to the Great Elm, or even with Mehris. He was walking deeper into populated areas. Areas that under normal circumstances would make many of the nature's servants more than a little uncomfortable.

That was why it was a ruse. That was why it was a trap. Eigron was going to double back and flank Mehris to try to see who was stalking them. Jenhiro would not be fooled, though he gave the druid a slight nod of credit for the plan.

Jenhiro looked up at the bright midday sun looming high in the sky. Eigron told Brodea that everything would be as she had demanded by the next convening of the council. A week from today.

Brodea specifically said that Avrimae die of natural causes. Yet would the Council of Elm even care if she was poisoned? Would they bother to look at a skewer? Jenhiro realized they might. There were those who opposed Brodea's war. If someone on the council even suspected that the human skewer was poisoned, then they may dig deeper and order the druids to investigate. Eigron could not cover it up if the druids became involved. Especially the Elder of Vines.

Even though Brodea was willing to kill Avrimae in order to get the dui Nuchada to talk, she would not want anything negative to lead to her now. She had too much at stake in trying to get something out of the dui Nuchada. If the council held a vote of no confidence against her...

It wouldn't be poison. Even though no one would question Mehris if he administered it. The hunter had been long seen as an aide of Eigron's over the last few weeks.

Jenhiro was torn. He knew he should follow Eigron, and that the druid would double back, but he couldn't take the two of them together. He was a hym of the forests. Wild and free. Though a trained killer, he didn't have the true skills necessary to put forward and stop the druid and his accomplice. Logically he should kill one now, in public. He probably could, but if Brodea spotted him...

He needed a distraction. One that would force Brodea away. One that would keep her occupied while he targeted the others. To do that, he needed help. And the only person left alive that he trusted was nowhere to be found.

That wasn't true.

A sick dawning gripped his stomach. There was one other he put his trust in that had never let him down, even when things were the most dire. Someone who knew the ways of misdirection. Someone who would want to help Avrimae. Someone who could help him. Someone who would be discreet and that no one would expect. Someone he couldn't even believe he was considering.

The dui Nuchada.

PART III

DUI NUCHADA

TOME III

What we see is often a curious thing. Our minds work quickly, generating a perception of this single, often first, image we see, and then we forever associate something to that image. So many inaccuracies often stem from that single generalization we make about a person, race, or religion in that instant. The first time we see someone not carrying their load, immediately they are lazy. And that laziness stays in our minds every time we see them, no matter how hard they are working.

If someone tries to contradict that precept by saying, "no, they are a hard worker," our minds create fictitious barriers around such assaulting words. We justify such precepts as, they were just caught on those days, or they are trying to look good to someone. Because, Maker forbid, our initial perception of them is wrong. And when we see them again, not carrying the load, all the work they have done before is immediately negated because our initial perception takes over as the dominant one. "I was right! They are lazy!"

This thought process extends beyond people, and incorporates everything. A tavern becomes dangerous because a fight broke out there once, a house becomes haunted because a whistling noise was heard, a race is nothing but a bunch of thugs and hooligans because of a mugging by one of them, or in my case, all wizards are evil…

Perception is NOT reality no matter how much our minds may be counter to it, no matter how much culture embraces such a mentality.

I am not preaching, nor am I above such petty-minded thinking myself. It took an enemy, who became an ally, to teach me that everyone can rise above that narrow-tunneled, line-of-sight mentality that each of us takes.

I, like my mentor Xexial Bontain, thought all Wild Elves were the same. That they were zealous, close-minded savages, bent on murder for the sake of self-aggrandizing their own culture.

I was wrong. I was closed-minded.

Because of that one person, I now realize that perception is always a two-way street. If they can rise above such preconceived judgments bred into them from centuries of teaching, then I to shall do my best to view things with an open mind.

-Third journal of the Blood Wizard,
Ashyn Rune

STRANGEST OF DAYS

Jenhiro could scarcely breathe as he approached the Water Pens. He still held his disguise as an Earthshorn. For all they knew he may be heading to those forlorn skewers to use as leverage against workers in the fields.

It felt insane. It was insane.

It seemed like all eyes were on him, and yet he knew that Brodea had her potent gaze cast elsewhere. This may be his best chance at talking with the dui Nuchada. It may be his only chance.

The long wooden poles that separated the humans from the Ferhym jutted skyward like young saplings. They looked easy enough to pry apart and release the dui Nuchada, but Jenhiro knew they were a druid's work. There would be no bending or twisting those wooden shoots. Not unless you wanted to be impaled by dozens of thriving, living vines.

Jenhiro could make out the massive bulk of the bull creature hunkered down in one of the corners by the pungent waters. He still couldn't believe they kept it alive.

It kept its head low and its thick fingers drifted through the foul liquid indiscriminately. Now visible to him, and bent low, it looked far less threatening than when it had towered over him, high in the sequoias. He realized that this was the creature that the druids saw. A creature cowed and fearful. Not the mighty wraithlike hunter that pursued him ardently for weeks, with only the thoughts of his death on its mind.

The dui Nuchada sat on the other end of the same pen, his back against the bars that divided his pen from the one that held more of the humans. Why they left him in this cell with a creature that once hunted him mercilessly, Jenhiro didn't know. Nor did he know why they stopped torturing him, or let him live for that matter. Either way, it was to Jenhiro's advantage. Or so he hoped. The dui Nuchada may have very different opinions about him now.

Jenhiro noted with some oddity, that the dui Nuchada's hand was also buried in the muck, similar to the bull. His eyes were closed, and his now shorn head was pressed against the naked wood of the bars. His olive skin was ashen. He looked nothing like a Wood Elf any longer. If anything, he looked worn. Jenhiro had put him there.

The Ferhym hoped to approach the dui Nuchada without making a scene. He wanted as little knowledge of his presence made public as possible, but when he came within a few yards of the pens, the Bull suddenly sprang to its feet snorting wildly. Amber eyes quickly turned in his direction, glaring savagely. Jenhiro froze, thinking immediately that it was a bad idea in coming here.

It stomped its hooves on the ground as if preparing to charge. As if it were going to barrel completely through the cage that it was in. Jenhiro didn't fear that though. He feared the recognition. If this bull could do it, how many others did as well? It only took a second for Jenhiro to understand. Woad meant nothing to the creature. It recognized his scent. Still it was making a ruckus, and Jenhiro knew within moments others would come to see what the cause was. He didn't have long.

The dui Nuchada opened his eyes at the disruption and looked in Jenhiro's direction. Those grey eyes sparkled with the same intensity as when they first met. Though the dui Nuchada's body was worn, his mind was as sharp as ever. This man was not ready to acquiesce to defeat. Not yet.

He pulled himself to his feet, and stumbled towards the beast. Jenhiro noted that the bull did not wheel on him, the obvious threat, but kept its ireful eyes boring on Jenhiro alone. How could the druids not see its intelligence?

The dui Nuchada then did something most peculiar. He splashed the water with his foot. At first there was no reaction, but then he did again. Jenhiro saw the bull's ears flicker. The dui Nuchada splashed once more, and that was when the beast turned on him.

Jenhiro tensed for a moment, thinking he may have just committed the dui Nuchada to a horrendous death when he saw, ever so slightly, the dui Nuchada shake his head. The beast wheeled back towards Jenhiro and snorted again. The dui Nuchada splashed one last time, and with it, the bull suddenly stormed off back to its corner.

The Ferhym, though curious about the interaction that just happened between mortal enemies, knew his window of opportunity was dwindling by a matter of heartbeats. He quickly moved towards the pen, looking swiftly for any signs of hunters or Councilors to witness their interaction. There was none, yet.

The dui Nuchada shambled forward, his body clearly stiff. He pressed himself to the bars, and stared at Jenhiro with a penetrating hawk-like gaze. "Tell me you've found her."

Jenhiro nodded, for even though he hadn't found her, thanks to Brodea, he was certain he knew where she was. "The druids have her in the Cove of Vines. I have not seen her, though I know she lives. That is all."

There was a sudden kindling in the dui Nuchada's eyes. It was a renewed sense of purpose. "Thank you," he said. "I had almost given up hope. We are even now I suppose."

Jenhiro nodded. "We are even." Quickly he looked back and forth, no Ferhym were curious yet of the creature's bellows, but he could see movement on the rocks of the other Water Pens. He couldn't afford to be seen any more than he already was. This was taking too long. "I have little time, but I need your help once more."

The dui Nuchada surprised him, by actually laughing. "There is little…"

Time was too short. Jenhiro had to interrupt. "It is about your friend, Avrimae."

It got the dui Nuchada's attention. "Go on."

"A druid is going to kill her, and I must put a stop to it. I need a way to protect her, but there are too many against me. Even the First Councilor is hunting for me."

The dui Nuchada bit his lip in frustration. His eyes, like lances, pierced Jenhiro trying to bury them deep into his core to find the truth. "If this is some sort of trick to get me to translate the tome…"

"No!" he said frustrated. "I don't even know what you're talking about."

"I'm sure," the dui Nuchada said.

Jenhiro looked to the other pen, the bodies within were growing curious. He was losing precious seconds; he needed to get through to the dui Nuchada. He needed his trust. But he didn't have anything! Nothing that would garner such blind faith. The dui Nuchada was right not to trust him, they, after all were enemies, by his own declaration.

The branch commander leaned his head against the bars in frustration. He was going to have to leave. It was a stupid idea to think he could persuade the man he committed to torture and punishment to help him. The dui Nuchada had already seen what they had done to Avrimae. How could he trust an elf after that?

Then Jenhiro's eyes fell upon something he hadn't seen since the night they had last spoken in camp together. The braid of platinum hair. It was dirty and frayed now, but he recognized it. Quickly he reached between the bars and grabbed the dui Nuchada's thin wrist. "When we met, you pretended to be a Lefhym. I assumed this came from a Voïre dui Ceremeia of your people, but it didn't, did it?" He whispered urgently as realization washed over him. He remembered hearing the whispers and tales from the druids. That the Voïre dui Ceremeia marked a dui Nuchada. He trusted an elf. "It's you, isn't it? The one from the story." At the time it seemed inconceivable. A folktale made up to share under the moonlight. "She gave it to you, didn't she? You were marked by a Ferhym Voïre?"

The dui Nuchada pulled his wrist from Jenhiro's grasp. "What do you know?" he demanded.

Jenhiro was excited now. Yes! She could help him after all! She could be the bridge that connected them! He spoke fast now. "She is with me. She helped me see our reality. See the truth."

"And what is your reality?" the dui Nuchada asked.

"That the Council of Elm is wrong. Not all skewers are evil just because of what they are. What they become determines their fate. Our own ignorance is our truest enemy. We fear what we don't understand."

The dui Nuchada's eyes showed his disbelief that Jenhiro had spoken the words. Jenhiro could hardly believe it himself, but as he said the words aloud he knew them to be true. He no longer believed in the Council of Elm. He no longer had faith in their view of the cause.

The dui Nuchada pulled away from the bars and looked to the moving throng of bodies now making their way to see the disturbance. "Tell her to contact me. She knows how," he said swiftly, and then he looked at the people. "I'll distract Brodea for you. Save Avrimae."

Jenhiro nodded.

"Run, Jenhiro."

The elf didn't question. He ran.

~ ~ ~

Brodea watched Eigron as he circuitously weaved his way through the midday throngs of elves. These hym busily hauled crops, moved and tended elk, and directed skewers with a propensity for the land. Those with a green thumb she heard more than one skewer mutter occasionally to each other.

Eigron was trying to cover himself by making his accomplice, Mehris, the bait for whomever may hunt them. Brodea thought he was acting irrationally and moving far too fast. A single day passed since Hengrit was found dead. Now at the sun's zenith, it appeared as if the druid was going to use the hunter to kill off Avrimae. She wondered how the druid convinced the hunter to do it so readily? Were all her subjects so stupid?

The druid scanned the crowds of humans and hym looking for any hunter that may be pursuing Mehris. The hunter was not moving fast, he was giving their pursuer every opportunity to find him and follow him. Under normal circumstances it might have seemed like a good plan. It was not.

Eigron proved himself capable of many things, but his inexperience in shadow games was wholly clear to her. Did he think moving about in broad daylight would somehow make his stalker easier to spot? Did he think that the crowds would keep the hunter from actually acting? It was chaos out there. No one would be the wiser when he fell.

The druid was making errors that were not only asinine, but ultimately costly. He was advertising himself, and his only ally, and placing himself within their hunter's control whether he knew it or not.

Brodea could see Eigron, like any druid would be, was out of his element. He didn't know the hym; he knew only his circle and the council. He was the stranger here. The hunter was not. They would become one with the people, because they were the people.

Eigron looked aloof and alien. His caste was intimidating to simpler hym like the Earthshorn, and the deeper he went into the populace, the more looks he received. He was attracting too much attention. While up ahead, Mehris easily slipped by without a second glance.

Eigron's actions, his juvenility, made him a liability to Brodea. She knew it was likely that she would have to sever her connection with the druid. He messed up badly. It was only a matter of time before it would be too big to cover up. If the councilors thought for a moment that she was unable to guide her people...

Would they think she was a liability too? Would there be others who would begin to plot against her? If she allowed Eigron to continue as he was, she could very well find herself in the same position that Tehirs had been.

No. It was all too clear. Eigron needed containment. Already a hunter knew this; it could even be a Councilor. She puzzled at the thought, thinking this stalker may be more of a boon then Eigron was. The idea also made her angry. The death of Eigron might benefit her and the cause ultimately, but whoever was going about this had no right to supersede her. She was the First Councilor. She was the Spear Maiden who led her people. She was the spiritual connection. She was going to bring about the end of the wizards. This was a vigilante and nothing more. That made them against her. Against the cause of balance.

Her dark gaze flitted through the crowds of people. The realization of it made what she was going to do next all the easier. Her conscience was no longer burdened with the thought of a good hym dying. It was a skewer. And she had long ago sworn to do everything it took to maintain balance. She had no choice but to uphold it. It was her life.

With the sun now at its apex, the elves were at their busiest. The murder of Eigron, or Mehris, would be so easy in this chaos. Eigron thought he was safe in the throngs. The truth was, unless someone intervened, he was a dead hym walking. How he seemed so capable in the weeks before was beyond her. Perhaps it was simply the capture of the dui Nuchada that brought the heat to her blood. The impulse of having the tome translated and used as a weapon. Eigron acted as that conduit to the Cove for her. An easily moldable conduit.

She stared at the back of his wild dark hair. Bits of hollowed bird bones jutted from the madness. There would be other druids. Others more capable, and just as willing.

She wondered how the stalker would do it? Poison? A puncture to the lungs? It would be close; that was often the easiest way. She almost desired to see the artistry unfold.

Brodea knew it couldn't happen, yet. He was her access into the cove, the weapons, and Julietta. Cultivating his replacement would take too long.

The First Councilor would ensure Eigron's survival, at least for the week. Perhaps this conflict would help him add wisdom to his naïve mind. If not, when the week was up, well, accidents happened all the time.

She heard it before she saw it. In the distance, something unrecognizable screamed. It was a curious sound, a whistling. An animal's cry.

Then she noticed others in the crowd turning their head in alarm. Something was happening. Something by the Great Elm. Brodea risked averting her eyes from the druid. Was this it? A distraction? Would the hunter make a move?

The crowd panicked as the strange whistling grew louder, more frantic. It caused the elk handled by the Earthshorn to grow skittish making them harder to control. Soon they, too, panicked, whistling and rearing up on hind legs.

"Rune," she growled. She somehow knew Ashyn had a hand in this. She had given him too long of a reprieve. He was growing strong.

It became increasingly difficult to see Eigron in the growing frenzy. Brodea now had to make a decision. Locate the source of the disturbance and quell it, or extract Eigron? She didn't like what her gut told her so she jumped into the hot waves of elven flesh.

Only a wizard could unnerve nature so. Could terrify them and send them off balance. It was that, or a druid was controlling them, which meant Eigron's hunter had a potential ally. That thought Brodea did not like at all. If the druids were turning on her...

Either way her decision was made. Eigron would survive one more day.

Brodea had always been fleet of foot and acrobatic, and a few months as First Councilor had not yet taken away centuries of skill. She dodged, maneuvered, and swept her way to the stunted druid. Before he even realized it, she was there.

Eigron startled at the sight of her. His fearful reaction disgusted her. If not for her, this druid would be a dead hym fast. "Your ruse has failed. You are an active target."

Her words confused the inept druid for only a moment, before he caught on. "Spirits preserve me!" He mumbled in shock. "Mehris..."

Eigron looked up towards the direction of his hunter aide, and Brodea looked to follow his gaze. "We need to get you out of this crowd first, and then we'll worry about the hunter."

"But..."

Brodea slapped him hard. He looked at her in shock. "If you are truly being hunted, now is the time they will strike a druid. You are lucky that I have agreed to stop this hunter for you, because it is looking like you would be more useful to me dead than alive if you are going to remain so ignorant. Now follow me, closely."

Eigron nodded. "Where are we going?"

Brodea looked at the crowd as it scattered. Anyone could kill Eigron at any moment. The situation was bad, and he had placed himself there. She needed to secure him, and fast. Normally the safest place he would be would be at the lodges where the hunters trained. Surrounded by the warrior Ferhym. That wasn't an option now since one had gone rogue.

The Cove of Vines was the next logical choice, but if the stalker found an ally druid, then it was almost expected that Eigron would flee there. They would be waiting.

No, she needed something one wouldn't expect. The last place one would think to look, or dare to go. She knew exactly where to take Eigron, and she knew exactly how it was going to look. "Just shut up, keep your head down, and follow," she snapped. Anger grew with every step she took. Eigron's mistake had now put her directly where she hadn't wanted to be, in the open.

"Well played, adversary," she seethed. "Well played."

~ ~ ~

Jenhiro couldn't believe what he was seeing as the First Councilor pushed right passed him dragging a bewildered Eigron with her. She hadn't even seen him! Nor had Eigron. More jarring to him though, was until she was right next to him he hadn't noticed her either! The First Councilor of all people!

The most respected person in Feydras' Anula. She blended with the other Ferhym seamlessly. She had painted over the seared markings in her flesh, and disappeared even more easily than he had. Jenhiro now fully realized without a doubt the person he was dealing with. Brodea was a hunter without peer.

The hunter only gave it a moment's thought about following them to try to get at Eigron. It was a fleeting gesture, because he knew that the dui Nuchada had come through for him and distracted Brodea as he had said he would. It was now up to him to protect Avrimae. It may be the only window he had that Mehris and Eigron were apart.

He was amazed by the dui Nuchada's effectiveness. How had he done that? How had he managed to rile up all the elk from inside a cage?

He looked into the panicked and dispersing crowds until his eyes caught the distinctive pattern of Willowfallen. The hunter was still pushing towards his objective. Perhaps he thought Eigron was still following him from a distance. Jenhiro maneuvered his way forward, closing the gap on his way to Avrimae's cell.

The elk were out of control. Many of the elves gave up and instead of fighting the reins of the powerful beasts, they let go and ran for the safety of cover. Soon the animals were bucking, kicking, and sprinting in all directions, turning the congregation of elves into a frenzied mob. Many Ferhym screamed as they fled for their lives, and Jenhiro knew at that point the only ones that would be able to get the animals under control were the druids. Jenhiro didn't miss the irony of it. A druid was there right now, and he was fleeing!

An elk came for Jenhiro suddenly. It threatened to gore anyone in its path with its great four-foot crest of antlers. The nimble hunter rolled beneath the raging creature and came up on its other side. Only intent on escape, the elk continued on its way further into masses of people. That was too close.

Then the worst happened. Whether the dui Nuchada's intention or not, the elk did what all fearful pack animals do. They congregated and ran. In the narrow streets of the district, they formed a perfect deadly funnel of destruction. They became a stampede.

Jenhiro knew he needed to get out of the madness and on track before he lost Mehris. His window of opportunity was beginning to close fast. The cell that Avrimae was in was only a few blocks away. With a stampede at his back and terrified elves in front of him, Jenhiro knew the chances of reaching Mehris before he had a chance to kill Avrimae were grim. If had any hope of catching up to Mehris in time, he needed to do something desperate. He didn't hide. He went for Mehris directly in a dead run.

Jenhiro pulled ahead of the stampeding elk and bore down on Mehris. He hoped that the sound of the rampaging creatures would distract Mehris enough not to notice the Earthshorn barreling towards him. He got close too. So close.

With only a few yards to go before the hunter would be in Jenhiro's grasp, Mehris turned. Jenhiro was at a point of no return and he lashed out at the hunter. Mehris' reacted to the threat instantly. Jenhiro's punch was blocked and his momentum was used against him as Mehris lifted him up and over, throwing him away.

Jenhiro flew head over heels, crashing hard into a wooden trough. Wood exploded, and water doused him as stars dotted his vision and pain shot through his body.

Jenhiro fought to keep conscious. He stumbled back to his feet, sliding in the water-slickened dirt that was fast turning to mud. His head spun, but he struggled to keep cognizant of his surroundings. He knew at any moment the trained hunter would counterstrike.

The ground rumbled beneath his feet, and his teeth chattered, but the attack never came. Not from Mehris. He shook the stars from his vision and saw that Mehris was running away from him with all haste towards the cells. Not just him. Jenhiro felt the growing tremble beneath his feet. The stampede was closing fast.

Jenhiro stumbled out of the wreckage of the water trough and chased after Mehris. His head was still woozy, and he knew his luck wouldn't hold against the elf a second time.

The two ran for all they had down the main section of the farmers' district. The elves who heard the stampede coming were smart enough to get off the streets and into their homes, so the pathway in front of them was mostly vacant. "Mostly" being the operative word.

Small push carts and wagons full of anything from fruits and vegetables to grains and lumber littered the abandoned pathway ahead. It became a blurred frenzy of leaps, sways, and harrowing sidesteps to avoid the obstacles. Behind him he could hear the elk having less luck as they crashed through the barriers in their crazed attempt to escape their unseen threat, goaded onward by that whistling cry.

Mehris was good. Jenhiro struggled to keep up with the hunter as he deftly maneuvered through the blockaded passage. It didn't take long before Jenhiro felt the taxing on his lungs that the collision with the trough gave him. His vision was getting murky in the corners. A stitch developed in his side. He could only stare forlornly as Mehris pulled ahead, and was eventually gone.

Jenhiro thought quickly. He knew that Mehris would still have to get inside Avrimae's cell and then perform the act so that it appeared as a natural cause. That would take time. Long enough for the branch commander to save her? He couldn't be sure. As he rounded the corner, Jenhiro was given his answer. His gut tightened even more. The answer was "yes."

Mehris had Avrimae out of her cell, and he was half-dragging, half-carrying the inert woman down the road. To onlookers it appeared as if the hunter was trying to rescue the skewer. Jenhiro realized Mehris was planning to use the stampede to his advantage. Just drop her and escape at the last possible second, so that the woman would be trampled to death.

No one on the council would question it. No one could after what happened here today. Brodea and her entourage would get away with murder.

He dug his bare feet into the earth harder and pushed forward with every bit of energy he had. He was only a handful of seconds in front of the stampeding elk. Whatever could be done to save Avrimae would have to be done now.

Jenhiro saw it. His only chance. He ran for a cart, closing the distance and leapt off it screaming wildly.

Mehris spun around surprised. Before he could react this time, Jenhiro collided into the two in a frenzy of limbs. Avrimae was ripped from Mehris' arms as the hunters rolled through the dirt road. Jenhiro tried to absorb the impact of the road by diffusing the inertia with his wild roll. Mehris held on tight, fighting to maintain dominance. When they finally came to a stop, the two were covered in dust and bled in a hundred places. Jenhiro ambled to his feet and saw Mehris was lying still, blood pooling on the ground from his mouth. Avrimae was on the ground a few feet away. The stampede was rounding corner he had just come from; it would be on him in a few breaths.

Jenhiro ran to Avrimae. She looked no worse for the wear after being dumped unceremoniously on the ground. Thunder roared in his ears as the stampede closed in on them. Jenhiro didn't know where he was going to go. Still he had to try. He bent over to pick the human up, when he was suddenly tackled from behind. His skull slammed hard against the packed earth. His head swam and his vision spun.

He was vaguely aware of someone climbing atop him, and then he realized with growing horror that he couldn't breathe! His vision snapped in place to see Mehris straddled on him. Blood and dirt matted his hair and obscured most of the Willowfallen markings, but it did nothing to hide the look of murder in the Wild Elf's eyes.

Panic filled his body in the absence of air. He clawed at the strong hands wrapped around his throat, but they held firm. Jenhiro's eyes darted from the killer on top of him to the still form of Avrimae only two feet away. The tremors against his back rumbled like an earthquake. A roar filled his ears. In mere seconds all three of them would be crushed to death.

Jenhiro swung wildly at the hunter on top of him, but Mehris reach was longer than his was. He hammered at Mehris forearms but the hunter's grip was as solid as oak. He would ride this task out until the end.

Jenhiro's vision began to close in from the sides. Air deprivation burned at his lungs. His chest was on fire, and it felt like his eyes were bulging from his skull. Blindly he groped around the ground for something, anything to leverage against his assailer.

His vision was but a pinprick and the rumble in his ears drown out all other sound, when his tingling fingers touched something round and hard. He fought to grab onto whatever it was, but the reverberation pushed it away. That was it. All hope was gone.

His hand fell open and his fingers slackened. Blackness closed in.

Jenhiro had failed.

Distantly he felt something roll back into his awaiting fingers. They closed around it. Something solid. Strong.

Rejuvenated, his hand latched onto it and he swung the object with all of his might towards Mehris. It was just long enough that it connected with the corner of the hunter's jaw.

The impact of the foreign object was powerful enough to rip the hunter off Jenhiro and into the downturned crown of a rampaging elk. The three-point crown of antlers slammed into Mehris' chest, goring him and tearing him from the ground.

With air flooding into his lungs, and knowing that it was the end, Jenhiro scrambled beneath the crashing hooves, and fell on top of Avrimae. There he covered her, ready to take the blows in place of her and hope that giving his life would spare hers.

He screamed as the heavy hoof falls rained down around him. He closed his eyes tight waiting to feel the crushing pain of thousands of pounds slamming down on him over and over again.

All around him his world was nothing but vibration, sound, and choking dust. Thunder pounded his ears and, the hammering of hooves shook his bones. He knew that any moment would be the end.

But it continued on and on until before he knew it, there was no more. The ground continued to shudder but it was distant. His ears still throbbed with sound but it was faint. Slowly Jenhiro opened his eyes, and he was rewarded with the sight of Avrimae beneath him, her lips slightly parted and drawing in small breaths.

The branch commander forced himself to his feet. His body hurt in a dozen places, and he found it difficult to breathe, but he didn't care. He was alive! He looked down to see what it was that he grasped that had saved his life from Mehris.

In his hand he held the broken end of a something large and green. A zucchini saved him. Jenhiro laughed and then cried. He couldn't help it. It was a miracle! No not a miracle, but maybe a sign from the Spirits! He was doing their work, their true work! It was what the cause was supposed to be.

Almost twenty feet away he saw the remains of Mehris. The body was twisted, broken, and doused in blood. The crumpled hunter drew no air, and his face mutilated by hooves, his eyes destroyed.

Jenhiro accepted this death, as he knew he must. Renewed in his belief in the cause, he reached down and lifted the sleeping form of Avrimae. She no longer deserved to be in a cell. He needed to find a place to hide her. He needed to take her home.

A FINAL WARNING

Ashyn heard the screams and wild cries of the elk in the distance and he knew that his distraction worked. He just hoped it was enough for the Wild Elf to save Avrimae. He stared down at the gaur who was bent over, its head supplanted onto the cold hard ground. After several moments its amber eyes opened, and it looked up at him.

Ashyn never saw the creature look more exhausted, not even when they had battled each other. Feedback was draining Rizen mercilessly.

Rizen nodded his weary head towards the water, and Ashyn obliged him. They walked to the filthy shore and sat down. Ashyn stuck his fingers into the muck right after the gaur. *It is much harder without my totem,* Rizen told him wearily, *but it is done.*

How many did you reach? Ashyn asked.

The gaur's amber eyes looked out beyond the water pens. *Most of them. The elk are in a panic. Tell me Totem-Brother, how will what I have done to nature aid us?*

Ashyn wasn't surprised to hear that question. In fact, if anything, he was surprised to hear it so late. After Jenhiro left, Ashyn told Rizen what he wanted the Shaman to do, and the creature did it on blind faith alone. They went from trying to kill each other, to becoming totally dependent upon one and other in the span of a day. He was grateful for it too, because his alternative was to attack the perimeter fences until the druids came and stopped the magical bars from killing him.

He wanted to chuckle at fickle fingers of fate, and how their reach plucked up the most unlikely of allies, but he knew he had some explaining to do first.

I know you hate the elf that came to this cell. He was rewarded with a snort of anger. It didn't bother Ashyn; he already knew what Jenhiro had done to warrant such seething hatred. Instead he appealed to the gaur's own inner conflict. *Like you, he made a terrible mistake. In killing your herd, he has paid a terrible price. I think he is trying to atone.*

Nothing will make up for the loss of my herd, my pundit, and my life. The gaur complained.

No, Ashyn agreed. *But that does not preclude one from trying does it?*

Rizen didn't answer. Ashyn knew he was thinking and thinking was a good thing. The Gaur was far from simple-minded and he wasn't letting his anger drive him, not this time.

I believe Jenhiro truly wants to help. And in time, with a lot of luck, I think he could be instrumental in our escape.

And what would make you trust your gaoler? Rizen asked.

It was a good question, and Ashyn was not certain why he trusted the hunter. That he did gave him hope. Jenhiro had the opportunity long ago to kill Ashyn and hadn't. To beat Ashyn like the other elves and he hadn't. And once, when Ashyn hung in the Council of Elm like some perverse decoration, he felt Jenhiro there, watching him, conflicted. Ashyn believed with Jenhiro's help, they actually had a real chance at saving his sister.

I understand, Rizen's thoughts interrupted his own.

Right. Ashyn supposed he didn't really need to explain at all, not while they were connected through water.

These droods, they have your sister? The bull's thoughts continued.

Yes.

The gaur nodded its massive head. *Then that is where we need to be. I know of the place; it was where they first studied me.* Rizen let the words linger. Ashyn was certain the druids were not kind in their study, just as Brodea had not been kind in her attempt to get Ashyn to translate the tome.

Can you find it again?

The gaur nodded. *But I will need rest,* he added. *And we will need to find a way through these bars if we are to save your sister and escape this place.*

Ashyn's gaze drifted from the monstrous form of the Gaur to the wooden poles that kept them from their freedom. *You have never tried to manipulate them?*

No, Rizen returned quickly. *That ability is too advanced for me.*

Ashyn thought about their predicament. If Rizen was unable to open the bars then someone else would have to do it. Either they would both have to be on the other side of the pens, or they would need to use a druid.

Ashyn sighed and rubbed his hand over the coarse stubble on his head. They could never sway a druid to their cause. Druids worked too closely with the council, and Ashyn was a wizard, worse he was the dui Nuchada. No druid would work with him, or get to know him on the level that Jenhiro had. They would rather die than free a skewer.

Then a thought hit him. A dangerous and terrible idea. It was three parts foolish, one part brilliant. Could he do it? Could he pull it off?

You have thought of something? the large bull remarked, still sharing each other's thoughts.

Ashyn nodded. *I need to fine tune it. I need to think it all the way through.*

I know not what these images mean, totem-brother, but I know the feeling, Rizen cautioned. *These ideas, they feel treacherous. They feel deadly.*

I don't think we have a choice. Ashyn projected back to the bull. *We know where she is, and we know where we are. We can't be in both.*

Rizen nodded his agreement. *Do not be impulsive on this, totem-brother. A lot can, and likely will, go wrong. If what I feel from you is true, you will only have one shot, and if it fails you damn everything and everyone.*

Then I can't get this wrong, can I?

Ashyn felt the bull's eyes studying him intensely. The wizard knew he was being reckless, and that he was going to break every rule that mattered to him over the last decade of life, but he believed he had no choice.

I am going to sleep. I suggest you do the same, Rizen said quietly into his mind. *We will discuss this again, after you have had a better chance to think things through.*

Ashyn couldn't argue with that. All he needed was time to sort it out and a little rest.

~ ~ ~

Ashyn was just about to drift off into his usual restless sleep when his body was ripped violently off the ground. He yelped in surprise. Hard appendages like bones wrapped around his arms and legs pinning them to his sides. He was lifted up and over, left hanging upside down by his legs.

There standing in front of him, right side up, was Brodea, Eigron, and two Exemplars.

Rizen whistled in surprise as Ashyn watched the bars come alive with wooden vines and wrap the great gaur up as well.

The vines lifted Ashyn higher so that he was almost eye level with Brodea. Behind her, he could see the druid looked angry. Nausea filled his gut. Did Jenhiro fail?

Brodea stepped into the cell just as confidently as when he first met her in the council chambers. Her copper hand reached out and grabbed his face, her sharp nails bit into his cheeks. "I hope you've had time to heal," her head turned to the gaur, "and perhaps get attached to a pet?"

Ashyn didn't say anything. He didn't want to give away Rizen's intelligence. The druids discounted him as a stupid animal. It was the only advantage they had, and he wouldn't lose it now.

She stepped aside and one of the Exemplar stepped in with her. It was the one he encountered in the chambers. The one that had tried to control him.

"Tell me if our dangerous wizard friend has his powers back," Brodea commanded sinisterly.

Swirling platinum eyes danced before him, quickly Ashyn shut his eyes.

"Oh no, not this time, wizard," Brodea said mercilessly. "I do not have time for these games."

Ashyn heard a startled scream from the other pen. Soon there was a commotion and then a cry of pain. Finally, seconds later there was whimpering.

Her mouth inches from his ear, her hot breath against his skin, she said, "Open your eyes or I will have Father Mactonal's bones removed from his legs in front of you." She continued to whisper, "And then after I have hurt him in the most terrible of ways, I will stop feeding the skewers in the pens. How long do you think they will last this time, before they eat your precious friend alive?"

Ashyn quivered with rage. She had him again! Already! "You are a monster."

"I am a votarist. I will do whatever it takes to balance nature in this world. If that means I have to use abhorrent methods to see balance restored, then I am willing to make that sacrifice. Now open your eyes or the next sound you will hear will be the sounds of bones being pulled out of flesh. Tell me wizard, have you ever seen poultry deboned? I wonder if it will sound like that, but with screams. I couldn't even imagine what that will feel like."

Ashyn knew he didn't have a choice. He couldn't do it to Macky, not again, not over this. He beat the will of the Exemplar once before; he would do it again. Ashyn opened his eyes, and she was there.

A swirl of silver gripped him and pulled him towards her like a strong current of water. It was stronger, more powerful than before, and it was insistent.

"Well?" he vaguely heard in the far off distance.

Then just as suddenly as the pull was there, it was gone. His mind reeled and his head swooned.

"He still has no connection," the Exemplar answered. "But we are fast running out of time. The magic is there; I can see it. It is denied to him, but it is so strong." Her voice was breathless. "It's out of his reach. Imagine it is on the other end of a gorge. Too far for him to reach. He must have hurt his mind terribly to cause such a wound."

"You are certain he still has no power."

Amid the haze of spinning objects Ashyn saw the elf in front of him nod. "Yes, First Councilor. But not for much longer."

My magic is there, Ashyn thought to himself. *She could see it. It is there!* Then he felt his stomach tighten even more at Brodea's next words.

"What about the beast? Check it for a connection."

No! No! Ashyn wanted to scream. She couldn't unravel it, not now. They were close, he could feel it, and they were so close!

The druid interjected, "First Councilor, my peers did extensive tests on the animal, we found no indications of any kind of connection to magic, let alone any real sentience. A simpleton monster landed its hands on a powerful artifact. If anything, what branch commander Jenhiro saw from it was from the artifact not the beast."

Ashyn watched Brodea wheel on the servant of nature. "I would trust the word of a Voïre dui Ceremeia child before I would listen to a druid again. Your knowledge has been severely lacking as of late," she chastised before turning and regarding the other Exemplar with a polite bow. "If you would, check the creature, my Voïre?" Brodea asked, with a surprising courtesy and compassion.

"Of course, First Councilor," the Exemplar said.

Ashyn tried to struggle in the vines to see what they were doing behind him. He wanted to look at the Exemplar. He wanted to see Rizen. Could the gaur fight off the power of her will?

Agonizing seconds ticked by before Ashyn heard her melodious voice once more. "It is as Genrus Eigron declares First Councilor. I detect nothing from this beast but a very limited intelligence, and fear. It knows fear."

Ashyn let out a breath. He wanted to cheer. It was a small victory against the Wild Elves, but it was their first. Ashyn wanted to smile in Brodea's face to rub it in as the Exemplar moved out of her way; instead he kept his face passive. Well as passive as he could will all the blood beginning to rush to his head. Already pressure was building in his ears.

Brodea leaned forward right in his face. He felt the druid tightening the vines against his body so he couldn't even so much as spit at her. "If I find out you were responsible for this afternoon's little excitement, I promise you that I will be back, but it isn't you that I will break. It's Mactonal."

She turned and strode through the bars. The other elves beyond the vines retreated into the bars, which unceremoniously dropped the two prisoners to the ground. Ashyn landed hard on his shoulder. Pain raced up his nerves like lightning.

"Stop feeding the neighboring pens," Brodea ordered, her eyes never leaving Ashyn's. "Let them all know that their starvation is because the Blood Wizard refuses to cooperate."

The druid nodded. "Shall I order his rations cut as well?"

"No. Feed him and the large cow well. I want his peers to see how little he regards their lives. And if the wizard is caught giving any of them food…" She trailed off.

"Yes, First Councilor?"

Brodea's dark eyes glittered, "Cut off their hands and let them bleed out."

Ashyn lowered his head onto the hard ground defeated. She had snatched his small victory against her right out of his hands, crumpled it up, and threw it away. He was running out of time. He needed to begin his plan.

"Perhaps it's for the best that you are no longer with us Xexial," Ashyn whispered to himself. "You would damn me for what I am about to do."

TOMB

Dumbfounded. That was the word he best used to describe himself. The old wizard thought Khyriaxx's breakthrough in locating the word Craetorian would make things easier in his search, but it did not.

The first days were fruitful. A smattering of uses of the words were scattered here and there, most detailing the myth and lore of ancient creatures of previous ages. But the lore was incredibly vague. They spoke of titan-like individuals the size of buildings fighting epic battles in the Forgotten Era. Monsters, really, that nearly destroyed the world. Neither Xexial, nor Khyriaxx could find anything stable that looked like it might have at one time been rooted in fact. It was too wildly fictitious. They were fables, nothing more.

Like everything else, the truth of the Craetorian was lost in the emptiness of the fifth era. A blight in their history and mar on their culture.

What truly happened five thousand winters ago that warranted the eradication of all lore and history? What could have truly been so terrible that the combined agreement of their ancestors decided it was better that one not know?

The sun rose and set day after day, as Xexial desperately searched for these answers. As he did, a grim tone of finality settled in on the veteran wizard. The time for excuses was ending. When Grind finally returned to the Onyx Tower the hunt would resume, in earnest. Any hope of finding the truth of Ashyn Rune was going to be lost to him, and soon so would the boy.

Once the scales learned nothing of use at the capital of the Dark Elves, he would come back angry and refueled to resume his campaign against the recreant. Xexial figured if they were lucky they had two days left. A week if the Maba-Heth found a false lead.

Still, it burned at Xexial. What was Ashyn Rune? What was this siphoner that was mentioned in the journal of Patrius Monerch? What were the Craetorian Purges?

He knew of only two factions who might bear the answers he desperately sought: the Enclave itself and the Seven. Both were on opposite corners of the continent, weeks, even months, away. Xexial didn't have weeks. He had days.

He slammed the tome shut and stood up with a huff. His bones creaked and his muscles tightened in protest. He fought through it in his anger, but he was still stooped from the ordeal. He was old now. Old and feeble, and the legacy of wizards he was hoping to leave behind was going to be hunted and killed.

"Do not be abandoning hope," Khyriaxx said without looking up from his tome. "There always be a solution."

Xexial shook his head. "Not for this, lad. Not for this." He said feeling ancient. "There's nothing that can save Ashyn from being a Recreant."

"Oh?" Khyriaxx said as he finally looked up from the tome he was diligently researching. The monocle in his right eye made it massive compared to the left. The ridiculous eye blinked once before the spriggan took off the lens. "Is there not you? Are you not his master?"

Xexial leaned heavily on the chair. "I was his master. Until he decided to declare himself rogue to the Seven."

"The boy thought you dead," Khyriaxx pointed out. "He had to make a choice."

"He choose poorly," Xexial groused.

"As do we all, sometimes..." Khyriaxx looked back at the tome. "Can you not recant the Recreant status? He be your apprentice after all."

Xexial was about to snap back at the diminutive creature, when he stopped. "I don't rightly know."

"Well if you could, would you? I suppose that be the important question."

Xexial hung his head. All the long winters of his life weighing on him like bags of sand. "I have never broken the Wizard's

Covenant. It is what binds us on our important mission. My boy, he violated that Covenant, our most sacred vow."

"Again I be reiterating. He thought you be dead. I be sure that swayed his opinion more than a little bit. Would you not try to save the only family you had left if everything else be gone? Have you never broken a single rule, ever?"

The simplicity of the last question hit Xexial like a hammer. He pulled the seat back and dropped his weary bones back into it. "I was sent on a mission, long ago to kill my errant master."

Khyriaxx stared up at him impassively, so Xexial continued, "It was over ten winters ago now I'd guess. Noumenon, my master, had been thought dead for several winters before that, but the Seven learned of an artifact that he created that; if in the wrong hands could prove devastating. They thought it destroyed when Noumenon died. It turned out they were wrong. It was out in Kuldarr, and it was being abused."

"How be this your old master's fault?" Khyriaxx queried.

Xexial shrugged, "A wizard is always held accountable for his actions. We already bear the stigma of being evil because we make the hard choices. His artifact was dangerous. It was a fool's gesture to try to make something of its power under the guise of aid. It should have been more secured.

"The Seven feared this in fact. They feared that he had been careless and the artifact stolen. Worse they feared he might have faked his death and gone Recreant with the artifact, using it for his own malevolent devices."

"So they sent his apprentice after him, not the Maba-Heth? Rather heartless."

Xexial sighed, leaning back into the hard wooden chair. "I was the closest. Not to mention I knew how Noumenon worked. They wanted to make sure he was truly dead. They wanted the artifact neutralized, and the Recreant, if any, dead. They knew it was personal to me. I hunted him for weeks."

"And was it your old master?"

Xexial shook his head; he saw Khyriaxx looked almost relieved. "It was a thief who managed to break into the Onyx Tower. A young man who made too many bad choices in life."

"And what did you do?"

Xexial stared coldly at the spriggan. "I did what I was told. I neutralized the threat."

The old wizard watched as the spry figure shifted uncomfortably in his chair. "And you destroyed this artifact?"

Xexial looked down at his bare hands. He flexed them slowly feeling the tightness of his joints. Age spots crept up the backs of them, like lily pads on the surface of a pond. He answered in a low voice, "Not immediately. They represented something that I lost. They filled a void of loneliness I hadn't truly known until I held them."

"They?" Khyriaxx asked.

Xexial took a deep breath and looked up at the spriggan, "Yes, I have, in the past, not followed the Seven's decrees word for word, but I did it for the best of intentions."

"And Ashyn's intentions in saving one he loves be not good enough?" Khyriaxx challenged. "Is he not filling a void of loss?"

Xexial buried his face in his hand in frustration. "Our burden as wizards is to always look at the whole picture. It is terrible to have to choose the many, and sacrifice the few, but it must be done. Ashyn has gone against this. He has chosen the few. He has turned his back on our beliefs, our teachings, and our mission. On me."

Xexial ran the hand over his face and through his thin hair. "In a single action he has made himself a Recreant. Any other way, there might," he said again with emphasis, "might, have been a chance. But he sent the Seven a letter stating exactly what he was going to do. Not just one letter, but several just to make sure they got it. He condemned himself by his own hand. I can see no way of undoing this. I originally hoped if I found out more about what he really was I could find some loophole."

"This not be sounding like a path to a solution. Your variables, they don't add up. What does finding out what Ashyn is have to do with his choice go Recreant?"

"I have to come to terms that it has nothing to do with it. I was grasping at straws, hoping that somehow finding out what he was would answer the why he went rogue."

"But…"

Xexial stared at him coldly. "Everything I wanted to learn about Ashyn was to answer how he saved my life. I did not think the boy a rogue. I thought he was completing his mission."

Khyriaxx shook his head, "But you've been stalling Grind all this time. It was to help the boy, yes?"

Xexial nodded. "It was. There was also another reason."

Khyriaxx cocked his head, confused. Xexial finished, "If Ashyn is capable of paying the price of feedback for another, I need to know if the reverse is true."

Khyriaxx's eyes went wide as he suddenly understood, "You want to make sure you can defeat him."

"Ashyn's chances of running will be obsolete when the Maba-Heth returns. The scales will have no choice but to enter the Shalis-Fey. No Recreant has ever escaped for long. When Grind calls upon me again, I will have to do my duty."

Khyriaxx stood up and backed away from the table. "This whole time, I thought I be helping you to save him."

"If there was a way, tinkerer, I would gladly consider it."

"You must be having records on Recreants, those who have come back into the fold?"

Xexial shook his head, "Wizards do not count rogues among their numbers. We have no logs on Recreants. When they are defeated, any traces of them are abolished as well. It eliminates any chances for dissension amongst our very limited ranks."

"So that's it? Because you can't find the answer you are looking for, you're just going to kill him!" Khyriaxx yelled.

Xexial stood up with a start. His body popped in pain but he ignored it in his anger and frustration, "What can I do? He made his choice!" Xexial roared. "You think I want to kill him? He's the closest thing to a brother I have!"

"Then fight!" Khyriaxx retorted. "Find a way! Convince the Seven that he not be Recreant!"

"How? We have nothing, spriggan. Nothing but a series of terrible choices that started with the day I rescued that boy from Bremingham. I am sorry, Khyriaxx, I am. I want the boy to live. I want him to be a wizard. But he has betrayed everything I value. If you no longer desire to help I understand. I am sure the Ferhym have left long ago, your home should be safe to you now."

The small creature put his hands on his hips; Xexial watched the quills on his head begin to rise defensively. "I can't believe a mighty wizard, feared and fabled, is going to give up. All because his apprentice did the obvious. He is going after his family. I think that perhaps the people are right, perhaps wizards are evil. I may no longer be with my people, but I would never betray them for making the right decision."

Xexial growled, "He is not making the right decision, he is being selfish!"

"And you are not?" the spriggan barked with surprising authority. "You would rather condemn a boy you raised, than stand up to the Maba-Heth? To the Seven? That sounds more like a coward to me!"

"How dare you!"

"No, how dare you!" the spriggan yelled. "I nursed you to health because you served a purpose."

"Inadvertently," Xexial said disbelievingly.

"Still, I did it because it was the right thing to do! You must find in your heart what be the right thing to do and you know it! I say, we go find Ashyn, his sister, and see if he be this siphoner. If he be, we have a new problem to deal with. One the Seven not be seeing before, no? That be fair! No immediate executions. What if sister be siphoner too, no?"

Xexial shook his head, "You have absolutely no idea what you are asking. You could die in those woods!"

The spriggan's erect quills drooped as his eyes turned soft. "I be fearing many things Xexial, I do not deny this. I am no fighter. I not be having skill with any type of weapon. I just tinker.

"I fear pain. I fear death. More than that, I fear people. That is why I be hiding in the shadow of the Onyx Tower for all these winters. Being around people frightens me."

"Then why even suggest going into the Shalis-Fey?" The flabbergasted wizard responded.

"I would rather die facing my fears, than live my life with the knowledge that I did not try to see if there could be another way."

Xexial opened his mouth to reply, ready to throw a flippant remark the spriggan's way, but no words escaped his lips.

"He didn't make the selfish choice Xexial, he made the logical one. I think you be knowing that."

Xexial didn't answer. He didn't need to. Instead, he did the only thing he could. He walked away. The wizard needed time to think, and he needed to think alone.

Khyriaxx made no obvious move to follow him. Xexial glanced back once to see the spriggan sitting back down amongst the tomes to continue researching all he could on Craetorians. Xexial turned around, walked to the doorway, and stepped through. He would go where he always did when he needed guidance.

~ ~ ~

Everything in the Onyx tower was black, except for a single door deep in the cellars. This door was solid white. A relief was carved within of a man hatching out of an egg. The detail was exquisite. It was almost as if he were staring at something real. He could see the muscular definition of the naked man, the lines and creases of his well-developed frame. A flock of curls adorned his head and made up his beard. But that wasn't what drew him in. It was the eyes. So detailed, so real, these eyes looked into the very depths of his being as if reading his soul like an open book. It was as if this carved man knew what Xexial was thinking. And in a way, he did.

Xexial knew the door only opened to those that it found a connection to magic with. While the essence of life flowed through every being, the door only opened for those who could touch that ethereal essence..

It was a bizarre trait. A unique spell placed upon the door that no known creationist knew how to replicate today. Another lost prize of their history due to the ignorance that was the Forgotten Era.

It should have been Xexial's first flag that Ashyn was more than a half-elf. His injury had broken the bridge that tied him to magic. He was severed from harnessing it. The door should have identified that, and like those who had no knowledge of connecting to magic, he should have been denied entrance. But the door opened. It found a reason. Xexial should have known then and there.

He placed his hand upon the ivory door. It was smooth and hard beneath his touch, but not cool like stone or marble. It was warm and dry.

Dragonbone. Xexial had long known that a dragon's bones kept its magic within them when they died, and that a skilled practitioner could use that magic to create anything from magical arms and armor to magical doors. This door, though, was beyond any still living person's capacity.

Suddenly the door rumbled beneath the touch of his skin. Normally Xexial would feel his flesh grow warm, then hot. A deep thrumming would fill his ears, vibrating so hard that his chest would shake and his teeth would chatter. None of this happened.

Cautiously he drew his hand away from the ivory portal. He was worried. He did this same thing often before. The tremors should be coursing through his body, but they were not.

Often the pulsations continued down to his very core. In the past he felt the liquids in his body rushing to the surface of his skin, flushing him with an internal heat that was as hot as fire. That was when it would read the magic. Find his capacity and his skill and evaluate his worth.

Was he no longer worthy? Just as quickly as it started the shuddering door subsided. Steam rose around him in the corridor. The trial was complete. But was he worthy?

The door in front of him slid open into a recess in the wall, with little sound. He found it more than a little odd. Did Ashyn do something to the door as well? Were his progenitors still safe? One look within answered his question. As usual the sight before him brought with it a new rush of emotion.

Within the doorway was a portico overlooking a great gallery below. Xexial stepped through. He took two ivory steps downward to the balustrades that would stop him from falling over thirty feet to the floor below. The curved supports were made of the same beautiful crème-colored marble as the steps he took, yet they beheld a myriad of iridescent blue-laced symbols that flowed flawlessly up and around the thick railing and supporting balusters.

The gallery was circular in shape, a gentle reminder that he was still in a tower after all. Above him was a ceiling that rested like an apse. A fresco was painted across the ceiling. Thousands of men in battle against every known color of dragon. It was a battle in the Forgotten Era, or before.

Many minutes passed before he pulled his gaze away from the massive war depiction. The sight of it always pulled him to wonder what that age was like? Was it as dark as everyone painted it out to be? Or was there life to it? A vibrancy of magic and lore, a renaissance lost to the ages? Some things survived, the statues, a few towers, all of them beautiful.

The old wizard looked below. There, thirty feet down, were twenty-three great statues of men, all facing one another. Twelve were in poses that suggested they were casting great spells. Ten were posed in silent contemplation, palms pressed firmly together at the center of their chest. Each man was robed in traditional wizard fashion, though the style seemed to change minutely from one man to the next. They all bore beards and long hair, except for the last one. The final statue stood at the center of the circle, the northern point.

This statue was unlike the rest. The man stood in full battle regalia. An intricately-carved breastplate that bore runes of protection and warding. It made Xexial chuckle briefly. He forced Ashyn to read the runes dozens of times in manuscripts and tomes.

Across the center of this breastplate was a great dragon taking flight, its wings spread from collarbone to collarbone and its great bony tail trailing down the stomach and wrapping along the left side towards its back. Even from his vantage, he could see the minute details that made it a majesty of the artwork.

Gauntlets covered the hands of the statue. They were adorned with runic symbols, much like his armor, and held a large gem-like object on the back of each hand. Underneath that armor were layered robes, just like any of the other twenty-two statues around him.

That was not the only way in which he stood apart. His head was bald, and he had a short-cropped beard that hugged his cheeks and chin. Nothing like the long, gangly beards he was used to seeing on the other statues, or with many of the Seven that he spoke with in the past. Above the carving of facial hair there were deep etches in the marble that was the man's flesh. Xexial knew they were tattoos.

The tattoos covered over his eyes and nose, and ran across his bald pate, his ears, and down the back of his head and neck. They were savage and barbaric, swirls and contoured marks that cut across his face, miring his visage in gouged lines. They made him look primal and fierce.

Xexial slowly descended the steps to the floor below. Each step felt heavier than the one prior did. He thought back to the last time he was here. How he watched his struggling apprentice who was lost in thought. When Ashyn was weighing the difficult decision that eventuaklly led him into becoming a Recreant. The irony of the fact that it was this room that helped bring about Ashyn's final decision to turn on Xexial was not lost on him. Here he was now weighing if he should do the same against the Maba-Heth and the Seven to save the boy.

Xexial stood before the twenty-three statues, his thoughts delving deeply into everything that led to this point in his life. Were the Seven worth killing for? Was the wizard's covenant? If he stood up against the Maba-Heth, he would be labeling himself as well. He didn't doubt that he could dispatch the Maba-Heth, but then what? They would only send another, and then another, until they came to personally deal with the problem.

Xexial wasn't nearly arrogant enough to think he could stand to the combined power of the Seven. But what did that say about him? Was he ready to let Grind kill Ashyn? His apprentice, his friend, his adopted brother?

Xexial paced around the circle of wizards. His thoughts didn't get any easier. There was no clear choice. He looked up at the center statue clad in armor. The old wizard approached this bald, tattooed statue. He felt reverence to the deceased of this tomb. These were his peers. Progenitors of the craft that he so loved. Carefully, he ran his worn, pale fingertips over the placard at the pedestal by the statue's sandaled feet. Xexial read it aloud. "Magelord Rheynnaus Craëgolshien, Bastard of Ashyreus, First of his name, and last born heir of Mysticarus."

Heir of Mysticarus. Xexial wished he knew more about the man. He always wished it every time he came to seek guidance. He only knew what his master, Noumenon, told him. That there were no details on Rheynnaus, only beliefs. Belief that it was he who constructed the Onyx Tower. Belief that his life was full of pain and strife. Belief that he was tested day after day, winter after winter, on what it meant to be a wizard, what it meant to do what was right.

Noumenon told him when he was a younger man that Rheynnaus never once surrendered to defeat. He never gave up. He endured all the horrors that were thrown at him, and judging by what Xexial saw in the Onyx Tower he was certain those horrors were many.

Rheynnaus represented hope and strong will to wizards in questioning times. He wasn't a god, not by any stretch, and Xexial knew that was what made him relatable. He was a wizard, a Magelord of wizards, who made the difficult choices.

Today, Rheynnaus offered no insights. Today, he did not give Xexial the supernal clarity that he hoped. Today, Rheynnaus was merely a statue, and Xexial was forced to make the most difficult choice of his life on his own.

His fingers slid from the placard on the pedestal toward the smooth marble sandal. He was momentarily startled when the placard buckled slightly as his fingers broke its threshold.

He stared. He never touched it before now. It was the first time. He hoped he hadn't damaged it in his musings. He reached out to make sure the brass placard that survived millennia wasn't broken. As his fingers grazed the metal it creaked and wobbled slightly again.

Xexial was curious now, so bent over to look at the seam of metal against marble. He placed the side of his face on the pedestal next to the placard and pushed lightly again. Ever so minutely the bottom of the placard jetted out a small gust of dust from beneath it.

It was hollow underneath!

Xexial never knew it existed, and Noumenon never mentioned such a thing. He searched the brass more diligently now. Growing excited. How did he miss this his entire life?

In moments he found a cleverly concealed hasp. He lifted it and the whole placard popped upwards and swung away on a hidden hinge. Beneath it sat a small alcove, and inside a parcel wrapped in oilskin and covered in no less than a century of dust.

He reached in to the small alcove and immediately he felt the pressure of a ward against his bare skin. He pulled his hand back for a moment and studied the small cubby that held this bizarre treasure.

Xexial was a master of wards, and he knew with enough time he could probably find his way around this one, but time wasn't much of an option. Slowly he took his fingers to the edge of the ward once more. As he pushed he felt a slight pang of electricity shoot up his arm. He knew the ward then; it was the very same that he placed on the front entrance of the Onyx Tower many winters before.

It was a Rend Ward. Should anyone attempt to pass the threshold that wasn't allowed, they would receive a jolt of energy that they would not soon forget. Should one be persistent and attempt to force their way through, they would find the result to be quite fatal. Attempting to go through would be like trying to push through water, and if one was persistent, they would be rewarded by having the flesh rent from their bones.

Xexial however knew a way around this very problem. All it required was a piece of the creator. Or what the creator likely had in their possession at the time of the ward's creation. He looked back up at the gauntlet covered hands of the statue.

"I will only borrow this," he promised the statue.

Xexial reached up to the marble hand and wrapped his fingers around the gem-inlaid gauntlets. Slowly, but firmly, he pulled down. In moments he felt the marble give way and the gauntlet slid off the statue's hand. As it broke the threshold of the white marble, the runic symbols of the gauntlets shimmered, and then color filled in the white voids.

Soon Xexial was holding a leather gauntlet in his hand. The runic symbols glittered and the large gem on the back of the gauntlet swirled and swayed with a cloud-like radiant crimson energy within it. Noumenon had shown him the gloves when he had graduated to the Second Circle of wizardry. It was a secret entrusted only to him, and eventually he was going to give the knowledge to Ashyn.

As the enchantment faded away and the gauntlet resumed its natural suede hue, he slipped it onto his hand. Like many forms of enchanted apparel, it formed to his hand.

Looking at the gauntlet against his hand, it made him keenly realize the loss of his gloves. Gloves he was the caretaker of for a long time. "One more loose end."

He stuck his hand back into the alcove, and as he knew they would, his fingers passed through as if pushing into the rolling wave of the ocean. There was a slight thrumming, and he felt a faint vibration in his forearm and then he was there! Gingerly, he removed the alien package for he was uncertain as to how old the item might truly be. He unfolded the corners of the oilskin and gasped in shock. It was a tome. It was not much larger than the palm of his hand, and no thicker than the tip of his smallest finger. He wiped the dust off his hand onto his robes and then carefully opened the leather binding of the ancient manuscript.

He was surprised to find the words on the inside to be written in the same hand as he learned his spell-craft. It was a written language unique to wizards, Hacroá. It was created so that strangers could never decipher their magic and use the arts of destruction. It it was only for spells, or so Xexial had thought.

As he read the words on the first page, he realized that at one point this language was used for more than spells. As he translated the words, he swooned. He was wrong. Rheynnaus did give him insight, more clarity than he ever gave the surly wizard in the past. Written across the page it said simply, *I am Magelord Rheynnaus Craëgolshien. Bastard of Ashyreus, First of his name, and last born heir of Mysticarus.*

Last living Craetorian wizard.

CRAETORIAN

*To understand one's nature is to first understand oneself. As of the beginning of this journal, I find myself to be, quite possibly the last of my kind. Until this moment, until I wrote these words onto this page in this very instant, I did not really grasp the magnitude of such a thing. It is overwhelming, really. I **am** the last of my kind.*

It has been impressed upon me by my colleagues and peers to begin this journal in the hopes of understanding what it means to be the last. I expect this to be no easy question for me to come to terms with, and I am told that it may take countless journals until I reach such an understanding, but I am to try. So to do that, I am to define, by nature what I am.

Craetorian.

To me that word does not harness the awe or fear that I see in others when uttered. To me the word has no meaning other than to express the race that I have derived from. I feel no different than I think a human, a picayune, or a hym feels when hearing their race designated to them.

My heritage does not control who I am. I am my own person. Yet, to others, the word craetorian now carries such weight that to be labeled as such has marked me with a stigma that I will carry for the remainder of my days.

Romerik tells me that it is important to chronicle this journal because that, as of now, I must hide what I am to all those around me. All but my trusted circle, we the twenty-three.

Even then, my most invaluable sage and friend Romerik Rillerion cautions that twenty-two with the knowledge of my bloodline is twenty-two too many. But it is already done, and I would not see it changed. This war has taken too much from me already.

Yet, I move ahead too much. Romerik tells me to narrow my focus to one topic at a time, and it needs to start with an understanding of what it means to be craetorian.

But how does one understand such a nature? Does the color of my flesh truly dictate that I am so different inside from those around me? Do I not feel the same emotion? Do I not bleed as they?

Romerik looks no different from me, and yet through bloodline we are worlds apart. So then I ask myself, in this journal, what does it truly mean to be a craetorian?

I say it means nothing. I am alive, and I simply am. Yet for the sake of argument, and because I do not need the chattering in my ear from the bearded loon, I shall endeavor to do as he says and take this first accounting of what it means to be craetorian. So, to that end, here is an endeavor to explain the origins of the craetorian, as I know them.

It all starts with humans. My kin. I consider myself one of them, even though they do not consider me one of them. Humans, special and magical in their own way. Short lived, violent, adaptable, and fiercely intelligent. Yet, that is not what makes them more special than the other races, no. It is that the human species has its own will to survive. The body, the structure, of the human is able to co-habitate with so many races it is truly staggering. No other race in existence outside of the human can reproduce outside of its species. A picayune and a hym, impossible. The Kii' Aur and a picayune, well the thought of it in itself is a little hard to stomach, and still impossible. But a human and a hym? Absolutely. A human and a picayune, while improbable, has happened. A human and a dragon… the stuff of legend. Living legend.

Humans' ability to cross-reproduce was important to dragons. For dragons, the original keepers of Nature have always found us mortals interesting. They've never made it a secret. Well, a scant five-hundred winters ago, they set their eyes upon the hym. Nature's other servants.

Magically attuned to nature in such a way that their bodies even adapt to their surroundings enthralled the omnipotent dragons. Yet the hym considered dragons traitors to the natural order. Why? It is hard to say.

It could have been a disagreement in how they believed the world and its inhabitants were meant to play out. It could have been because hym prefer to eat vegetation, while a dragon has no choice but to devour meat. It could have been a spiritual conflict. Religion has always been at the forefront of adversity. We kill each other over arguments about what happens when we die, and then fail to see the irony in that. Either way, the hym would not parlay with the dragons, ever. Dragons sought to change this.

Dragons have a unique ability through their attunement to magic to alter form, yet the hym have always been beyond their grasp. The ever-changing ability to adapt to nature made the hym impossible to duplicate. The dragons tried, of course. And the hym have caught them each and every time. So dragons turned to co-habitation.

They knew that Humans and hym could sire offspring, and that offspring was generally well accepted by both parties. So the dragons hoped that by cross-breeding their race into the hym, it would force the two races closer together. But the draknai, the offspring of a human and a dragon, could never mate with any race outside of a fellow draknai, or a human. Much the same as the offspring of a hym and human can only then pair with another human, hym, or the hybrid man-Hym and bear children. The half-breed cannot then procreate with a picayune or dragon. It is as impossible as a hym and a picayune, but I digress.

Rather than carrying the human ability to reproduce outside the species, they are limited to the reproductive abilities of the other species. They cannot intermingle with another race outside of their progenitors. To bridge this seemingly natural gap of evolution, dragons decided the best course of action was to create a new species, one capable of the genetic diversity of humanity, but with the genes of the dragon. And so they did, using the power of the Nether Plane. They magically infused the human reproductive fluids into the egg of a dragon.

The egg was magically nurtured throughout its incubation process. I have been told that the gestation period for those created that way was lengthy, much longer than a dragon ever believed possible, but the results of that experimentation were quite unexpected, especially for a trial.

As the egg hatched, the first of what would come to be known as the craetorian was born. For all intents and purposes, this first generation Craetorian looked human. It being only a trial, the dragons were not disappointed with this outcome. Over time, however, the dragons realized that this boy, this first born, was not human at all. They noticed telltale differences, first in his features: eyes of no natural human tone, a duskier skin hue, or more vibrant hair coloration. Later they noticed it in his inhuman strength and his natural ability to connect deeply with magic. Something no human has ever displayed without intense training. They also noticed that the boy had a very unnatural ability to relate to them. Physically, culturally, and spiritually, the boy was attuned to their highly logical way of thinking. This made him very different from the humans they studied.

Dragons were overjoyed at the success of their creation, and when the boy came of age they sent him out immediately to sire as many children as he could. There was no room for love for the boy. No room for emotion, which was largely devoid in dragons. His only goal in life was the exponential growth of his new species. He was, after all, only a trial.

Dragons continued to create more first generation Craetorians from those that would donate their precious eggs as well. Between the first boy and the volunteers there was an insurgence of a new race in the world, as Craetorians procreated like wildfire, our reproductive abilities just as capable as the humans'. It wasn't until decades later that the dragons noticed there was a flaw in their 'infallible' design.

As I write this, I now see the irony in such an act as they committed. Creatures of nature, protectors and guardians of natural balance, and they performed an act that was counter to it all. They made an aberration.

Nature is balance, always. An area becomes over populated; a disease or plague will wash through and reduce the swollen numbers. A species lives longer than others do; nature imbues it with a lower birthrate. An elf and a human couple and bear the fruits of birth, that child will carry a bit of both parents in them. Appearance, temperament, emotions, even strength and character of will may be displayed. The term, like father like son, is often used to explain such characteristics.

One thing that the nature always adheres to though is balance. The boy may be mostly like his father in looks, and mannerisms, but rest-assured something, the eyes, his emotions, his level of intelligence, are determined by the mother.

It may never be half and half, but the two parts always make a whole. Never more, never less.

A draknai for instance stands on two legs like a man, but bears the scales and crest of its dragon father. Those scales' color always match the scales of the father as well. Yet, the draknai will forever be locked to the earth at his feet, for even though he is born with wings, they lack the strength or length to bear him aloft on the winds. A genetic marker carried over from father to offspring, but one that serves no function at all. It is not some cruel handicap, but a balancing of properties. It is what nature does. Its great design is to keep things in check.

That is where dragons overstepped their bounds. Where they truly became the very monstrous traitors that the hym claimed them to be. For Craetorians are not bound to the natural lock of balance. The Nether Plane, not the mundane to which our lives are lived, created them. We are violators of order. We are outsiders in our own world.

Craetorians not only possess all the properties of a human on the inside and out, but all of the properties of a dragon as well. We are two complete races in a single vessel. We lack the balanced dilution of genes that nature produces. We are the purest possible blend, unmarred by the trappings of evolution. The hym have often preached to us that within our being are two souls. One dragon, one human. They are trapped in a cage that is our flesh fighting each other for dominance. To this I cannot disagree for at times I do feel like there is something within me, a beast trying to escape. Is it the human or the dragon? I am unsure.

What's even more incredible of our people is that, because we were artificially created through magic, nature has no say in the evolution of our species. We are not bound to any mutation based on the location of our upbringing. If we procreate with a human, our bloodline is not diluted like other species. Our genes stay superior, sovereign, and dominant. There is no washing out of what we are with anything from the other parent, with the minor exception of general appearance. We look human not reptilian like our draknai cousins. Our might, our intelligence, our endurance all caries over from the Craetorian. We are all Craetorian, each and every time. We do not blend. As long as we mate with humans or Craetorians.

Dragons thought this feat a marvel at first. The power of their creation grew continuously as the Craetorian mingled with human societies, and even the hym. But as the decades wore on dragons realized that this unnatural trait was actually a horrible oversight that they made. And that is because evolution has no control.

Humans are unique and wondrous in many ways. One is that they are incredibly short-lived compared to most other races. Because of this, they reproduce far more quickly and are naturally aggressive. They accomplish more in that limited span than any of the longer lived races. Martially, they are strong, and their skill is superior to almost every race. Moreover, their incredible desire to learn has put them at the forefront of technology. This thirst for knowledge and power has also made them superior in magical endeavors as well.

These are true boons of the human people. Now couple these traits with the durability, extended lifespan, raw strength, and pure magical power of a dragon. It is not so hard to see how dangerous a Craetorian is capable of becoming.

While humans may be many wonderful things, and I shall always call them kin, there are also some very dark things about them. Greed, tyranny, lust, and wrath are but a few. Of all races, none knows war as intimately as the human does. Conflicts arise for many reasons: religions, territory, even love.

It pains me to say that we Craetorians adopted those traits as well. If one positive thing can be said about dragons in all of this, it is that they have millennia upon millennia to learn how to not let emotions like passion drive them. Curiosity may be their greatest flaw. Anger and violence are not.

The same cannot be said for humans or for us Craetorians. We are creatures of pure emotion. And that emotion is transferred the easiest way we know how. Through violence and aggression.

It was because of this and the overwhelming numbers that we created with no limited life span, that Dragon kind decided to end its project. They decided, through much deliberation, that the flaws of humanity out-weighed that of the ability that they sought. And so it was decided, rather dispassionately I am told, that the remnants of the project needed to be collected and culled.

It was the first purging of the Craetorian people. Dragons hunted down and exterminated all men, women, and children. We were only entering into our third generation, we hardly had a chance to blossom into our own identity and we were marked to die.

I don't know whether I should be, but I am proud to say that my ancestors retaliated against their hunters and oppressors on an unprecedented scale. Victims of their own creation, Dragons were not prepared to meet a combatant equally as powerful as they in every way.

Dragons never considered themselves the most powerful race to navigate the world, but I would say if they had any emotion they displayed at all, it would be pride. They are a confident race, and that confidence was shaken.

Soon the Craetorians, being the passionate creatures we are, we went from retaliation to revenge. Craetorians hunted dragons. In fact, my kind was so successful at it, that in the end, it was the dragons who disappeared into solitude.

Driven by anger and power, that is when the people of the project declared their sovereignty. They named themselves Craetorian, which roughly translates into Exiles, and with no equal to stand in their way, they marched across the continent to rule all of its inhabitants, unabated for centuries.

That is where I come from. The legacy put to parchment as my peers feel I need to do. I do not know if I will ever show this journal to anyone, but I must confess that in writing it, it does help bring to focus the true gravitas of the nature of my being.

I am a Craetorian.

I am the magelord amongst wizards.

I am.

~ ~ ~

Xexial put the journal down, and leaned his head back against the hard marble toes of Rheynnaus Craëgolshien. This was his journal. A journal that was thousands upon thousands of winters old. It was a relic of the Fifth Era, perhaps the only one in existence, aside from the gauntlet on his hand, that wasn't a piece of art. It survived, trapped in a hidden cubby by a statue's feet.

His eyes fell to the dragonbone door and the relief of the naked man emerging from the shell of an egg. It made much more sense to him now. The door, its purpose, why it read magic.

He now knew the story the fresco on the ceiling told him. It wasn't lost to guess or speculations any longer. He knew facts from the mouth of one who had known such.

He looked down at the little tome between his fingers. Though he wanted to read every page, though he wanted to absorb it like a sponge, he withheld. His focus was on Ashyn, not on Rheynnaus, and to that end he only re-read the first section of the journal. It was clearly the most important for him. He read it again and again until he committed it to memory.

Craetorian.

Reading those few words it seemed impossible and yet possible all at once. Craetorians? A mythical, magical race of, what? Super-people? Xexial shook his head, not super. Just, advanced. Altered. It explained so much, and yet seemed so, fanciful. Like it was only a matter of convenience.

And yet, as he thought to the boy's eyes in times of anger, the emotional responses, the bursts of magic, his attunement to fire. Xexial had met half-elves in his time, and never in his life had he seen such a raw connection to the weaves of magic as Ashyn displayed. He tried to tell himself that Ashyn was special, that he displayed more elven traits than human, but now, with the small book in hand, Xexial felt as if he was just trying to convince himself the boy was part-hym.

"Maker help me," he whispered suddenly as he thought back to that day by the brook, when the small platinum haired Exemplar had called Ashyn the Nuchada. Xexial had translated it as Spirit Eyes

Xexial assumed that she was just enthralled with meeting a little boy with curious grey eyes. Then later, he figured it was because of Ashyn's unique ability to call on magic that she sensed.

He knew their language well. He knew that in it the word "dui" meant the word in conjunction was something that was plural. But now he realized that the word Nuchada in itself meant two words in Trade Tongue. That meant that both words were plural, Spirits Eyes. It didn't seem right. It came to him: spirits within eyes.

The Ferhym knew! The Ferhym knew what Ashyn was all along! Of course they knew. They were ancient! A Craetorian was just the type of person that the Ferhym would hunt. The ultimate skewer. That is why they would track a little boy relentlessly through the woods. Why they would give him no quarter. He was the ultimate sin, made by their greatest adversary, dragons.

Even the Jasian Enclave would view them as monsters. Hence the Craetorian Purges. It all made sense now. Every single bit of it.

Xexial let his own knowledge cloud his judgment over the tribal and feral elves. He ignored the very words handed to him when Ashyn had been but a small boy. He discounted the Exemplar for the musings of a little girl. She knew more than even he did about Ashyn. He was a fool.

Khyriaxx stated that a red dragon pursued Ashyn. Watched by a dragon. Ashyn was a siphoner, and that unique ability was well-documented about dragons. They could take and hold magic within themselves, storing it like a living container. This way they always had a surplus before feedback would set in. It was what made their bones so valuable at their death. They could take, hold, and disperse magic.

His mental connection may be severed to magic because of his injury, but his body physically adapted to magic like a sponge in water. It just took it in, just like a dragon's.

Xexial's gut wrenched as he looked from the tome to the wall knowing his apprentice was out there, in those woods, with the enemy.

Ashyn was not a Nuchada. He was the dui Nuchada. The Ferhym's mortal adversary. Ashyn Rune was a Craetorian. And he was all alone.

THE ALLEGIANT

The three days after the stampede seemed to be all about making sure Ashyn wouldn't die from infections in the Water Pens. Many times throughout the day Eigron would visit him, smear more of the green ichor upon his lacerated abdomen, chant a few words, and stare at him with hate-filled eyes. There was always something else too. Eigron had a pent up nervousness about him. He was always looking over his shoulder as if he were going to be attacked at any moment.

When he would leave, Rizen would assist with the mending flesh, making sure that the muscles healed correctly so that they wouldn't bunch or spasm in any harmful ways.

Ashyn noted that both of their Creative magics felt very similar, and yet he knew not to mention it to the gaur, or risk angering the bull.

Brodea came to see him once a day, usually in conjunction with Eigron, and he made sure to look at her with as much malice as he could muster. To his surprise, the First Councilor did not look at him with disdain as she had in the past, but almost with a sense of accomplishment.

Over the course of those three days, there were many new patrols. They were constantly watched by all manner of Ferhym from hunters to druids to actual Councilors. Brodea wasn't taking any chances anymore. She was looking for anything that might show the use of his gift was rekindled. She clearly believed he was responsible for the stampede.

At those times when the elves were present, Ashyn was amazed to see the simpleton creature act that the gaur put on. Cowed and almost oblivious to its penned up state, Rizen appeared docile, domesticated really, and it paid off. The elves believed he was nothing, and he was ignored completely by almost everyone.

Everyone but the First Councilor. Brodea wasn't as lax around the bull. She watched Rizen carefully, as if she knew the truth. She recognized the game that he played, but had no proof to bring to light.

Now, with days of no longer being tortured, Ashyn's mind fully cleared from the haze of pain, and he saw how much of a threat Brodea truly represented. Her presence forced obedience from her subordinates. She was naturally charismatic, and possessed strong leadership skills. Yet, there was a vindictive streak to her. One her daughter clearly adopted. This vengeful nature, Ashyn soon understood, would never let her stop her quest to defeat wizards, unless she was given strong reason to stop.

Ashyn was well fed, which helped gather his returning strength. He stretched his muscles and moved around his pen more, memorizing the layout of his surroundings, and the areas he could see.

He was sorry to watch his neighbors stare at him with hatred and longing, but he believed Brodea's warning against sharing. He settled for their hatred. It meant their continued survival.

He talked to Macky every day, catching up on the last decade he missed in Czynsk. Macky told him everything that happened after he left the hospice. Of course the topic, as it had when they were children, inevitably fell to Avrimae. It pained Ashyn to see his friend so in love with the woman, only to know that it could never be reciprocated.

What surprised Ashyn, though he didn't mention it, was how Macky left Uriel out of much of the conversations they shared. Uriel had been Macky's best friend, and though Ashyn knew that Avrimae had inevitably come between the two of them, he thought Macky would have spoken more of the better days.

Macky also provided service for the people in the pens every day, and Ashyn found himself listening in. Macky gave his people hope. Something Xexial said the boy would never do. Macky made the transformation from sheep to shepherd.

The priest also confirmed that no one knew of Julietta at all. Ashyn would have found that strange, but Jenhiro already notified him that Julietta was with the druids. It would be obvious that she was an unknown quantity, the druid Ferhym were even more reclusive then their average Ferhym brethren.

In that time, Ashyn conversed frequently with his cellmate on all manner of things. Strategies going forward. Optimism in not surrendering to hopelessness. The gaur often questioned him on the motives of humans. Like the gaur were a strange species to Ashyn, humans were a great unknown to Rizen as well. So Ashyn did his best to put humanity in a proper light. Telling everything they had accomplished, but not shying away from their moments of ugliness as well.

That open rapport had unlocked something in the silent gaur. *My people are not violent as you saw with me,* Rizen began suddenly on the third day at the water's edge.

Ashyn, his mind on his plan looked up in surprise, *Excuse me?*

The gaur are goat-herders. A snort followed, and Ashyn didn't know if it was one of disdain, or in acceptance that Rizen was sharing this with him. *We hail from the Broken Teeth Mountains.*

Ashyn glanced in what he thought was the direction of the range. He had looked at the mountains often as a child in Czynsk. He was taught that they were the home of the Dakhym, Dark Elves, but he never imagined that within the mountains themselves was a race of peaceful shepherds.

You saw me at my worst, Totem-Brother. I was lost. My herd was gone, my spirit damned. I never thought before that I would be capable of hurting anyone, but the idea of losing my spirit's ability to return to the cycle… His mental voice drifted.

The gaur shared a brief look with him before directing it back to stare longingly at the water. *I know some of the values of what you call the Maker. They are much different than our own. Our entire existence is based on the philosophy that our spirit does not die and go to a heaven when the vessel of our flesh does, but that it is natural energy that returns to the Cycle of Energy where we find a new host when another gaur is born in this world. We are reincarnated.*

Ashyn nodded in understanding. *So for that time that your vessel couldn't be destroyed…*

I couldn't return to the cycle. It doomed me. It broke my mind. My people, because of our beliefs, are all intrinsically connected you see. We are all family because we are shared energy. The death of my herd, while crushing, I could accept because I knew they were one with the cycle, and that one day they would all be reborn. But my unlife… it was maddening to know that I was forever apart from them. Brahma is our great shepherd of the cycle. We are 'his' herd. And I thought for certain I was exiled from the herd forever. A terrible fate for any gaur, but something infinitely worse for a Shaman.

Why?

Rizen stirred the putrid waters in a slow spiral with a thick finger. *Because I am a caretaker of my people. I am a caretaker of their energy. The elements you have seen me manipulate comes from energy.*

Magic. Ashyn agreed.

Again Rizen snorted, but Ashyn knew this was no agreement. *You may call it such, but I have heard of this magic. A shaman pulls from energy.* He rapped hard against his broad chest. *Our energy.*

Understanding was revealed in Ashyn's eyes. *Your soul?*

Rizen nodded. *We borrow from the Spirits. They give to us their energy, we use of it. When I call the elements, or when I knit your flesh I am asking for the spirit energy of my fallen people, and then I place that energy upon my own spirit to do it. It has to hold up to the rigors I am asking of the others after all.*

All of his life Ashyn was raised under a single defining belief. Magic came from only two fonts, Creation and Destruction. Everyone who used magic, inherently pulled from the wells of Creation, while only those specially trained could tap into the Nether and harness Destruction. What the Shaman was telling him was stunning, and yet it made a certain amount of sense, given his knowledge of feedback. Rizen claimed that the strength of one's spirit measured the amount of influence they had over elements and nature. This different philosophy gave Ashyn a new appreciation for magic.

Like Macky, whose mindset with the Jasian Enclave was ingrained into one way of thinking, Ashyn too found it hard to stray from his training. A decade of teaching was difficult to shake, but it was enlightening.

Do you desire to know more of my people? the gaur asked after a long silence.

Ashyn nodded, and said *I would.*

We are a caste society. Our lives chosen for us the moment we are brought to this world. Our Pundit, the head shaman, would read the newborn's spirit and declare what assignment we have as we grow in life.

Parentage? Ashyn asked.

Rizen replied immediately, *Irrelevant. The Shaman chooses caste, and the newborn goes. We are all family, all of the same energy, remember?*

The wizard nodded.

There is only one stipulation to this rule. The Shaman. For our herds, there can only be two Shamans: The Pundit and the Pan. A Pundit may go many winters never seeing a Pan at birth, or may find a Pan after just elevating to Pundit status themselves. Even if a Pan died, another may be born the very next day. It is always the will of Brahma and never easy to define.

Ashyn was always amazed at how many cultures shared similar philosophies without ever realizing it. The gaurs' Shaman balance was much like a wizards' master and apprentice.

It did raise a question though. *What happens if a Pan becomes Pundit while the other Pundit is still alive?*

That Pundit often becomes revered as Paragon. They are the wise elder that the Pundit could go to in times of need, yet they no longer perform the role of Shaman or possess a totem. They become a proud and celebrated elder. Still, a Paragon is capable of using energy, and if the Pundit were to perish before the Pan was ready to fulfill the role of Pundit, it isn't uncommon for the Paragon to fulfill the role until the Pan was ready.

The Shaman is the spiritual advisor of the herd leader, called the Bos Gaurus, and they are the religious preacher to the people.

So in a way you are one part me, and one part Macky? Ashyn reasoned aloud.

The wizard watched as Rizen's gaze swept to the frail man now giving a surmons about the Maker in the neighboring pen. *That is an accurate, if somewhat crude assessment,* the gaur noted, *but yes.*

Rizen fell silent then, his education on the gaur finished for the day. Ashyn knew that it must have taken a lot for Rizen to even say that much. It was no difficulty to see how insular his culture was. That had taken a large measure of trust. It was a huge step for the two of them. Ashyn was glad he had not ended Rizen's life when he had the chance.

That night Ashyn decided repay that trust and explain to Rizen what his elaborate plan was and how he arrived at it.

From Brodea's reaction three days prior, Ashyn had to assume that Jenhiro was successful in liberating Avrimae. The fact that Brodea never mentioned it, made him certain that if

Avrimae had been recaptured or killed, the First Councilor would have used it against him.

Deciding to hold nothing back, he told Rizen of his connection to the silver-eyed elf. Ashyn confided with his cellmate that he used to talk to the Exemplar in visions, and he was waiting to hear from her now. It was part of the agreement he made with Jenhiro.

Rizen turned out to be adaptable to the idea. He didn't make any argument against his claims or accuse him conspiring with the enemy. He just accepted Ashyn's words. The gaur was a remarkable sounding board for ideas, including on how Ashyn might regain his connection to magic.

Ashyn figured that his use of magic right now was sporadic at best, worthless at worst. But he knew the only time he was fully in control of magic was when he held the totem. Ashyn figured if he could get a hold of the totem again, he would be reconnected with his magic, even if it was a temporary solution.

Rizen, much to Ashyn's surprise, never objected to any of his plan. The Shaman only stated that he trusted his totem-brother to make the right choices, and to be aware of how disastrous all of it could be if it went the wrong way. Ashyn agreed with the gaur completely. It would only be a matter of days before Brodea was ready for the next phase of his torture, and he knew that she would use everyone against him.

In the end, Ashyn knew that regardless of what happened once he was placed before the tome, there were only two real outcomes. Strangely, he felt contented with both.

The few for the many, he told Rizen after the explanation of his plan. *I am not worth the lives of all those that will suffer if I don't give Brodea what she wants. Worse, I will endanger more lives if I do give her what she wants. I have become the few. My life is a small sacrifice, if it means protecting all those that would be hurt because of me.*

The gaur didn't answer him. Finally, he let out a snort and pulled his fingers from the murky waters. Ashyn wasn't sure if that was a snort of agreement, or resentment. The young wizard pulled his fingers from the pool of refuse, folded his arms across his chest and closed his eyes. His mind was made up.

No more people would die because of him. Either he would free them, or he was going to die trying.

~ ~ ~

Neither Ashyn nor Rizen ever looked up to see the lone figure of a Ferhym watching the duo curiously night after night from the council chambers. She watched on in silence as they buried their fingers in the disgusting and fetid waters, pondering what could be going through the mind of Ashyn Rune.

FORGING TRUST

He heard the door shut in the other room with a dull thud. This was it. The real moment of truth.

She walked into the room. Her foot falls delicate and soft. Her green dress swayed with the rhythm of her fine movements. Her copper, unadorned flesh was radiant in the flickering candlelight of the room. Her platinum hair reflected the soft light, casting the chambers in the glow of her presence. Her silver eyes fell upon the dormant form of a woman spread out against one of the chaises and she froze.

"I am sorry. We have been hiding for days, and I had nowhere left to go." Jenhiro said from the shadows as he stepped into her light.

The Voïre dui Ceremeia looked up in surprise from the woman asleep on her chair. He did not look away. "What have you done, Jenhiro?"

The use of his name startled him for only a moment. He blinked before composing himself, "The First Councilor ordered her execution. Genrus Eigron and his lackeys were going to carry it out. I... I had to stop it. I had to bring balance to nature."

The Voïre looked behind her towards the door. Jenhiro watched as she bit her lower lip. She was so young he realized. Perhaps right around the same age as the dui Nuchada. Still very much a youth in the eyes of the hym, albeit a very beautiful one.

When she turned to face him again, Jenhiro stood straight. He would take her decision standing tall. This moment would judge if all the Ferhym still believed in the code, or if they followed the corrupt First Councilor.

"Alright," she said at last.

Jenhiro's heart swelled with hope. He wasn't alone. His assessment was right. She would help; she bonded herself to the dui Nuchada when she was a small child. It was why he came. The dui Nuchada was his only ally in a world gone to chaos. Still, when the moment was upon them, he was afraid she would lose the nerve.

She came forward and checked on Avrimae. "How long since she was last sedated by the druids?"

Jenhiro shrugged as he bent to meet her. "Three days. Perhaps more. It should have worn off by now, but she won't wake up. I've been keeping her alive with honey and water."

Again he found the Voïre biting the corner of her lower lip. A tell that she was thinking. "She will awaken very soon. The restoration spells the druids use usually don't last much longer than three days. Before she does, what we need to do to her won't seem kind, Jenhiro. I have seen her when she isn't tempered. She is wild and fearful, and she screams and yells incoherently."

Jenhiro nodded.

"I need to look into her eyes, and you will need to hold her down while I do so." She paused to let it sink in. "We need to do it before she naturally awakens. It will seem inhumane, she will writhe and fight and perhaps even cause self-harm, but ultimately it will help her."

"How?"

The Voïre looked up at him. He felt the mirror of his own conscience looking heavily back at him. Weighing on him like sodden armor. "I have to reach inside of her mind, where she has locked herself in a cage of her own fear, and I have to free her. Afterwards, she should be able to come around on her own. She will still be fearful of us, probably of you in particular. You need to understand this. What she has gone through, it cannot be forgotten just because you liberated her from her assailers. There are scars and torments deep within her that will last the rest of her life."

"All the more reason to save her."

The Voïre sighed, "I do not blame you for saving her, Jenhiro, but you've painted yourself a target now."

"No one saw me."

"The First Councilor will piece it together." She rubbed her neck. "She's a cunning opponent, Jenhiro, and she rarely loses. It's only a matter of time before she connects your absence and the absence of Avrimae."

Jenhiro nodded, "I know this, but Eigron and his kind must be stopped. What is happening is wrong, and I couldn't allow it to continue. I couldn't let them kill her, just so I could be safe. It isn't right. It would be a hollow existence."

The Voïre let out a weak smile. "No. I suppose it would be, wouldn't it?" Then her expression grew more serious as she looked Jenhiro over. "You're hurt."

Jenhiro shrugged. "I'm fine," he lied. "Let's help Avrimae first."

The Voïre stood up, hovering above the bent over hunter. "She'll sleep at least for another hour. We need to see to your wounds first. I won't have you passing out on me when I need you most."

Jenhiro wanted to object, but as he looked up, her eyes ensnared his. Quickly he looked back down. "Fine," he agreed. "My wounds first, then we help Avrimae."

"I will fetch water," the Voïre replied matter-of-factly. "Strip and wait for me."

Minutes later she was back with multiple buckets of water and some of the healing supplies that Jenhiro often saw druids use to aid in their healing. She guided him to a small alcove in her home where it would be easiest to clean up the water, but secluded enough that one could not see the two of them through her home's open portals.

The Voïre hoisted up the sleeves of her green dress, squatted down, and dipped a clean cloth in one of the buckets. She lifted it up and twisted the excess water off before touching it to the green and purple bruised flesh of his ribs. Jenhiro sucked in a gasp of air as she pressed hard against him.

"Sorry. I don't normally do this."

"It's okay," Jenhiro grunted. "Out in the woods, we don't often have a druid with us and we are forced to make do on our own."

Jenhiro watched her platinum head bob in agreement. She worked in silence as she cleaned out the cuts on his lower torso and legs. Days had passed, and they were starting to show signs of infection.

She neither paid any mind to his genitalia as she worked at cleansing him, nor did her close proximity to him make the situation awkward. The Ferhym often bathed communally in the ponds, and Jenhiro suffered injuries far more often than the incident of the stampede. Previously, it had been Sendea's hands on him. Though they were never intimate, she had been extremely familiar with the contours of his body. She had patched him up more times than he could even count. Jenhiro involuntarily shuddered and sniffled at the memory.

"Am I doing something to make you uncomfortable?"

Jenhiro shook his head. "Just a memory."

"Do you want to talk about it?"

"No," he replied a little too sharply.

"I understand."

She worked her way up his abdomen, picking fibers and granules of dirt from the cuts when she asked him, "Why are you bearing the woad of an Earthshorn?"

"Cover," he answered her.

"Cover for what?"

Jenhiro looked down at her as she in turn looked up curious. It felt so strange looking at the Voïre dui Ceremeia after being trained all his life not to look into their eyes. Almost immediately out of habit he broke the gaze first. He described his plan and how he arrived at it. It was then that he remembered the dui Nuchada's last words. "He asked that you contact him. He said you knew how."

Perplexed the Voïre asked, "Who?"

"The dui Nuchada."

The Voïre smiled. "His name is Ashyn, Jenhiro. Ashyn Rune."

Jenhiro looked down at his feet in shock. He never bothered to learn the dui Nuchada's name. In the beginning, it was out of survival. He just lost his team, and he wanted someone capable of hunting those that took the team out. The dui Nuchada's name was negligible. Later though, Jenhiro realized he should have asked.

"I... I didn't know."

"Well, now you do." With with humor in her voice, she asked, "Does that change things?"

"I'm not sure," he said, and to Jenhiro's surprise she actually laughed a little.

"Yes, well I'm sure he's becoming quite tired of being called dui Nuchada, or skewer, or whatever other terrible thing they are calling him."

"Do you have a name?" Jenhiro asked suddenly.

The Voïre dui Ceremeia kept working. "I do," she said a bit curtly, as her motions became harsh and jerky.

"When was the last time someone asked you what your name was?"

The silver-haired beauty stopped working, and looked to the floor. Jenhiro waited for a moment for her to answer, but nothing came. Slowly he reached out and lifted her head up. He was surprised to see her eyes glistening with tears.

"I'm sorry. Have I offended you?"

The Voïre shook her head no. "No one has asked me or called me by name since I was a very small child. Not even my family. Sometimes, well, sometimes I miss it."

Jenhiro couldn't even guess what her life was like. Never to be looked in the eyes, never to be addressed as anything other than Voïre dui Ceremeia. To be practically revered at all times. To be so isolated and alone even when surrounded by a people who worship you.

"What is your name?" he asked her.

The Voïre sniffed once and wiped her eyes. "Relm."

"Relm," Jenhiro replied. "That is a very beautiful name, Relm. It is a shame that it cannot be used more."

She replied in a near whisper, "Thank you." Slowly she went back to work cleaning him up.

When she was tending to the wound on the side of his head from where he had slammed it on the ground, Jenhiro could not help but to ask, "Why are you doing this? Why are you helping me?"

Relm paused before ministering the wound some more. "Because it is the right thing to do."

Jenhiro reached out and pulled her hands away from his head. Her wrists were so thin, so delicate. "I am soon to be a fugitive to my own people. People that I love very much. How is it the right thing?"

Relm put the cleaning supplies down and handed him a clean damp cloth for his head. He took it and she turned away from him, walking back into the main living quarters. "When I was only a little girl, my family nominated me to go out on a great hunt for skewers," she began. "I was six-winters-old."

Relm reached out, picked one of the lit candles up, and brought it to a small wicker couch that she sat upon. Jenhiro followed quickly redressing before sitting next to her.

"A war party of orcs was discovered using our woods as a staging ground. Many hunters were going to be sent to eliminate the scourge to the balance of the natural world."

Jenhiro nodded, "I remember that. My branch was far to the east. We learned about it when we came back. The orcs attacked a human settlement, just south of the Shalis-Fey."

Relm nodded. "It was a gathering of orcs of a magnitude that allegedly hadn't been seen in over a century. Such a massing of orcs could mean only one thing. They found a dui Nuchada.

"Being a Voïre dui Ceremeia is an amazing privilege. I wasn't chosen by the people for this responsibility, but by the Spirits and nature itself. Still, my mother, she loved the Council of Elm so dearly, and she wanted to do all she could for them. So, she nominated that I go out in place of the much older, much more seasoned Voïre dui Ceremeia. I was special to my mother. A gift from the Spirits, she would call me.

"She wanted to show everyone how sacred I was, so she convinced the branch commander to bring me to identify the dui Nuchada, should the orcs find one, and to kill it."

Relm looked up at him, and her swirling eyes suddenly entranced Jenhiro. Part of his mind told him to look away, but he found he could not. Her will was strong. So unbelievably strong. He found himself looking through the eyes of a little girl.

"Well they did find one," her voice echoed in the background.

~ ~ ~

"Stay down!" Whisper commanded.

Relm did as the huntress bade and kept low. There were noises all around her. Screams of pain, roars of fury, and the drums. The beating of drums.

Whisper hissed and ran into the woods, javelin in hand ready to bring the monsters to heel. Relm screamed for her not to go, but the Ferhym was gone leaving her alone with nothing but the sounds, and the rustling of a forest alive with danger.

As Relm lay in terror, prostrate against the verge, a large foot suddenly slammed in front of her face. Relm sucked in her breath at the sight of it. Grey, gnarled flesh, laced with inky, black veins, flexed thick shin muscles. She followed the foot upward to see the rest of a massive orc looming over her. Moist gore and slick sweat clung to his bulky frame. In his hand, he held one of the spears of her people. Fresh blood ran off the bladed tip.

The savage moved with purpose, his nose crinkled, sniffing, trying to find the scent of his next victim. It swayed its lumbering head as greasy hair slapped wetly back and forth across his neck. The orc's jowls moved as it breathed, revealing yellow tusks. It knew there was someone near.

Relm didn't move. She didn't even exhale.

Unable to find what it could smell, the monstrous humanoid roared in displeasure and ran further into the woods at an amazing pace.

"I can't stay here," Relm whispered.

Slowly, she picked herself out of the bushes and searched for Whísper or Shedalia, the only two huntresses she really knew. If she stayed, one of the orcs might find her and hurt her.

Relm stumbled forward, pushing through the tangle of vines and bramble. The fingers of vegetation pulled at her naked flesh like skeletal hands of a monster.

The continuing sounds of combat heightened her fear, and every few seconds came the pounding of war drums. BOOM, BOOM, BOOM.

Her heart beat manically, and her chest heaved. She wanted to call out to Whísper or to Shedalia, but she was afraid that the orcs would hear her. Why did Whísper leave her? Where did she go?

All around her the forest exploded into disarray. She couldn't see the Hunters but she knew they were there. They all moved so fast. The orcs, on the other hand were easy to spot. Massive lumbering forms of pallid grey covered in the viscera of their kills. They scattered like insects as the Hunters dove into their numbers with spear and javelin.

Relm realized quickly that the Ferhym held the clear advantage, regardless of the orc numbers. The savage species seemed to recognize this too, and turned to their quickest defense. Fires lit up all across the Shalis-Fey. All around her within the emerald woods, hot flickering lights of yellow and orange speckled the shadowed tree line.

She caught sight of some hunters in the trees lobbing down volleys of javelins onto the forest floor. The elves were deadly accurate with the weapons.

Perforated orcs dropped to the ground resembling the pin cushions of a seamstress. The creatures still kept moving forward, relentless in their savagery, brutal in their own defense.

Relm saw a hunter make his first and only mistake. He feinted an attack that brought him forward too slowly. The orc made up for this and brought his sword flashing forward, cutting the elf down as swiftly as summer lightning. Relm quickly turned away hoping not to see the eyes of the dying elf as he tried to pack his own innards back into his body.

All around her, she could smell the refuse of dying orcs and elves as their bodies expired mixed with burning pitch and vegetation. She wanted to wretch. She could feel the very desire upon the orcs. Their need to slaughter.

The Ferhym hunters were unrelenting in doling out cold murder. Each strike was a kill. And soon the forest floor was thick with the red morass of blood.

An orc ran right by Relm in its haste to escape the vengeance of the elves. She could see its small, beady, black eyes beneath its heavy brow, darting back and forth looking for an escape. It never even noticed her in the tangle of bushes as it moved on.

Screams of suffering intermingled with the war cries of the Ferhym and the yelling of orcs. It created a din of intensity and violence that assailed her young senses. The carnage overloaded her fragile mind and she couldn't help but cry.

Slowly, the conflict subsided and Relm walked amongst the wreckage of the Shalis-Fey. Those who weren't dead, lay scattered against the ground, holding rent body parts, some seeking fretfully to find their amputated appendages. All had glossy-eyed, vacant expressions, and though she was only a child, she felt the emotion of it. All of it. All the hate, anger, fear, and terror as it saturated her mind, covering her in a veil of unbridled despair.

Hunters walked through the sundered forest carving paths of ruddy mud as they executed the surviving orcs. Relm looked down at her own bare feet drenched in crimson. The forest had become a bloody mire.

Once again, the need to vomit rushed within her stomach to her throat as she noticed that strewn around her were the entrails of orcs. They looked like large, undulating worms as the last vestiges of life leaked out of them.

She saw the short-haired huntress, Shedalia, slapping gore soaked leaves against flames that were beginning to climb one of the large sequoias. The viscera against the leaves crackled and popped from the searing heat. A new and even more revolting smell filled the air.

"I told you to stay down!" Whísper yelled at her from behind. Relm spun to see the huntress.

The warrior-elf was covered in the blood of the savages. She looked savage herself. Something perverse and alien. Tears poured down Relm's face. She never wanted to see Whísper like this. She seemed polluted now, blighted in a bog of cruor and gore.

The huntress moved forward, and Relm took a step backward.

"You need to stay down!" she yelled, "There are still more skewers!"

Relm wasn't listening. All she saw was Whísper as something she never envisioned before. A killer. Unable to take anymore, she turned and ran off into the woods, ignoring Whísper's pleas to stop.

It felt like hours, but Relm knew it was only minutes when she finally collapsed to the ground in a fit of crying. She had seen so much, too much evil, in the span of a few moments to think that such violence could be justifiable in this world.

In the distance she could hear the howls of victory coming from her kin, but to her it might as well have been the howls of Bristle Wolves. She knew what her people were. They were predators.

As her sobs lessened, she heard what she first thought was a bizarre echo. Then after several seconds of no longer crying, she realized that there was someone else crying. Someone nearby.

At first she sat petrified, as if she were a statue of stone. Was it an orc? It didn't sound like an orc. Her mind tried to process the crying sound, but it was hard to think. *It sounds like... no that can't be*, she thought. It sounded like another little girl.

Slowly, she picked herself up and followed the sounds of the whimpering. As she stumbled through the woods, the noise of the elves behind her faded until there was only the sound of the girl crying.

She ducked under a low hanging branch to see the slumped over form of an orc. As she cautiously approached she saw that a javelin or spear had cut deeply into his inner right thigh. She knew that the brute must have run away from the fight, only to bleed out a short distance away. Still in his hand, burning slowly were dying remains of a torch. It had begun to kindle a bush, and Relm could tell by the smoldering that it wouldn't be long before this vegetation ignited too. She could see a handful of the orcs arrows had fallen from its hip quiver and were laying against the fire, the metal arrowheads red hot.

She was about to back away from the dead creature when she heard the whimpering again. It was just on the other side of the orc. With terror rising in her chest, she cautiously stepped forward and peered around the body.

A mass of burgundy hair sat curled up against the base of a tree. It was a girl! How did another elf get so far away from her family? Relm wondered if she should track down Whísper and let her know of the lost child.

The moment she thought of it, she discounted the idea. Whísper was a monster to her right now. A cold killer. It was likely she would ignore the small girl, or worse.

Relm decided that she would help the girl. It was clear that the red-head was larger than she was, but she knew that the girl couldn't be too much older.

So she reached slowly into the alcove that the girl crawled into. As she did, she accidently snapped a branch. The loud crack echoed in their tight chamber. Suddenly, the red-head stopped moving, and looked up. Relm was also surprised. It wasn't a Ferhym child at all. It was a human!

The red-headed girl was maybe in her early teens, and she had a very pretty, albeit dirty face, and bright hazel eyes. Instantly, Relm felt the connection between them.

The girl froze solid like a statue.

It was the magic, Relm understood. Being what her people called the Voïre dui Ceremeia, she had an unusual talent for compelling people with her eyes. Or so she was told. It didn't seem to work on any of the elves in her town, and especially not on her mother. Now though, she could see this human was mesmerized.

As she looked at Relm, Relm found herself looking into the girl. It was a disconcerting experience, and yet, she wanted to see more. Her eyes probed deeper into the human's. She could see fear. Fear of the orcs. Fear of what she would do now. Relm could feel the terror and uncertainty in her because of the death of her family. She could feel an overwhelming sadness. More than that though, she could feel a raw connection to magic.

This girl was like a river, and Relm felt as if she were being swallowed completely inside the torrent of magical waters that this child had within her. She dove into that current and followed it. Drinking deeply the well of energy she felt from the human. She took the ride all the way to the core of the young teen. There seemed to be more to this girl. As if there were not a single core, but more a complex maze to her.

Before her, in the pools of energy that represented the spirit of the girl, she felt the presence of something more, another pool, a greater pool. She moved to it confused. The elder Voïre dui Ceremeia told her that people contained only one center, and that this life pool within them was their connection to everything that they were. Their memories, their emotions, their dreams and desires. It was what made them individual and unique. It was their soul.

But there was so much more to this girl. She had not one font, but two. How was such a thing possible? How could a person bear more than one soul? And that was when Relm realized that this girl was why she had come. This is who they were looking for. This was the creature birthed by magic. She was the beholder of two species: human and dragon. She was everything there was to being human, and everything there was to being dragon. She was the dui Nuchada.

Relm explored the mystery of this rare form, enamored by the majesty of the idea of two spirits being in one. She followed the channels as they wove around one and other. It was like a braid. Relm knew then that though it may carry the independent weaves of two races, they had bonded perfectly together. There weren't two spirits within the eyes, but one massive, immensely complex spirit that was beautiful and terrifying all at once. She felt like she could stay lost in this place for a lifetime.

"Voïre!" a voice said hazily in the distance. Relm was confused to hear such an odd sound. "Voïre!" another yelled, this one still murky, but sounding much closer.

Relm snapped back into her own body and looked at the girl before her. The girl still sat there looking glamoured and dumbfounded by the sight of Relm.

The elf child heard noise just outside of the alcove they were hidden in. She knew if Whisper, Shedalia, or Branch Commander Elumin caught sight of this girl and asked Relm if she was the dui Nuchada, they would kill her with the same aggression and violence as they killed the orcs. It was their mission.

Relm had seen into the depths of the girl before her. No, not girl, Julietta. Her name was Julietta. She knew the most recent memories she witnessed of the family Julietta lost. Julietta was scared and alone. There was no one for her anymore, and everyone in these woods wanted her dead for reasons that she would never know.

Relm could lie, she decided. She could say that Julietta was not the dui Nuchada. But what would they do to her? She was so deep in the Shalis-Fey, and Whísper seemed so cold that it was likely they would kill her just for being too close to Feydras' Anula.

Would they? Would they kill a child? Relm asked herself. And she knew the answer was yes. And even if they didn't they would take her in as a skewer to slave off the toils of her insolence. Worse, if the other Voïre dui Ceremeia saw her, she would know the truth too!

Relm bit her lip in frustration. She didn't know what to do! She didn't want to see Julietta die, not after witnessing all the horrors she saw already. It just wasn't right. She was only a girl. An innocent girl, whose only fault was that she was unlucky enough to be born a dui Nuchada.

Relm's eyes scanned around looking for anything that could help hide her. Help protect this poor girl. She immediately knew she couldn't. The fire was beginning to catch on the bush, if she left her here, Julietta would burn alive. Julietta would never make it away from the hunters either. She would be captured for sure.

There was only one thing she could hope to do, the young elf decided. Relm would have to save Julietta, but prevent anyone else from discovering the truth about her being a dui Nuchada.

The thought turned her stomach even more. She looked into Julietta's bright hazel eyes, knowing that the only way to protect her was to ensure that Relm's face was the last thing she would ever see.

With a shaky hand the elf child reached out and pulled one of the arrows away from the torch. The steel arrow head glowed a rich red. It would work. It had to work.

Relm raised the arrowhead up in front of Julietta. The girl didn't even blink as the heat sweltered her skin, flushing her olive complexion a shade of pink. Carefully she moved the weapon forward until it hovered just in front of Julietta's left eye. All she needed to do was stab forward real quick and it would all be over.

Still she couldn't do it. Her hand stayed rock still, the arrow a hair's breadth away from the dui Nuchada's eye.

Tears flooded down Relm's face. She couldn't do this. She couldn't! She didn't want to hurt this girl.

"Relm!" Whisper yelled her real name so close it startled her.

She had to do it. She had to help Julietta. The little girl sniffled, and wiped the snot and tears away from her face with her free hand. She would be strong. She would help Julietta. Even if it meant dedicating the rest of her life to taking care of this poor girl.

Relm steeled herself. She would be Julietta's caretaker now, and always. She jabbed the weapon forward. Once. Twice.

Julietta never even moved.

BOND

J enhiro blinked away the memory. Relm's memory. He stared into her eyes. They were no longer pools of quicksilver, but still. "That was…"

Relm looked away. "I have never shared that memory with anyone." She stood up and paced the room. "I just wanted you to know where my heart was, and why. Why I am helping you now."

Jenhiro sat dumbfounded for a moment, trying to collect his thoughts before speaking again. "So that was why Julietta was never executed."

Relm nodded. "I denied the council their dui Nuchada, though they never stopped claiming her to be such. Still there was no proof. I would never confirm it, nor could the other Voïre. Shedalia and Whísper, they wanted to kill her instantly. If not for Branch Commander Elumin, they would have. He showed considerable mercy in sparing Julietta, though I'm sure he had motives of his own."

Jenhiro watched as his Voïre dui Ceremeia looked over to the still form of Avrimae. "The druid did what he could to heal her wounds, but I'm afraid the damage I did was quite extensive. He had to hollow out her eye sockets to save her from infection." Her voice trembled as her lip quivered, "I blinded her, to save her. And still they accused her of being a dui Nuchada, but because they had no proof, they kept her as a skewer to repay a debt for a crime she never committed. I didn't think they'd do that. I thought…" She shook her head. "I don't know what I thought, that they would take her to the humans I guess. I was just a silly little girl."

Tears leaked out of the sides of her beautiful eyes, and Jenhiro quickly moved to her. He took her in his arms and she fell into him sobbing. He whispered to her reassuringly, "You did the right thing." He was surprised by his own words, and how right they felt. Now he understood the Earthshorn's words when he said Relm watched Julietta working the fields.

Jenhiro saw through Relm's eyes. He made the journey into the depths of Julietta, and what he saw was nothing evil, but beautiful and innocent. She might be a dui Nuchada, but she was no monster.

Relm stayed there in his arms for a long time, crying. And he knew why. She held that entire burden to herself since she was only a small child. She grew up secluded and alone with no one to lean on, no one to trust. The pain festered inside of her. The doubt and indecision. Everything he was going through for the last few months, she had endured for winters.

"You know my pain as well, don't you?" he asked.

She nodded against his chest. "When we first made eye contact in front of the druid's cove, I saw it. A Voïre's gift and curse, to see everything in a person. That one moment though, it was truly a gift. It was the first time I saw someone like me, another Ferhym who questioned. I knew I wasn't alone anymore. I had someone I could finally confide in."

He looked down at her, and she looked into his eyes. "I knew in that moment, I could trust you, Jenhiro."

He turned away, "Yet I have condemned Ashyn. I have let him be imprisoned and tortured after he saved my very life, because he is a dui Nuchada, a skewer. How can I be trusted after such a betrayal?"

Relm reached up and gently touched his jaw, guiding him to look into her depthless eyes once more. "You were doing your duty. The fact that you questioned such is truly a testament to your character."

Jenhiro's jaw muscles clenched. "And yet, his pain..."

Relm leaned in. "This was always his destination. He has always known the risks."

Jenhiro blinked in surprised. His face was so close to hers that he suddenly had the urge to kiss those lips that were there, so close, so full. He felt himself drawn to her. A kindred spirit. It was so long since he had companionship.

His hand reached up and touched her cheek. His strong coarse fingertips pushed back the platinum hair on the side of her cheek, so he could take in her whole face. Suddenly the sight of the brilliant silver hair sent his mind to the braid on Ashyn's wrist. He pulled back. "You've marked another. Why Ashyn?"

Relm's eyes widened for only a moment, and she too pulled away. Perhaps she realized how close they were to each other as well. How intimate their last few moments had become. Sharing each other's memories would do that, Jenhiro supposed.

"It is so very complicated," she told him over her shoulder, not daring to look at him anymore. "It was just, the right thing to do."

"I don't understand."

"We learned shortly after the druid sent Julietta to Feydras' Anula to be healed, that a wizard was traveling through the woods with another survivor from the human town. A small boy with olive skin and red hair."

Jenhiro stood with his mouth agape. "Just like Julietta."

Relm nodded. "Since they were unable to determine the truth of Julietta being a dui Nuchada or not, the druid was informed to tell the branch commander and the other hunters that she died in transport due to impact. It was meant to gauge the reaction of the wizard and child when we encountered them. But I saw into his eyes, and I knew the truth. They already wanted Ashyn; they wanted to see his reaction. If it were family, then they would know for sure that Julietta was a dui Nuchada. They wanted to capture Ashyn for that purpose. Ashyn would condemn Julietta and himself in one quick motion.

"They set the trap, but were too leery of me after Julietta. No one questioned if I stabbed her eyes out or the orcs, but they didn't want to take chances. Elumin placed me in a very open pool of water where I wouldn't miss him, and no Ferhym could miss me.

"I confess I was excited this time to meet the dui Nuchada. As you saw in my memory with Julietta, there is nothing evil about her, just magical. This time the councilor in charge of the operation clearly informed Elumin we were to use no violence. We had a treaty with wizards. Our mission was to talk to the wizard and this potential dui Nuchada, nothing more. If it was a dui Nuchada, we were to negotiate for him. I believed them, what's more, I wanted to be the one to let the dui Nuchada know his family was alive, if it were the case."

Jenhiro looked at her. "What happened?"

Relm chuckled slightly. "He didn't speak our language. I was so excited, I tried to tell him he was a dui Nuchada and that I encountered a girl that looked just like him in the woods, and he didn't understand me!"

Jenhiro shook his head and laughed as well. "Terrible irony."

"I know!" Relm agreed passionately. "Since we couldn't communicate that way, I tried looking him in the eyes, but he wouldn't meet my gaze, not long enough to let me convey the message in a way he would understand. It was like a game, he kept weaving and dodging and avoiding my eyes!" She folded her arms over her chest. "It was infuriating."

"Then what happened?"

Relm shrugged, "Elumin had enough. He revealed himself and questioned the wizard directly. He fed the wizard exactly the same information that was conveyed by the druid, and every time I tried to speak, he would only cut me off. The wizard refused to relinquish his charge. He was adamant in fact.

"Finally, Elumin demanded the wizard hand Ashyn over. It ended poorly. The wizard threatened to destroy the Shalis-Fey and make it uninhabitable for generations."

Now it was Jenhiro's turn to be surprised. "Just like the Maze."

"Exactly," Relm replied. "It was still a fresh wound against us being only a few winters old. Brodea said a wizard was responsible for that very thing, and now another was threatening to do it again. Knowing he could make good on his threat, they let him go. That was when I got one good look into Ashyn's eyes. It was only a glimpse, but it was enough."

Jenhiro perked up at this.

Once more Relm bit her lip as she thought about how to proceed. "Have you ever looked at someone and just knew this person is destined for something? It's as if all the stars align just for them, and that one day they will do something momentous."

Jenhiro shook his head, "No."

Relm sighed. "I know. I told you, it was complicated. Here was this boy, and I just saved, but wounded his potential family, we couldn't communicate at all, and yet I had this feeling as if he was meant for something. Something beyond our comprehension. It seems silly, I know."

"So you marked him because you think Ashyn is some type of chosen one?" Jenhiro remarked almost snidely.

"No!" Relm snapped quickly, her eyes livid. "He's not some chosen one, and I don't profess to be some type of prophet claiming to know why he's on this road, but I do know that I sense something in him. A warrior. Something that we need. Not just his people, but our people too. I think Ashyn is destined for something big. Something that may bridge a gap between our races that has gone on for too long. That was why I marked him. Because I knew he was special, and I knew that somehow, someday he would need me."

Jenhiro shook his head. "I don't understand."

"Trust me, neither do I. I've wondered for over a decade now why I made the decision I did. But I tell you now, if you ask me would I do it again, I have to answer the same. Yes, I would. We need Ashyn Rune. I need Ashyn Rune. I just don't know the how or the why. Not yet."

"Then your heart is not bonded to him?" Jenhiro queried.

Relm looked to the floor. "I honestly don't know. I do feel something for him, but it may just be the magic of the mark that binds us."

"I see."

Relm waved her hand dismissively. "It matters little anyway. Ever since then I haven't been allowed to see him. Once Elumin tried to attack the wizard, and the wizard retaliated by killing the branch commander and several others, I was quickly sent back to Feydras' Anula and any queries to the status of Ashyn were quickly ignored."

Jenhiro was nonplussed, "But he said you know how to get a hold of him."

Relm smirked. "I do."

"And you're not going to tell me?" he asked slightly defensively.

Sadness filled Relm's eyes. "I'm sorry, Jenhiro. I trust you, I do. It is why I shared my memories with you, to let you know that you are not alone. We both question what's happening in our beloved society. It's safer if you don't know the details."

Though he was angry, Jenhiro reluctantly nodded. He did understand. Branch commanders often did not tell all facets of a complex plan to every member of their branch. He didn't begrudge Relm for doing the same. "So what do we do now?"

At this, Relm revealed a large, pristine, white smile that felt eerily familiar to Jenhiro. "It's time that Ashyn Rune and Avrimae be on their way home. Julietta too, she's long overdue." The smile disappeared, and she looked at him with all seriousness. "Can I count on you?"

Jenhiro folded his arms over his chest. Something about her smile bothered him. Some lingering thought in the back of his mind about its familiarity, but he dismissed it. She was the Voïre dui Ceremeia, and she was his only ally right now. "I believe you can." He answered.

"Good. First I will explain my plan, hopefully you can fill in the holes to the areas I'm weakest. Then I'll let Ashyn know, and see what he has planned. He's had more than enough time, and he's disturbingly clever, that one."

Jenhiro snickered. "Tell me about it."

"Finally we'll get Avrimae stabilized. Though I'm very concerned about her, we need to get things underway, and quickly. We don't have much time left."

Jenhiro nodded.

It was time to save Avrimae.

It was time to save Julietta.

It was time to set the Blood Wizard free.

Spirits help him; he hoped he was making the right choice.

~ ~ ~

Ashyn smiled as he felt himself floating on a cloud. It was warm and inviting, and he hadn't felt this way in weeks now. As usual, he couldn't open his eyes. "I see Jenhiro delivered my message."

The ethereal sing-song voice answered him, "He has."

"And was he successful? Is Avrimae safe?"

"She is."

Ashyn let out a sigh of relief. It was better news than he hoped for, considering the circumstances.

"You asked for me?"

Ashyn nodded, and wondered for a moment if she could see him. "I need your help."

"How?"

"I need you to find the magic within me, and reconnect it."

He heard her sigh. "It doesn't work like that Ashyn. I can't just connect you to magic. It is not some extraneous item like a sword or a bow. It is not a possession. It is life."

"I know," he answered quickly. He couldn't afford to lose her on this. "But an Exemplar saw it in me tonight. She said it's there, but I can't reach it. I don't understand what that means. You know what I am; you know about magic. I need you to help me reach it."

Ashyn sat in silence for a long time, wondering if this dream state was going to keep him like this indefinitely. Finally, she spoke again, "Ashyn, to do what you are asking we will need to be together, and it isn't something that we can do between a barrier. If I come to you, it will give away our connection. The risks are too great for everyone. If they learned of what we can do, they'd kill you, instantly. Brodea couldn't risk the Voïre, not in front of the Council, not even for the Tome she desperately wants translated."

Ashyn was stunned. He hadn't thought it common knowledge that Brodea was trying to have a wizard's artifact translated. He suddenly had reservations on whether or not he could trust this Exemplar.

Still, he was running out of options, and he was drastically low on time. People were going to starve soon, and Brodea was going to have Macky killed in a horrible way. After witnessing what she was willing to do to others to just get him to talk, Ashyn knew that if he wanted to save his friends, he needed to take the risk.

"What if I convinced Brodea to let us work together?"

The Exemplar laughed. The full-bodied sound was unexpected and somehow familiar. He discounted it. He needed to drive it home. "I don't know how much time I have before she starts torturing me again, but I know it won't be me she hurts. With Avrimae now gone, she'll target Macky next, countless others until she gets what she wants. The people of the Water Pens have stopped being fed."

"I know," Relm answered.

"Then I have to try something…"

"You have less than a week, Ashyn. Brodea is so confident that you will talk in four days' time that she is going to put you on display before the Council of Elm to start to decipher the tome to them."

Bewildered, he whispered, "How do you know this?"

"Because I was there when she told Councilor Vooken this evening. It isn't Macky. Jenhiro and I know who she'll torture to get you to talk Ashyn."

Ashyn felt weak, at the thought of who else the Exemplar was going to name.

"It's Julietta, Ashyn. Brodea's finally been assured to get her before the next council gathering."

RELM ADVISES

66"I am sorry Ashyn," the Exemplar whispered compassionately.

His voice paper-thin, he squeaked, "You know who Julietta is?"

"I have always known."

Anger filled him. He yelled, "Then why have you never said anything? For winters, I'd been living with the thought that my sister was dead, when you've known the whole time! You've known how to contact me and let me know she's safe! That's she's alive!"

He shook his head as rage extended to every fiber of his being. "I've trusted you! And you let me go on thinking that she was dead while she was being tortured, mutilated, and probably worse!"

She whispered weakly, "I did it to protect you both."

"Protect me!" he roared. "I am a Recreant now because I've given up everything to save her! There is no safe haven for me no matter where I go! I've made this choice because I felt I needed to get her away from the Ferhym. Now you're telling me that at any time you could have bestowed this information upon me and you chose not to, to protect me?" He turned away disgusted, "Fuck you."

Ashyn heard her sob, but he didn't care. He was livid beyond his own understanding of the word. He wanted to hurt something, someone. He was willing to sacrifice everything for his sister, and in some ways he had. Now the Exemplar told him she knew the truth of his sister and chose not to share it. Still beside himself, his tone suddenly shifted. Meekly he asked, "How? How would this protect me?"

Her voice trembled as she spoke, and Ashyn listened as Relm explained, "Twice. I tried to reunite you with your sister, and twice I failed. The first time was at the waterfall, before I marked you. I tried to communicate with you, and even with the wizard, but you didn't understand me. I tried to make eye contact so I could show you, but you avoided me."

Ashyn responded flatly, "Xexial told me that the elves told him that Julietta was dead."

"It is true, they did. When I tried to interject, I was talked over by Elumin, or just ignored. And because we couldn't communicate, I couldn't tell you the truth of your sister."

"And the second time?"

"Czynsk. I was placed on Whísper's vanguard to identify the wizard, and any other potential skewers. I was allowed to take a small contingent with me, and for that, I nominated Julietta. They allowed it. I wasn't certain you would arrive with the wizard, but I knew you lived, and I knew you had gone to Czynsk as a child. I hoped that you would be there. After we arrived, and I identified you, well Whísper made the connection first between you and Julietta, and she made other plans."

"And you did nothing to stop those plans, did you? You let my sister be used as bait. Food for Bristle Wolves, to lure me out."

"I didn't know!" she swore. "I was immediately sent back to Feydras' Anula, under guard by her most trusted huntress, after you left with the wizard. Whísper denied me my entourage so I knew something was happening, but I didn't realize that she remembered that Julietta was your sister. It was a decade past, and so much happened in her life after that singular moment."

"You could have warned me before; you had eleven bloody winters to do it in!"

Though he couldn't see her face to know she was crying, he could hear the trembling of her voice. "Wards."

"What?" he asked.

"You were behind a wizard's wards. Our connection cannot penetrate a wizard's wards."

Ashyn was astonished. His own tower had denied him the truth from the Exemplar all this time. When she spoke again, she was much quieter.

"After Whisper returned, she was in no condition to talk about Julietta. By the time she was, Brodea was already aware of her and aware of the connection. It was as I feared all along. Identifying your sister to you had now placed her in danger. Up until the moment you recognized Julietta as your sister, the Council of Elm could not confirm that she truly was a dui Nuchada. Because of this indecision, members of the council would not let her be killed, but they wouldn't let her go into the world either. She would have to remain watched until such time that her true nature itself became known. So they kept her here, safe in the fields, for the last eleven winters."

"But they burned out her eyes…" Ashyn cried.

There was another prolonged silence. "Her eyes were lost to Julietta in the forests of the Shalis-Fey. No Councilor or hunter was responsible for her going blind."

Ashyn felt all his rage leave him. He asked in a low voice, "They haven't tortured her?"

"I've kept an eye on her almost every day since we were children. No one in Feydras' Anula has ever laid a hand upon her in harm. I cannot say that they have been friendly or kind, because they have not, but no one has ever tortured her. The cause calls for the balance of nature, Ashyn. Not for the punishment of children for no reason. While I don't agree on many things with the Council of Elm, most of them are not the monsters you think they are. Julietta never displayed the propensity for magic like you have. And without her eyes, no Voïre dui Ceremeia can peer within her to see what she truly is. That is why she wasn't killed for being a dui Nuchada."

Ashyn's legs grew weak and he fell to the ground, or whatever it was in the dream state. "Then Xexial was right. I should have gone to the Seven first. I never should have come here. Julietta was safe."

Ashyn felt tears building up; his face grew hot, not with anger, but with shame. He betrayed his master, condemned his life, endured torture, and his sister had been safe the entire time. He failed Xexial, and now he was failing Julietta.

"She is not safe any longer, Ashyn." Relm told him. "Brodea knows, and come the week's end when the council convenes, they will know. When Brodea starts torturing her, you will do everything you can to stop it, and they will see the truth. Julietta is a dui Nuchada. They will have no choice but to swiftly balance this skewer that has been in their midst for far too long. That is the power Brodea will hold over you. For only she can stop the execution of Julietta, if you translate the book for her."

Ashyn buried his face into his hands in defeat. Brodea was going to win. Ashyn would have no choice. She was the reason he was here. She was the only reason he cared to draw breath. If Brodea took that away from him, it would destroy him.

"She will not bluff with this, Ashyn," Relm said as if reading his mind. "This is it. If you refuse to translate the tome, Julietta dies, and then you will die too."

Ashyn whispered, "Then Brodea has won. I won't let my sister die."

"I know."

"In a few days, this will all be over and I will unleash the Netherphage."

"Do you know what it is?"

"I read enough," he admitted, not caring anymore. He failed. Ashyn failed everyone.

"Then it's time you read all of it."

Ashyn lifted his head up in surprise.

"I have a plan. We," she corrected, "have a plan. But first I know you've been planning as well. Tell me, and tell me why you need me to help guide you back to magic so badly."

Ashyn felt his chest grow tight. The Exemplar had help, and he was fairly certain he knew who that help was.

"And Ashyn, if we're going to make this work, call me Relm."

THE MABA-HETH RETURNS

Xexial stared at Khyriaxx impassively as he finished relaying the journal's chapter. The sun was burning the last rays of light into the slotted windows of the library. It cast the entire chamber in a blazing orange hue. The spriggan in front of Xexial poured over his own paperwork as he took notes from everything that Xexial told him. When the Xexial was done recounting the chapter for the umpteenth time, the small creature reached up and removed the monocle from his eye.

He said excitedly, "Incredible. I never be thinking I be hearing a tale of something so ancient. I greatly desire to read the whole thing sometime soon."

Xexial nodded in agreement. "Indeed. But I am afraid that will never be." Xexial looked down at his naked hands once more. He returned the journal to its warded alcove and the gauntlet to the hand of Rheynnaus where it resumed the texture and appearance of marble.

Xexial could see the indignation in the eyes of Khyriaxx, but before he could defend why he had not brought the ancient parcel out of the tombs the spriggan continued, "I see. Then it appears you be correct all along. Ashyn Rune is indeed not a human, or a half-elf. His tendencies and mannerisms be following the same pattern as what is in both the journal you found, and the one by Patrius Monerch. He must be a Craetorian, or at least be something very similar. Perhaps he be distant descendant. There be too many ironies."

"And we now know that the Craetorians did not all perish with Magelord Craëgolshien, but continued on, at least in some secrecy, as the Enclave's Craetorian Purges indicate," the old wizard pointed out. "Plus, it is entirely possible at least one bloodline lived on. All it would take is for them continue having offspring with a human. Something that could be easily done since they appear human enough."

"This is a knowledge the Ferhym be knowing for a long time then. That Craetorians existed when others have thought them extinct," the tinkerer commented.

"They are one step ahead of us it seems," Xexial grumbled.

"I say this be good news. There may be more of them now. More Craetorians."

"I can confirm at least one more, Ashyn's sister, Julietta."

Khyriaxx steepled his small three fingered hands together and spoke so quietly that Xexial could barely hear it, "Yes. At least two. They must be powerful indeed. Very powerful."

Xexial looked at the spriggan with curiosity. It was the first time he ever made a comment regarding the nature of someone's power. "Ashyn is not powerful enough to avoid injury. The boy lost his connection to magic just like any other Creationist that takes it too far."

Khyriaxx nodded recouping from his previous statement. "You be right. He be mortal after all, and susceptible to everything we be. I just find the act of siphoning and storing to be very intriguing."

Xexial could definitely see where a tinkerer would like that concept. Especially in someone living that wasn't an armor-plated beast that could swallow him in a single bite. Xexial thought back to waking up in the spriggan's small home and witnessing all the strange contraptions Khyriaxx worked on. How he used the power of wind to fuel many of his contraptions. Yes, the wizard could definitely see it now, a living breathing man that could store an eldritch energy that the spriggan could barely begin the fathom. The questions Khyriaxx must have.

"His power is irrelevant for now. What we must figure out is how to find him."

The spriggan's eyebrows raised. "Oh? And have you figured out what you are going to do when you do find the boy?"

There was a sudden loud click in the circular library as the locking mechanism on the double doors turned to open. The doors swung wide, and Xexial looked away from Khyriaxx in alarm. None of his wards triggered an entrant. He should have known if someone else was in the tower with them! Instead he was caught by surprise as the familiar piercing, deep emerald eyes leered at him from just outside the chamber.

"The wizard is going to kill him of course," Gavius Grind answered in Xexial's stead.

The senior wizard was speechless. Not so much out of surprise, but more from anger and quite a bit of concern. The Maba-Heth purposely avoided Xexial's wards, again, even knowing that he was cleared to pass through them all. It bothered Xexial to know how capable Grind was at circumventing his own protection system. Enough to eavesdrop on the duo at least. Worse it made Xexial realize that he wouldn't be safe from the wizard hunter in his own home, even while he slept.

On top of that, he was angry that this young wizard had the audacity to speak for him, as if Xexial answered to Grind. Then the unsettling truth sank in. He did answer to Grind. The scales wizard hunter was acting on behest of the Seven, and therefore Xexial was bound to serve the reptile to the best of his capacity.

"Of course," Xexial replied through gritted teeth. "Have you learned anything from Tilliatemma that may aid us?" he added, trying to deflect some of his surprise away, as if he knew Grind had been in the tower all along.

The sharp-toothed grin from the scales immediately told Xexial that ploy failed. "Nothing of notable relevance to the Recreant. However, it was surprising to see that the Dakhym have undergone a change in government."

Xexial perked up at this. "The Singh Imperium?"

"This helps us how?" Khyriaxx interrupted. "I thought you be here to hunt a Recreant, not discuss the politics of other nations."

Xexial watched the scales' frill flush a golden hue in anger. "Khyriaxx is right," Xexial intervened before the Maba-Heth lost his patience. "Politics are not for a wizard. We should be focused on Ashyn and his whereabouts."

The slit eyes of the wizard hunter fell back to Xexial. He could still read the menace in them. Grind never agreed with the spriggan's presence, never thought it necessary. Had Xexial been asked the same question six months prior he would have been much like the Maba-Heth in his assessment of the tinkerer. Now though, things changed. Xexial needed the squat little creature. It was as if Khyriaxx had become a confidant for Xexial's own conscience.

Xexial held his icy gaze on the Maba-Heth, his conviction set. Finally, the scales looked away. "Agreed."

"Good. So then, if nothing was learned from Tilliatemma pertaining to Ashyn, what is your next step?" the elder wizard pushed.

Xexial watched as the scales paced quietly around the circular room. Though his reptilian features were indistinguishable in determining his emotion, the frill on the back of his head told a different tale. It shifted between a golden hue and a burnt orange, and Xexial knew that Grind was deeply conflicted. The old wizard assumed the Maba-Heth wanted to head west into the deserts of Malten, or south east into the realms of the Gnomes, but deep down he felt that Grind knew he was right. Grind knew they needed to go into the Shalis-Fey.

"There are many paths still available to us. But, after all this time, and without his blood, the recreant could be virtually anywhere. You seem determined that we head south, and now that choice is just as good as any, I will agree. We hunt your way."

"About damn time," Xexial said firmly. He looked away from the angry wizard hunter and down to Khyriaxx. "Gather our things. We leave at first light tomorrow. It's time to pay a visit to the Ferhym and find out where my wayward apprentice has gone."

Khyriaxx nodded and quickly hopped off the chair. "Don't forget to stop by my house first. I still think there be items that will help."

Xexial nodded and Khyriaxx promptly left the room. Xexial knew he owed the creature some sort of apology for the way that he acted before, but he wasn't sure exactly what he should say. He was torn in his loyalties to both the Seven and to Ashyn. Finding out what Ashyn was helped answer to him some desperately needed questions, but it still didn't give him the cognizance on choosing a correct path to take. The boy or his service?

He didn't even bother to look at the scales. "Get a good night's rest, Maba-Heth. Tomorrow we will be at war with the Ferhym. Have no doubt they will know it the moment we set foot in those woods, and they will be relentless."

The caiman-like wizard folded his scaled arms over his black robes. "And you still think the Recreant is in there? After all this time?"

"There's only one way to find out."

TENOUS

Brodea stared down below towards the Water Pens. She could see the wizard leaning against the posts of his cell, one foot in the mire, while he was talking to the skewer named Mactonal on the other side. Her gut clenched excitedly at the thought of what was to come in a mere three days.

"You are absolutely sure, Eigron?" she asked again, just desiring to hear the words.

"Yes, First Councilor. The Elder of Vines has transferred custody of Julietta to the council in the event that it will indeed get the Blood Wizard to relinquish his knowledge of the tome. She will be yours on the evening before the council convening, but not a moment before."

Brodea let out a relieved sigh of victory. Finally! Finally, the druids were coming around to her way of thinking. This Julietta was a dui Nuchada, and Ashyn would confirm that. Over a decade of sitting on their laurels and now the council would see that she was correct all along. Better still, she would use the woman to get the boy wizard to translate the tome, of that she had no doubt.

Ashyn tried to sacrifice himself to stop Avrimae's pain. There was no way he would endure the same to his sister.

"And what about my hunter?" Eigron said. "Mehris is dead, surely you are not going to try and say it was the elk's fault?"

"Surely not," Brodea said turning away from her view of the Water Pens to look at the druid. "I tipped my hat early. To save you before you too would have fallen victim to the killer, or have you forgotten?" she asked, her dark eyes flashing with menace.

Eigron lowered his head, "Of course not, First Councilor. I am grateful of course."

"And Avrimae is... lost, because of it, remember that." She added just as darkly. "If that skewer is pregnant..."

"We will find her," Eigron pressed.

"And you will have your killer," she said simply, and then added, "Before he kills you, preferably."

Eigron glowered at this, and it made Brodea smile even more. "Eigron, dear, you have delivered as you said you would. When have I not done the same?"

She turned back around and watched the large bull thing lumber to the water opposite of Ashyn. It was curious how much time they spent near the brackish refuse.

Still she could see that Ashyn was paying the monster no mind, and instead continued talking to the other human as if the beast weren't even there. The boy was enduring and brave, she would give him that. But in a few days' time, he would be broken.

"If there is nothing else, please send the Voïre up; she's been waiting patiently to see me," she added without looking back at the druid.

She heard Eigron exit, pleased with the outcome. He was worried, and that was good. He had pushed his authority, painted himself as more important than he was, and was quickly brought back to heel with the deaths of his two accomplices. Once she delivered the killer, he would be hers forever. The need for his elimination had passed. The stampede had ultimately helped her, and she used it. Now only if she could zero in on the hunter that was attacking all of her pawns...

The beautiful melodic voice of the Voïre dui Ceremeia chimed from by the stairs, "You wanted to see me?"

Brodea turned, smiling, averting her eyes only slightly so that she was staring at the Voïre's chin. "Yes. Please." She extended her hand to the center of the chamber, where a small pedestal stood holding the traditional basin of water and next to it the tome.

The Voïre walked beside her, her verdant green dress swishing along the polished floor towards the basin. As they approached, she watched as the Voïre looked into the water and saw the image of Ashyn and the bull creature.

"Watching them from here even though you can just look down and see them?" the Voïre asked.

"I find it good to have a wider perspective on the situation. This particular angle has been very enlightening," Brodea replied with a smile.

"As to?"

Brodea reached down and gently caressed the surface of the water where Ashyn was sitting. "This Mactonal means a lot to the boy. Almost as much as Avrimae did." Brodea looked up to study the Voïre's reaction to the past tense usage of Avrimae. The Voïre's mercury eyes studied the dui Nuchada impassively.

"So you seek to influence the dui Nuchada next using Mactonal?"

"Perhaps. I seek to invoke the next stage."

The Voïre looked up at her First Councilor, and Brodea stared down to the tome, but not quickly enough. She felt the electricity of the Voïre's magic course through her, tingling her entire body. It never got any easier dealing with the Voïre.

Brodea's fingers reached out and caressed the leather jacket that covered the powerful pages beneath. "Before the convening in a few days' time, I want you to read this."

Brodea could see the Voïre was clearly confused, even without looking in her swirling eyes. "But, if the druids cannot read it, how can I hope to? I know not the meaning of this language, let alone Trade Tongue that you speak to the humans with."

Brodea noticed that last part came out a little bitter. "You are a Voïre; you will never have to use such a barbaric language as that of the skewers."

"And yet you trained Whisper..."

Brodea scoffed, "She is a branch commander, and was vanguard to my campaign against wizards. Of course she needed to recognize the foul tongue. You are the purest hym. You should not be soiled with their perversities."

"Yet you want me to look at this," the Voïre replied pointing to the book beneath Brodea's fingers.

"Call it a hunch."

"Hunch?"

"You are a beautiful creature of constant and glorious connection to Creative magic. The druids virtually worship your commands. The council even listens to your words, when the Spirits take notice of you. I have a feeling, that even if you read these words, regardless of meaning, they will stay in your head. You just might not know what to do with them."

"And how would that help? How does that help the cause?" the Voïre asked skepticism clearly in her voice.

"Well, if anything happens to this tome, at least we know its contents will be safe in your head, right?"

"Even could I understand such a thing, I could not memorize such a tome in a few days. It would take winters of recital. Reading over and over, being queried constantly," the Voïre admitted.

Brodea smiled again, "Just humor me, my dear."

The Voïre reached down with her smooth, unadorned skin and touched the ancient manuscript. Brodea watched her intently. Finally, the Voïre dui Ceremeia picked it up. "If it is your will First Councilor, I shall endeavor not to disappoint you."

Brodea reached out and touched the side of the Voïre's face gently. "You are special. You are the Voïre dui Ceremeia, the perfection of the Ferhym people. I trust you, implicitly." Brodea dropped her hand and turned from the young elf. "Now go. I'm sure you have much to do, and I know you have a lot of reading before you."

The Voïre nodded and began to take the stairs, when she stopped and turned to face the First Councilor.

Brodea looked up, curious.

"I'm glad you found somebody, Brodea."

Brodea raised a perfectly sculpted eyebrow. "Oh?"

The Voïre nodded. "Feydras' Anula is alight with whispers, about how Eigron has been staying with you these last few days. He seems a pleasant hym." With that, the Voïre turned and descended the stairs, not waiting for a reply from Brodea.

Brodea scowled. Though it came as no surprise to her in the least. She knew this would happen the moment she decided to protect him. Ideally, she shouldn't care. But she did.

She needed to get it off her mind. Brodea decided that she needed Vooken.

~ ~ ~

A short while later Brodea lay naked, spooned in Vooken's arms against the hardwood of the council chamber floor. Their bodies were still slick with sweat from their lusting, but Brodea found herself contented to just lie there in his arms with his chest against her back as they looked out into the night. The stars up above glowed brightly, casting everything in a tranquil pale blue hue.

Brodea knew she should be out, searching for the hunter that was going to try to end Eigron's life, but she was enjoying, just for this moment, being with Vooken and feeling like a female, not the First Councilor. To have her only responsibility be in pleasing her companion, and in his pleasing her.

As they lay there, she became aware of him tracing the lines of her Windsong crest against her abdomen. The raised flesh of her permanently fused woad was sensitive under the lightly brushing strokes of his calloused fingertips.

He whispered, and Brodea could hear an almost solemn pitch to his voice, "It can never change."

"Not while I still draw breath," she agreed. "That is the nature of the Spirit's test when the poison was painted upon my flesh."

She felt his fingers slide across her stomach, over her breasts, and against her long, slender copper neck, until they were slow massaging the cartilage of her pointed ears. Slightly somberly, he responded, "Yes. I know."

Brodea lifted her head and looked away from the stars and into his deep brown eyes. "Do you wish differently?" She asked, suddenly nervous.

"No," Vooken said a little too quickly.

"Then what is it?"

"I make no claim to your body Brodea, I never have," he said quietly, while running his fingers through her raven hair. "And yet I cannot help but feel disquiet at the time you have been spending in the company of another."

Brodea arched an eyebrow. "I have spent time with no other."

Now it was Vooken's turn to look at her in a questioning manner. "You need not cover up anything Brodea; we have lived many centuries around one and other. I know that Eigron has been staying in your home for the last several days, and verily he has not often left your side."

Brodea burst into laughter, which only seemed to aggravate Vooken more. "Not you too! The Voïre commented this just early this evening!"

"It still is what it is," Vooken replied.

"Are you jealous?" she said indignantly.

Vooken visibly stiffened in front of her. Clearly it was no laughing matter to him. Brodea turned fully around so that they were face to face. Gently she stroked his cheek with the back of her hand. He reached up and pulled it away. "I do not need coddling, Brodea. I want an answer. If you want to spend time with another, that is your choice, and I will honor it. But I am long past the age and patience for infidelities. I will always support you as my friend and as the First Councilor; you need never fear this. In that we will always be unified. But when it comes to this, I will not share you."

"You always were bold," Brodea said with a small smile. "I respect that most about you."

He returned dispassionately, "Then you are making the counter choice, I take it?"

Brodea wasn't sure how to respond. She knew she should tell him everything. He was right after all. They began this road together many winters back, after he lost his best friend, and she her husband, to the foul pestilence that was the wizard. He was always by her side, her staunchest supporter. That flag never wavered, that alliance never questionable.

And yet, she knew how much he would object to what she was doing now. She was hunting a Ferhym. Their kind. And though she could justify it to herself that this Ferhym was a skewer, she wasn't sure any other could truly understand. Understand what the cause meant to her above all else. Not even Vooken.

She looked at him sadly. She didn't want this part of their friendship to end. Brodea desperately needed this closeness from someone, and she surely didn't want it from Eigron. Though the young elf was helpful in all things, there were things he had done that he could never cleanse himself of. And even while she wasn't above doing what was completely necessary for the cause, his actions burned at her.

She knew Vooken was the only one she could turn to when she needed to feel like less of the First Councilor, and more of just herself. And yet, she felt the cause demanded that she remain silent in her actions. If she let Vooken know about this errant killer, about the threat to Eigron, he wouldn't be able to contain it. He would send out hunters to find this killer and bring him to the Council. There would be uproar. Worse there would be an investigation as to why such a hunter turned. The council may even learn about the rape of Avrimae.

Though she was only a skewer, it was an unprecedented act of cruelty. They believed in the balance of nature, not the torture of the misguided. How would the council handle the rape, or worse, the knowledge that the now missing Avrimae may very well be carrying the aberrant spawn of such an action? That outcome itself was worse in the Council's eyes then the action that caused it. And all of this done on her order, more or less.

No, she couldn't tell Vooken. As much as she craved the way his eyes drank her in, in a way that saw her as a woman, not as First Councilor. As much as she enjoyed the touch of his body to hers, and the closeness and companionship she felt from that connection, she couldn't let him in on this. Not yet. Not until she had it under control. But she didn't need give him the guise that she was interested in Eigron either.

"I bear no intimacy with the Genrus Eigron," Brodea breathed at last while wrapping her arms around Vooken. "But I will not lie to you. He is staying with me."

"Why?" He both asked, and desperately searched with his dark eyes. "Why do you dare keep a male hym at length in your dwelling, if not for intimate companionship?"

"Because he is my deepest connection to the druids," she confirmed. "Though the Elder of Vines works diligently for the council in trying to decipher the tome, and to identify weapons that will help us against the wizards, they keep much from us as well."

"We are not wielders of the gifts of nature like they are," Vooken defended.

"True. But we've had need for Julietta for weeks, no, months, and they have denied her to us. To the Council of Elm, to the First Councilor!" She felt her heartbeat quicken as her own words incited her to truths that Eigron had told her that even she was unaware of.

"Because of her ability to not be burned." Again Vooken tried to remain neutral.

Brodea shook her head. "She was never theirs, and when we had need of the skewer to help maintain balance, they kept her. It was so they could hold a modicum of power over us. Over the councilors."

Vooken leaned away from her, protesting, "Never. The druids believe in the Council; they need the Council just as we need them. Our nature is symbiotic. We cannot survive without the other."

"That is true, Vooken, but that does not mean that they do not keep secrets from us. The Blood Wizard arrived with more than just his bow. He had many relics upon his person and in his travel pack. We have been given no updates on any of these things."

"Perhaps they are useless. They told us of the staff brought in."

Angrily, she replied, "Only because of Jenhiro. And only because he saw its use. He was not privy to the artifacts in the wizard's bag. They knew that we would laud the hunter as a hero. He brought us the Blood Wizard after all."

Something about her own words bothered her, like there was something obvious in the statement but she was missing it. Then Vooken sat up, and she caught glistening chest reflected in the moonlight. It cast deep shadows against his firm muscular frame that helped accentuate his familial markings. It was no wonder he came from Moonspear, the night light radiated well off his body. She blinked away the distraction of his flesh as the councilor spoke.

"What did Eigron say was in the bag?"

Brodea scooted herself up next to him and shook her head in frustration. Their talk was becoming conspiratorial now. "A pair of gloves. Ringed he says. Other than, that he doesn't know any more. The elder would not permit him near it; he is only a Genrus after all. He was only allowed access to the staff from the bull, and of course the bow of the wizard because of Eigron's firsthand knowledge of the weapon."

Brodea wasn't lying to Vooken about any of this. It was known to her the moment Eigron had begun reporting directly to her in place of the Elder of Vines. They were hiding something, and while she was not happy about it, she let it go. Just that knowledge was enough to exploit them when need be. She was going to use it to get Julietta if they had taken much longer, so now she could use it another day. Still, it hadn't been a burden of knowledge that weighed on her. Not like everything else happening lately. Still it gave her something to give to Vooken to hold him over.

"I don't like these words Brodea. Do you think the druids have found a weapon that could be used and they are hiding it?"

"That is one of the reasons I keep Eigron close. He is trying to find out. And I need to know at all times, regardless of the hour." And that was her lie. That was the one mistruth she gave him in the litany of truths she laid before him. It was absolutely not why he was there.

Vooken stared at her for a moment, as if processing this information and trying to decipher if she was lying. To Brodea's own knowledge, she had never lied to him, and so Vooken had no reason to believe what she was saying wasn't true.

But this was a big step. Though it may be a small lie, female elves only let the males into their homes for extended periods for two reasons: they were visiting family, or they had begun to mate. There was no other reason to keep a male for more than a single evening unless they were in coitus. Breeding their species was difficult for the Ferhym, and so it was widely accepted that they do it copiously in spurts, generally for the few weeks that their bodies were the most fertile.

Brodea knew the implication of what it looked like was happening between Eigron and herself. She knew that the moment she decided to secure him in her own home. Word would spread. She was willing to accept that rumor, as long as it kept him alive for the week. She knew the hunter wouldn't be brazen enough to strike at the First Councilor's home.

Vooken still visibly bristled at the notion of Eigron staying with her. Brodea and Vooken had never practiced the act in an effort to mate, and so they had never stayed with each other more than one night at a time. Since it was their tradition that the male came to the female, he had only ever come to her abode. She never stayed the night in his.

She knew now it looked like she was trying to conceive another child with Eigron, and that is how it would be perceived by the masses. It was widely known that Vooken was close to Brodea. This act, though not for the reasons that either he, or everyone else thought, was a direct slight to his manhood and honor. She was asking him to be okay with that, and yet insuring him that it was not a slight.

"When do you foresee the time that Eigron is no longer needed to stay with you?" he finally asked.

Brodea shrugged. "Soon, I hope." And it was an honest answer. The quicker she could catch their rogue, the quicker Eigron, and the constant reminder of what he did, would be out of her home.

Vooken stood up, his naked frame casting her in shadow. "Then until that time, this must end," Vooken said with finality.

Though Brodea knew those words were coming, it still felt like a blow to her chest. She lost a part of Vooken with this, and they both knew it.

"I still stand by you Brodea. But we cannot do this until things return as they were."

Brodea nodded in agreement. She was a strong female hym. She always had been. In the times of her being a hunter, while she was raising her children, and even while she was married to Ambit, she remained firm and stoic, never displaying weakness. Even now her face was impassive at Vooken's declaration. She said quietly, "I understand."

While she was strong, and fierce, and even independent in a way, she was also female. It wasn't that she had some sort of ravenous sexual appetite. It was that she still craved closeness. She still had the need to feel soft, beautiful, and desired. She found that solace with Vooken, and it worked. Until now. And that made her feel weak.

Vooken collected his loincloth and dressed quickly. Brodea stayed sitting on the floor, looking out into Feydras' Anula.

Before he left, her now ex-lover stopped behind her. She felt him hovering there. Was he waiting for her to stop him? Was he waiting for her to promise to eject Eigron at first light, cut a piece of her hair away and braid it for him, marking herself to him for eternity? Or was there something he wanted to say?

She wanted to do many of these things. Plead to him not to do this. To change his mind and not take insult to his manhood by Eigron. In her own mind she thought about debasing herself before him. Let him do things to her that would be below her stature. To let him stay standing while she instead pleased him with only her mouth, something that was considered extremely wasteful and criminal to her very culture.

She thought about not being strong, but being soft, and weak. Being vulnerable. She thought these thoughts, but she knew she was none of them. No tears flooded her midnight eyes. She would not grovel; she would not beg. She would let him walk, and either he would come back when Eigron was gone, or he wouldn't.

Finally, in silence, Vooken walked away from her, as she knew he would, and Brodea looked on to her city without uttering a single word to him, not wasting a single breath.

Brodea was strong. The Spirits demanded it be so.

BAD REALITY

Relm reported calmly to Jenhiro, "I have done it."

Jenhiro's tense muscles finally relaxed as Avrimae's shoulders and head fell limply into his arms. Relm had been right about her fighting. He hadn't known the worn woman had so much energy left. His left forearm still throbbed with pain where she bit him hard in an effort to escape from Relm's shifting silver eyes.

For two days between Relm's obligations to the council and the First Councilor directly, she repeatedly entered Avrimae's mind and tried to coax and calm down the tortured woman. Each time Avrimae would fight, kick, scream, and try to attack anything in sight. It was a grueling experience.

Jenhiro carefully set the human back down on the chaise, while he watched an exhausted Relm move toward the other chair. Once more, her hands were shaking.

"Are you alright?" he asked as he moved next to her.

When Relm looked up, her eyes were glistening when she whispered, "I had no idea."

Jenhiro sat down with her, and held her hands in his.

"I had to dive deep into her fears and agonies. I had to assuage a pain that runs through her soul. Her mind, it's so fragile now. Her cage wasn't bars of iron, but more like a cube of glass. It was like trying to cross a frozen river of thin ice. Even now, with all I've helped, her mind is still ready to run back into that small box and shatter," Relm told him. "I didn't realize the magnitude of what they've done to her." Her voice a whisper, she added, "And of what you did to them."

Jenhiro nodded quietly.

Relm sniffled and looked to Avrimae who now appeared to be sleeping. "It is truly terrible what we are capable of doing as a species."

He reminded her softly, "All species are capable of such acts."

"But we are supposed to be above this!" she argued fervently. "It is why we have the cause! Why we are maintainers of the balance of nature!"

Again, Jenhiro opted not to answer, letting her vent.

"What I have just seen has solidified my desire to help people, now more than ever before. Though it hurts my heart to even say this, I am glad."

Jenhiro was perplexed, "Glad?"

She nodded with firm resolve. "Glad for what you have done. You made your choice and issued their fate."

Jenhiro clenched his jaw tightly and nodded. Though it felt good to have someone approve of his decision, it still burned him deeply that he was directly responsible for the deaths of two of his people.

Relm read this in his eyes, and she reached up and touched the side of his face. "I am sorry, that was extremely inconsiderate of me."

Jenhiro took her delicate fingers into his own. "It's okay." He looked over to the sleeping form of Avrimae. "What can we do to help?"

Relm also looked at the still woman. "A great deal actually. I have helped her, but outside of my constantly entering her mind, I have no way of communicating with her, neither of us does. Ashyn is our only link; he's the only one who can speak both of our languages, outside of Brodea."

"And Whisper," Jenhiro added.

Relm nodded. "Yes, she has learned from her mother well."

Jenhiro thought he detected bitterness in her voice at the comment. Was it resentment toward Whisper, or against Brodea? He wasn't sure. Perhaps it was both.

He remembered Relm's memory. Until she had seen Whisper bathed in blood, she had looked up to the Ferhym huntress. Maybe that was it, the loss of a role model.

Stressing the point of "we," Jenhiro asked, "How do we communicate with her in the mean time? How can we help her now? She needs to be ready to go and soon."

Relm blinked for a moment before her eyes focused on Jenhiro. "We need to give her a reason to trust us. To do that, I have promised her something."

"And what is that?"

Relm looked at him with all seriousness. "We have to rescue another person, someone dear to her."

"Well that shouldn't be too hard," he answered, "They are in the Water Pens I assume?"

Relm shook her head no. "The mines."

Jenhiro swore to the Spirits under his breath. "That's completely on the other end of the hunters' living quarters. It's taking us exactly where we don't want to go! We don't have time to save all the cells. We discussed this. Helping Avrimae has already taken considerably longer than we thought."

Relm nodded as she looked empathetically towards Avrimae. "She needs a friend right now, Jenhiro. Someone she feels she can trust. I can't let her down. We'll just need to modify the plan."

He hated to be the negative one, but he had to remain objective. "You have said that Ashyn is already aware of his part of the plan. He has somehow swayed the bull miraculously to his side, but if we change now, you have to reach out to him. As far as I can tell, and I am no expert, but it looks like you both have to be asleep to do this."

Jenhiro watched her head subtly bob in agreement. "Something likes that, yes."

"Unless one of us risks informing him in person, can we really afford to sacrifice anymore time? And if we made a move to liberate this friend of Avrimae's tonight, with little planning I might add, what if we are seen? This could jeopardize everything, and we only have one real shot at this, Relm."

Jenhiro saw her thinking so he pressed, "What if Brodea moves early? They might move Julietta sooner. There's too many what-ifs and not enough whens. We have to act, before she does. Otherwise, we lose our only opportunity to save Ashyn and all those in the Water Pens as well."

Relm stood firm. "If we cannot do it beforehand, then we have to do it at the same time. We can split up. You go to the cells, and I'll take Avrimae."

Jenhiro shook his head. "No, that's a terrible idea! It is too dangerous for you. What if Avrimae loses control?"

"Well we can't leave her here," Relm argued. "The moment we move, we are committed, Jenhiro."

Jenhiro grunted and turned away from the Voïre dui Ceremeia. Whether intentional or not, when she got emotional, her natural abilities leaked through, and that meant falling in a trance when he looked into her eyes. It was so easy when the Voïre were children and their abilities didn't affect their own kind.

"There has to be common ground we can reach," Relm said.

And it hit Jenhiro. It was so simple. "Prisoner transfer."

"What?"

Jenhiro turned back around excited as a plan formed in his head. He didn't look in her eyes, though. He fell back to the safety of tradition. He had an idea and didn't want to lose it by the distraction her magic would cause him. "I know a way to get this friend out of the mines for Avrimae. We transfer them to the Water Pens instead."

"Why would you want to do that? It's worse than the mines right now. I am trying to get Avrimae to trust us; putting her friend in the pens would only intensify that distrust."

Jenhiro tapped the side of his head fiercely, "Think about it, Relm. They would be in position already for our escape. They only need endure two days of no food. It's terrible, I know, but it's the safest way. Put this friend in the Water Pens. It will work, and we don't need to separate come time."

Jenhiro saw Relm's face light up, as she understood his reasoning. But then a curious look fell about her expression. "And yet a moment ago you were afraid of being caught?"

"That is the real problem, I agree. But it can be greatly mitigated if no one is looking for an escapee. Avrimae was a special circumstance. They are trying to kill her. So they want to keep it as quiet as possible.

"If we try and free this companion from the mines, then we will draw a lot of attention. However, if there is no break out, there is no hiding another skewer in this home or anywhere else. They are simply transferred from one cell to another. Accountability is still there, and since the council doesn't convene until we are planning the true escape…"

"…the skewers manifest and mining notes won't be seen by them until then either! The First Councilor won't know what's happened until it's too late." Relm beamed now. "I'm impressed Jenhiro."

"Thanks," came the snarky reply. "Now to do this before I convince myself how bad of an idea it really is."

~ ~ ~

Long after Jenhiro settled down to sleep on the floor of the main room, Relm grazed her fingers gently over the leather tome. Briefly she closed her eyes and reached out to him. He was there, waiting. Relm smiled.

She whispered to Ashyn, "I've never tried anything like this before."

"Talk to people in their dreams, often?" Ashyn asked a trace of humor in his voice.

It was good to hear that humor. She knew he had hope, that he trusted her. "You were right, Ashyn, Brodea gave me the tome. I think she suspects our connection. She wants me to read it to see if I can remember it."

"Then we better get started. We don't want to let the First Councilor down now, do we?" he said mirthlessly.

"It doesn't bother you that she knows?" Relm asked him.

"I'm more concerned about your well-being. You are the one in danger. There's little more that Brodea can do to me than what she is about to do in a few days."

Relm nodded, it was true. "You don't have to worry about me now, Ashyn, not yet. The danger is yet to come."

"Then let's get started." As simple as that.

"My mind will forget it, as soon as I utter the words, Ashyn. That is why the druids can't decipher it," she reminded him.

"Well, let's find out if mine does not."

Relm opened her eyes and stared at the words on the page, she never attempted to make a connection with him in a waking state before. She hadn't thought it could even be done, not until Whisper commented on it in their fight. Perhaps she should thank her.

Relm pushed the thoughts of Whisper aside. "Are you ready?" she asked. She knew it was going to take all night.

"I hope so."

Relm read from the tome. As she feared, the words were lost to her even as she read them. But Ashyn…

She could feel Ashyn begin to learn.

~ ~ ~

An hour before the dawn light first cast its golden rays into the swallet that was Feydras' Anula, Jenhiro found himself standing face to face with the druid who was about to lift up the miners for another day of hard labor.

Two hunters, now guards, stood on either side of the druid, poignantly reminding the branch commander of Eigron and his lackeys, Mehris and Hengrit. Lackeys that were now successfully balanced. That thought gave Jenhiro a small measure of resolve as he stood before the druid.

"I've heard of no such transfer," the druid baulked.

"Consult with Genrus Eigron, if you'd like. Waste his time when right now he is preparing for the Blood Wizard," Jenhiro returned swiftly. "In fact, I am certain that right now he is with the First Councilor, you could ask her too, if you'd like." While he wasn't lying, he wasn't telling the truth either.

Jenhiro only hoped the druid would be distracted by the mention of Eigron. Judging by the druid's blanches, he clearly did not agree with the young druid's meteoric rise to power either. "That is not necessary."

Quickly, the druid turned around and moved his fingers in elaborate patterns in the air. As he did, the vines holding the cell below pulled themselves upwards. Within minutes, the wooden cell was at eye level.

Forlorn, hard-worked faces stared at him with depressed and hopeless eyes. For many it was time to work again. Not for one of them, though.

Jenhiro looked through the throng of foul smelling bodies until he spotted who he was looking for. Near the back of the gaggle of humans he could see a man sitting down with his back against the bars of the cell. Like the others he was filthy and in tattered and worn garments, but he fit the description Relm gave him.

His hair was coal black and long, tied behind his head in a greasy ponytail. His face was round, almost comically fat compared to his button nose. Yet his cheeks appeared gaunt and hollow. Jenhiro knew this one missed too many meals in recent months. His eyes were a darker shade of brown, but like his nose, they appeared small and beady to his oversized face.

Jenhiro pointed. "That one."

The druid chittered to the two hunters guarding the cell. The duo nodded, stepped into the cell and went straight for the dark-haired human.

Many of the humans squealed and got out of the elves' way. Some who were not so fast were pushed away. The man made no effort to move at all. Once on top of him, they forced him roughly to his feet. The man spoke harshly and aggressively to the elves, but none, including Jenhiro knew what he was saying.

Still the smaller Ferhym overpowered the tired and emaciated human and brought him forward. Jenhiro could see that at one time he was a very large, possibly imposing, form of a man. Now, his tattered clothing hung limply on an emaciated frame.

He tried to use that bulk now to appear intimidating, but Jenhiro had gone up against much larger, far more deadly opponents. This human did not scare him, nor apparently did he threaten his captors in any way. They forced him to stand before Jenhiro at spear point.

"Will you need assistance with this escort?" the druid asked?

Jenhiro drew his own spear. "No, brother. I have this skewer, thank you," he answered with a polite nod of his head.

Jenhiro then leveled his spear right at his chest and motioned it slightly to the east. Luckily for him, the human was not completely stupid. He looked down his nose at Jenhiro, snorted, hocked a wad of phlegm at the druid, and then walked in the direction the hunter motioned.

The druid wrinkled his nose in disgust. Jenhiro commented, "His right to reclamation is revoked." He said with as much conviction as he could, "He shall now meet his balancing at the Water Pens."

The druid nodded and smiled at him, contented with the fate that awaited this man. Jenhiro did not let it affect his judgment. He knew, as did Relm, that their people believed in the cause, just as he did, but were misguided. It would take time to set things right and put his people on their righteous path once more.

Over the course of the next several minutes, the large human asked countless questions, but Jenhiro had no way of answering him, so the Ferhym remained silent. The man hesitated, and relentlessly continued to speak loudly to Jenhiro. How Avrimae considered this one a trusted ally was beyond him. Then again, he truly knew very little about the woman either.

He thought of her for the next hour as he guided the human through town on an escort, much as Ashyn had taken. And just like that escort weeks past, many of the morning-going Ferhym quickly moved away from the hunter and the large human who was bound for the pens. They had seen it before.

No hunter stopped him. No one questioned him. He looked exactly as he should, a hunter, confident in his own skin. The woad upon his body was fitting, as he was Willowfallen. Should any report the escort, it would send ripples of confusion among the lower hunters until it was time to leave. By then, it would be too late for them.

He reported to the druid on the eastern end of the water pens and gave the same spiel he fed the other druid. There was no difficulty in the task, and that worried him. Everything was going too smoothly. At least, until he heard the druid whisper to another, "If Eigron thinks that by giving the spear to Lady Windsong, it grants him some supreme authority over his peers, he's sadly mistaken."

Jenhiro took the comment in stride. He followed the druid and the extra hunter around to far eastern side of the pens, right near the base of the tree. He knew the steps leading to the Council of Elm were only twenty paces away. This was the most dangerous part. At any moment Whisper, Vooken, Eigron, or even Brodea could come down those stairs and the ruse would be up. They all knew his face. He tried to stay nonchalant, but he couldn't help looking back to those stairs.

"She won't be coming down," the druid remarked, apparently detecting his apprehension.

"Excuse me?" Jenhiro said, rather alarmed that even after so many seasons in the field he could still seem so green that a druid could read him like a tome.

"Our First Councilor went up there only a few moments before you arrived. Stone's throw really. You just missed her, and the Voïre dui Ceremeia."

Jenhiro startled at this. Relm was with her? Who was watching Avrimae? He looked to the two hunters that stood guard at the stairs. They looked everywhere but at him. Seeing and hearing everything, but also ignoring everyone.

"A shame," Jenhiro lied covering up his rising alarm. "I've only had the pleasure of ever talking with her once."

The druid raised an eyebrow at Jenhiro as he held out his hand, warping and manipulating the bars. "She's a damn fine hym. Blessed by the Spirits really. Three child-bearing daughters. Only hym to ever successfully balance a wizard, alone, and a right good First Councilor."

Jenhiro absorbed his words, wondering if the druid had ever heard the words come from Lady Windsong's mouth as he had. Or if he heard the duplicity, knew of the rape she allowed, or witnessed the atrocities of torture that she committed on Ashyn. "And yet, you slandered her moments before?" He said, before he could think better of it.

The druid gave him a dark eyed glare, "Not the First Councilor. Young Genrus Eigron," he corrected. "I do not fault the Lady Windsong for her attraction to young, firm flesh, so recently turned full adult. I think we all secretly have such lustings within us. I blame our little Genrus who thinks he can use that twig between his legs to manipulate our beloved First Councilor and make her sing for him."

The cage opened and he nodded. Jenhiro, still forced to maintain his act slammed the shaft of his spear against Avrimae's friend causing him to shout and tumble into the pens. The druid laughed and quickly animated the poles shut. He then turned to Jenhiro. "She'll come to her senses soon enough, and our little Genrus will come tumbling down to the ground, just like that skewer. We are supposed to be a humble people. I am not jealous of Eigron; I am annoyed that he is not humble like we, and it is permitted. I am not angry at Lady Windsong, but disheartened, because I feel she is being used for her desires to mate."

Jenhiro bowed his head. "I understand, I meant no offense, brother."

The druid clasped his shoulder. "None taken, brother," he replied kindly. "I spoke out of kind, and you heard it, nothing to be apologetic for."

Jenhiro clasped the druid's shoulder in return, and they both nodded. Jenhiro stepped happily away from those stairs, eager to be back at Relm's. He had some choice words for why she chose to leave Avrimae alone.

Jenhiro barely made it a half a dozen feet when he heard a scream of rage coming from the cage he just placed the skewer into. He quickly turned his head in surprise to see Avrimae's friend charging another person in the cell. The one Ashyn conversed with. The one Relm called Macky. Jenhiro recognized the look in the skewer's eyes. It was murder.

OLD... FRIEND

Ashyn was just reviewing everything he learned for the tenth time with Rizen when he heard a guttural scream erupt from the cage behind him. It was so angry and so fierce that it ripped his concentration from the water and slammed him back into reality with bone-jarring force. He blinked away the confusion and ambled to his feet looking towards the cage.

The other cell was much larger than the one he shared with Rizen, and so all he could see was a large group of humans gathered around two people that were on the ground. The one on top was large, with black hair, and tattered darkened clothing, like he had spent time in the mines. He must be new in the Water Pens, because he still had hair on his head.

The other on the ground was harder to see. He was clearly smaller, and skinnier, but it was hard to determine how much so because he was balled up with his hands protectively over his head.

The man on top was an animal. His screams were indecipherable. He was tearing and swinging at the body beneath him with the savagery of a predator pouncing on its kill. Ashyn knew the man underneath would likely die if no one did anything. Where was Macky? Why didn't he stop this?

Ashyn's heart dropped as he saw a glimpse of the man's face. Small eyes and a button nose. It was Uriel.

The man he was attacking was Macky!

"Ashyn!" a stressed voiced called him to his right.

Surprised at hearing his own name, the wizard looked up immediately. It was Jenhiro. The Ferhym once again wore different marking across his skin. Ashyn was amazed that the simplicity of the disguise worked so easily on these Elves. No wonder they thought he was a Wood Elf for far longer than he thought possible.

Jenhiro seemed deeply troubled at the events happening within the cell. Ashyn was terrified for the safety of his friend, but to see such a reaction from a hym dismayed him. "You have to do something!" Jenhiro said urgently, and then placed his hand against his chest so it was hard to notice and pointed upwards. "If she sees, this whole plan will fail."

"What did you do?" Ashyn asked quickly before catching a glance at Uriel. The man was wild, but Macky was defending himself well. It seemed like most of Uriel's attacks were rapidly losing power. Still Ashyn knew it would only take one good hit to lay Macky out. If that happened, it didn't matter how tired Uriel was. He could still smother him or choke him to death.

Jenhiro looked towards the other elves who were looking into the cage with amused interest. They hadn't noticed him speaking with Ashyn. Not yet.

"Relm needed to convince Avrimae to trust us. To do that we had to move her friend." Jenhiro looked into the cage. "If Brodea sees him though, she'll know something is amiss. It will jeopardize everything!"

Ashyn cursed as he looked upwards. He didn't see anyone looking back down at him yet. Fights in the cages below were commonplace enough. But he knew that she would soon react to the chaos coming from beneath her if Jenhiro became involved. When that happened she would, see Uriel. Would it matter? Would she know who he was? Probably. She knew everything else about Ashyn's childhood in Czynsk.

"Can you handle this alone? I should leave before someone recognizes me, or worse realizes that we are working together."

Ashyn nodded. "Go. I will think of something."

Jenhiro clasped his fist to his heart. "Soon." He moved swiftly off towards the Ferhym homesteads.

Ashyn looked back and saw that Macky was in bad shape. As quickly as Uriel had been losing wind, Macky's defense had also been breaking down. Ashyn could see a small, but growing, puddle of blood beneath Macky's head. Blood poured liberally from his nose and mouth.

Impulsively, Ashyn wanted to yell at Uriel to stop. Yet he knew Brodea would recognize his voice immediately, worse it may bring the druid over, or the guards, and they just might kill Macky outright. Thanks to Relm, Ashyn now knew that Brodea didn't need Macky anymore. She had stronger leverage now. That made the priest expendable. If he was judged too wounded, they might just kill him anyhow to provide meat for the starving people in the pens.

No, Ashyn needed another solution, without screaming at the top of his lungs at Uriel.

"They killed her!" Uriel screamed with every weakening swing. "They killed her! She's dead!"

Macky was laying still now, the pummeling too much for him. Passed out and bleeding, but still breathing. Ashyn thought Uriel might choke him or suffocate him, or just beat him to death, but he didn't. He stopped at looked down at his bloody and worn hands.

"My wife is gone. They told me so! Taunted me with it! The scarred elf bitch just laughed at me!" He whispered hoarsely, "Because of you!" Uriel's enraged eyes came up searching, probably for a means with which to end the priest's life. Ashyn was alarmed that no one was coming to Macky's aid. Not a single person was trying to stop Uriel at all. Their cellmate, their partner, their spiritual leader, and they were just going to watch his murder. Ashyn was too, unless he figured something out fast.

Yet his mind was in a fog! As much as he wanted to save his childhood friend, any yelling he did would cost them Jenhiro, or even Relm. Their whole plan would unravel and more than just Macky would perish. Few for the many, reverberated in his head once more. Always the few.

Uriel looked right at him and Ashyn hoped for a moment there might have been recognition, but just as quickly he cast his murderous gaze elsewhere. Ashyn could tell by the growing smile on Uriel's face he found something suitable for Macky's death.

Ashyn followed that gaze to the sewage, and the wizard knew what Uriel had in mind for Macky.

ADAPT OR DIE

Ashyn moved swiftly towards the foul waterline and without thinking plunged his hand into the foul murk. Instantly Rizen's thoughts touched his. Far too calmly for the situation demanded he said, *Your kind seems bent on the destruction of each other.*

Yes. The wizard agreed.

Ashyn looked back to see Uriel dragging Macky's limp form across the rocky surface. The larger man was clearly exhausted, and it was only hatred that was fueling him now.

Ashyn projected his thoughts to the shaman, *Can I communicate with others through the water, as I speak with you?*

If you learned how, yes.

Ashyn shook his head, he had no connection to magic like that, and he didn't have the time. *Could you connect me to another person?*

To emphasize this point, he looked away from the duo and towards the gaur. The large beast scrutinized him for what felt like an eternity before answering, *If the other person is cooperative, perhaps.*

And if they are not?

The large bull shook his head. *They have to be adaptive to the idea first. Think of your shock the first time we communicated. Since then as we have talked I have come to see you have a clear understanding of how the spirit energy around us works. If you lacked that understanding, you shall have no such true connection.*

Even if they understand my voice? Ashyn pressed.

Your mind does not carry the same pattern that comes from your mouth. It does not use the same muscles.

Ashyn hadn't thought of that. He had hoped that his voice might dissuade Uriel from his act. But it wasn't his voice at all. It was his thoughts and his mind. Still he had to try.

This would expose me as well, the gaur projected. *One of their nature wielders is very near, and if this human begins to panic once he is exposed to the water, and they see me in the water...*

The gaur didn't need to finish. Ashyn's mind reeled. He turned back just to see Uriel dragging Macky right to the water's edge. He was cajoling the unconscious priest. Telling him how he would join the rest of the worthless shit in the water.

Let them see me instead, Ashyn told Rizen.

The gaur cocked his head in confusion.

They are in constant fear of my abilities returning at any time. If anyone is to be questioned for the act, let it clearly be me. Lay as far away from the waterline as you can, with only your hoof in the water. I will walk knee deep into it.

It is waste Ashyn, Rizen direly warned. *Touching this filth with the hands you eat with is foul enough. To wade into this murk, you could get deathly ill. There are many ways this poison will pollute your body. You still have cuts. Many of your wounds have yet to properly heal even with all of our aid. If this gets into your blood stream there is little I can do to aid you.*

I must try, or many will die, Ashyn said determinedly.

If you die, then we all die, Rizen countered. *You are the one thing that ties us all together. Our lives are all braided around you now, totem-brother. If you fray, then the strand that binds us will fall apart.*

Ashyn followed the gaur's line of sight to the druid who was only interested in fight happening in the skewer pen. *If someone need be sacrificed for this, it should be your friend Macky, or me.*

I will not let Macky be the few for the many, Ashyn persisted.

Then I will do this.

Ashyn felt the conviction behind his thoughts. The bull turned away from everyone, as if oblivious to the fight. *Try to act interested in the goings-on in that cell.*

That shouldn't be hard, Ashyn thought. His friend was about to drown.

Tell me what you want me to say, and when to say it. I don't know if we will get through, or if we do, if it will be in enough time. But I will do this. Also there is a risk with the aggressor's emotions. I will feel them; I am uncertain how that will affect me. Last time, the emotions almost made me end your life, Rizen said plainly.

Ashyn nodded. He understood. *Thank you for this.* Ashyn told him sincerely.

Don't thank me, yet. Rizen cautioned. *This may end badly for all of us.*

~ ~ ~

It had been a long time since Pan, now named Rizen, felt truly alive. Given that second chance by his totem-brother he was compelled to offer the same measure of life to the creature Ashyn called Macky. Though to his culture, Macky's soul would simply enter the great Cycle to be born a new, fresh and away from the worries of imprisonment, Rizen saw how this moment mattered to Ashyn, his own savior from unlife.

So he would try, at least, to reach out to the angry human and stop it from murdering its own kind. Rizen snorted in displeasure at the very idea of hurting his own herd. It seemed so obtuse to him. It was against everything it meant to be a gaur. The gaur did not hurt each other. They thrived together. Humans at their very nature seemed built for conflict. Rizen would have never thought to find himself allied with such small, angry creatures. But he never thought he would have wound up losing his life and gathering salvation either.

He pushed the thought away, for he did not want Ashyn to feel his own displeasure at the acts of his herd. Instead, he focused on the crud that floated past his hoof. As he did, he felt the life within the soiled waters.

As always, Rizen could feel their suffering. The choking bloat that toxified the fish, and the crustaceans that speckled the contaminated waters. He could feel the poison that ate at their scales and devoured their insides. He sensed the great tree's displeasure. Did these pointy-eared cretins not understand how cyclical this filth was? Did they not realize the harm they were causing their own icon? The ones Ashyn called druids surely must. They had strong ties to the nature. How could they condone such a thing?

Again he pushed these ponderings aside and instead focused on the moment. He felt Ashyn in the water only a few steps away. Like his first interaction when they shared the totem, he marveled at the uniqueness of the beast within Ashyn. It was powerful, this part of Ashyn's soul. It was a beast, and it was primal. That was why he connected with the totem. It was why he connected so easily with Rizen in the waters. Far easier than it was going to be to reach out to a human. Still he would try.

Rizen waited for another fresh being to enter the polluted pool. It didn't take long.

There was a wake of water and the life went scattering away. With his ears he clearly could hear the splash as the beaten and unconscious man was thrown into the lake. Were the waters frigid like the cool springs he was used to in the mountains, it might be enough to bring the man to sudden consciousness, but they were not. The waters were tepid.

Luckily, Macky's unconsciousness actually served him well. By nature of his body, it protected him while he was dormant. His own internal defenses shut his body off from drawing water into his lungs, at least for the moment. He would last far longer in this state than if he were conscious and panicking. But, he would also offer no resistance to his assailer. It was only a matter of time, internal defenses or not, that his body would crave the oxygen that it was being denied, and then it would be over for Macky.

Rizen felt the foot of another penetrate the briny waters. Immediately the waters were assailed with such anger and such hatred, that it sent him reeling. These were feelings he had not had since the witnessing of his herd's massacre, and losing his soul to the unlife.

He knew the emotions of the human would batter him, but he felt confident in his spiritual connection with nature to overcome the onslaught, but he didn't have his totem to lean upon for guidance and strength. The power of such raw emotion wrestled with him and stirred up memories of the dark time. It made him feel lost like before and long for a death he thought he couldn't receive. The man in the waters wanted to either kill this Macky, or be killed. He wanted nothing else.

There is too much pain. He told Ashyn. *This man will not hear me, even if I try. I can call to him and call to him, plead for him to stop his actions but it will not matter. He is committed in this act Ashyn. Fully with his very soul.*

His name is Uriel. Ashyn's mind flooded into his own. *There has to be a way in. Something that will make him see reason. Macky used to be his best friend! Surely that means something?* The gaur shook his head, and though he knew Ashyn did not see it, he would feel the act mentally.

Now that it was absolutely clear that the human was intent on murdering Macky, Rizen could hear the commotion of the people in the pen with Uriel. Almost a half dozen people in the muck and grim trying futilely to get the large miner off the scrawny priest. The range of emotions tried to latch onto Rizen but he was able to deflect them far easier than those of Uriel.

And like with his own powerful emotions, Uriel had more strength than they did, even as tired as he was. He was driven by rage and not nearly as starved as those in the cell.

Rizen felt Uriel fling the people away, one and two at a time as they pulled at his body. Each distraction from the pen-mates gave Macky a little more time as the unconscious form bobbed to the surface allowing his face to just break the surface of the water. Though they would wear quickly, they kept Uriel from pushing Macky further underwater.

Again, Rizen reached out to the man. He tried to send his thoughts through the water and seep into the pours of the violent human. He tried to enter the blood vessels and ride the journey into Uriel's mind. But at every turn he was only met with feelings of despair and the desire for murder.

Rizen felt his hands begin to shake as the violence filled his own mind. Once more, the loss of his Pundit wracked his own spirit. Reflexively he reached out to one of the posts for support. He grabbed onto it so tightly the wood splintered, and vines shot forth and pecked at his fur viciously. But he couldn't let go, otherwise he was afraid the rage might consume him too and he'd revert to the same bull he as when he had hunted Ashyn for days on end.

Unable to keep his mind sheltered from Ashyn, Rizen poured his thoughts into the wizard. To warn him, if anything.

~ ~ ~

Rizen was losing. Ashyn could feel it. He was losing the battle with what he had become when he had gone mad. The wizard couldn't afford to have that happen again. There would be no way he could stop Rizen again. No way could he save Rizen, not from the Ferhym, and not from himself.

Don't succumb, Rizen. You are stronger than this!

The only other time he felt this, was when they had held the totem together, and he had needed power. Then, with the help of such a powerful artifact, he used it as a conduit to pull the essence of it all into him. The act allowed him to save Jenhiro's life, and even Rizen's. Without the totem though, he felt disconnected from it. Like the Exemplar told Brodea, it was there, but too far way. It was across a chasm that he had no way to cross.

It was frustrating and infuriating to know that he was defenseless. He could feel the magic, touch it, but he couldn't connect to it without aid.

But the Exemplar could touch the magic within him. Did that mean Rizen could too?

In me. He told the gaur. *Dump the emotion into me; let me be your aid!*

~ ~ ~

Rizen heard the words in his mind and responded. Immediately, he shifted all the anger, pain, and fury away from himself, and directed it into the powerful receptacle he marveled at.

Ashyn was like an open basin, and the hatred and bitterness poured into him far less forcefully than with Rizen. Immediately it began to lift, and Rizen started to feel the meaning behind the raw wound of pure emotion.

Within that unbridled fury that was coiled in the human named Uriel, he felt the pain of utter loss and despair. He felt the emptying of everything he cherished. Everything he loved. He felt an aching pain of separation from his daughter. He felt the worry of whether or not she was okay. The turmoil that shifted around within him like a whirlpool. The betrayal of the woman he loved desperately to a man he once thought was his closest friend. He felt the brutal sting of being told she was dead. He felt the utter hopelessness at the loss of his wife…

~ ~ ~

Ashyn looked up suddenly at this. His eyes focusing on Uriel and the murder he was committing. Of course! That was why the two didn't talk anymore. That was why, even after countless winters of friendship, they didn't even like to mention the other's name. Avrimae left Macky for Uriel and then became his wife!

She then betrayed Uriel by siding once more with her former lover! Uriel thought she was dead. Uriel believed Avrimae was killed and he blamed Macky because she rallied against the elves with the priest. They had both said that she was the first to stand beside him!

Ashyn knew what to do. What to say. He knew how to get through.

~ ~ ~

The rage was strong. The hate pulled at the shaman so much that he knew he was teetering close to oblivion. Even with everything he was dumping into Ashyn, it was not enough. He wanted to let go. He needed to let go or become lost in the hate once more. Become a creature of malice and violence. Everything his people were against.

She's alive! Ashyn's mind flared into his. *Listen to me,* he repeated. *Just push with everything you have and repeat over and over that Avrimae is alive!*

Rizen focused on those three words, and those words alone. The pecking at his hand faded into the distance. The pain of the repeated stabs became little more the pinpricks to his subconscious. The screaming coming from fifteen feet away evaporated into white noise. The boiling rage within him kept him hot and ready to spill blood. He desired it, craved it, but he tried to focus on those three words. Though they meant nothing to him, he knew to Ashyn they carried weight and they would to Uriel, too.

He repeated them over and over in his head and he felt the roaring fury in his ears subside. He felt the vibrations of his body settle. Again, and again, and again he said it. And Rizen knew that somehow, someway it was helping him. He released his grip from the post not needing its support any longer. As he repeated the words he heard them echoed, and soon he realized why they were helping him. They weren't just his thoughts any longer, but Uriel's. He broke through.

Rizen dared to look at the man, though he was supposed to be masking himself.

Uriel was no longer pushing down on Macky, but holding his jaw just above the waterline. He wasn't looking at Rizen, but at Ashyn. The two were staring at each other. There was a terrible ire still in Uriel's expression, but there was also comprehension, and unbelievably, hope.

Rizen felt the heartbeat within Macky. He was still alive.

They had done it.

The towering gaur collapsed next to the side of the water, exhausted. This was in Ashyn's small hands now.

~ ~ ~

Ashyn stood up, broke his connection from Rizen, and walked to the bars. Ashyn felt heat radiating off his body. His vision was painted in an ocherous glow. He felt the anger. He felt the righteous rage within him.

"Pull him from the water," he commanded Uriel.

All around the large man, the other people scattered away. He watched as Uriel drug Macky out of the water and dropped him unceremoniously on to the rocky ground. Uriel was afraid of Ashyn, but at the same time he was reckless. Ashyn knew it was because he thought he had nothing to live for. The large, dark-haired human walked to the bars and stared hard at Ashyn .

He growled at him, "Ye better be right, witch." He stepped closer. "Ana' I want proof!"

"Your wife is alive, Uriel." Ashyn told him. He saw the man's face contort in shock. "And you'll have your proof soon enough. It is the very reason you are here."

"Ye will git her now!" Uriel threatened and reached through the bars for Ashyn. "I don't care what ye are!"

Ashyn, expected that. Uriel moved so slowly. With little effort, Ashyn took a single step backward, avoiding Uriel's strong grasp. Vines came alive from the bars and quickly wrapped around the surprised miner, pinning him in place.

"Soon," Ashyn said and he turned away. He felt the power of all the hatred Rizen poured into him ebbing. It was leaving him, spent, physically and emotionally.

"I will kill 'em, I swear it!" Uriel spit.

Ashyn stopped and turned back around to face the angered man, calmly telling him, "Then you will have to get in line. Because if you kill him before they get to," he pointed upward, "I'll tell you who will take his place, and it won't be you. They are using you, Uriel. They are using all three of you."

Uriel looked away from the council and back at Ashyn. "I dunna understand. Why?"

Ashyn sat down with a sigh. The color of everything around him returned to normal. "To hurt me, Uriel. To hurt me."

Uriel writhed in anger, shouting, "Then ye are the one who needs to die!"

Ashyn shrugged. "You may be correct. But the fact is we need to work together if we want to survive. That means all of us. We all have to do our part and whether I deserve death or not, it is of moot point until we can leave this place."

The wizard watched as small beaks slithered from the vines Uriel was struggling in. "You'll want to stop moving, or things will become extremely unpleasant for you in a matter of moments."

Uriel stared at the moving vines in alarm. He whispered, his voice growing from aggressive to panicky, "Call them off!"

"I can't." He watched the man a moment. "I'm not that kind of 'witch,' though I doubt someone like you would even pay attention. Wizards don't have that kind of power. Neither do witches, which are girls, if you remember. Only Creation-wielding druids can manipulate nature as they do. And that means these Wild Elves. So I suggest you hold very still and they will let you go.

"Also don't touch Macky again, and I promise you, you will see Avrimae."

Ashyn turned his back on the lumbering man with finality. It wasn't to reject the man, or to show him who was in control. It was to hide the tears that were beginning to tumble down his face. Ashyn may have taken in all of Uriel's anger and his hatred, but he also took in all of his despair. Right now Ashyn's friends were being hurt and mentally torn apart.

Uriel's inner pain coupled with his own sorrow. He wasn't sure how much more he could take. Ashyn wanted to be strong for Julietta, but everything was taking its toll.

He took a deep breath so he wouldn't sob and let Uriel know just how deep his anguish ran. He just let the tears flow in silence. Jenhiro was on his side. So was Relm. In two days it was going to happen. He only had two days left and it would be all over. One way or another, Brodea wouldn't be able to use Julietta or his friends against him, anymore. That thought brought him a small measure of peace.

Moments later the vines released the angry man, and he stormed away, ignoring Macky completely.

~ ~ ~

Quiet over the passing weeks since he followed Ashyn into Feydras' Anula, Xao looked up from his hiding spot and stared with wide yellow eyes at his charge. He felt him! For the first time in months, Xao actually felt Ashyn again through their connection in magic! The boy was finally healing, not just physically, but mentally. Ashyn was growing stronger, even if he didn't realize it yet. Soon the elves would be in for a reckoning.

The Watcher smiled a toothy grin. Though terrified of his own impotence in deciding to let things play their own course with the Ferhym and Ashyn, his patience paid off.

The only time he had interjected was when Ashyn had been thrown from the Great Elm. Xao had risked it all, interjecting on Ashyn's behalf. The dragon had flown up and guided the young wizard down, shielding himself around Ashyn like a protective cocoon. Xao was the first one to hit the water, and soften the way for Ashyn. After that, everything had proceeded well. Ashyn had a plan when he entered the Shalis-Fey, and now he was finally going to see it through.

When Xao's mother asked him to watch the Rune family, she had stated the whole family. Xao thought he had failed when he made the choice to only save Ashyn, clearly the most self-destructive of the bunch. It turns out, he was wrong.

Ashyn was going to save Julietta, and Xao would be ready to help in any way he could. He stood up and stretched out his muscles, his orange fur rippling as he did so. He wondered how the elves would act when they found out Ashyn Rune had the aid of a dragon?

Xao looked away from the boy and to the other inhabitant of the cell. He found the creature merely staring at him, as it always did.

FIRST STEPS

Xexial looked out at the looming forest in front of him. The trees stood as imposing sentinels, custodians of a great many secrets that lay within. Secrets that only they were the true keepers of.

Xexial had spent a great deal of his very experienced life in proximity of the Shalis-Fey woods, and never once were they ever as dangerous as since he met Ashyn Rune. The last time he entered, he was looking for traces of the boy he thought he lost. Now he was doing it again.

"Why are we lingering?" the Maba-Heth groused.

Xexial ignored him, continuing to focus on the woods. He felt a slight tug at the sleeve of his tan robes. He looked down to see something he never thought he would see. An ally. An ally to a wizard. "You be having second thoughts?" Khyriaxx asked.

Xexial's eyes drifted to the strange brass contraption affixed to the spriggan's back. He didn't know what in the hells it did, but Khyriaxx was adamant that it would help.

Xexial shook his head. "No," the old wizard answered as he looked back up at the ancient wooded line of conifers.

"Then what be your quandary?" Khyriaxx asked.

"The moment we step into those woods, wizards will fully be at war with the Ferhym," Xexial announced flatly.

"The Recreant's letter already said we were at war," Grind commented impatiently. "So what does it matter? We have a job to do."

Xexial didn't bother to look at the anxious wizard hunter. "Because, willingly or not, the moment we step foot through this line of trees, we will begin a retaliatory strike against the Wild Elves. Further, if they captured Ashyn, we will be heading into the heart of their civilization. We will be assaulting Feydras' Anula."

Grind scoffed, his frill turning a dull yellow in agitation. "My job is to kill the Recreant. I don't care about anything else. Especially not some tribal tree-jumpers."

Xexial winced at the comment. He still wasn't certain what he was going to do when he finally found Ashyn. His heart and mind were in turmoil, and he knew that he would only be able to make that final wrenching decision when he stood before his apprentice himself.

"We are ready," Khyriaxx encouraged.

"Long past it," Grind added.

Xexial instead looked beyond the trees and into the belly of the woods. "Then we go," he said with firm conviction. "May history be gentle upon us when they reflect how this war began."

Xexial stepped into the Shalis-Fey.

~ ~ ~

Brodea smiled widely at the Elder of Vines as he and Genrus Eigron walked towards her. Only an hour before there was a commotion in the Water Pens, and she was getting ready to pay a visit to the Blood Wizard with the Voïre in tow, who had become so invaluable as of late.

On their way down the stairs they ran into Eigron, eager to see her.

"He's ready," was all the druid told her. It was all he needed to say, she understood. Releasing the services of the Voïre, Brodea now stood in the druid's cove, a rare guest to the elusive servants of nature. And the two before her were giving her exactly what she desired.

In the senior druid's hands, she saw the weapon that Eigron promised her, and following behind Eigron, tethered by a rope was what she longed for most of all, her weapon, Julietta.

The Elder of Vines closed the distance between them; Brodea could see a look of anger and disappointment written clearly across his aged features. "This is for our people," Brodea assured him.

"So you say," the elder remarked, unafraid of Brodea's position.

Brodea raised an eyebrow, "You disagree with what the Spirits decree?"

The old Ferhym looked around between the trees and ferns of the druid's cove, and finally glanced to the sky before settling back on her. "I've been a part of this land now for quite some time, my dear First Councilor. You now make the fourth First Councilor I have the honor of serving, and you are by far the most gifted and loveliest."

Brodea beamed at the compliment.

"But you are also the most dangerous," the elder added, wiping the smile off her face. She looked to Eigron who was looking at the ground, embarrassed. The Elder of Vines continued. "Both for the skewers and our own people."

He walked. Brodea reluctantly accompanied him. "When you asked me to research the tome and the shard, I did so gladly, eagerly even, because I knew they were the weapons of unbalancers most foul," he told her.

The First Councilor nodded in agreement. Part of her wanted to cut the old elf off, especially at the insult, but he was their oldest living Ferhym in Feydras' Anula. That alone provided him a miniscule measure of leeway. She would stay her rebuttal, if only until the druid finished what he had to say.

"When we hit an impasse, and Branch Commander Jenhiro brought us this artifact, I again sought to please you because of your disappointment in our failure in deciphering the tome. We thought it would be easy to manipulate this item. The laws of Creation, unlike the tome and the shard, bind it. Also a vessel contains an unusually powerful connection to the earth itself. We, being nature's primary caretakers, knew that the item would eventually unlock its secrets to us.

"I did this for you Lady Windsong, even at the expense of a very talented hunter. This hunter warned us vehemently about what he witnessed from both the creature who wielded the device, and this artifact itself. We turned our back on him and his warnings to delve into this device, to research how it can help you. We turned on our own hym to do it, and we did, for you." He shook his head in sorrow. "Now, I am told Jenhiro has not been seen for some time. He was a hym in need, and I fear that in our negligence, we have lost him forever. We possibly sacrificed a good Ferhym because we believe in the council and the cause."

Brodea nodded in silence. It was an honest survey, and one she made many times upon herself. She knew much of sacrifice. She assumed the Elder of Vines was done, that he said his piece so that she knew the extremes he went to for his belief in the cause. She was wrong. She watched as the Elder's expression turned disgusted and angry.

"But your request of this woman to use to humiliate and torture the wizard," he took a breath before continuing, "I find it quite simply abhorrent. You intentionally desire to inflict horrors upon her, and it is shameful. Though she not be Ferhym, she is part of this natural world."

Brodea's patience had run its course. How dare he call her shameful! "She is a skewer just like the wizard!" she spit. "The worst kind, in fact. She is dui Nuchada."

The elder shook his head. "She is different, yes," he agreed. "Her resistance to Creation magic, namely fire, is perplexing, absolutely. But never once has she demonstrated any of the other properties of the dui Nuchada!" Brodea saw his mouth form into a thin line of conviction. "I have seen ten of them in my lifetime, First Councilor. Ten! I tell you now this one is harmless. We should study it, learn from it, and learn how to balance the skewers by adopting her powers. You will kill a boon to us, First Councilor. A boon from the Spirits!"

Brodea glowered at him. "Are you suggesting we turn away from the edicts of our ancestors? Betray the Spirits and the sacred cause they have bestowed upon us, because this little ginger-haired tart has placed an enchantment upon you?" Her voice was cold and dispassionate. "I respect you, Elder of Vines. I respect all the druids."

Brodea pointed to Eigron, "It is why I felt it important to bring one closer to the doings of the Council of Elm. Long have we gone without having a druid as a Councilor. Sixty winters at least. While Eigron is young, I feel he has proven some worth by his relaying to us recent events that have transpired with the wizards. Namely in identifying the Blood Wizard to us. As such, it is why I have held him in as a liaison for the last several weeks. Does that not show the measure of respect for what I believe you contribute to our society and the cause?"

Brodea was lying, but she didn't give the elder a chance to call her out on it, instead she compounded it with truths. At least truths as she saw them. She pointed at the elder and the staff like object he held. "Not once have I questioned your methods to you. Not once, even when I asked for Julietta weeks past. You held her when the council needed her, and though I did not like it, I did not question your motives to you. That shows how important you are to the Ferhym. But this? You dare to challenge my methods against skewers most foul? Against the Blood Wizard? The only wizard we have ever captured. He can release to us the weapons necessary to destroy their menace to nature forever! You say you want to learn. How can that not be worth the sacrifice? I would gladly destroy a dozen evil skewers and their families, in the hopes that one could translate the tome. How is the potential to bring real balance for the first time in thousands of winters not worth one possible skewer?"

The Elder of Vines stared straight forward. His bushy eyebrows furrowed in intense thought. Only once did he risk glancing back at Julietta, before looking down at the artifact once more.

"She has been in the care of the Earthshorn for a decade. Though I would never say we showed affection towards her, we have watched her bloom from adolescence into adulthood, and never once has she posed a threat," he told her quietly. "What is true balance, if we sacrifice who we are?"

"We can change this world for the better," Brodea pressed.

"Would you sacrifice your daughter?"

Instantly she thought back winters before when she had Whisper kill a druid to protect their secrets. Brodea already did far worse for what she believed was necessary. Whisper knew all of it. Whisper's recent lack of restraint made her a liability to the cause. "If it meant true balance, I would." She wasn't lying.

The elder sighed, and Brodea wasn't sure if it was in resignation or disappointment. He handed over the artifact. Brodea took the smooth mahogany staff. She marveled at the egg-shaped stone that sat atop the long shaft, and the sharp point, so much like a spear, on the bottom.

"It is a totem. A powerful, mystical object that wards off enemies and gives the bearer strength and power."

"How do we use this against the wizard?"

"'We cannot." The Elder's eyes held a deep sadness as he uttered the words. "A totem is rare. We Ferhym have not used such devices since our separation from the other hym, long ago. It is not an art that is lost to us. Only one we have merely strayed away from. Totems are very specific to their wielder.

Ferhym work together. Such an artifact would have little use to us, since we share almost everything communally.

"When a totem is crafted, it is built around the wielder. It enhances that which the wielder excels at. So to use the totem of another is not impossible, rather incredibly rare. We discovered that only a select few could wield this particular device. It only answers to the most bestial natured. Like the creature in the pens."

Brodea looked down at his slumped form. "What does that mean for the Ferhym?"

He looked up at her with tired, sad eyes. "In order to use it, it has to find something within you that most elves simply do not possess."

"And that is?" Brodea replied testily her patience waning.

"A monster," he told her. Brodea looked at him in confusion, and he added sadly, "but I don't think that will be a problem for you."

The Elder of Vines walked away. Though his words were meant as both a warning and a barb to Brodea, she didn't care. She held the totem up, enamored by its majesty. This weapon could take down the Blood Wizard. Now she would use it against all wizards. Brodea could become that monster.

When she looked at Eigron, he looked back at her sheepishly. She didn't know what was going through the young druid's mind, and frankly, now that she had what she wanted, she didn't care. Brodea smiled, she had the weapon, and she had Julietta. She had control of the druids. And soon she would have control of the Blood Wizard as well.

Ashyn Rune was hers. And that meant the secrets of the tome would finally be, too. She planned all along not to wait for the Council of Elm. She would begin tonight, and tomorrow she would present to them a broken wizard and all the powers the Netherphage held.

That, or she would present them a corpse. Either way the council would be happy. And no one would question their First Councilor again.

~ ~ ~

Ashyn leaned against the bars, his eyes closed, replaying the diagrams repeatedly in his mind. On his back, he could feel the heat of Macky against him. Sitting only a few feet away, eyeing them both maliciously, he could sense Uriel.

"I can't concentrate with you staring like that," Ashyn said, opening his eyes and looking at Uriel.

"Ur' a monster," he said, spitting a wad of phlegm to his right. "Ana' I ain't takin' my eyes from ye, until you prove Avrimae's alive." He looked at Macky, too. "Neither of ya."

Ashyn shook his head. "No offense, Macky, but I can't believe she chose him over you."

Macky chuckled to the point where Ashyn knew it hurt him. "Tell me about it," he said between coughs.

Uriel's eyes went wide. "I's a successful man. She knows a real man when she sees one."

Macky angled himself for a rebuttal, but Ashyn touched his shoulder. "Not worth your time."

"Yeah. Lissen ta the little boy. Tis what ye always' did, Macky."

"Yes, because standing up for myself was such a terrible thing to do," Macky shot back.

"Ye challenged the Bishop!" Uriel returned.

"He was only human, Uriel. He made mistakes just like everyone else. I simply defended us against those mistakes."

Uriel scoffed, "And how well did that work out fer ye? Twice ye received *penance.* Once fer another person. No one would hire ye full on, once your charity was paid off, and the bishop forbade any of the priests to marry ye to Avrimae. Lissenin' ta the witch really worked out well fer ye!"

Ashyn soaked up everything Uriel was saying. It was the lost chapters of Macky's life that he refused to talk about. The poor choices. Avrimae was forbidden to marry Macky because of a vengeful Bishop. Should she have consented to being intimate with Macky and then bearing a child out of wedlock in an Enclave town, the results would have been horrendous for the woman.

It was considered sacrilegious. They were shunned and given little station, Often they were tattooed to indicate that they were marred. Regarded as little more than vagrants, treated as whores or prostitutes, chided and propositioned to become an exclusive sex slave for a pittance.

Ashyn knew it all too well. He studied the tattoo in the manuscripts he read within the Onyx Tower. It ran from elbow to shoulder, an interconnecting weave of two colors that looked much like grasping thorns. The color red symbolized impurity and stood for blood, to show the woman bore another bloodline's offspring; green marked the woman as a disease.

Ashyn knew that it was percieved that a woman giving herself to a man out of wedlock, was somehow a contagion and could be transmitted to others. Therefore, the impure woman was to keep that arm always exposed so all could see that she was tainted with sin. Should she attempt to hide it, then the punishment was often a public execution.

This was what had awaited Avrimae. This was what the bishop held over Macky, and ultimately guaranteed his friend's surrender.

Ashyn opened his eyes and looked at Macky. "Is what he says true?"

Macky shook his weary head. "It doesn't matter. I made my choices. That is in the past now."

"You lost the woman you loved because of me?" Ashyn almost couldn't believe it. It sounded horrible.

Macky looked Ashyn in the eyes. "No," the thin man answered passionately. "I lost her because of a spiteful, bulbous old man who became drunk on his own power. I joined the Enclave to change that. I didn't want anyone else to ever suffer what Avrimae and I suffered. I wanted her to be happy."

Uriel chuckled. "Yes, all that fighting and the bishop still won in the end dinna he?" With a sneer, he added, "I won, too."

Macky looked directly at Uriel. "You won, Uriel, because if I couldn't be with Avrimae, I wanted her to be with the one person in this entire world that I trusted enough to do right by her. That would treat her as she is meant to be treated, and to give her what I could not." Macky closed his eyes and leaned his head against the pole. "I never thought you'd turn into an asshole because of it."

Uriel's cocky grin was wiped from his face. "Ye wanted me ta be with Avrimae?"

Macky didn't open his eyes, instead Ashyn saw a single tear pool up in the corner and cascade down his face. "You love her, almost as much as I do. You are a hard worker, and were my best friend. If she couldn't be with me, of course I wanted her to be happy. I knew of no other who would treat her right."

Uriel looked down at his bruised hands. Bruises caused from beating on Macky. "Why dinna ya ever say anythin'?"

"Because," Macky sighed, "because, I thought if I said anything, you would think that her compassion for you was false.

That she just wanted a family, a family the bishop would never let me give her.

"Avrimae loves you, Yer. I wanted it to be real for the two of you, not just for her, but for both of you."

"So ye ne'er stopped bein' me friend all this time?" Uriel said, tears now forming in his own eyes. "Even after all I dun?"

Macky opened his eyes and looked at Uriel. "Oh, I stopped being your friend when you became a bullying assbag. But you always treated Avrimae like a treasure, and I respected that. And no matter how big a piece of shite you became to me, no, Uriel, I never stopped caring about your well-being."

Uriel continued to stare at his hands. "I am a piece o' shite ain't I?"

Macky took a deep breath and nodded, "Yes, you are. But you are also a good husband, and a loving father, and don't you forget that."

Ashyn could only watch the interaction between the two in silence. So many questions ran through his mind. He stared at Macky, realizing everything he sacrificed for his friends and his love. This man knew nothing of greed.

"No matter what anyone ever says, Macky," Ashyn whispered to him, "You are a good man. Don't ever forget that."

"Aye," Uriel echoed, hearing Ashyn's words. "He really is, ain't he?"

~ ~ ~

Brodea confidently walked down the well-worn walkways that led to the community district. Eigron fell in step behind her dragging Julietta on a leash like a disobedient animal.

Brodea's head was held high, her expression smug, as her raven hair billowed behind her. She had everything she needed, everything she wanted. She was anything but the humble creature that all Ferhym were supposed to be.

Jenhiro watched it all from a distance, analyzing how badly their situation was deteriorating. Transferring Uriel to the Water Pens had cost them Julietta, as he feared something like this may. If there were no Julietta, there would be no Ashyn. If there was no Ashyn, well, then they were stuck up a tall tree with no branches.

He warned Relm that this very thing might happen. It was why he wanted to push to move sooner. Now the worst was happening. Brodea was taking control, again.

The Hunter followed them, discreetly at a distance, until he came to the sector of housing that contained all of the Councilors. Warning whistles went off in his head. As of this moment, he knew he was entering the enemy's territory. This was Brodea's court.

Jenhiro slowed down. Unless he was directly invited into the Councilors' homesteads, even as honored as he was, he was not allowed in that sector. It was still early afternoon, and the sun was bright and full above their heads. There would be little hiding for him here. It didn't help that all the Councilors now on the Council of Elm were once previous hunters themselves. Every one of them had senses honed to detect someone slinking around in their domain. It was ingrained in them for centuries. Many, longer than Jenhiro had even been alive. He was looking at the entrance to the most elite of his people.

He navigated around the councilor sector and scanned every exit he came across. He saw no signs of the First Councilor, or Eigron, or even Julietta continuing through it.

Jenhiro's heart dropped into his stomach. The druid at the Water Pens was correct. Brodea was protecting Eigron the best way she knew how, by keeping him in her home. It was easy to see why the druid thought that Brodea was intimate with Eigron. Had Jenhiro not overheard their conversation, or even seen Brodea actively protecting the young Ferhym, he may have thought the same. Instead, Brodea had fortified Eigron in a wall of security. He was in a home surrounded by veteran killers. And if Eigron was there, that meant the Gaur's totem was there. Worse, that meant Julietta would be kept there.

Now they had a real problem. If they were going to save Ashyn and company, they were going to have to either break into Brodea's home or raid the Council of Elm. Either option meant entering into the realm of the Ferhym's most trained and lethal hunters to do it.

And there would be no more planning. It had to be done tonight or not at all.

THE SECRET IS IN THE WATER

As dusk settled in Feydras' Anula, Jenhiro grew even more agitated. He scouted every possible escape route twice. He checked the Water Pens, surprised that Macky and Avrimae's friend were still both alive, alarmed to see Ashyn asleep in the middle of the day. He left the wizard alone. He couldn't risk being seen.

He traced and retraced, hoping for some sign of Brodea, some sign of Eigron, but there was nothing. Either she eluded him, which was a real possibility, or she was secured within the Councilors' sector.

He made his way back to the Voïre, and now he stood before a strangely exhausted Ferhym.

"We must move tonight," Jenhiro pleaded with Relm.

Unsurprisingly, she shook her head no. "We've discussed this, Jenhiro. I've watched the Water Pens for months; we've planned this all week. You've seen how they're treated. There is no hope for reclamation from those in the pens, only suffering and death."

Jenhiro heard Relm's words, he really did, but he thought he had a better understanding of Brodea, or at least a better acceptance of what she was, than Relm was willing to accept or admit.

"Besides," the Voïre continued, "Avrimae is not ready to move."

Jenhiro looked over to the corner Avrimae curled against. She was cold. Jenhiro didn't know why, but she was. He could see her visibly shaking and her teeth chattered. The Ferhym picked up a blanket that Relm had nearby and offered Avrimae the woven fabric to wrap herself up with. Again she pushed herself harder into the corner to get away from him. She began shaking even harder, tears poured out of the corners of her eyes. He sighed and the placed parcel on the ground in front of her and backed away slowly.

"Avrimae will not befriend you in a single hour, or a single day," Relm said from behind him. "We'll be lucky if she realizes that we are allies even within a week's time."

Frustrated, Jenhiro ran his hands through his hair. It was all he could do to keep his own anxiety from growing.

"That didn't seem to bother you when you left to parlay with Brodea this morning? Why didn't you tell me?" He said, a little more anxiously then intended.

Relm stared at him in surprise, forcing Jenhiro to look away from her eyes. "I have obligations, Jenhiro. If I am summoned to the First Councilor, I go," she said firmly. "Besides, Avrimae was getting much needed, actual rest, not druid-induced sedation. I am not some housemate that watches the children while you are away balancing skewers!"

Jenhiro's ears flushed. "Your right, I'm sorry. I didn't mean it like that. That was foolish and I overreacted."

Relm visibly relaxed. "No, we are all on edge. It is a tumultuous time. You just need to sit down, Jenhiro, and breathe. Everything will come into play tomorrow."

Jenhiro shook his head. "I am telling you, Relm, we have to act now! Brodea is ready to move now, we must move first."

Relm surprised him by showing little signs of stress herself, she pointed at the human fiercely. "Avrimae has been a prisoner of ours for months, and the victim of repeated physical and sexual degradations by our people. We are enemies to her, Jenhiro. In her mind she is in the presence of her worst nightmares."

He wasn't getting through to Relm. Why wasn't she listening? He let out a deep breath from his lungs. "I saved her from that. Surely she must realize…"

Relm interrupted, "She doesn't know that yet. That was what Uriel was for. That was why he was moved in the same place as everyone else. Now they are all together, in one easy location. So relax. Just sit down already."

"Not exactly. I already told you that it cost us Julietta. She's nowhere near the pens," Jenhiro pointed out. "And I don't want to sit." He really didn't mean to sound negative; it wasn't usually in his nature, but with Julietta confined to Brodea's home, surrounded by councilors and guarded by a druid with the Gaur's totem things looked grim.

Relm pinched the bridge of her nose in frustration. "Brodea is a hym who controls the flow of a situation. Surely you've realized that by now. She always has. She's just ensuring the druids upheld their end of the bargain before the council gathering tomorrow. It would not do for the First Councilor to tell the council one thing, and then have our spiritual advisors not deliver on the appointed day."

Jenhiro realized that Relm wasn't the least bit surprised by Brodea's turn of events in taking Julietta from the cove. "You were expecting this!"

"I was there," she said. "Of course I knew it was going to happen."

"But…" Jenhiro was at a loss for words. Had Relm kept things from him? Vitally important things? "Our plan was to infiltrate the druid's cove for Julietta and Eigron."

"That was what we talked about, yes."

"They are not there now. So what happens next?" He asked. For the first time, the branch commander didn't quite know how to proceed.

Relm smiled sadly. She turned and entered her room leaving him alone in the foyer. She returned holding a strange leather bound object in her hands. "Plan B."

"What's Plan B?"

"Something most unpleasant," She said.

Jenhiro felt suddenly very cold. He didn't like how Relm was acting. How she was sounding. What was it she was holding? Was it? It couldn't be.

He looked at the way she was standing. Tall, erect, in charge. He saw the sternness on her face. He knew that face. Why did he know that face?

"What have you done, Relm?"

Her swirling eyes found everything but his, "I've done what was necessary to protect the interests of the people. All the people."

"And that is?" Jenhiro asked reaching for his spear.

"She came to the First Councilor, of course," a voice called from the other room. Jenhiro drew his weapon and turned, instantly ready to defend himself. As the owner of the voice walked into the room, Jenhiro felt a growing pain in his stomach.

Relm whispered, "Like I said. Brodea is a hym that controls the situation. I warned you she was not someone to go up against. I am sorry."

She had betrayed them. She had betrayed him.

Brodea smiled a bright white smile, "I am surprised Jenhiro. How long did you really think this farce could last? How could you possibly think that I wouldn't find out?"

Suddenly Relm's door flew open and Whisper and over a dozen hunters stormed into her small abode. Behind them all, followed Eigron, Jenhiro's last target.

Jenhiro watched as three hunters collected around Avrimae and leveled their weapons at the terrified woman. She shrieked. A keen wail that pierced Jenhiro's heart. There was no escape, no way to save her. He only had two options, surrender and hope they kept her alive, or fight to the death.

"I often wondered how it was that you of all people could defeat Ashyn where my daughter failed," Brodea said. "How could a branch commander capture the Blood Wizard? Then it occurred to me." Her dark eyes grew malicious, "By allying with him of course."

Jenhiro stared at her, his eyes wide.

"To have fallen so low, Jenhiro. How does it feel to know that you have become that which you once hunted?"

Jenhiro looked directly into Brodea's obsidian eyes, spitting, "You tell me. It was you who fell first."

Brodea's smile faltered for only a second. She looked over to the direction of Whisper and Relm. "Daughter, bring them, bring the tome, I want Ashyn to finally see that he has failed dismally."

"I won't come willingly," Jenhiro scoffed.

"But I think you will," Brodea answered. And then Jenhiro was looking into Relm's swirling platinum eyes. He knew no more.

~ ~ ~

A few hours later, Brodea stood with Whisper as they both looked down into the Water Pens over one hundred feet below. She could see the gaur and the dui Nuchada at opposite ends of their cage, acting as if they couldn't stand each other. But she knew. She knew the ruse. They were touching the water.

"I have you now, wizard," she said confidently.

"You should have just let me kill him," Whísper spit as she stared with hate down at the dui Nuchada. "I could have spared us the entire stampede."

Behind the two women, Brodea heard Eigron still defending his caste. "There is still no evidence that the bull is responsible for the restlessness of the elk, regardless of its skill. It has to be the wizard, or the work of this traitor."

Brodea turned and looked at the young hym condescendingly. Eigron was manipulating the wood of the great elm so that it encased Julietta's hands and feet solidly. He already sealed both Avrimae and Jenhiro in the same fashion. Not even an axe could free them in a single stroke, and if anyone tried, Brodea's people would be on them. Eigron was a fool, and a consistent failure, but he had skill, Brodea had to admit.

Jenhiro had fought like a Bristle Wolf against Relm's subjugation. It was almost admirable. Still, like all Voïre dui Ceremeia, her influence was just too strong, and the branch commander submitted in the end. Though she would never voice it, Brodea still had a hard time accepting it. Jenhiro, the humble hero, was actually the traitor and hunter of her own people.

She knew so little of the hunter. He seemed filled with such promise. Brodea could only think that it was perhaps the putrescent words of the Blood Wizard that somehow polluted his mind. There was no saving him after his actions, and it made her a little sad that she was going to have to balance one of her own. Not just a Ferhym, but also a hunter, and a talented one.

Julietta, on the other hand, never spoke up, not once. Brodea was sure the fiery-haired young woman understood every word they were speaking perfectly. Brodea was confident Julietta was fully aware of the situation she was in, but she handled it passively, almost serenely.

It was hard to read any emotion at all on her face. Without her eyes, or the full functionality of the muscles around her eyes, it gave the woman a stony appearance. If anything, Brodea thought she looked disinterested.

Then there was Avrimae. Her mind was a wreck. The sight of Eigron sent her into a fit of screaming and terror. Once more she hung sedated so that her wrenching cries wouldn't wake up all of Feydras' Anula.

The First Councilor had to admit, she was tempted to call for an immediate convening of the Council of Elm. She wanted to show them that their worries were in vain. She wanted to show them that the Spirits did speak to her, and that she was in control of the situation, but she couldn't. Not yet. Not until Ashyn was fully broken, or dead. Only then could she safely bring all to light, when the Netherphage was invoked.

Brodea looked back at Eigron. "It is the bull. It always has been."

"And how is that?" Whisper asked her mother.

"The secret is in the water," Brodea told her. "That is where you will find the beast's true intelligence. It is how I learned of everything," she added, looking to Relm who stood off to the side of the council chambers looking down below.

Eigron scoffed, but Brodea's icy glare back at him quickly stifled it. He approached the mother and daughter, and Brodea nodded at Whisper to move out of his way. She did, and Eigron leaned his head over the side.

"I don't understand. They aren't even looking at each other. All they are doing is staying near the edge of the murk. It's disgusting, but they are just animals," Whisper commented.

"They are intentionally ignoring each other," Brodea told her daft daughter. "To appear apart."

Whisper looked at her surprised, "Why would they do that?"

Brodea nodded with her eyes back to the Water Pens below. "The gaur has you all fooled. It is keenly intelligent. The wizard is helping keep its secret while still communicating with it. You underestimate the power of desperation. It can bring out the best and the worst in people."

"And how would you know that?" Eigron asked, almost challenging.

Whisper hissed, "Careful how you speak to the First Councilor, fool."

Brodea raised her hand to silence the two of them. She maneuvered the totem between the two so that the shimmering, egg-like stone on top divided them.

"I have watched them ever since Whisper threw the wizard into that cage. I have watched how the gaur acts around the boy, and how he acts around the hym." Looking back to Jenhiro, she went on, "I have never taken my eyes off of the dui

Nuchada. With the sole exception of when I was in the market saving a foolish druid."

"But how?" Jenhiro asked now. "How were you able to maintain such vigilance without anyone able to see you doing it?"

Brodea looked to the druid and nodded, "Show him."

Eigron walked away from the First Councilor, went to the basin of water and scooped up a small bowl. From there he took it to Jenhiro and held it up before him.

Even from where Brodea stood, she could hear the strange murmurings coming from the water. They were indistinct in form, but she recognized what it was. Communication. Ashyn and the bull were talking to each other. Though she couldn't see it, she knew that the traitor was looking up at the wizard and gaur through the water. He recognized it immediately. It was, after all, one of the chief ways Councilors communicated with their Branches in the Shalis-Fey.

"Day and night, I watched the two this way. When you brought the other human to the Water Pens this morning, and I heard the commotion I immediately went to the basin with the Voïre dui Ceremeia. The sounds intensified, and then I heard you, speaking to the Blood Wizard. It was only compounded later when a druid approached about a curious elf that lied to him. Lied!" Brodea looked at Jenhiro patronizingly, "You can't lie to a druid, Jenhiro. You know this."

She watched with confidence as Jenhiro closed his eyes in shame. "Yes, I knew it was you, Jenhiro. You merely let me know what they were planning. I already knew you had Avrimae. I knew you were up to something. But I knew where she was, so it was no concern to me."

Eigron stared at her in horror. "You knew where Avrimae was? And yet you let me live in fear of failure?"

"One does not drink all their water in the desert and hope for oasis," she answered. "In order to make the Blood Wizard think he has a chance of succeeding, everyone has to believe it. Even you."

"But what about the beast?" Whísper asked, truly in awe of her mother. "What gave it away to you?"

"I told her," Relm said.

Brodea savored the look of horror on Jenhiro's face when she spoke the words.

"Right after the stampede, when I looked into its eyes to sense its power. I just didn't want to give it away in front of the wizard."

"You bitch!" Jenhiro snarled. "You've been using me this whole time!"

Relm shook her head. "I told you not to act, Jenhiro. I told you not to do it from the very beginning, and what did you do? You killed a fellow Elf!" She said pleadingly, "You caused a stampede, and brought a skewer into my home! What was I supposed to do? I was terrified!"

"I trusted you," he hissed.

"You betrayed that trust first when you murdered our people!" Relm snapped. "I want what is best for the Ferhym. And I want what is best for the humans. That means balance."

"But you've marked the dui Nuchada. You are betraying the one you've bound yourself to!"

"Enough of this!" Brodea barked. It still ate at her what the Voïre had done so long ago. But her reasons, as she brought to light, paid off tenfold in the end. They were childish, and yet, in a small way, sound. The Voïre simply hadn't wanted to see a boy her age hurt. It scared her to think a child could be murdered.

Brodea realized it was her own fault. She was proud, too proud for a Ferhym rightly to be, and she pushed the council to allow the child on the hunt for the dui Nuchada, when the elder, more experienced Voïre should have gone. It was a bitter lesson learned. Humbling, really.

"Bring the dui Nuchada, and bring the gaur." She told Eigron and Whisper. "And round up the skewers in the water pens and corral them all to one location where we can see them from here."

"Should I bring up the one the dui Nuchada is attached to?" Eigron asked.

"No. I want him out of reach."

FALLING APART

You are sure this will work?

Ashyn looked away from the barrier separating him from the humans and instead glanced toward the massive Gaur who was diligently studying the massive elm. *I have no clue.* Only two days before, he began to translate the tome. Now he was getting ready to stage a breakout with two Ferhym, a Gaur, and a bunch of emaciated, clueless humans.

If she is watching...

Rizen didn't need to elaborate. Ashyn knew exactly whom the gaur meant. Ashyn risked a glance up as well. He could see the flickering amber lights of burning torches in the chamber above. It was impossible to know if she was up there, the stairs that led up the tree began on the north-east side and he hadn't seen anyone come or go down the stairs in many hours. Yet, he knew if Brodea was up there, she would signal an alarm the instant she knew something was happening. He only hoped Relm was up to the task, because it was going to be dangerous. No dangerous was to light a word for it. It would be downright lethal if they got it wrong.

I wish I had words to encourage you, Ashyn confessed. *Only, when it starts, be strong.*

I understand... The gaur began, but his pose suddenly froze. Ashyn was not alarmed by the reaction; he had seen it repeatedly over the past week with the creature. Rizen reached out and put his large three-fingered hand to the ground, his snout sniffing deeply into the air. *The one you call Eigron approaches.*

Ashyn broke from the water just in time as Eigron and Whisper came surging around the corner with a dozen armed hunters. Ashyn stood and waited, but he felt the tension rise in his guts and the hackles raise on his neck. Something was different. Something was wrong.

Whisper was the first one to the bars. Her gnarled, pink scars contorted in what appeared to be a painful smile on her once beautiful face. "It's time for the big event dui Nuchada. The games are over."

Eigron's fingers danced and Ashyn heard Rizen whistle in surprise. Ashyn spun to see sludge covered vines creeping from the water wrapping themselves up the thick tree trunk like legs of the gaur. Rizen fought and scrambled, but he was already in the water.

His amber eyes darted to Ashyn for help or confirmation. Then Ashyn heard screams of alarm come from the cage next to him. He looked in horror as the snapping vines were coming alive and viciously lashing out on the humans, pulling them to the ground and dragging them backwards towards the stiff wooden bars.

Macky and Uriel, though no longer friends, worked together, trying to pull back people as more and more vines darted forth from the bars like hundreds of angry snakes. The beaks were indiscriminate in their violence, pecking and stabbing at everything until they got a solid enough grip to wrap around and drag the humans back.

The young wizard could see the stones slicken with blood as some of the beaks drove deeper into the flesh of their victims than others.

Within seconds, Ashyn watched helplessly as Macky and Uriel were taken down and driven violently to the bars. Someone failed. Someone was captured or worse. They needed to take their chances and try to escape now. At best, they could at least make it to Julietta before they died. Ashyn spun quickly and dove towards the gaur, all pretenses of their hatred towards each other gone.

Rizen was trying to battle the excrement-soaked vines with all he had. Ashyn could see the bull's large muscles flex and bow under the pressure of the constricting vines. Dozens were covering him now, creeping up his torso and working their way to his chest. He tore vigorously at them.

As Ashyn waded into the water he screamed, *They know! Use your talents do not hide it anymore!*

Before the gaur could even respond, Ashyn felt the snaring grip of one of the tendrils latch on to his own leg. He looked down to see it creeping up his thigh like a slug. He reached down to slap it away.

Freeze the water like you did on me! He screamed into Rizen's mind.

Ashyn could feel the fear emanating from the bull now. It was real fear. The vines pulled Rizen down into the murky waters.

"No!" Ashyn screamed as he dove for the gaur. Deeper and deeper they pulled. Ashyn tried to help, but the two-thousand-pound creature was too heavy. He watched as the beast that had become his ally, and then his friend, was pulled under the water. Rizen's amber eyes never left his own, and he saw in one last moment the look of sheer terror in Rizen's eyes before he disappeared into the murk. A small jetty of bubbles followed, and within a minute they were gone.

"Not so tough," Eigron commented. "Jenhiro greatly overestimated the beast's skill."

Ashyn turned with bitter hatred in his eyes. He tried fiercely to call on his anger. His righteous rage to resuscitate the long dormant magic within him that only seemed to flare out in spurts of dire need. Well now that need was dire indeed.

"You're next," Whisper said with glee. "Feel free to scream. I like the way it sounds coming from your throat."

Ashyn felt the tendrils of vines roll up his body. He tried to fight them off. He tried to pry them away, but it was in vain. He looked over to the humans in the other pens, and pain wracked at his chest. They were all pinned against the bars; fear and agony painted across their faces as the vines kept tightening, kept attacking. Many were covered in lacerations, and the bright red of their life's essence flowed like streams down their bodies.

As Ashyn was driven to his knees, the anger in him ignited a spark. Beneath him he could feel the mud and filth sucking him downward, pulling him into the water. He felt the languid waters pouring over his skin. Brackish fluid burned the wounds in his chest as it forced him downward, just like Rizen.

The waterline was at this chest, and then his neck. Steam rolled from him, from the water. His vision was painted in orange.

"Quicker," he heard Whisper say in the distance.

"I'm trying," Eigron huffed.

Vines rose and fell against him, some ruptured from the heat pouring from his body like an inferno. The exploding guts splashed his face with waste. He wanted to wretch, but knew that would only bring the filth into his mouth. His eyes bore down on Whisper who had a worried look on her face. He knew why, he felt why. He only needed a second more.

Then those words entered his ear, and he watched the victory of the moment glow from her eyes like a blazing torch, erasing all worry, "I have him."

His head was driven below the water, and he closed his eyes. The world became muted around him as he struggled to hold his breath, and wondered how long it would be before his lungs let go.

Then he heard a voice. It was crystal clear, like she was right next to him. In fact, it sounded like she was all around him. "Your little rebellion has failed," Brodea whispered.

Ashyn knew at that moment how Brodea found out. Macky told him they put Ashyn's picture on the water. He told him! Ashyn repeatedly noted how similar the gaur's magic and the Ferhym magic was, and still he spoke to it, day in and day out, using the same techniques the Ferhym did. Ashyn was a fool.

"It all ends. Tonight," Brodea echoed with confidence around him.

Ashyn Rune was pulled away.

THE BOOK OF BALANCE

The first thing that he noticed was that everything sounded dull. He could hear voices, but they were muted, and inconsistent. Like trying to hear underwater. But he wasn't underwater, not anymore.

Wind whistled by his face tickling his nose. He could smell the sap of trees. The fresh scent of the verge, and the wooded smell of elm.

Ashyn opened his eyes. He knew where he was.

Dim orange light flickered in front of him casting the four figures before him in odd, misshapen silhouettes. He still could understand most of their forms though. Three females and a male. Every one of them had the signature long pointed ears of the Ferhym.

A pearly white smile pierced through the obscured shape. Ashyn ignored it and instead took in the rest of the room. He knew it so well. The council chambers. These wooden walls had been his prison for weeks, his endless torment. Pain engulfed everything he had known for that short time, and now it looked like that is what was planned again. He was ready for it. He would do his part.

Behind the four elves, he could make out four other figures. They a much wider assortment than the Ferhym in the front. The wood was alive and it swallowed the four trapped individuals' hands and feet in an impenetrable grip. They all hung, suspended by their arms, their shoulders extended out painfully wide.

Rizen was the easiest to make out due to his sheer size, but he also saw Avrimae and Jenhiro and he felt his eyes begin to water when they took in the last one: Julietta.

Brodea stepped forward, blocking Ashyn's view of his sister. Ashyn directed his angry hawk's gaze to her. Brodea's smile never wavered. "I see I finally have your attention, Blood Wizard."

"I still won't do it Brodea," he announced. "I will not translate the tome."

The challenge seemed to entice her all the more. She walked to him, grabbed him by the shoulders and spun him around. He was facing out into nothing but the night. Ashyn had no idea he was so close to the edge. Brodea leaned the chair he was bound to forward, her strength and control an impressive feat as Ashyn felt himself slide forward.

Brodea's eyes flickered with intensity, saying simply, "Look down." Ashyn obeyed.

What he saw below made his heart sink. The Water Pens were emptied. Instead he saw the people lined up side by side, all of them on their knees. Vines bound their hands. Behind them stood multiple Ferhym all holding lowered spears.

The lead Ferhym, painted some sort of dark lacquer onto his blade. He was standing directly behind Uriel.

No, no, no, no, no, no. It wasn't supposed to be like this, Ashyn thought. *Brodea was supposed to focus on me, on the people in this chamber.*

"Watch carefully," she told him.

"Don't do this!"

"Will you read for me?"

Ashyn closed his eyes. He knew he was at a point of no return. *Xexial forgive me,* he whispered in his own mind. Ashyn nodded. "I will."

Brodea sucked in a deep breath through her teeth. He knew she was savoring in this victory. He felt her eyes on him, wild and savage. She was a predator who had captured her prey in a death grip and now she was savoring his blood on her lips.

"Too late."

"No!" Ashyn pleaded.

"First Councilor!" a new high-pitched, song-like voice said in alarm. "He agrees." She quickly added, "He agrees to decipher the tome, like I told you he would."

Brodea nodded. It was the first time Ashyn had heard her voice since they were children. Truly heard her voice. Had the situation been different, he would have found it beautiful.

"And a penalty for his disobedience must be given," the First Councilor said harshly. "Bring Avrimae; let her watch her mate's death."

Ashyn fought against the vines binding his arms and legs to the chair. This is not how it was supposed to be! He watched, as the world seemingly slowed before him.

The wood warped and manipulated as it moved Avrimae forward. It was so seamless, so natural. No deformations remained behind where the wood was altered as it slid her forward.

The she bent forward, hanging over the emptiness, next to him. Eigron thrust something underneath her nose, some sort of salt, and her eyes flared to life. Immediately she panicked at seeing nothingness, but they focused, and Avrimae smiled for an instant as Ashyn knew they locked on her husband, Uriel.

"Avrimae!" Ashyn heard both Macky and Uriel cry in unison at the sight of her.

Ashyn watched as her eyes fell to the spear behind Uriel, at the realization of what was about to happen.

Her voice came out slowly, alien, "No," It became a bellow, "No, Yer. Yer!"

"It's okay, baby," Uriel said calmly. "I love you. Watch out for little Mackenzie for us. Raise our daughter right. Make her proud of her papa."

Ashyn saw as Macky was jarred by the name of Avrimae and Uriel's daughter. He mustn't have known.

Avrimae was crying. "I love you," she mumbled repeatedly between tears.

Ashyn looked away from her, and instead focused on the one thing he had grown to hate most: Brodea's wide bright smile.

He watched as she turned her head to face below. With her free hand she reached up, ever so slowly towards her brow. Her hand crept up a few inches, and then a few more. It reached her face and the first two fingers of her hand rested upon her brow.

Her eyes looked deep into Ashyn's own. Those eyes, a black so deep they glistened like onyx, radiated one thing and one alone: absolute victory. She had won. She beat him.

Her fingers left her brow in a short and decisive salute. Ashyn looked down in horror as the elf with the lacquered spear nodded. He reared back his weapon, and then thrust it forward with all of his strength.

Ashyn screamed. It was guttural, long, and harsh. Uriel stared at him, accepting his death.

Macky however, was quite different. The man looked up at him, his beaten and bruised face a swollen mass of purples and greens. But Ashyn could still see his eyes. His brown, pure, innocent eyes. Macky wanted nothing in life but the love of a woman. He was simple and devout. He was easy to get along with and wore a big heart for all people.

Macky nodded to Ashyn and to Avrimae, his love. It was a slight nod, but Ashyn saw it, and he understood it. Macky knew what was going to happen, and he accepted it. Accepted it, because he must. Self-sacrifice. It's what Jasia would do. What she had done. For love.

Ashyn's world caught up to him, as Macky, in a last ditch effort of strength and love, lunged suddenly to the left, bowling into Uriel, and knocking the large man over.

Ashyn felt his heart wrench from his chest as the tip of the spear was driven violently into Macky's back. Macky's eyes went wide, and his back arched forward from the impact. Macky cried out, but it was small, subtle.

The Ferhym withdrew the spear. The dark lacquer gone, now replaced with a layer of crimson. Macky fell to his side, shivering.

Ashyn felt Brodea's hot breath on his ear. "Unexpected," she admitted, "But just as effective. It won't be long now…"

Ashyn had no choice but to watch as the poison worked its way through Macky's system. Immediately, by the short gasps his friend was taking, Ashyn could tell the poison was restricting his breathing. Soon, the man was covered in sweat and his nose ran. Then he fell into convulsions. After several seconds, Mactonal Turgenssen finally fell still.

Ashyn was breathing heavily. Tears ran down his face, and he did nothing to try to staunch the flow. Macky was innocent. Innocent and he was dead because of Brodea. No! Because of him! He should have foreseen this! He should have known she would do this!

Avrimae screamed and writhed against wooden bindings. Tears and mucus poured from her face as she wailed for the death of her friend and former lover.

The elf next to him nodded, and Ashyn watched as the hunter below reapplied the lacquer, just as Uriel picked himself up. Disbelief written across his face at Macky's sacrifice for him.

"Do we need another demonstration?" Brodea asked.

"No," Ashyn grunted, his inside hollow. Macky was dead. Probably the best friend he had ever had the pleasure of knowing, and the man was now dead. He turned and faced Brodea. He promised in a dark whisper, "One day, I will make you suffer."

It only caused the First Councilor to smile broadly. "There will be plenty of time to dream for hopeless vanities later."

Avrimae's bindings pulled her away from the ledge as she screamed her love for her husband.

Brodea turned Ashyn back around. He could now clearly see Whisper painting a similar poison onto her spear as well. "Now that was the best scream yet," she said sadistically. "Can we hear it again?"

Whisper raised the poison brandished weapon up to Avrimae's chin, as Eigron repositioned her by the others. "Even a small nick is enough to kill some."

Brodea grabbed Ashyn's chin and turned his head to face hers. When she spoke to him, it was surprisingly compassionate. "These are skewers dui Nuchada, but I promise you that I will let them all go, even your sister, if you translate the tome tonight. No more need to die for you."

"F...F...First Councilor!" Eigron stuttered. "Jenhiro has murdered our people! He cannot be released!"

Brodea's eyes flashed with annoyance at Eigron's outcry. Quickly the First Councilor tried to mask it with her usual charisma, but Ashyn saw it. Brodea was fed up with this one.

"Of course not, my dear druid." She told Eigron with her usual charm. "I meant Julietta, Avrimae, and the animal."

Brodea released Ashyn's chin and she walked away from him. "Bring him the tome. It's high time we learned more than the pittance the druids could teach us."

~ ~ ~

A small table was brought before him, and the tome and a candle were placed atop it. Ashyn's bindings were cut from his hands and he wiped at the corners of his eyes.

His fingers shook as he reached for the leather bound cover. *Months ago I chose the many for the few, and now the few were dying or,* he looked at Avrimae, *worse.* Ashyn had already decoded the nature of the tome. It wasn't large, and in only a few days' time he was able to commit most of the book to memory. He had always been able to do that.

Xexial used to joke that the day he could actually harness the magic the way he could memorize the incantations was the day he would be the strongest wizard in Kuldarr. So reenacting the incantation within the book was not the problem. The problem was Eigron.

It was proven with Relm that they would never be able to duplicate what he was saying and what he was doing. Relm couldn't recite one word he said, or even repeat what she said, unless she read it from the tome. It vanished from her mind the moment it left her lips. It was his only advantage, yet the obvious thing he couldn't do in front of the druid was lie. The druid would know that.

Brodea had just shown him that she was not above disciplining him for his insolence. Avrimae would die next, followed by Uriel, Rizen, Jenhiro, and then eventually Julietta.

Macky paid the price for Ashyn's ignorance. He would not condemn Avrimae as well. He would keep her alive for Macky.

Ashyn looked down at the archaic scrawl written across the first page. Again he saw the word: Craetorian. Ashyn cleared his throat, turned the page, and read the first line of draconic text aloud. "Balance can only be achieved through the Nether. The Nether can only be achieved through **Destruction. Destruction** can only be achieved through the wizard. The wizard can only achieve balance through the phage.

"Netherphage."

Brodea's eyes lit up at the word of balance. "Only a Ferhym knows true balance," she proclaimed with conviction.

Ashyn didn't have the heart to argue with her. Didn't have the spirit to bother to explain that his whole purpose was the balance of life. And through life, he was the balance of magic. Yet he knew the philosophies of the Ferhym well, none more so than the Council of Elm's. It was impossible to convince them otherwise. He turned the page and read on. "The phage is the answer. The phage is restoration. The phage is extermination. The phage is balance."

"How do we make the Netherphage work?" Brodea asked. Ashyn looked up to see what the druid knew. It was they after all who had possession of the tome for almost two decades.

Eigron shrugged. "We learned very little from the tome outside of the fact that only a wizard or a dui Nuchada can translate its components. Past the first few pages the whole of the tome becomes one long invocation of some sort. A spell is woven into the very text as it is read. It cannot be bypassed, that we know of. Only the answer to the Netherphage lies within. A wizard has to decode the invocation from the spell that makes one forget."

Ashyn vaguely heard the words, but he did hear them. In the back of his mind he realized that the druid said only a wizard or a dui Nuchada could translate it. Why? By now they could have located any linguist or historian with a passing knowledge of draconic. He knew Relm couldn't hold on to it, for the very reason Eigron explained, but he thought that it was because magic worked very differently in her. Ashyn assumed the Druids knew far more about the Netherphage, and that was why they wanted it so badly.

Ashyn looked at them both. "Are you telling me you have no idea what this says past the first few pages at all?"

Brodea shot Eigron a murderous look for sharing that revelation. Eigron looked to the ground in shame. It was enough to make the cogs in Ashyn's mind begin to turn. This is what Relm was talking about. This was why they needed him. The tome was warded in such a way that the idea formed by the words was immediately destroyed upon reading the information. The reason they hadn't made it farther was that no one could remember it. The only ones that could were wizards. It wasn't just Relm. It was everyone!

Ashyn was silent for a moment as he thought it out. It was clear Brodea did not enjoy the sentiment of his silence. She spoke up, giving Ashyn a reason to be knocked out of his personal torpor, hearing her say loudly to Whísper, "Give the wizard incentive to keep going."

"Wait!" he yelled watching as Whísper moved to nick Avrimae with her poison-coated spear.

Ashyn's mind whirred. Why could he read the tome? If only a wizard could do it because of his affinity for **Destruction,** it was in order to avoid the effects of having his memories killed as soon as they were formed. He would need to have a defense for that. He didn't. He was broken right now, yet he already memorized the tome after two days. There had to be another reason.

He flipped back to the first page, and he read the translation of the single word written there: Craetorian. Only a wizard or the dui Nuchada could read the tome, they said, and if he had no trained defense then it had to be that which was innate. If his mind was blocking itself from the memory damage, then that meant he needed to have the ability to do it on a subconscious level. That meant he had to have access to something he felt was denied to him for so long.

Ashyn understood. His eyes widened at the realization. Even though his psyche was broken from the connection of magic, like the snapping of a string on a bow, it didn't make him any less of a threat. After all, a bow could still be used as a weapon, just not the weapon it was intended to be until it was restrung.

"I've heard that the dui Nuchada are the descendants of dragons..." Whisper told him before she threw him from the ledge. Dragons can siphon magic. Ashyn had always had a connection to magic, because the magic was in his bones. That was the beast inside him trying to escape! This epiphany made him look around the room. He was going about it all wrong. He was trying to pull the magic in from the world around him. He needed to pull the magic out from within him. Just like the gaur. He was storing it.

His gaze fell on the Voïre dui Ceremeia, their eyes locked. He saw them watering in the corners. She was as distraught about Macky as he was. She nodded at him ever so slightly, and he knew. He knew he was right.

Whisper's spear poked against Avrimae's flesh. She whimpered and cried, in seconds the tip would pierce through the small protective outer layer of skin and the poison on it would enter her blood stream.

Ashyn looked to Jenhiro; his eyes were locked on him as well. They were terrified, but not for what was happening to him, or due to any lack of courage on his part. He was afraid for Avrimae. He sacrificed everything he was to help her, and now it seemed as if she were going to die anyhow as a means of simple punishment against Ashyn.

His mind kept going back to the word: Craetorian. At first Ashyn thought that perhaps it was the title of the book, but now he wasn't so sure. It seemed now more like a prerequisite. His eyes lit up, as he understood. A dui Nuchada was a Craetorian.

The reason he could read it was that his mind absorbed things differently. The threads of **Destruction** could erase only what a single spirit could read, but his mind was threaded, like a braid. The spell focused on only one piece of the braid. He simply had more strands.

His fingers caressed the page. "This is very complex," he said at last. "You must give me a moment to sort it out."

Brodea raised her hand and Whísper froze.

"They are just words," the Huntress hissed. "He's stalling."

Brodea looked at him, "Are you stalling Blood Wizard? Because if you are, I plan on being very unpleasant about it."

"I am stalling, because I am thinking," Ashyn answered. And he was thinking, thinking hard. "If what Eigron says is true, and this whole tome is an invocation, then you don't need me to translate it, you need me to cast it, because you cannot do it yourself."

Brodea slowly clapped her hands. It was mocking and condescending but Ashyn locked his gaze with her dark orbs. "You dazzle me, Ashyn. Simply marvelous."

Eigron looked at the floor in shame. Ashyn knew his last statement gave away too much. It finally gave Ashyn all the knowledge he needed to figure it out.

"Dui Nuchada," Ashyn told them, "is Craetorian."

Brodea nodded. "The council has known about the spell for a long time. A wizard told me, before I slew him, that Craetorians were the progenitors of the wizard. Arbiters of the magic of Destruction. He boasted that the tome in your hands is the true nature of Destruction.

"I've known what it can do ever since I watched a part of the Shalis-Fey die and form the Maze. What we cannot do is cast the spell. For that, we need a wizard, and not just any wizard, but a Craetorian wizard. It took me many winters, but we figured it out.

"The dui Nuchada and the Craetorian are one and the same. It is you who will cast the spell, wizard, and bring about the first age of prosperity, and growth, among those that understand this world the best."

"By destroying it?" Ashyn asked baffled. "I've been to the maze. There is nothing in there but death."

"No," Brodea answered. She reached behind her and withdrew the same small shard of crystal that he saw before when he first arrived in Feydras' Anula. She held it before him.

"This killed the wizard and destroyed the forest because it wasn't controlled by that spell. The Nether, it needs a focus. It is the great balancing of the world. I broke the original focus; you must build a new one with this." Brodea held forth the gaur's totem.

"What will it do?"

Brodea's eye shone with intensity. "Why, it will destroy magic, Blood Wizard. It will destroy all magic."

THE RITUAL

66 "That's impossible. You cannot destroy magic," Ashyn proclaimed.

Brodea laughed. "Just because you've never heard of it being done, does not make the task impossible."

Ashyn shook his head in disagreement. "Magic is life. It is in everything! If you attempt to remove magic, you will, in effect, being taking out everything it means to be alive. That's counter to all your people stand for! No life means no nature. No nature means no balance."

"You think so extreme," Brodea said humorously. "I do not wish to destroy life, nor unbalance nature. I wish to eliminate its influence on your kind that skews this world so! I simply wish to separate those that seek to twist and perverse the gifts of nature from it all together." She raised the totem. "Monsters such as this bull should not be capable of such defilement."

"Such a thing as separating someone from magic is not possible. They would die," Ashyn spat.

Brodea snickered, while she idly played with the stone that sat on the top of the totem. "Tell me wizard, are you yourself not broken to your connection to magic?"

Ashyn paused.

It only made Brodea laugh louder.

Ashyn looked around to see if the others were in agreement with her decision. Their faces were impassive, all except for Whisper who was smiling at the idea. "You can't tell me you agree with this?" Ashyn asked Eigron, whose face was a stone. "You are part of nature. Part of magic, this will affect you too."

"It is the will of the Spirits," Eigron replied. "She speaks directly to them. I cannot judge what it is they decree; only they can. If this will bring balance to nature and end the scourge of wizards, then I cannot disagree."

Ashyn ran his fingers over the stubble on his head. He blew out a large gust of air. This is crazy. It was all suddenly ludicrous. He knew the book, the invocation to the spell, but he didn't realize until this moment what Brodea had in mind. They wanted him to destroy magic, or they would kill his sister. His sister who was a dui Nuchada, who was part of magic. No. He couldn't do it. He couldn't be responsible for the deaths of so many. Even for his sister's life. Even for his life. Ashyn attempted to close the book.

And she was on him. Faster than he thought was possible for a Ferhym to move she was there. She wrapped around him swiftly like a striking asp. She pinned his right arm behind his back like a chicken wing and wrapped her left arm around his head, her sharp nails piercing through his eyelids pinning them in place.

"You will not take this from me," she hissed. "Voïre, now!"

There she was. The Voïre dui Ceremeia. The Exemplar. Relm. Her eyes were a swirling maelstrom of energy. A torrent of pure magic that drew him in so quickly he couldn't even breathe.

It all happened so fast. Faster than his mind even processed. He heard the clink of the totem and crystal shard striking the ground. The totem, up until a second ago, that Brodea had been holding.

Now he was swimming, lost in the captivity that was Relm's amazing eyes. The quicksilver danced, swayed, and pulled him deeper into her world and away from his reality. And he knew then, once more, he was hers.

~ ~ ~

"I have him," Relm said to Brodea.

Brodea smiled and slowly released the wizard. "Very good, Voïre. That was fast. You are far more powerful than your elder. She couldn't hold the wizard at bay."

Whisper scowled in displeasure.

"I have developed a connection with him, like we discussed. It was far easier to let him in," Relm said confidently.

"You bitch." Jenhiro snapped.

Brodea stepped away from Ashyn, who was now under Relm's complete control. She moved up to Jenhiro with purpose. He stared at her, unafraid. When she was only inches away Brodea struck him hard against his jaw. She then grabbed his cheeks with her razor sharp nails, cutting grooves deeply into his flesh. "Do not speak to the Voïre in such a fashion."

She released her grip with a flick of her arm. Jenhiro could feel the beating of his pulse through those holes in his cheeks, and he could feel the blood ooze out of the five small wounds.

Brodea strode away from him. "At last we can finally begin. What do we need to start this ritual, Ashyn?"

Jenhiro watched in horror as Ashyn clearly recounted the list of ingredients he needed in order to make the invocation successful. Worse, he saw that Eigron was already prepared for much of it as he moved repeatedly behind him and came back with parcels that clearly came from the druid's cove. "You knew?"

Whisper sniggered at Jenhiro.

Brodea looked at him smugly. "Everything has proceeded exactly as planned. Vooken and I have been plotting this moment since we found out about Julietta. When we learned we had a dui Nuchada already amongst us, it made things so much easier."

Julietta raised her head at this, but still didn't say a word. Jenhiro wondered if the girl was mute as well as blind. Clearly she had to know her brother was in front of her. Brodea called him "Ashyn" amongst other things. How did she not know? Did she not care?

Brodea waved a hand at Whisper that Jenhiro caught with his peripheral vision. The huntress lowered her spear. From there she walked to the ledge and waved down at the guard below. Brodea was in absolute control, and there was nothing they could do.

"Is this space sufficient?" Brodea asked Ashyn.

The boy, the dui Nuchada, looked around the room, and then consulted the tome once more. "It seems so."

"Good," Brodea answered. "Then if we have everything, let us begin. Ashyn has the spell memorized?"

Relm nodded. "His mind is like a sponge. We have been studying the tome together for the last two days. He knows enough to at least complete a trial of the spell, with help."

Jenhiro hung his head in shame. Relm had played Ashyn too.

"Excellent. Eigron, assist the wizard as necessary."

The druid nodded. Jenhiro looked up to see the pride on his face. Eigron was doing something beyond what was called for by the druids. He was doing the Spirits' work as decreed by his First Councilor.

Ashyn also did as he was told. He was a servant of Relm, subjugated by the power of her abilities. Ashyn read from the book and told his assistant exactly how to position the spell components against the floor.

Jenhiro watched transfixed as Ashyn picked up a piece of their blood bark, an item they used for leaving symbols for their dead drops and caches in the woods, or so they could be tracked by their own in times of trouble. Ashyn drew symbols upon the floor, geometric patterns that were perfectly done and arranged so that the blood red sap glistened directly in the moonlight.

Jenhiro watched Ashyn's motions, the surety of his actions. The movements he made while walking back and forth and consulting the tome repeatedly. Though the former branch commander knew little of magic, and even less about how a wizard operated, the skill and technical details that Ashyn possessed while ordering Eigron around seemed impressive, if nothing else.

Soon another member joined them in the council chambers. It was Vooken. The pony-tailed Councilor walked up next to Brodea and gave a curious glance towards Jenhiro.

"Is it working?" Vooken asked, hopeful.

"Just like we spoke of," Brodea answered jubilantly. "Finally, the Spirits will reward us by eliminating the powers the skewers hold over warping nature."

"You will go down in the history of our reliefs as the First Councilor who destroyed the wizards once and for all," Vooken stated.

Jenhiro watched as Brodea reached out and touched his hand, ever so gently. "I didn't do it alone."

Jenhiro was surprised to see Vooken turn away from her. He told her a little coldly, "No. You will always have my aide First Councilor."

The captive Ferhym pondered their interaction as he looked towards the others. Avrimae stopped crying and seemed almost captivated as Ashyn worked at creating the bizarre symbols on the floor over and over. It relieved him to see her at total ease for the first time in weeks.

He looked over to the gaur. His stalker. The gaur was quiet, contemplative. Its intelligent eyes also watching diligently as Ashyn worked on the hard wooden flooring of the great tree. If the beast knew what the wizard was doing, it didn't show.

Jenhiro also noted that its gaze periodically went to the staff that was lying on the ground. Brodea had never picked it back up, and had instead chosen to forget about it. Peculiar, considering she held such reverence in it a short while earlier. Ashyn worked around it. Moving it when necessary, ignoring it otherwise. None seemed to pay the proximity any mind, and why should they? Relm, the person who had earned Jenhiro's trust, subjugated him.

Though Jenhiro hated Eigron for what he did to Avrimae, and he detested Brodea for twisting the ideals of the cause, he now felt the most betrayed by the Voïre dui Ceremeia. Relm was supposed to be the best of his people. The paragon of the Ferhym. The symbol of purity. Yet she deceived him. She used him as a pawn. She twisted and manipulated him so that everyone was at this point, under Brodea's complete control. Brodea had the entire rebellion in one place, at her fingertips.

That sense of betrayal burned stronger from her than any of the others. He trusted Relm. Trusted her with everything and she turned that trust into his undoing.

As the night progressed and the bright silver moon shone full in the sky, Jenhiro felt himself growing tired. It wasn't the tired of an exhaustive day, but drained. A curious feeling.

As his eyes grew heavier, he noticed that the other prisoners were acting the same way. It was strange, and yet it was a quandary he would try to solve, he figured, after he woke up, for he was so tired.

Then pain flashed through him, and his eyes flew open. He felt the epicenter of the pain at his calf. Before his mind could register calling out, he looked down to see yellow eyes flashing up at him. It took him a second to understand what he was looking at, but as it slinked towards the gaur, out of sight of all the others, it was unmistakable. It was the wildcat Ashyn called Ginger.

As with him, he saw the cat swipe up at the back of the tranquil gaur, it snorted in equal surprise as Jenhiro could see the pain registering in the bull's eyes. It looked around the room seeing if anyone noticed him. Rizen's eyes locked with Jenhiro's, and ever so slightly, Rizen nodded to him. What in the name of the Spirits was going on?

"The precision of the symbols is perfect," Ashyn said woodenly to Eigron. "For the next part of the ritual that will draw the Nether, we need a sacrifice."

"You have four to choose from," Brodea said with a sinister smile as she waved to the four bound to the tree.

Ashyn approached the gaur. Jenhiro could see him studying the bull intently. He reached out and touched its furry chest, studied its musculature, and grabbed its head and turned it left and right. The gaur resisted Ashyn and roared in his face. Ashyn didn't jump in fright, or shudder, or even budge. He simply said, "No, too primal," turned, and stepped in front of Avrimae.

Again the Blood Wizard repeated the procedure. He seemed completely indifferent to her sexuality as he touched her chest and studied the musculature of her body. "No, she's been soiled."

Brodea stared seething at Eigron.

Ashyn then stepped up to Julietta and at a simple glance said, "Blind, won't work." And before Jenhiro knew it, Ashyn was in front of him.

Jenhiro stared into those piercing hawk-like eyes of the young man he had traveled with, fought with, and grew to understand. They were flat, disinterested. If Ashyn was in there, he was lost somewhere.

"Ashyn," Jenhiro whispered. "Ashyn you have to hear me."

Ashyn ignored him, or perhaps didn't even hear him. "Ashyn this isn't you. You don't know what you are doing. You have to fight it, fight Relm."

Again, Ashyn said nothing. Not even a flicker of recognition. "If you do this, you will be hurting innocent people. Killing them, hundreds, perhaps thousands. I may not know you well, but I don't think you want this. You have to stop it. Stop yourself."

Ashyn turned from him. "He lacks a strong enough connection," he said to Brodea. "None of them are capable."

Brodea, who up until this point stood with her hands on her hips, folded them across her chest aggressively. "Well then who is capable?"

Ashyn turned stiffly and observed the room. He then pointed at three people. Relm, Eigron, and then himself. "We all have the connection required."

"Connection for what?" Brodea demanded.

"In order to trigger the phage, it needs a conduit to travel from the Nether into the Mundane. Only those that are capable of manipulating magic fully can act as the proper conduits."

Angrily, Brodea said, "The gaur can."

Ashyn shook his head and then pointed to the totem. "He requires his own conduit to cast magic."

"But he spoke to you through the water!"

"A conduit."

Brodea looked away from him and stared at Eigron. "Is what he is saying true?"

Eigron shrugged. "In the sense of the ritual, yes. I sense no deception from him in that regard. The beast? Again, yes, as the dui Nuchada has seen it, the beast has always needed a conduit. Whether it has to be one of the three of us?" He looked intently at the wizard. "I cannot say I trust him."

Brodea nodded at Whisper and she quickly moved the spear tip to Avrimae's chin. Ashyn's eyes followed in a disinterested fashion.

"I will have her killed."

Ashyn didn't move.

"I think he is calling your bluff mother," Whisper said aloud. "Let me kill her so we can find out."

"It's not a bluff," Relm said her eyes still a maelstrom of silver fury. "He'll do it himself if you order it. Tell me your will."

Brodea smiled. "Let's put your control to the test then Voïre. Ashyn Rune."

The wizard turned to the First Councilor.

"Kill your sister."

THE SACRIFICE

Ashyn looked around for a weapon. He found one. Brodea watched with amusement as he stepped over to the totem and hefted if up. He spun it over so that the spear-like side was facing to the front and began walking to Julietta.

"Ashyn, no! Don't do this Ashyn! It's your sister!" Jenhiro pleaded as the wizard moved slowly, but with purpose towards Julietta.

He's really going to do it, Brodea marveled as she watched Ashyn heft the weapon at chest level to the suspended woman.

In the background, Brodea heard Jenhiro pleading with Ashyn to stop. The dui Nuchada didn't listen; he just kept moving menacingly forward, the totem raised, ready to impale his sister. Brodea savored the delicious irony of the fact that he was going to kill the person he was intent on saving.

He reached Julietta. There was no hesitation. Jenhiro writhed and screamed to get Ashyn to stop. Brodea looked at Relm whose quicksilver eyes were swirling wildly as she maintained control of the wizard.

Brodea loved it. Now this was balance. The way it was meant to be. Ashyn lined the spear tip up to Julietta's chest. He pressed firmly so that a small nodule of blood balled against the penetrating tip. She held her head high.

Ashyn reared back and then thrust forward.

Brodea smiled and then said simply, "Stop."

Ashyn froze. The pointed tip of the totem only a fraction of an inch from Julietta's chest.

"Well, he's not lying," she said perfectly.

Eigron stared at her in confusion, "Yes, yes he is."

"Will you kill Julietta?" Brodea asked.

"If it is your will," Ashyn answered.

"Will you be the sacrifice?"

"If it is your will," Ashyn repeated.

Brodea bit her lip as she thought. "Will it conclude the ritual? Will the phage be released?"

"No," he answered. "There is a single step remaining. To invoke Destruction."

"But you are broken," Brodea said bluntly.

"I can fix him," Relm replied. "Here and now. He is almost healed anyhow. Another day, or week, it won't matter. His psychological wound is healed. He'll have his power back and unless I am controlling him, we will not be able to stop him, we will have to kill him." Relm turned to face Brodea.

Brodea felt the jolt of the Voïre's power course through her, "You picked the right night to act, First Councilor. He may have very well had his power when facing the council tomorrow. Tonight, with this action, you have saved many Ferhym lives."

Those words solidified it for her. Brodea did everything, sacrificed everything for the cause. It was time someone else sacrificed as she had. A single thought came to mind. She looked at Eigron whose usefulness had long waned. "Do it. Heal him."

Vooken dissented, "You can't! He's a wizard!"

"He is under our control," Brodea replied mirthlessly, putting the witnessing Councilor in place. "The Spirits demand the Netherphage, and the Blood Wizard will be the undoing of skewers everywhere. To do that, we need him whole."

"You are wise," Relm said and she fell silent. Busy remedying whatever malady kept Ashyn's connection to magic gone for so long.

"I have vowed to stand by your side in all things, Brodea, even this. But I do not agree," he said folding his arms. "This is beyond reckless."

"Noted," Brodea said, not in the least bit distressed by his choice. He made his decision as he always did. Brodea looked at Eigron almost apologetically. Almost. "I guess the choice is made." She told him before looking to her middle daughter. "Whisper, do as the Blood Wizard instructs."

Whisper withdrew her spear quickly from the woman's chin leaving a small red line. She looked over to Eigron maliciously. "With pleasure, mother."

Brodea saw, with some amusement, the look of horror that crossed Eigron's face. "You can't be serious? I am a servant of nature! The cove will never tolerate this!"

"And you are serving nature," Brodea replied.

"After all I have done! After all I have helped you accomplish!" Eigron shouted. "You'll start a war with the druids, Brodea! They will never let this slight pass. The Elder of Vines will demand balance from you!"

Brodea looked at him almost bored. "The elder and many druids have felt you have become a liability to them already. Have you not listened to the whispers? They think you are power hungry. They think you know nothing of humility. And you know what? They are right. Now you get the opportunity to do something great for our people again. You get to help annihilate wizards through nature's means. A phage is a plague, Eigron. Nature's greatest balancer. And it will be your sacrifice that sets it in motion. You will be praised."

He took a step back from Whisper as she leveled her spear towards him. She asked harshly, "What must I do, dui Nuchada?"

Ashyn turned and pointed with the totem to the center of a strange diagram etched upon the wooden surface. Brodea looked with growing interest. "Place him in the center of the Çaez'eth Durí. You must stand in it, too."

"No, no! I will fight you! I will not submit!" Eigron blurted as he raised his hands to control the elements of the Great Elm.

The wood groaned and creaked as the bindings on the four splintered and weakened. Eigron was close to releasing them, but he wasn't fast enough.

Whisper lashed out like lightning before Eigron could react enough to pull his hands back. There was a flash of her spear tip and bellow of panic as Eigron tried to protect himself.

Eight digits struck the wooden surface. Blood oozed from them. Eigron looked to his hands, all his fingers cut into stumps, and he screamed. Only his thumbs remained. His control of nature was gone.

Brodea risked a glance at their captives, how close had he come to letting them out. Luckily their bindings, now withered and splintered, still held. They were going nowhere. Her eyes fell to Jenhiro and she thought for a moment she saw him smile.

Yes, those hands had touched Avrimae, she surmised. There's a hunter in him still. It's a shame he tainted himself with the perfidiousness of the wizard's words.

Whisper grabbed the screaming druid by his throat; her strong forearms bulged as she cut off his air, the yell of terror dying like a whisper on the wind.

She drug him like a sack of potatoes over to the center of the symbol that Ashyn had called the Çaez'eth Durí. "Now what?"

Ashyn looked to Brodea and pointed to the other symbol. Her brow furrowed. "I am no sacrifice."

Ashyn shook his head no. "In that glyph the focus or the wielder must stand. They will be the one who will control the Netherphage. It is to be you, correct?"

"I can direct this great balancing upon the targets of my choosing, without the totem?" Brodea was hesitant, but hopeful.

Ashyn nodded. "More or less. Think of it as broad strokes with a thick brush. You cannot make precise details on your tapestry, but you can give it a general outline."

Brodea hesitated no more. If she chose wizards and it targeted human sorcerers as well, then all the better. None should wield the power of Creation except those worthy of the Spirits, the hym. No, only the Ferhym. Even her elven cousins lacked the piety necessary. They needed to earn it back.

She stepped into the center of the Çaez'eth Durí. Vooken looked at her worriedly. She whispered to him, "For the cause."

"I will complete the ritual," Ashyn said as he turned and walked by Jenhiro. Brodea watched as the former branch commander tried to lunge at Ashyn and then tried to talk Ashyn out of what he was doing. The subjugated wizard paid the elf no mind. Relm was strong, Brodea realized with some pride. If she would have used her from the start, much of this pointless delaying could have been avoided. A foolish decision on her own part, but one now remedied.

"As the wielder of Netherphage, you must order the sacrifice. As the wielder of Netherphage you may also pick another," he waved his hand to the four prisoners, "who will be added to the sacrifice to strengthen the power of the phage. They do not need the same connection as the first sacrifice. Any will do."

Brodea smiled at this, "Eigron?"

The whimpering druid looked over at Brodea. His bulging eyes pleading for mercy from the First Councilor. Begging her to stop her daughter. She dangled the carrot. "Is he still lying?"

Whisper relaxed her grip and Eigron hung his head low gasping for air. After several seconds he shook his head. "He speaks the truth. Two sacrifices will be more powerful than one." He looked up quickly urging, "But he's still lying about it needing to be me!"

Whisper tightened her grip again cutting off the rest of his cries.

"Then I shall do what you could not," Brodea said. "I choose Avrimae."

"No!" Jenhiro screamed. "Choose me! Ashyn, choose me! Don't listen to her. Don't sacrifice Avrimae. She's innocent, Ashyn. Innocent!"

Jenhiro's screams tore through the chamber. Brodea noted that they were so passionate, so strained, that they even roused both women from their slumbers.

Slumbers? Brodea found it suddenly suspicious that the women would fall asleep at a time like this.

Down below past the pens, she heard another wail. It was the sound of a man. Clearly he heard Jenhiro's cry. *Ah yes,* she thought, *the husband.*

"Order it," Ashyn said.

Brodea looked at him.

"Order the sacrifice," he told her as he raised the pointed end of the totem to Avrimae's throat. "Claim the Netherphage for your own."

Brodea pushed the oddity of their sleeping aside. This wizard was right. With this power she could strike down all of the skewers in a single pass. They would all perish, and the reliefs of the Council of Elm would be bursting with accolades. Accolades she brought to her people and to the Spirits. She, Brodea Windsong, and her daughters. She looked at Ashyn and said with absolute confidence, "Kill them! Kill them for Balance. Kill them for the Netherphage!"

Ashyn nodded.

Brodea watched, as she knew she must, as her daughter didn't hesitate in the slightest. Whisper drove the spear into Eigron. His eyes widened in shock and pain, his body quaked and convulsed, but her iron grip did not lessen.

She drove the poisoned metal head under his ribcage passed the sternum, severing his aorta. Eigron's eyes lolled and his tongue bulged from his mouth. Whisper twisted the spear, his body writhing, her own muscles flexing as she held him in place.

Whísper ripped the spear from his body, tearing open the wound and spilling gouts of blood and viscera all about the glyph. Red light emanated from the outlines of the Çaez'eth Durí and then Whísper didn't move.

Brodea smiled as she saw her own Çaez'eth Durí begin to emanate a faint crimson light. She was ready for the power. Ready to feel the control of the magic within her. Ready to feel the power of the Netherphage. She turned her head; it felt strange, sluggish as if she was trying to pass through water.

"What is happening?" she demanded. It felt like a gelatin was covering over her body and it was beginning to harden. Invisible viscous goo was holding her in place. Was this part of the ritual?

Brodea watched as Ashyn rolled the totem and drove the spike deep into the tree. The great elm absorbed it as if it were a part of the plant. Immediately the bindings around the quartet of hostages receded.

"Kill her!" Brodea ordered. "Kill Avrimae now!"

With the order again, the light intensified around her, and she found that she could move only her jaw and eyes. Those eyes bore into one person: the Blood Wizard.

Ashyn stared directly at her. His fierce gaze pierced into her own. Just like when she saw him before. When she saw him through Shedalia's memory. She realized that all the same intensity was there. Only this time there was power too, the power of the dui Nuchada.

"No," he told her.

Ashyn Rune was in control.

THE RELEASE

Ashyn could feel the connection once more. It was alive! He could feel the magic driven by the totem, just like before. It made him feel whole.

Ashyn looked to Whisper and Brodea now bound by the glyphs he created. Xexial once told him he had a natural affinity for wards and glyphs. Looks like the old man had been right. Fitting, really. His first connection once more with magic, and the first use of it was something that Xexial would have done.

Ashyn watched as the roots binding Avrimae receded. Behind him Brodea was issuing a litany of increasingly slurring curses in the Ferhym language. He would deal with her shortly. First he needed to make sure Avrimae was okay, and then his sister.

In Whisper's bloodlust she inadvertently nicked Avrimae with the poison-tipped spear. Right now a trace amount of the neurotoxin was seeping through her bloodstream. Was it enough to be fatal? Ashyn hoped not.

Suddenly, he felt someone behind him. He could feel the heat wash over him and it wasn't that of Brodea or Whisper. It wasn't Eigron either. That threat was neutralized forever. The four were still trapped, so who?

Vooken.

Ashyn couldn't remove the totem, otherwise the four would remain bound, and he needed desperately to check Avrimae. He let go of the totem and rolled away just as a kick flew where his head had been milliseconds before.

Ashyn turned to face his opponent. He stared into the light brown eyes of the councilor. A trained hunter, perhaps fiercer than even Shedalia. Definitely wiser. Ashyn knew he was no contest for this elf in hand to hand combat. Vooken knew it too.

The hunter picked up Brodea's spear and wielded it deftly, maneuvering it between himself and Ashyn. Vooken was deadly. His knowledge of the spear far more evident than any Ashyn fought before. Ashyn just needed time for the totem to do its work on the roots holding Jenhiro and Rizen. Once those two were free, it would be a different matter entirely.

"Kill the wizard Vooken!" Brodea mumbled through a clenched jaw.

Ashyn backed away from Avrimae guiding Vooken with him. The councilor moved deftly, his footing sure. He stabbed at Ashyn once, twice. Ashyn barely had a chance to avoid either attack. Vooken was toying with him. He could end it quickly, and Ashyn didn't like the feeling. What neither knew, was that Ashyn was not alone right then.

Vooken came forward with a feint that Ashyn fell for. He was exposed, and vulnerable. The spear flashed out, ready to take his throat in a single precise slice. And then Vooken screamed. His attack went high, sliding across Ashyn's cheek and bouncing off his cheek bone.

The cut burned, but Brodea's spear wasn't poisoned. Dumbfounded, he looked at Vooken who was struggling with something.

Something orange.

Ashyn recognized the big ball of fur, a flurry of claws and teeth as it gnashed and tore at the Ferhym's exposed legs. He couldn't believe it. "Ginger?"

The cat's yellow eyes flashed once at Ashyn in confirmation and it then resumed harrying the councilor. Tying him up for those last few precious seconds.

Ashyn ran to the totem and grabbed it. He felt the power, the magic. He let it flow into him, filling his bones. The remaining bindings crept back into the tree and disappeared.

Ashyn immediately rushed to Avrimae as she tumbled forward. He caught her in his arms and lowered her to the floor. Her heart rate was quick, and her pupils were heavily dilated. The poison was doing its work.

"No," Ashyn growled. He needed to save her. Save her for Macky. He couldn't let both of his friends die.

Between the hissing of Ginger and the yelps of Vooken, there was a sudden cry of surprise. Ashyn turned to see that Jenhiro had disarmed Vooken. The councilor was now in a dire situation surrounded by a traitor Ferhym and a large pissed off cat.

"Surrender," Ashyn ordered the elf. Vooken stared at him in furious defiance.

"I shall see your kind perish dui Nuchada." He spit. "Perhaps not this day. But I shall see it!"

Vooken moved to attack Jenhiro. Jenhiro raised his weapon to defend himself, but again the senior councilor was wise to the ways of combat. The move was a feint, and even as Vooken dove away from his pair of assailers, he was cognizant of his surroundings enough that he directed his roll right towards the crystal and the tome.

"Shit," Ashyn said. He tried setting Avrimae down, quickly but delicately, but there was no time. Vooken came out of his roll and grabbed both the crystal and tome.

Rizen bellowed and charged after him. Even then, the wily councilor was quicker than they all were. He deftly did a handstand over the chair that had bound Ashyn, and then lunged off the side of the council chambers into open space.

Both Jenhiro and Rizen skidded to a stop at the edge of the opening. Ashyn knew neither was interested in taking a drop like that again. They had done it once together, and that was enough. Ashyn made it to the edge last. Already he could see the councilor making his way to the shoreline of the cage. The people of the Water Pens were on their knees still with only four elves behind them.

Vooken was waving frantically at those hunters and Ashyn knew what would happen next.

He looked down right at Uriel. The man's beady dark eyes were staring right up at him. "Fight!" Ashyn yelled as loudly as he could, "Fight for Macky!" It was virtually imperceptible to anyone else, but Ashyn saw Uriel nod.

The large human, imprisoned for so long, launched to his feet and tackled his detainer. "For Father Macky!" he bellowed as he did.

The prisoners all scrambled to their feet as well. There were more than a dozen angry prisoners and only three remaining guards. Even then those hunters below were well trained and armed. Ashyn knew he didn't have much time. Quickly he made his way back to Avrimae.

Jenhiro was next to him in a flash. He was bent low, his fingers checking the quickening pulse in her neck. Avrimae's breathing rattled. "No. No. You have to stop it, wizard. You have to," he pleaded. But there was little he could do. Ashyn lacked the skill.

Whísper laughed at them. "She couldn't even survive a single scratch. Humans are pathetic and weak. I will enjoy watching her die."

Jenhiro turned on her, his gaze menacing, his voice a hiss, "If she dies, there are no bounds to the torture I will inflict upon you, before you follow her."

Whísper scoffed him. "You can try, traitor. You can try."

Rizen approached them, and Jenhiro looked up quickly. He growled, bringing the woman closer to him. "Get away from her."

Rizen, now unable to speak with Ashyn held out his large hand. Ashyn looked to the massive gaur, and then to his own hands. He wanted the totem.

It was the moment of truth. For weeks the gaur had hounded them, tried to kill them. For only a handful of days they had been reluctant cellmates. Yet in that short time, Ashyn learned much about the gaur, much about its people and its society. He hoped that knowledge and his alliance as a totem-brother were strong enough. He couldn't survive another encounter against the gaur, not now.

"Don't do it Ashyn," Jenhiro warned. "It can't be trusted."

Rizen's amber eyes glared at Jenhiro. Though Ashyn knew he couldn't understand the Ferhym's words, the body language conveyed more than enough.

"We had a deal, Jenhiro," Ashyn said flatly. "And we need him."

Ashyn handed over the totem.

Rizen took it and looked at it reverently. Immediately, Ashyn felt his connection to magic diminish once more. It hit him hard, and made him woozy, but he tried not to let it show.

Rizen touched the shaft, ran his thick fingers over the smooth mahogany. Ashyn knew what this reunion meant for the gaur. Redemption.

Immediately, Rizen looked at Ashyn, snorted, and nodded at Avrimae. Though they could no longer speak to each other's minds, the wizard thought he understood. "Can you?" He asked hopefully.

Rizen shook the totem in front of the two of them and then nodded to Avrimae again.

"What is he saying?" Jenhiro asked.

"I think he wants to heal Avrimae," Ashyn answered.

"Is that possible?" Jenhiro queried.

"I don't know. But when he stalked us, we watched his wounds close time and again."

"Yes," Jenhiro acknowledged. "Yes," he said again more firmly. He bent down and gently lifted the woman up, her hoarse breathing more of a death rattle now.

Brodea laughed at them, "Yes, waste your time on the dead woman Ashyn Rune." She sneered, "Vooken shall return with hunters and you will have nowhere to go."

"She's right," Jenhiro said. "Now is your chance. You need to leave. I will stay, with Avrimae, until the end. Take your sister and go."

Ashyn looked up at Julietta, the one he had yearned to save for so long. He stepped forward hesitantly. Though she was blindfolded, she made as if to look directly at him. The crescent scars around her covered sockets were white against her olive skin. In little more than a whisper, Julietta asked, "Is it really you?"

Ashyn reached out to touch her hand. Julietta let him. Once more Ashyn could feel the tears forming at the corners of his eyes. He could leave, right now, with Julietta. He could get away, so simply. He knew he could. But he was a wizard. And he had made a vow. A vow to protect life, all life. He was the few. His needs were the few. And they, the many."

"We stay."

"And then I will destroy you," Brodea declared.

Ashyn ignored her, focusing instead on Rizen. "Do it." He stepped aside and the Shaman lowered his mentor's totem to Avrimae.

As soon as the egg-shaped stone touched Avrimae's chest, her back arched violently and she screamed. Jenhiro moved to stop Rizen, but Ashyn put his hand softly on Jenhiro's shoulder. "Let him try," he whispered. "She will die otherwise."

Avrimae screamed as deep green lines spider webbed across her flesh connecting with the stone. All across her chest and shoulders the veins protruded from her flesh. Veins Ashyn wasn't even aware could be visible.

Rizen's eyes were closed as he concentrated. Slowly he mumbled something in his deep, natural voice. It was incoherent to Ashyn, and even though the wizard knew many languages, this dialect was completely unknown to him.

Soon the veins faded beneath her pink flesh, and the viridian webbing slowly disappeared into the totem. At the moment the last drop of green disappeared from her skin, she collapsed, panting heavily. Jenhiro was back on her, stroking her sweat-soaked hair.

"Excellent work, Jenhiro. You let a monster kill her," Whisper taunted. "Do you see now why you can never trust a skewer's magic?"

Avrimae's eyes fluttered open. Jenhiro saw them, and he smiled. They were clear. For the first time in weeks, they were clear. Her incoherence, her daze was gone.

A shaky hand came up and touched Jenhiro's copper skin. "I've seen this face," she whispered hoarsely. "I know this face, and it does not frighten me."

Jenhiro looked up in wide-eyed wonder at the gaur. "How...how did you do that?"

Tired amber eyes only stared down at them. He had no answer for them.

"Sometimes we must see people with more than just our eyes, Jenhiro." Ashyn said. "We must see them with our hearts."

"Lies. Treacherous lies!" Brodea yelled. "They poison you, Jenhiro. The wizard's words are just as polluting as the toxins that are in her body."

"Toxins we placed there," Jenhiro replied darkly. The branch commander stood and walked to the imprisoned First Councilor. "We judge for actions we are too ignorant to understand, and then perpetuate it by using similar methods on our enemies all in the name of balance!

"I have seen more honesty, humility, and trustworthiness from this dui Nuchada, this enemy, than I have seen from any of my kin in the last few months. If you call this poison, then it is a poison I gladly consume for it has set me free."

Jenhiro leveled the spear at Brodea's throat, her own spear. "I believe in the cause. I believe in balance. I believe in the Council of Elm and in the druids, but it is you that has become the disease. You fester inside the heart of the council; you eat away at everything we have represented for millennia. You are the skewer Brodea; it is my duty as a hunter to see balance is set."

"You know nothing of the cause!" Brodea hissed. "You know nothing of sacrifice, of what must be done to ensure that our world, our way of life is safe from the pestilence of evil that stands behind you! You can strike me down, but another will take my place! Another who believes just as I that there is no room in this world for the evil of wizards or the aberrations that are the dui Nuchada!"

"Then I shall strike down every First Councilor that takes your place until I find one who will listen to reason!" Jenhiro yelled.

He hefted the spear and pulled back, accepting his actions. He would plunge the weapon into her dark heart, and save his council from her misguided ways.

"Jenhiro, no," Ashyn told him. "This is not the answer."

"She will only keep fueling this battle against wizards. She will find a way to destroy you. She must die."

"And what would that solve?" Ashyn asked. "Brodea is right; another would only take her place. Carving out the sickness won't stop the disease once it's spread; it will only become more aggressive."

"And what would you suggest?"

"We treat it, by curing the whole disease." He stepped up beside Brodea. "You are going to let us go," he told her, "All of us, including the survivors of the Water Pens."

Brodea laughed at him. "You are in my city, in the heart of my forest, what makes you think that I would do such a thing?"

Ashyn smiled. "Because while you may know so much about me, I have learned something very important about you."

Ashyn walked over and picked up Relm, who up until this point had been cowering out of sight. She seemed terrified, weak, and exhausted. Brodea sneered at him.

"While she was in my mind, part of me was in hers, and do you know what it was I saw in there, Brodea Windsong?"

She didn't answer with words, only her eyes. Those dark obsidian chips conveyed a thousand words. Hatred, dark promises she one day meant to fulfill, and fear. Fear of what this tortured wizard may do to Relm.

"I saw her mother," he said confidently, and then he looked over at Whisper, "And I saw the sister that she used to idolize, until she learned her sister was a murderer."

Jenhiro looked between the three Ferhym women in shock, and he understood. He understood the quirks in Relm that he had thought seemed familiar. He now recognized the animosity towards Whisper. The sounds of neglect when she spoke of Brodea. He understood her facial gestures. Her bodily mannerisms that he knew he had seen before. The way she bit her lip when she was concentrating, her smile, her confidence. Just like Brodea.

Just like her mother. It was well known that Brodea had three daughters.

"Relm Windsong," he said as it all made sense. Only Brodea would have pushed to have her young child witness a massacre, if only to identify the legendary dui Nuchada.

"That's Voïre dui Ceremeia to you!" Whísper hissed. "She's due the proper respect, hunter."

"I now understand why you betrayed me," Jenhiro told Relm. Relm refused to make eye contact with him. "You have lost your way, just like your mother."

"It is you that has lost your way Jenhiro," Brodea responded.

Ashyn drove himself between the two of them, still holding Relm by the arm. "You tortured me, raped and whipped Avrimae. You killed Macky. You threatened to kill my sister. I have reason to return such pain upon you tenfold. And I would use your precious daughter to inflict such pain."

"You wouldn't dare!"

"Relm is coming with us. And you will let us leave Feydras' Anula and the Shalis-Fey. When we are safely away from the tree line, I will release her to return to you. Consider this a stalemate Brodea. I will not kill you, though I want to, as an offer of peace between wizards and the Ferhym."

For the first time he saw genuine fear in Brodea's eyes. "If you hurt her…"

Ashyn was not deterred by her weak threat. "Know that I will hurt her if we are threatened by the Ferhym on our exit. I keep Relm only for safe passage. When we are free, I promise to let her return to your people unmarred."

"How do I know you will keep your word?" Brodea asked, and Ashyn knew she was beaten.

"Because you don't have a choice, Brodea," Ashyn replied with finality.

The First Councilor lowered her head and nodded. "Go," she whispered.

"Mother?" Whísper said shocked.

"Leave Feydras' Anula. You will have safe passage through the Shalis-Fey."

"Mother, no!" Whísper argued. "He killed Shedalia! He needs to die! They all need to die!"

"Not today," Brodea said quietly. "Not today."

~ ~ ~

Ashyn strode down the steps with Rizen, Avrimae, Jenhiro, Relm, and his sister, Julietta. There was so much he wanted to say to her. So much emotion he wanted to convey. So much he wanted to hear. He wanted to get to know her again. But it was not time yet.

Right now, Ashyn needed to be a leader. He needed to get the people of the Water Pens free of Feydras' Anula and the Shalis-Fey.

When they hit the lower steps, he saw it was not a pretty sight. Though the men and women of the pens had overwhelmed the four hunters and taken their weapons, it was not without heavy cost. There were only five of them left, including Uriel.

Avrimae saw him and immediately ran to him crying. She embraced him tightly, crying into his chest, and he stroked her hair and held her tight. When he looked up to Ashyn, it was with eyes full of wonder and gratitude.

"Thank you," he mouthed, and he buried his head in her neck, crying as well.

Jenhiro stood next to Ashyn, "Well he is not the man I expected, after what I had seen of him."

"We all have a dark side," Ashyn admitted. "And we all have a good side, even someone like Uriel."

Ashyn walked slowly to the still body on the ground. He bent low and turned Macky over. Aside from the large red stain upon his clothing, one might mistake the priest for sleeping. Ashyn felt his face flush, and the tributaries begin to roll down his cheeks.

He cried because he failed Macky. He cried because his best friend was dead. Ashyn felt a strong hand on his shoulder, and when he looked up, he saw it was Uriel. His eyes were bloodshot as well. Ashyn stood and joined Uriel and Avrimae in a hug, and they cried together in silence for many moments.

Finally, Jenhiro approached respectfully. "We must move, dui Nuchada. It isn't safe."

Ashyn sniffed and he nodded. He thought briefly about heading to the druid's cove to collect his things, the bow, everything of value in his bag, the gloves. There was no time. Jenhiro was right. He looked to the Ferhym who had a strong grip on the Exemplar. He was doing everything possible to avoid her eyes. Luckily he had a century of training.

Jenhiro still didn't know something. And he wouldn't know until they were all safe.

"Let's go."

WINDSONGS

I t took almost four hours for the effects of the Çaez'eth Durí to wear off. The Council of Elm was now crawling with councilors, hunters, and druids. It was a complete travesty.

Brodea sat on her throne watching the Elder of Vines pray to the Spirits over the deceased body of Eigron. No one, not even Vooken, admitted that Whísper was the druid's killer. They all claimed that Jenhiro did it when he had turned rogue and facilitated the escape of the Blood Wizard, the skewers in the pens, and the blind girl, Julietta.

Vooken was clever in his accounting of the details to the Elder of Vines, and Brodea expounded upon it when she exclaimed how the wizard took their precious Voïre dui Ceremeia hostage. She didn't tell them it was her daughter. She didn't have to.

Whísper was smart to keep her mouth shut. Brodea and Vooken were covering for her, and the only other witnesses to any of it all lay dead from the escape at the Water Pens.

Right now, she knew Ashyn was deep within the Shalis-Fey, and with Jenhiro as a guide, it wouldn't take them long to escape the threshold of the sequoias. When they hit the outskirts of the forest and the regular conifers, they would think her control over the situation weakened significantly. What they didn't know was that the outskirts were where she had the most control. She suspected she had two days at the least until they hit the forest's edge. Let them get comfortable. Let them get confident.

Brodea knew that if it wasn't for Vooken's quick thinking with the tome, all might have truly been lost. Where at first she thought he had abandoned her, she now realized that he had done the best possible thing. He did what the cause dictated. The loss of Brodea may have wounded the people a little, but there would always be another First Councilor. The loss of the Netherphage weapon though...

It was a weapon; they could not afford to part with. It was the great balancer. It was a gift from the Spirits given to Brodea at the cost of her husband, Ambit. Though Vooken questioned her timing, she knew he did not question the effectiveness of the weapon or the cause. Never the cause.

In hindsight, Brodea acted impulsively in the end. She knew that now. Everything had been following the correct course so perfectly; she had weakened the Blood Wizard so well that she grew overconfident. She should have followed the original course she and Vooken had set.

"I will never exclude you from anything again," she whispered to Vooken while the druids scoured the council chambers for a means with which to weaken the wizard. Vooken reached over and laced her fingers with his. "Never again."

Vooken gave her a small smile. It was a good smile.

~ ~ ~

Whísper did not take the escape of the Blood Wizard as confidently as Brodea did. It bothered her that Brodea accepted the dui Nuchada's terms so quickly. It bothered her that as First Councilor she would let one of their precious Voïre dui Ceremeia go, just like that, without a fight. Regardless of Whísper's feelings for her odd, revered baby sister, she was trained not to ever negotiate with skewers. They were terrorists of nature, and the Ferhym did not parlay with terrorists.

That was all Brodea had done since the arrival of the dui Nuchada. She had talked. Sure she issued a little pain here and there to the boy, she did not break the threshold to gain that information. She rode it. Sat by and didn't take it to the next level. She had been too cautious, and now it had cost Brodea.

Whísper realized that her mother was growing weak. Soft. She was losing her devotion to the cause. That fire in her was ebbing.

Brodea told her, after Vooken arrived, not to pursue the dui Nuchada or the traitor Jenhiro. That it was too dangerous for the Voïre. That they would have to hope that the Blood Wizard kept his word.

Whísper had whipped Avrimae. Cut, and burned, and stabbed, and prodded Ashyn over and over again. She had made him bleed in ways he had never thought possible. She had thrown him off the tree into a pond of sewage.

No. Ashyn would not be merciful. The Voïre dui Ceremeia was in danger. Her sister was in danger.

And so when dawn broke that next morning, and Brodea was giving an accounting of the escape of the wizard for the thirtieth time to the council, Whísper was nowhere to be found. She was doing what she had been trained to do. She was hunting.

WIND, SONG, AND FIRE

Relm was thrown roughly to the ground and the spear was trained at her face. "Don't ever look at me," Jenhiro ordered, "or I will cut out those eyes."

Sweat coated her green dress and her platinum hair hung limp and wet at her sides. Ashyn knew she wasn't used to the rigorous pace they were moving, but they had to put as much distance as possible between them and Feydras' Anula.

Ashyn reached out and lifted the spear away from her. He said calmly to Jenhiro, "She's our guest. Not an object."

The rogue Ferhym spit to the ground. "She betrayed us, Ashyn. She cost your friend his life. How can you not hate her? We trusted her, and she betrayed us all."

Ashyn looked up at the monstrous sequoias around him. Anywhere the Ferhym could be waiting, watching. Ashyn asked Jenhiro repeatedly to scout ahead, to scale the trees, but he didn't want to be one inch from the Exemplar.

Ashyn knew he was taking Relm's duplicity very hard. Just when the damaged elf had tried to trust his own kind again, she turned on him. "I am a man of my word, Jenhiro." He continued firmly, "We will not harm her unless we are threatened. Am I clear?"

"And if she takes control of you again?" Jenhiro pressed.

"She can't," he answered with all conviction.

Jenhiro harrumphed and stormed away, kicking foliage as he went.

Ashyn extended his hand and Relm took it. He helped her up. "He hates me so much," she said with tears in her quicksilver eyes. "I want to tell him everything."

Ashyn nodded. "I know, but not yet."

Rizen approached before they could continue their conversation. *Well timed*, Ashyn thought sarcastically. The gaur held a small bowl with only a smattering of water. Ashyn immediately put his fingers in the bowl.

Our movement progresses well. Few Ferhym have followed from their big residence, he said in Ashyn's mind, referring to Feydras' Anula. *Spies, nothing more. Though, I know there are more here. In the trees. I don't want this caravan to meet the same fate as my herd's.* After a moment, Rizen added, *this is my new herd now. You are my Bos until I return home.*

Ashyn nodded. He feared as much, too. When they had entered the Shalis-Fey he had known they were in the trees, but they were so good at hiding. It was only through the help of Jenhiro that he had actively avoided patrols. He had not wanted Rizen to harm anymore of the elves after losing his whole branch to the Pundit before. Now, Jenhiro had just been tasked with getting them out as quickly as possible. Avoiding patrols in the manner he had before had taken weeks. They needed to be out in days.

Do you still trust your pointy-eared ally? Rizen asked.

Ashyn glanced down at Relm before answering; *Jenhiro has come through at every turn, has he not?*

He has.

And yet you two, knowing each have made grievous errors, have not found it capable to trust one and other? Ashyn asked.

Rizen snorted. *He killed my herd.*

And his branch is dead. You hunted us mercilessly for weeks.

Again Rizen snorted in disdain.

I don't need you two to be friends. I need you to work together.

Rizen was quiet for a long time, before Ashyn heard the words in his head. *I will keep my bargain, totem-brother.*

The massive gaur pulled the bowl from Ashyn's fingers and then fell back to the end of the caravan.

Ashyn sighed. He had never wanted to be a leader. Politics is not for a wizard, Xexial used to advise. It made Ashyn smirk. Would he be proud? Angry? Probably both.

Ashyn held out his hand, and after a moment a single spark flashed to life. That spark intensified into a small flickering flame.

He whispered, "Two parts deadly, one part ridiculous. A Blood Wizard, indeed." Though it was still very weak, Relm had not lied to Brodea. She had guided him, healed him. He truly was a wizard once more.

Ginger bounded up on a nearby rock and meowed at him. He was the one thing in all of this that brought the biggest smile to his face. He walked over and scratched the cat's chin. "I don't know how you found me my little friend, but your timing was fantastic. You are my hero, you know that?"

Ginger purred contentedly, walked in a circle, and then hopped off the rock, to do whatever it was a cat like him did. Ashyn thought it was curious that the tabby had found him like that, but it was also a blessing. Since the day he had allied with the massive feline, he had no more loyal a companion.

Ashyn was about to continue moving when he felt the hairs on his neck stand on end. He turned with the feeling, and he saw her watching him, again.

Though watching wasn't exactly the right word. Julietta stood there, facing him, her head directed toward him, and yet he knew that she saw nothing.

As she approached him, she walked with her palms out, face down. She maneuvered deftly around obstacles letting her finger tips guide her. He really found her movements quite impressive.

Ashyn smiled at her. She smiled back.

"How do you do that?" he asked.

"What?"

"How did you know that I was smiling?"

Julietta shrugged as she fell into step next to him. "It would take a long time to explain."

"It's going to be a long walk," Ashyn remarked.

Julietta nodded, "And you are going to be very busy with this walk. Tell me, how is it my little brother became a vigilante and a leader to these people? That is not the small boy who coveted insects that I remember."

Ashyn looked at the ground. "I'm far from a child anymore."

Julietta nodded. "Yes. Now you are what the Ferhym called a wizard. What is that?"

Surprise apparent in his voice, he asked, "You don't know what a wizard is?"

Julietta shook her head. "I only know things I have heard from the druids and the Earthshorn. I'm afraid that my knowledge is very limited. The Ferhym can be biased."

Ashyn laughed at her comment. "It would take a long time to explain."

Julietta smiled again. "It's going to be a long walk."

Ashyn Rune laughed. "Yes, it is sister. Yes, it is."

And so he explained what a wizard was, only leaving out some of the minor details. Like, why the world hated and feared him. And that his title was the Blood Wizard.

~ ~ ~

Xao watched Ashyn and Julietta interact with one another and his heart swelled. *You would be proud of me Mireanthia,* he thought. *You would be proud of them.*

Xao always kept close now, and he knew that they were far from free of the danger the Ferhym represented, but the Runes were reunited. They were whole.

The small red dragon would never leave Ashyn's side again. Not while either of them drew breath. Not because it was his duty as a Watcher, no. It was because Ashyn Rune had become his friend.

Xao blinked at the two with his large yellow eyes as they walked deeper into the Shalis-Fey. They followed a Ferhym and a gaur, and they had an Exemplar amongst them. To say they were in for a wild ride was quite the understatement. But wherever the Blood Wizard went, his faithful cat Ginger would follow.

Always.

EPILOGUE

exial was asleep and it would stay that way until he was done doing what it was that he needed to do.

Carefully, he maneuvered through the underbrush, completely silent. His small feet padding gently on the mossy surface without making so much of a whisper.

They were at a small pond that Ashyn used. It was evident by the arrow they found nearby, and a handful of spears that littered the area.

Something had died. Something large, but the scavengers of the Shalis-Fey had drug it off and consumed it long before. He was not concerned. No beast of these woods could harm him.

As he made his way around the dense foliage, he could make out the form just on the other side. Large and brooding, it stared at him as he approached with its deep emerald green irises.

As the light took form around the person, he could make out its scaly skin and a small ridge of horns and frills upon its head. There were no ears visible, instead there were disc-shaped membranes beyond its jaw line.

It bore a blunt snout with two nostrils located above its oversized mouth. The creature before him had a pronounced overbite, its sharp dagger-like yellow-tinged teeth extended low over its lips.

Gavius Grind.

This was the first time they could converse since the wizard entered into the Shalis-Fey with Xexial.

"Last night, you felt it?" Grind said, with no preamble. Time was short, Xexial may be recharging, but he could only hold the old man at bay for so long.

He nodded. "**Destruction** has been used to great effect."

"The Recreant?" the scales asked disbelievingly. "Could Bontain really have taught him of such power?"

"Or it was the artifact."

Grind looked up into the woods. "It is in play?"

He shrugged. "Perhaps."

"Then we must find the Recreant quickly and kill him before the Seven become aware of what happened." Grind pressed. "Now more than ever. We must stop dallying with the damned old man, and just do what needs to be done!"

He held up a small three-fingered hand. "Patience apprentice. Ashyn Rune will die. Though first…" He reached into the folds of his tunic and produced a small diary. "We must find a way to take his power." He opened the small book penned by Rheynnaus Craëgolshien.

"This be what we've been waiting for," he said passionately. "If a Craetorian be alive, there is no telling what power we can derive from it. We must be finding a way to make this happen. That is why I continue to build trust with the Bontain."

Grind snorted. "You can just control him; I don't see why we need go through this farce."

He shook his head, his locks slapping against his shoulders. "It must seem real for it to be real."

He directed his hazel gaze over to the sleeping form of Xexial Bontain. "Xexial must be as convincing as possible when we finally encounter the boy. Only if I win his trust will we be able to see if it is true. If Ashyn Rune be the son of the Jadis Khan. If Ashyn Rune be Craetorian.

"And if he isn't?" Grind asked.

Khyriaxx looked to the younger wizard. "Then we kill him, of course. We kill all of them."

The sharp yellow-stained teeth smiled back at him. "Yes, Maba-Heth. Yes."

The Maba-Heth worked in pairs.

Always.

~ ~ ~

The Elder of Vines stood in the council chambers looking at the markings that were permanently etched across the hardwood surface of the Great Elm. A travesty was committed here. A travesty in one of their most sacred places.

"Can we duplicate it?" Vooken asked him.

The elder nodded and pointed to the basin of water. Vooken followed and looked inside. There, the memory of the entire ritual panned out before them. Nothing was erased from his memory as it had been every time they tried to translate the tome. The druids found a loophole. It only cost them the death of Eigron.

"What has been committed here is heresy!" The elder shook with rage. "We should have been consulted. It should not have been left to the devices of this child," he said referring to Eigron.

Vooken bowed his head. "I agree."

The elder's dark eyes softened. "I am sorry; I know this must be hard for you."

The councilor shook his head. "No harder than it will be for anyone else. When Brodea took position as First Councilor, I backed her so strongly because I felt she was a Ferhym of great vision. One that would lead us into a glorious future. She loves the cause over all else." Vooken looked to the Elder of Vines, "And it is clear that it will be the ruin of us all."

Vooken held up the tome. "This weapon, this Netherphage, has the ability to change everything. Bring nature back to its true balance. But in her hands, there is no telling what could happen. This needs to be controlled by someone more capable. Someone older, wiser."

The elder raised a graying eyebrow. "Someone like you?"

Vooken shook his head. "I am not versed with the intricacies of magic like the druids. My control is rudimentary at best. No, I am thinking it has been too long that there were a druid on the council. One here to truly represent the cause and the true balance of nature."

"Are you saying there will be an opening?" the elder queried.

"If a druid were capable of engaging the Netherphage, and they did all that Brodea has failed to do, I think there will be **the** opening."

The elder thought long about what Vooken was saying. His words were dark; he was talking about a coup. He was talking about overthrowing Brodea Windsong.

"But we still need a wizard," Vooken said sadly.

The elder held up his left hand in front of the councilor. He wore a heavy leather glove with thick fingers. Inlaid in the hide were iridescent sapphire lines that ran from the circles of his fingertips down his fingers and hands to his wrists. "I don't think that will be a problem anymore."

Vooken smiled at the Elder of Vines. Brodea overstepped her bounds. She used the position as First Councilor to fuel her own personal vendetta and veiled it as being the will of the Spirits.

Brodea was a poison. The Elder of Vines would be the antidote. He was an elf of the earth. A Hym of true balance. An avatar of nature.

And nature was vengeance.

The Netherphage would come.

~ ~ ~

ABOUT THE AUTHOR

JAY ERICKSON grew up in Midwestern USA before joining the United States Air Force at the age of nineteen as an aircraft mechanic. During his active tour, he earned two Associates' degrees in Computer Applications and Aerospace Maintenance. In 2001, he separated from active service and became an Air Force Reservist.

Since that time, he has held a variety of jobs from working at a casino, to crane operation, to masonry. Even with a myriad of different careers, though, writing has been his primary interest and hobby. As an avid reader, he has always held a deep love for Fantasy and Science Fiction. It was a natural fit for his writing. Now he's taking that hobby one step further by joining Halsbren Publishing LLC.

Mr. Erickson resides in Northwest Indiana with his wife and two children.

Made in the USA
Middletown, DE
02 July 2022

68309688R00295